Secrets of a Happy Marriage

Secrets of a Happy Marriage

CATHY KELLY

First published in Great Britain in 2017
This edition published in 2016
by Orion Books,
an imprint of The Orion Publishing Group Ltd
Carmelite House, 50 Victoria Embankment,
London EC4Y 0DZ

An Hachette UK company

1 3 5 7 9 10 8 6 4 2

A CIP catalogue record for this book is
available from the British Library.

ISBN (Hardback) 978 1 4091 7059 4
ISBN (Export trade paperback) 978 1 4091 5368 9

Typeset at The Spartan Press Ltd,
Lymington, Hants

Printed in Australia by McPhersons Printing Group

MIX
Paper from
responsible sources
FSC® C104740

www.orionbooks.co.uk

For Lucy,
my incredible sister without whom I would be lost,
and for Emma,
who is like another sister to me.
Love you both.

Prologue

In the San Francisco February dawn, Faenia Lennox sat at an off-white chalk-painted desk facing the Bay with its familiar and beloved fog visible beyond the Japanese maples in her garden and typed at speed, the same speed she'd learned from Mrs Farmsworth's classes in New York all those years ago. Over forty years ago, in fact.

'Do not look at the keyboard, girls!' Mrs Farmsworth had said in those commanding tones that made immigrants like Faenia wonder if she'd been a lady general in the war. Faenia, fingers quivering with tiredness and heart leaden with loneliness, had wondered if she'd ever have the strength of someone like Mrs Farmsworth, who stood ramrod straight and yet whose old eyes were kind beneath sharp-edged spectacles that edged off the end of her patrician nose.

Faenia had grown strong, with time.

Once a quivering skinny little thing in darned pantyhose given to her by her housemates in the narrow, creaking house in Brooklyn, Faenia Lennox had become a woman Mrs Farmsworth would be proud of.

She was strong enough in her sixties to take time away from her life to reassess.

It was a lesson she'd learned a long time ago but lessons sometimes needed to be relearned, returned to, particularly where love and marriage were concerned.

Faenia looked down at slender tanned fingers, now manicured, with a ring on each ring finger – a Celtic Claddagh ring on her wedding finger and a gold and blue chrysoprase ring on the other hand – and a pretty stainless-steel Cartier tank watch on her wrist.

In Lisowen, the tiny Kerry town where she'd grown up, nobody had jewellery like this. Or a house like this art deco one, perched on the hill like an adorable eyrie, full of exotic plants the likes of which the gardeners of Lisowen couldn't imagine, and real art – not expensive – on the walls, and books filling up white bookcases so that when Faenia came home from work, she could slip off her work clothes, put on soft shoes and sink into a couch with a book, lamplight warming her home.

And Nic's home – if Nic wanted it. But Nic wasn't brave enough to take the step, to walk out of the façade of a complicated life.

'Dearest Isobel,' wrote Faenia,

'Thank you for news. I still can't get my head around it all, to be honest. I knew it was coming and yet so much has been going on here at work and everything. But Eddie turning seventy – how did *that* happen? It seems like only yesterday we were kids playing round the back of Lady Margaret's orchard in Lisowen, stealing crab apples and hoping nobody knew because Lady Margaret, for all that she let the crab apples rot on the avenue, would have had a fit if she knew we'd stolen them. I do feel sorry for her now: her whole world was changing. At the time, we hated her, remember? She was rich, we were poor: it was all so simple in our heads. When nothing's simple, is it?

I don't know what I'd do without your telling me all the gossip – I'd know nothing. Although, it seems so distant to me now. Lisowen, Eddie, Mick, Kit and Nora. From another world and another life. Do you ever feel that?'

Faenia broke off the email at that point, feeling stupid.

Isobel, who'd been to the tiny, wooden-framed school with her in Lisowen all those years ago, would not feel the same at all. Isobel had stayed in Kerry and had married a man who'd gone on to be a police sergeant in Lisowen itself, which gave her an interesting view into the inner workings of a busy Kerry tourist spot.

It also meant Isobel had had to remain on the outskirts of things. She could be involved but people didn't always tell her things as she was considered an unpaid part of the police force.

The person who asked how Isobel was feeling was her long-time friend so many thousands of miles away, the friend who'd reached out to her from New York all those years ago because Faenia knew Isobel would never tell anyone, that her secret would be safe.

There was a comfort, Faenia knew, in telling someone you never saw so many personal things. An email to an old friend in another country was like therapy without the 170-dollar price tag – one could be straightforward and honest, knowing the person you were writing to would not meet the other parties described, knowing there would be no judgement. Just kindness, understanding and the odd comment of such clarity that it cut through hours of meaningless chatter from other people.

And yet, Faenia could not say everything, not any more.

Thirty years before, she'd told Isobel, via the flimsy paper of an airmail letter, that her marriage to Chuck had broken up and the hideous irony of why.

Years later, when Isobel and Faenia herself had thought she was married to her job, she'd revealed how surprising and wonderful it had been to meet the much-older Marvin, and how they'd married in a civil ceremony that made it easier to meld Jewish and lapsed Catholic faiths. She'd written, when email had eventually taken over, about Marvin's adult children and grandchildren and what a joy they were in her life.

She'd written about Marvin's inexorable decline into demen-tia, how that cruel disease made her feel like a widow for four years before she'd actually become one, how she'd cared for Marvin with such love, how her heart had broken when he'd had to go into full-time care.

And she'd written about the shock of his death, how she'd slowly come out of the ache of widowhood from a marriage that had for months been in name only with a man who would smile that familiar smile at her in the care home and say: 'Who are you?' when she'd visit. She went every day: it was only right. Marvin had cared for her and her last act of kindness to him had to be caring for him.

In the same way, Isobel had written and later emailed about the goings-on of Lisowen, of her own family and why her daughter was still going out with that lout who ran the tour bus company.

'I can't say it to anyone else, Faenia, in case she finds out that I hate him but he won't ever marry her, she's stone mad about him and her fertile years have practically slipped away waiting for him.'

Faenia, who worked in a chic downtown department store as *the* personal shopper to the rich women of San Francisco, had seen many of her staff and many of her clients caught in the same trap.

All the arguing and convincing in the world could never convince these women that their man – the man they adored – might one day leave them for a younger woman when their chance of babies was gone.

'He loves me. We need each other!' they'd say to Faenia, starkly elegant in her work uniform of Marc Jacobs dark tailored pants – the best for small, slender women – crisp white shirt, a cotton blend with stretch added for all the racing around the store she did all day, and a piece of giant costume jewellery like one of her Navajo silver and turquoise pieces.

With her urchin-cut silver-white hair that clung to that fine-boned face, that air of wisdom, of having *seen*, Faenia was considered a guru on all things, not just which blouse would work with which jacket for which event or should couture be considered for a society wedding. Her clients told her things, asked her things.

But even then, the lovely young women never listened. Neither did women of nearly forty, like Isobel's daughter.

She told Isobel this: 'There is almost nothing you can do, Isobel. Except tell her how you feel, just once. And explain that you are there for her, always, no matter what.'

Wisdom was so easy to pass on – much harder to practise.

If only she could practise some wisdom about Nic.

This was the love story she'd waited all her life for without actually knowing she was waiting or what she was waiting for. She'd met Nic when she was sixty and it had been like the clouds had parted and shone rays of divine sunlight upon this glorious late romance.

Had shone. Past tense.

If they couldn't be together, then she didn't want a half-hearted relationship. Faenia was too old to do anything half-hearted now.

The eighteen-year-old child who'd come to America was long gone, her wide-eyed innocence a thing of the past. In her place was a sophisticated woman who would hardly be recognised in her hometown.

'I have some time due to me at work,' Faenia typed, which was an understatement, as she had weeks of holidays stored over the twenty years she'd worked at the store, a job for which she'd been headhunted from Bergdorf's in New York.

'It will be strange to come back to Ireland after so long. They'll have cardiac arrests if they see me after so many years. I keep thinking the past is best left in the past and that Ed will have to be seventy without me. And how do I explain...?'

She knew that Isobel would email back that explanations were useless, that people forgot about the past and only worried about themselves.

Faenia stopped typing, thinking sadly of so many things lost in those years since she'd left Lisowen. She had lived far more of her life away from Lisowen than in it. She was American now, had a US passport, had completed the citizenship exam.

Her accent no longer made people look at her strangely: she spoke with the cadences of a well-travelled American woman.

But she could still see her birth home in her mind's eye: the tiny town, with great swathes of green, shades of glorious trees bent by the Atlantic, rocky fields leading down to the darkening sea, and the stone monolith of the castle standing feudally over it all, the small farms scattered around like windfall apples dropped from a great tree.

In another era, the castle had belonged to some powerful lord and not much had changed when Faenia had been a child apart from the powerful owner. This time, no warrior lord stood in the keep and looked over people who could die on his word: instead, the grand, if impoverished Villiers family owned the castle, both a part of and not a part of the small village.

Faenia had been a different person growing up in the Kerry coast: innocent, stupid perhaps, and more trusting.

Information was certainly power.

Her life in America had helped her grow up and her whole life was here: her beloved stepchildren, Lola and Marc, and their families. The friends she'd made over the years, her friends from work, her work itself which she adored.

She had built a life here and she was thinking of dropping out of it to visit a country that had not treated her well so long ago.

But the fight with Nic – 'I can't do it, Faenia, I can't move in. It would kill the kids if I left' – had left her shattered.

This from an adult with adult children who had their own lives. It was an excuse and Faenia had grown weary of excuses.

The Claddagh ring Nic had given her sat in front of the keyboard because she'd taken it off to put cream on her hands. Funny how hands showed your age. Your skin could be discreetly firmed up on your face thanks to the gentle caress of dermal fillers but the hands so often gave it all away: liver spots, skin as crêpey as an old gown, veins like snakes. Faenia had tried to take care of her hands, but still they gave away her age like nothing else about her, the Irish skin coming to the fore with its paleness and tendency towards sun spots.

She was a California sixty, which was the same as fifty anywhere else, as long as you stayed out of the sun and took care of all the beautiful dermatology work that had cost a fortune.

The ring Nic had given her gleamed at her. It was the prettiest Claddagh ring Faenia had ever seen: white gold, delicate and with a sheeny opal stone shining iridescently in place of the traditional heart.

With a traditional Irish Claddagh ring, one wore it with the apex of the heart towards oneself if one was attached and away from oneself, and on the right hand, if one was not.

A handy way for people long ago to tell who was affianced and who was not.

It was time to wear it away from her heart, Faenia thought, wanting to cry and not letting herself.

Or maybe she should not wear it at all any more. Maybe she should go home for the grand birthday party in Lisowen just to get away.

She'd visited so much of the world over the years but had never gone back to Ireland. It had felt too painful. How could she tell them what had happened, about all the mistakes she'd made...?

And yet with Nic gone from her life – and there was no doubt, Nic was gone – perhaps this was her chance to visit her homeland and make peace with the past.

One

In London, Cari Brannigan kicked the door of the empty office shut with one of her killer heels and went over to the window where she stared out at the imposing metropolitan skyline.

Most of the time, the view from Cambridge Publishing, a whole building housing a veritable pantheon of imprints, made Cari feel proud to be part of such an organisation.

Right now, she just wondered if the windows were plate glass or not and if there was a TV set anywhere on this floor full of books and conference rooms so she could fling the TV out, just to watch it ricochet fifteen floors down as if she were Aerosmith or Led Zeppelin or some wild rock band hellbent on 1970s-style destruction.

Half an hour ago, she'd thought she had a good career, a brilliant career for a thirty-four-year-old woman on the verge of total breakthrough with the possibility of moving to London from the Irish division – a move she'd never considered possible three years before when everything about her life had fallen apart because of The Break Up.

Cari called it The Break Up in her mind because Wedding Called Off at the Altar made her feel like such a loser, as if Jerry Springer and Jeremy Kyle would fight to the death to go through the grisly details on TV: 'And you didn't have a clue your fiancé was cheating on you till you were standing at the altar in your dress…?'

'No!' the TV Cari would have sobbed and then launched

8

herself at Bastard/Barney and ripped his eyes or other important bits out with her gel nails – she'd need gel nails, right? – in
front of a chanting audience telling her to 'Get him, girl!'

Post The Break Up, everything in her life had felt hellish, but
she'd clambered her way out thanks to work, finding a fabulous
author, the author who meant that career wise she was finally
on top of the world.

She'd won Editor of the Year at the prestigious trade industry
awards. Her author was one of the company's top three authors
in terms of both earnings and prizes won.

Next stop: Cari Brannigan moving to London to take a
higher-up job as publisher which would mean leaving her
family and her cousin Jojo, who was her best friend: the people
who'd helped her through her pain. But there was a position
open in the company, and she was tipped to take over the job,
desperate for it…

And then, just twenty minutes ago, another man had tripped
her career plans up as neatly as if he'd dumped her at the altar.
Which was why the idea of throwing something or someone
out of the glassy Cambridge building was so tempting.

Cari had been sitting at the monthly sales and editorial meeting of the Xenon imprint along with lots of other editors
and five of the Irish team who'd flown over from Dublin that
morning on the red-eye. She should have been listening to the
presentation about the heartbreaking new non-fiction title the
rights department had bought from a Swedish agent – a tale of
animal cruelty and how one scarred fighting dog had changed
the lives of several hardened criminals.

Instead, and this was weird because she loved dogs, she'd
found herself thinking about what sort of apartment she'd
get when she moved to London. Cool loft? Quirky mews. A
houseboat, even? Or a swish apartment she could decorate
in classic New York style with an all-white bathroom with
those subway tiles? All rented, obviously: no way she could

afford to buy anything. Her cousin Paul and his wife, Lena, had just such a New York-style apartment in Manhattan and Cari loved it.

She was getting better, she decided. She was recovering, coming out of the last stage of grief – what was it: raging fury? Whatever. Cari had made up her own stages of grief, ones far more fun than the Kübler-Ross ones.

Wanting to kill someone was first. Next up was buying shoes she couldn't afford. She forgot what three was but four was misery-eating ice cream and promising never to touch a man again.

Yes, she'd come through all those stages and had graduated with honours.

A little twinkle of joy filled her. In London, she could shop for shoes all the time. Despite her coolly androgynous look – straight, mannish trousers, dark shirts to hide her D-cup breasts, minimal make-up and midnight-dark hair cut short and curving round a face emphasised with eyeliner and glossy nude lips – Cari Brannigan loved shoes. Soft leather. Teeny bows in surprising places, suede with narrow straps to wrap elegantly round her slender ankles, insane colours like from an artists' palette: she loved them all. The higher the better.

Also, high shoes made her look taller, which was handy because since The Break Up, she had developed a wild hunger for chocolate. Not any old muck, no. But fabulous quality chocolate: proper stuff that cost proper money.

It still made you put on weight, though. With gorgeous high heels, Cari could hide the extra pounds and pretend she was a lean five foot seven, instead of a not-so-lean five foot four in flats, which she almost never wore.

She'd already scanned the list and knew she needed to pay attention in about five minutes' time, when the talk would move on to books likely to sell in her territory, because with so many books released every moment, a person would go mad trying to remember them all. Books that sold well in Australia might do zilch in Ireland and vice versa. A wise publishing person knew the difference.

New book meetings were long and exhausting and Cari was dying for the afternoon ten-minute tea break so she could fill her mug with strong coffee, snaffle a chocolate biscuit, and be ready for the final round.

Cari had hoped to get a moment alone with the UK office's publishing director, Jennifer, a charming but tough woman with a Cleopatra black bob rippled through with grey streaks, but Jennifer hadn't returned her email earlier in the week and throughout the day-long meeting had appeared to be in a very bad mood and hadn't met Cari's eyes. Strange and unsettling.

When tea break finally rolled around, Edwin Miller, the managing director of all of Cambridge, had gently asked her to stay back for a moment.

Gavin Watson, a publisher in London and therefore higher on the food chain than Cari, stayed in the room also, along with Jennifer, who was looking more annoyed than ever.

'I don't want the Irish contingent to miss your flights and I'd hoped to talk to you afterwards, Cari,' Edwin was saying.

He managed to shove Jeff Karan, the Irish MD and Cari's direct boss, out the door and Cari felt the danger.

Jeff was looking at her with that hangdog expression he often wore, as if he wanted to stay, wanted to protect her, but he was no match for Edwin, who had been managing director so long the joke was that his first printer had been a certain Herr Gutenberg.

Edwin closed the door.

Cari felt all her focus hone in on him. The animal instinct that told her danger was afoot had pinged up from 'mild emergency' to 'oh hell, sound the alarms, children and women first'.

'As I said, I'd hoped to get you on your own afterwards, Cari,' Edwin said in his charming way, 'but we're running late, as ever, so let's do it now.'

His complicit gaze at Gavin, who was beyond connected in the British publishing world, made Cari hit Anxiety Level Four. Gavin's grandfather had founded Cambridge Publishing, the grand old publishing house which was home to all the imprints. While the various imprints, like record labels, dealt with different areas, there were two other commercial imprints other than Xenon, but Xenon was the biggest.

Edwin wasn't just the managing director of Xenon, but deputy managing director of Cambridge.

Gavin was tipped for the top – mainly for his connections and his ruthlessless, certainly not for his ability to edit or to manage human beings, Cari thought.

'Cari, do sit,' said Edwin, and she knew then things were bad.

She sat, nervously, like colt about to run.

'This is going to be hard,' Edwin began, shooting his cuffs which were, as always, French and decorated with cufflinks from some wealthy, aristocratic ancestor, 'but we have to think of the company and of the authors. You know how they are – capricious, certainly. Tricky. And sometimes—' Edwin faltered. 'Sometimes they want change.'

'Who wants change?' Cari said.

Sitting be damned, she got to her feet and began to pace. All her life, she'd been a pacer. If she was going to the scaffold, she wanted to be on her feet so she could poke a spike heel into a captor's foot.

She looked over at Gavin who was smirking. He was younger than her, certainly. Doing that cool thing with a beard and a fake-manly sort of shirt in a lumberjack style. Probably never held a damn axe in his life. She narrowed her eyes at him.

'John Steele wants a new editor.'

Edwin's words sucked all the air out of the room for a moment. Cari thought she might not be able to breathe.

'John wants what? A new editor? Not me? I'm the only person he trusts, you know that. Why didn't he tell me? We're on the phone all the time. Or get Freddie to talk to me. I'd have talked him out of it—' She stopped. She was babbling.

Freddie was John's agent, the only other person in publishing that John said he trusted, apart from Cari herself, who had discovered his first book on the slush pile and championed it fiercely.

'I told you this wasn't the way to do it, Edwin,' said Jennifer now. 'We should have discussed this in advance with you, Cari, but—'

'But John Steele's contract is coming up for renewal, Jennifer, and he is very important to the company,' said Edwin. 'It's all happened at very high speed but he wants Gavin to be his new editor,' Edwin added, putting the final nail into the coffin.

'It's a guy thing, Cari,' Gavin said, speaking for the first time and smirking.

'Authors sometimes like to change editors: John feels he's losing his edge, he wants change,' put in Edwin.

'Writers are artists, Cari, we must think of them,' interrupted Gavin.

'Bull,' snarled Cari, 'you always say they're spoiled little prima donnas who earn far too much and expect us to put in their commas. *I'm* the one who tries to make you see that they get anxious about writing, worried about what we think of their first drafts, and their second drafts, hideously anxious about selling books and letting us all down, and that yes, they *are* artists.'

Gavin, who had won, after all, smiled as she repeated his bitchy words back to him.

'I was afraid you'd take it like this,' he said, with a fake, pitying smile.

'Like what? Angrily?' snarled Cari. 'Honestly, why would I be angry when *you are stealing my best author?*'

Authors wanted lots of things but generally they told their editors, either in person or via their agents.

They didn't do it by discussing it with the MD, publishing

director and another editor, and then letting them stick the knife in at the tail end of a new books meeting.

'I told him I'd tell you, smooth it all over,' said Gavin silkily. 'As you know, John can't bear scenes. I was over at his place in Cork on Monday. That's a lovely new extension they're building onto the house, and the landscaping is exquisite, isn't it? I'm going to help him with the London flat he's thinking of buying. Go the extra mile. He'll need a base here as he's agreed to do more publicity. He's agreed to tour, by the way,' Gavin added, still smirking.

Cari heard herself gasp.

John Steele hated publicity, did perhaps one interview on each continent per book, which did not make him beloved of either the press or the publicity department. He had never toured, and had told Cari that the thought made him physically sick. Somehow, Gavin had succeeded where she had failed.

Cari knew there was no more to be said.

She stared at Edwin, who she'd admired, and Jennifer, who could have given her a heads-up to what was going on but hadn't.

'We need you in Dublin. You're a fabulous editor, Cari,' said Jennifer, dark eyes full of pity under that Cleopatra bob.

'You knew I wanted to move to London, move up the company,' Cari said to Jennifer, trying not to let her voice shake. 'I found John Steele for us, championed him. I coaxed that first edit out of him when nobody said we'd be able to cut the book from three hundred thousand words down to one hundred and sixty. I coaxed the difficult second book from him. And you let this' – she gestured in disgust at Gavin – 'steal him away from me. Fine,' she said, stalking to the door. 'Since you've already agreed, it seems I'm surplus to requirements.'

It wasn't the best way to leave a room when the company's managing director and the publishing director were both there and when you had had hopes of a big move to London, a move of which they would be in charge. But suddenly Cari didn't care.

Her career was in tatters. The move to London was all predicated on her involvement in John Steele's meteoric rise and now that he was no longer her author, she'd just taken a tumble down a snake in the corporate world of snakes and ladders.

Edwin and Jennifer let her go without another word. That told her a lot.

In the quiet of the lonely office she'd found to lick her wounds, Cari stared down at the street far below and stopped thinking about throwing a TV out the window. What good would that do? No, for the sake of all womankind, she needed to rid the world of Gavin Watson, the slimy, good-for-nothing toad who'd just shafted her.

Her editorial mind, used to dealing with killers from her beloved crime novels and how long it took for a person to die from a lung puncture, crystallised. What sort of weapon did she need? A retractable switchblade she could slide from her sleeve and flick into action, ready to put up against Gavin Watson's carotid artery? Was more hard core better? A handgun, something menacing and heavy with a silencer on the business end, that she could aim coolly and tell him the warning shots were going straight into his head?

Or perhaps a bit of street fighting: a sharp blow with the edge of her hand into the soft cartilage of his throat. Then he'd be lying on the floor, flailing and trying to breathe and she could tell him what she was going to do to him next for stealing her author. If only she'd bought that staple gun on sale in Lidl...

No: Cari felt a film of cold sweat break over her body.

Not just stealing an author – stealing her best author, the man she'd nurtured for four years, the crime genius who said nobody understood him like she did.

John Steele was one of Cambridge's biggest authors. A quiet, unassuming Sheffield man, he'd settled in West Cork in Ireland decades ago and had been writing ever since, although he'd supported his family by working as a carpenter of fine kitchens. When he'd finally summoned up the courage to send one of his novels to a publisher and it had landed on Cari's desk, she had felt the spark of excitement of which every editor dreamed.

The hairs on her arms had literally stood up. This, this crime thriller with a brilliant but broken – *naturally* – hero, was incredible. The book was quite unputdownable. She, who could speed read, had stayed up till three o'clock finishing the huge manuscript and she'd known they must have it. Yes, it needed vast tracts of editing because it was a huge book but it was clever, marvellously written *and* commercial, the holy grail of publishing.

A star was born.

For four years, she had been the conduit between John Steele and the outside world. She had taken care of him, helped make him one of the biggest writers in the world. She was the only person in publishing he trusted, apart from his agent, Freddie, another Sheffield man who also understood John's reticence with the press.

She was godmother to his young son, for heaven's sake! Not that she was the motherly type, she'd protested when he'd asked her, but still, John Steele, the man she'd pushed to number one on book sales' charts all around the world, had said he'd wanted it.

'I couldn't have done any of it without you, Cari,' he'd said. 'Mags and I want you to be Jake's godmother. You're family to us.'

As family, she'd bought two Minion teddies and a set of adorable clothes for Jake for his second birthday in September. Had braved Hamley's before Christmas to buy him a bag-load of things, had promised to be his spiritual helper for ever – OK, that had been pushing it because since the wedding, she still felt as if she might get ill every time she stepped into a church, but still – and now John Steele, her finest, most commercial, biggest-selling author, one of the entire company's biggest-selling authors *worldwide*, wanted to be edited by Gavin Watson.

Her position as 'family' was being usurped.

There had been no call from John, no call from his agent. Nothing. Nada. Zip. It was a bloody coup and Cari hadn't had the slightest idea it was going to happen.

She sat down heavily in the office's ergonomic chair and brooded.

The knife, definitely the knife. So she could watch the blood dripping out of him. Like in *Stone Cold Blue Killer*, not a John Steele book and one by a first-time Irish author, it had never sold much but she'd edited it years ago and liked it. The killer had been a hunter and he'd hung his victims up on a hunting trestle . . .

Somehow, Cari went back into the boardroom after tea break and sat through the rest of the meeting. She nailed a smile to her face but she couldn't bring herself to add much to the conversation, except when it came time to present her new books. As only one of two editors from Ireland, her remit covered many genres, unlike her UK colleagues who generally specialised, so Cari had fourteen books to present, nine non-fiction and five fiction.

With Jeff casting sympathetic looks at her across the table, Cari aced it with her acting.

She started with the small, sweet memoir about a childhood in a remote part of Ireland followed by a Broadway career of an Irish actress, a book she loved, and her presentation of it was delivered as if Cari had spent time on Broadway herself. The women's fiction novel that dealt with adoption and infidelity had everyone at the boardoom sighing, saying, 'This could be big.'

Someone – clearly John Steele's defection had been on a

need-to-know basis so far, although by tonight, everyone, their authors, their agents, their former agents, their former publishers, and the NSA would know – praised Cari's next book, a debut by a fledgling crime writer, by saying, 'She has shades of John Steele, not that anyone can beat John!'

Everyone smiled at Cari, none of them having a clue that he wasn't her author any more.

John Steele: saving careers left, right and centre, apart from the woman who'd made him and he was screwing up hers.

When the meeting finally ended, Cari was out the door faster than anyone else. Normally the small Irish team travelled together but not tonight. Tonight, Cari couldn't bear to hear any sympathy.

She threw herself into a taxi outside Cambridge House and went to Paddington where she sat in lonely splendour on the Heathrow Express.

The betrayal filled her mind.

She wasn't surprised at Gavin. Gavin would put his grandmother on the game if he thought it would give him an edge.

And as for Edwin – nobody could be that sweetly nice and remain as managing director for so long. He must have the negatives of so many hideously embarrassing/career-destroying photos. It was the only answer.

But John Steele... That betrayal was absolute. After the heartbreak of her wedding, she'd felt as if she couldn't trust anyone again and she'd learned to trust John as he, in turn, had learned to trust her. That he could turn his back on her now was devastating.

She rifled in her bag for a tissue, and found the post she'd grabbed from the hall floor that morning as she'd got the early flight. Bills, bills, and one hard card envelope, either a wedding invitation – to which she would not go – or maybe a party?

Her mind on Gavin, John and the pain, she ripped it open.

Expensive paper.

With a flashback to her own wedding, Cari remembered that she and He-Who-Must-Never-Be-Named-Again had spent good money on their invitations. Sage-green-lined envelopes, old gold writing on the card, a green card with gold writing for the RSVP.

Things of beauty. Expensive beauty. She'd burned the RSVPs and the few unused invitations ceremoniously in the back garden afterwards with her sister, Maggie, and cousins Trina and Jojo helping.

'Burn the bastard out of your life,' darling Jojo had said, and then opened a bottle of sparkling wine, because they were all a bit broke and, as Trina – who never had a ha'penny – said, 'Champagne would be a mistake in case you thought of champagne when you thought of—'

'Him!' said Jojo. 'We shall never say his name again.'

'Like Voldemort.'

Still thinking of this, she unthinkingly ripped open the envelope and stared at it in horror.

Edward and Bess Brannigan invite you to celebrate
Edward's seventieth birthday party in the glorious surroundings of
Lisowen Castle, Co. Kerry on the weekend of 25th March.
We would be delighted if you would be our guests for
a weekend of celebration.

She blinked: once, twice.

Was this a hallucination brought on by sheer temper? Or perhaps a sort of rare high blood pressure anomaly that made nightmares seem true by fizzing through the cerebral cortex with a last-ditch bypass into the optic nerve just to make the whole thing seem real.

Aeons ago, she'd edited a book about simple things to watch out for health-wise when she was an ultra-junior editor at Factual Anomalies, a small, slightly off-beat publisher of factual manuals. They'd been the sort of publishers who were ahead of the internet curve for oddball information and had plenty of 'Teach Yourself How To Perform the Heimlich Manoeuvre On Every Species'-type fare. It was harder with dogs than you'd think.

Unfortunately, the last chapter of said book: 'If that fails, here's a guide to speedy, low-risk tracheotomies – you don't need to be a doctor to do this!' had been the one that had caused the trouble.

Allegedly low-risk, non-medically performed tracheotomies never went well, no matter how many manuals you read or how often you'd seen it done on *Grey's Anatomy*.

Factual Anomalies had gone down after a slew of civil injury cases, but still, Cari had learned a lot. Like where the carotid artery was and how easily it might be pierced with a flick knife. That had come from their urban survival guide: 'How to survive after an apocalypse with just a knife, water treatment tablets and a car battery', the blurb had said.

It had sold shedloads. People, male readers particularly, liked being prepared. Cari could still vaguely recall how to build an A-frame shelter from planks of wood and some tarpaulin. Not that there was much call for this in her life. But still, you never knew. In the apocalypse/revolution, Gavin would be first up against the wall, that was for sure.

She refocused on the stiff card.

The words remained the same.

She was invited to her Uncle Ed's seventieth birthday at an all-expenses paid weekend in Lisowen Castle in Lisowen, the small, blink-and-you'd-miss-it town where her mother, Nora, father, Mick, and uncles Edward and Kit had grown up. The invitation made it plain that this party was one where the entire extended Brannigan family could get together to celebrate the whole dynasty.

The concept of the word 'extended' was the one which made her feel ill.

Just the family and she could cope.

She'd seen most of them since her disastrous wedding morning. The immediate family of three brothers and their families had been at the few family events, most notably at Uncle Ed's second wedding six months ago to Bess, whom her cousin Jojo called Bess the Impaler. Jojo's mother and Edward's wife, Lottie, had died horribly of cancer now more than three years before, and most of the family were astonished when he found a partner in Bess and then married her with what appeared to be unseemly haste.

However, Bess did not appear to be a touchy-feely sort of person and she had done a good impression of seeming utterly oblivious to the undercurrents of resentment coming from Jojo at the wedding. Cari had found herself feeling sorry for poor Amy, Bess's grown-up daughter, because she had the air of a pound puppy who kept getting left behind while other, cuter puppies went home with for ever families. It couldn't have been easy growing up with Bess as your mama and not being perfect.

Amy, all curves and falling over occasional tables and with a complete lack of small talk, was clearly not her mother's idea of the perfect daughter.

It had been a very small wedding and in respect over Lottie's recent death, all of the extended Brannigan family had *not* been invited. Luckily that meant no Traci, Cari's second cousin, who was married to Barney – the same Barney who'd left Cari stranded on the altar more than three years before, almost fainting with the scents of peonies and shock, after he'd said in a low, guilty voice: 'I'm so sorry, Cari, but I can't. I'm going to marry Traci.'

And then he'd left.

Marched down the aisle with half the guests staring at him open-mouthed and the other half staring at Cari, equally opened-mouthed at the sight of the groom legging it out the church while the bride stood shakily at the altar, alone. In creamy, Celtic-maiden silk, as well as beautiful Jimmy Choo slingbacks in crystal and old gold that had cost a fortune and were a tad too small and hurt.

Jojo, maid of honour and saviour, had bustled Cari to the side and into the vestry, which the priest hadn't liked, but before Jojo had a chance to say anything, her darling Mum had arrived with Lottie and between the two of them they'd conjured up black opaque tights from the bottom of someone's handbag, as well as a man's long, just-in-case-it-turns-cold sweater. The priest had been sent out and they'd unhooked Cari from the wedding dress and into these semi normal clothes in a flash. The sweater was long enough to look like a mini dress. Not at all bridal. Jojo grabbed the shoes and the dress, shoved both into a giant jute shopping bag with *Vincent de Paul Give At Christmas* written on it, then shoved it at her mother.

She whisked Cari out the back vestry door and into Paul's car before the guests had begun streaming out of the church gossiping like mad. Jojo, still in full bridesmaid regalia, had driven to her and Hugh's house, which was – thankfully – not done up like a bridal bower. While Cari had stared at the kettle, wondering how to turn it on because her faculties seemed to have abandoned her, Jojo had pulled off her matron of honour gown and wriggled into her jeans.

Nora and Cari's sister, Maggie, rolled up fifteen minutes later with Cari's handbag, which she had whisked from the second wedding car where Trina, another one of the bridesmaids, was supposed to be minding it.

All the time this flurry of activity was going on, Cari stared into space.

'He's going to marry Traci,' she said to herself over and over, in a haze that two cups of strong coffee with sugar, and one laced with brandy, could not penetrate.

Now, three years later, she would have to see him and Traci once again at this blasted birthday party. Because from the look of the glossy invitation, it was clear that Bess was going to invite every last member of the extended family to this big event. She'd make up for the small wedding now.

And Cari would have to face both Traci, fiancé-stealer, and Barney, ex-fiancé and total pig. Just great.

The Heathrow Express slid seamlessly into the airport. Cari ripped the invitation into very small pieces and, once off the train and in the steely caverns beneath Heathrow, threw the pieces into the first bin she saw.

That was one party she would not be attending.

She marched through the airport like a woman on a mission. She strode past the kind ladies wearily trying to flog perfume and through a hen party in stetsons and sparkles, with T-shirts announcing Little Devils Dublin Tour.

For a brief moment, Cari paused, wedge-booted Robert Clergerie's (wickedly expensive but good for airport travel) resting as she considered informing the bride-to-be (pink, sparkle-encrusted T-shirt in the middle of many black T-shirts) that marriage was insane and it was a far better bet to find herself a lover. Or even a few lovers, instead of plumping for just one man.

Several lovers meant you could have a fabulous-looking commitment-phobe, a muscular guy who specialised in carrying you into the bedroom *and* a bespectacled professor who could talk in bed afterwards, depending on what mood you were in on a particular day. These men couldn't meet, obviously. Or maybe they could? Just to keep them on their toes.

Why be stuck with just *one* man with all his faults, foibles and issues? When a man was one of three, he knew to leave his issues at the door to Cari's apartment. Well, a girl could dream. She had a lovely bed but, in truth, it wasn't getting much action these days. Her libido had died at that altar. No man had warmed her bed since Barney. She decided she had forgotten how to have sex and, actually, that was all right with her. Celibacy was the new…? The new *something*, she was sure.

'Kerry, you look wonderful!' squeaked one of the hen party and Cari noticed that they were running back and forth between the Clarins and the Charlotte Tilbury counters trying out all the make-up.

The bride now boasted sexily red lips and her eyes shone with both the brilliance of the latest palettes and a blusher that made her glow. Sheer happiness was written all over her face.

It was, Cari could see, too late.

She had been overtaken by the pod people.

Like Scrooge muttering 'bah, humbug', at Christmas, Cari stalked off, and made her way into a shoe shop.

Heels, unlike men, never let you down.

She dumped her leather briefcase beside a display shelf, took down a patent leather shoe with a heel like a rapier and checked the size. It was her size: thirty-eight. Perfect.

'Can I help?' said a sweet young salesman, hovering eagerly.

'Does this look like it would rip through a man's crotch if you stood on him?' Cari said, holding up the shoe.

The young man gulped. He was new. His boyfriend had said he should go to the high street store. The airport was full of nutters: everyone knew that.

'Depends,' he said hesitantly.

'On what?'

'How hard you pushed?' He was looking around for the *Candid Camera* people because it was a good job and he'd only just started, and perhaps this was some sort of hazing thing…

Cari ripped off one wedge, slipped her foot into the shoe and ground the heel into the hard shop floor. She thought of one face, one crotch, as she ground. Gavin's. No, Barney's. No, Gavin's.

She thought of the stupid girl getting married and going round announcing the fact, all happiness, stetsons and feather boas. Why wasn't there a warning with marriage? With life?

Everyone betrayed you in the end. Everyone except family. 'I'll try the other one,' she said, sitting down.

The assistant leapt off to the stockroom and returned quickly.

The woman looked normal: sleek business suit, dark coat, very masculine, a briefcase and a very nice Marc Jacobs handbag . . . But perhaps she was a dominatrix beneath it all? He'd seen male doms in the gay clubs but not many women ones. She didn't need a whip to be scary, she just was plain old scary.

The woman tried both shoes on and stomped around, long coat whirling around her like a female Batman. If Batman wore high heels and red lippie, she'd be a dead ringer for him.

'I'll take them,' she growled. 'In fact, I'll wear them.'

The sweet young man grabbed her own shoes and had them in the spike heels' box in a flash. He processed her credit card faster than he ever had in his life and then she was gone, stomping off.

He sighed with relief. He was definitely moving to the high street store.

Two

'A second marriage is a triumph
of hope over experience.'
Samuel Johnson

A glorious year lay ahead, with it a new life, and it was definitely time for new traditions. Parties as husband and wife, holidays, family time...

These were the thoughts running through Bess Brannigan's head as she sat at her computer at Tanglewood House that evening on that Thursday in late February and did what she'd been doing ever since she'd written it three months before: looking, almost furtively, at her Christmas letter. Edward was at a work event, so she had the place to herself.

He wouldn't understand how much she'd loved that letter, how much it had meant to her to send it.

Her joyous missive had long since gone, but the birthday invitations for Edward's seventieth had been posted two days before and, wondering if anyone would have replied just yet via email, she allowed herself another dip into her and Edward's Christmas letter before she checked her email.

She felt a giddy freedom that she, Bess Brannigan, neé Reynolds, a woman known for her iron resolve in business, had been able to send the Christmas letter of her dreams and kept returning to it just for the sheer joy of seeing how wonderfully life had turned out, despite everything.

Bess was not given to self-pity but others might say she had not had an easy life.

During those years as a single, working mother – with her own mother, Maura, performing a bitchy Greek chorus in the

26

background, the main refrain being 'I told you so!' – Bess would not have dreamed of sending out a Christmas letter with her cards.

She'd seen plenty of them and to be frank, had scoffed. *'Stevie has broken up with Fleur but we still see her and baby Rhianna all the time - we're just one big happy family!'*

Imagine that Christmas dinner.

Or *'Anthony is delighted that he took early redundancy because he has so much time for his garden now...'* which meant Anthony was banished to the shed in a vain attempt to keep him out of the pub, why he'd been pushed towards early redundancy in the first place.

'Clarissa has finished her degree in fine art and is looking for a new job, although it's hard out there now!!!! She's back in her old bedroom and is available for babysitting - until a fabulous opportunity comes up, of course!'

Fine arts indeed.

Bess had no time for such degrees, which had limited ways of being monetised. A chartered accountant – now *that* was a qualification. She'd been a C.A. when she was twenty-nine, at a time when women were something of a rarity in the job and when men in suits had tried to pat her behind and intimidate her in some way.

Not a mistake any of them had made twice.

Being older was easier. Nearly thirty years on Bess had a reputation for taking no prisoners; this along with her once brunette, now faintly greying, hair cut in a sculptural bob and a steely glare from her large dark eyes soon put manners on them.

Only men with a death wish would pat her behind and try to intimidate her now.

Funny that Edward could pat her behind fondly and she'd turn and smile at him, filled with love for this man who'd become her husband at this late stage, a time when she thought love had long since passed her by.

Love: it was a magic ingredient like no other.

'It's been a hectic year in the Brannigan household,' she had written in her first ever Christmas letter, sent with the vast number of Christmas cards she and Edward had dispatched. *Yes, folks, to all of you who've known me as Bess Reynolds for so long, I am officially Bess Brannigan since June and I love it.*

Edward and I have renovated Tanglewood on the North Dublin coast, I'm attaching photos, and it's now open plan with picture windows so you can see the bay. We have dolphins come to swim in the cove and Edward swears he saw a basking shark one day but I'm not sure. I know I've bored you all with the photos of our safari honeymoon but here are some more anyway!

To anyone who said they thought lions wouldn't eat me out of professional courtesy, well, ha!! Edward's a fabulous photographer and he got lovely photos of lions, all the big five, in fact. It was marvellous.'

Until she'd met Edward, Bess thought that women who married again must have been stark raving mad. At fifty-eight, she lived happily on her own, could sit at her own dinner table in her pyjamas if she felt like it and eat a salad while watching whatever she wanted on the box. The soaps, a soppy film, a documentary on cake making, whatever. Who needed someone else to cook and clean for?

In retrospect, Bess realised she'd never been even vaguely in love with her first husband, the charming, handsome and wandering Dennis. They'd been too young and his hands were more likely to be found on other women's derrières than on hers.

Neither had Dennis been much of a man for work. Or savings, come to that. After a few years of marriage, Bess had come to the conclusion that banknotes sang to him and if he had any number of them in his pocket, he had a wild urge to release their plaintive song into the world.

They were such opposites, they were almost different species, but Dennis had provided her with a daughter, Amy.

Amy was the return for her investment in Dennis.

It hadn't been hard to send him off to London to live so they could get divorced, divorce not being a possibility in Ireland in those days unless one of the parties lived abroad.

'No bother, lovie,' Dennis had said, still cheerful, despite the end of their five-year marriage.

His relentless cheerfulness drove Bess mad. They might have been discussing changing the wallpaper in the dining room instead of splitting up. 'You will pay the money into my account, like you promised, won't you?' he added.

Bess thought of how Dennis had never got up for a night feed with baby Amy; how he'd promise to put on a wash but would inevitably forget; how he'd always been late to pick Amy up from crèche on the days he was supposed to be doing it – even on those many days when he hadn't a job. She thought of herself hauling shopping bags and Amy's carry seat into their small starter home, and how Dennis would wait until she had finished putting it all away before noticing she'd returned in the first place.

If he was gone, if he divorced her, then he could never come back. He could skip from job to job and she would not have to worry about whose skirt his hand was sliding up or if he was going to embarrass her in front of the neighbours by sliding said hand up the wrong skirt.

'I'll pay,' she'd said.

At the age of thirty-two, Bess Reynolds had been paying maintenance to her former husband, had been the single mother of a quiet little girl called Amy, had a fabulous reputation as a brilliant accountant, and had the life of a plain clothes nun.

'I told you that Dennis was a waster,' Bess's mother, Maura, snapped with the regularity of the speaking clock. 'You lost your mind when you married him, had your head turned by his looks. Good-looking men are all useless. I did tell you—'

At least the speaking clock *varied* what it said.

Little Amy, with her strawberry-blonde hair, big blue eyes and a thumb that was always in her mouth despite all Bess's efforts, was afraid of her grandmother and Bess could see why. Only a person raised by her would not fear Maura, a woman for whom the expression 'tough as old boots' might have been invented.

Her mother, Bess often thought, had missed her calling: she'd have been a fabulous politician or else the perfect woman in charge of some last-chance-saloon addiction clinic/jail where people with denial issues went when all else had failed. Fear of failure when Maura was in charge would have ripped any desire to use/drink/reoffend right out of the patients. Both governments and addicts would have quailed before her.

The years after Dennis had been hard for Bess, both financially and personally, so there would never have been Christmas letters unless she had a taste for airing her dismally dirty laundry in public:

Dennis wants to marry again and still wants his maintenance money. He knows that if he marries, it stops. He says we never had a binding legal agreement that would stand up in Ireland anyway and he wants custody, which is just a ploy to frighten me. His new fiancée is a dancer.'

'Stripper,' her mother rasped when she heard the news, in a voice hardened by a lifetime's fondness for untipped cigarettes which she smoked out of the side of her mouth as she talked. 'Ballerinas only marry other ballerinas and what other sort of dancer would look at Dennis apart from a stripper?'

'Amy is not doing well at school,' Bess might have written in her putative Christmas letter, but would not, because it was as bad as her mother claiming Dennis's new love was a stripper.

'The head nun told me Amy cried today because she says she's the only girl in school without a father. We don't need one, I've told her, and I'm certainly not looking, but hilariously, all the other women think I'm after their half-bald men so I never get invited to the parents' nights out.

I'm the only divorced mother in the school which is like telling people you've killed several people and are out on bail. They think the very notion of divorce might be catching, except the ones who sidle up to me and ask me how exactly we did it, given that divorce is not yet legal in the Republic of Ireland. Lots of happy marriages out there!

I've told Amy that we do fine on our own, but she wants to be like everyone else. And where does that get a person? I want to cry. You might as well be yourself. It's not an easy road but at least you're true to yourself.

Also, my ex-husband is looking for more money, I don't have it and his new love is possibly a stripper - in which case, she might make more money than I do. But he does keep in touch with our daughter and I can't deny her that. If I stop sending him the odd few hundred quid, would he phoning her stop too? I can't take the risk - it's too important to the poor child.'

Yet again, not the stuff of which Christmas letters were made.

A few years later, the letter might have moved on to more worries:

'Amy blames me for not keeping the channels of communication open between her and Dennis. The channel was actually money. I can't tell her that, can I? No teenager wants to know that their father only rang on birthdays because he could remind his ex-wife where to send the cheques.'

And then – when Bess was fifty-eight, Amy was raised and Dennis was no longer on the payroll, having married and then divorced his dancer – Edward Brannigan had come into her life: Edward with his courtly ways, his wonderful sense of humour, low golf handicap so he could beat Bess on the course but not low enough that he bored her with tales of holes lost and won, and a sex appeal that made something inside Bess – something that had laid dormant for years – awaken.

They'd met at a business dinner and Bess had found herself seated beside Edward, widowed head of a big engineering company, supposedly very wealthy with vast investments but not flashy, rattling-giant-gold-Rolex rich. He was far more subtle and elegant, a silver fox, with that luxuriant silver-grey hair that looked so good on men. He was tanned from the golf course, yet had the strong wrists and shoulders that told of days reared on a farm.

Bess didn't notice men, not any more. She knew better. Divorced women who looked at men at events were labelled as manhunters. But she couldn't stop noticing this one.

He wore a soft jacket in a warm colour, like beech leaves turning in autumn, and in it he stood out among all the men in their greys and navys. His eyes were hazel and warm, and some sort of amber and vetivert scent surrounded him, making Bess think of sun holidays where she could find a private little beach, set herself up for the day with her books and let her skin warm gently.

'I'd been told you're a tough cookie, Ms Reynolds,' he'd said. 'Nobody mentioned how lovely you were.'

Bess, who could command a room in a moment and would have sworn she'd never blushed in her life, turned a faint pink colour. She was beyond the hot flush of menopausal hormones, she knew: *he* was making her blush, *he* was heating her up. Mr Silver Fox was flirting with her and she loved it.

That night as she took off her mascara, she told herself it was all ridiculous and she'd been imagining the attraction. Instead, she focused on one thing at a time, the way she always did. She patted her eyelids with the remover stuff, reflecting how she was forever promising to give up wearing mascara because removing it was a nuisance, and yet tonight, she was glad she had. She had good eyes: always had. Good bones, too, and a strong, handsome face as her mother said when she wasn't lamenting Bess's mistakes.

Somehow, she stopped removing her eye make-up and thought about how it felt to be sitting beside a man who both found her attractive and was obvious about it. The unusualness of the whole situation made her breathless. And it was a long, long time since Bess had been breathless over anything but a fast walk.

In the mirror was a woman reaching the cliff face of sixty, whose face said as much, but who still had the elegant collarbones of her youth, and whose dark hair still rippled around eyes that had once burned with passion for feckless Dennis.

She must have been mad, Bess told herself, and yet continued to rub the coconut body lotion into skin still tanned from that week in Sicily where she'd left the buttoned-up Bess Reynolds behind and let herself go, wearing flowing skirts, gypsy blouses and revelling in stripping down to her swimsuit to dive into the sea.

'Dinner?' The request, one single word written in a strong hand with fountain pen on Edward Brannigan's headed notepaper, delivered to her office with – oh joy, how original! – velvety white Vendela roses the following Monday had made her melt even more.

How could she reply with equal brevity and wit?

She drew a box, put a tick in it, and wrote 'YES' in capital letters under it as a reply.

An hour later, she sent a second note via courier – shocked at her own spendiness – and wrote 'Friday?'

She giggled, actually giggled, when he wrote back: *'I hope you mean this Friday but I'm not sure I can wait that long. Should I choose and pick you up? Did you like the roses? I thought red were too obvious for a woman like you.'*

Days before, Bess Reynolds would have thought that men sending roses and women being thrilled by that was too dully stupid for words, but now she thought it was the most original gesture ever. It was the person who sent them that mattered. Clearly, she had never met the right person before, had never known such a person existed.

Now, a year shy of her sixtieth birthday, Bess was at a new stage in her life. Amy was grown up and Dennis was a long-forgotten legal battle – 'try working', Bess had finally told him when he'd married his dancer and moaned about no more cheques from Ireland. 'The gravy train is stopping.'

He'd disappeared from both her and Amy's life when the money dried up, a fact for which Amy still blamed her mother.

And Bess, although she could hardly believe it herself, was married again.

'Mrs Bess Brannigan' – the very words still thrilled her in a way she thought she was far beyond feeling.

Her new husband loved her, adored her. He hugged fondly, said he needed a proper kiss after a day in work, brought her tea in bed at the weekends, and brought her flowers *for no reason*.

At weekends, they lay lazily in bed in the mornings, making love, then reading the papers, and when Bess took a bath in the giant cream stone oval bath that suited Edward's long frame, he sat on the edge of it, reading funny pieces from the newspapers to her, as if he couldn't bear to be parted from her.

Now she could write a Christmas letter.

'Amy is so happy with her new job—'

Bess paused. The absolute unvarnished truth was not required in these letters.

Bess adored Amy, yet despite trying very hard had never managed to be the uncritically adoring mother she'd planned to be.

'Don't be your mother!' would flash into Bess's head when Amy did something she disagreed with. But steely,

34

uncompromising Maura would somehow channel her way in and create a distance between Bess (trained and accustomed to a hard life) and her daughter (whom Bess had tried so very hard to insulate from pain).

Now thirty-two, Amy appeared to like the place where she now worked, but dressing shop windows for a cheap chain store was not a career by any stretch of the imagination. Bess had seen the windows: men's work trousers alongside cheap athletic gear and the odd bicycle from Lord knew where thrown into the mix. It was better than Amy's previous jobs, all of which had been random, none with any clearly defined path.

If only Amy had found a career she loved or even – the Bess of old would have never thought this but, newly married, she did – found a man she loved. Romantic love had come as a shock to Bess. She'd thought it didn't exist, but thanks to Edward she now knew it did and perhaps if Amy found proper love...

'Amy made a beautiful bridesmaid at our wedding in June, for all of you who couldn't make it.'

That was true at least. Bess had taken one look at photos of her soon-to-be stepdaughter, Jojo, and Jojo's three girl cousins early on and decided that if she and Edward ever did tie the knot, Amy would need a revamp with professional help. She would not blend into the background by comparison with Edward's admittedly stunning daughter and nieces. There were four Brannigan girls: Edward's daughter, Jojo, who was Viking blonde, and his nieces Cari, Maggie and Trina, all utterly stunning brunettes.

Stunning – there was no other word for it.

They were something, those Brannigan girls – in a quartet, they looked like an aristocratic portrait of European royalty shipped around the Empire in the 1800s to be shown as prospective brides to heirs to thrones in important kingdoms. There was something of the Ralph Lauren model thing about all of them that had annoyed Bess without her knowing why:

all good skin, all with incredible eyes, confident gazes ... yes, *that* was it. All four looked happy and confident in a way that Amy never had.

Bess, hit with the dual feeling of guilt that her daughter had no confidence in her, and terrified it was her fault, was fiercely determined that Amy would not feel lacking beside these girls. She would look just as good as the Brannigans.

Amy's dress had been a special order Vera Wang that had cost a small fortune, a gown in a subtle peach that suited her pale freckled skin and the rippling strawberry-blonde hair that was her most beautiful feature.

Amy wasn't slim like the four Brannigan girls, being more of a curvy girl, and she hadn't a clue about clothes or make-up, which Bess refused to feel guilty about, because she'd been earning a living when the girl was growing up and hadn't had time to sit and play dressing-up like some mothers did.

OK, she did feel guilty. Hideously guilty. But she did her best to quash the guilt. Relentlessly.

Before the actual wedding, guilt meant Bess insisted the make-up artist come three times to try out different looks.

Bess had felt like she was hitting a baby seal at the look in Amy's pale blue eyes that third night as Bess had instructed the make-up girl in layering on the make-up with a trowel.

'She has lovely eyes, she doesn't need it this heavy,' the make-up artist had said, while Amy had sat, mute.

'She does have nice eyes but you have to make the best of them,' Bess said desperately, ignoring Amy's sad face.

She had seen the endless photos of Edward's daughter, Jojo, and his son, Paul, and of their cousins, Cari, Maggie and Trina. All stunning with that rippling dark hair. Jojo was blonde like her mother.

She'd met Jojo too once, although Jojo had been white-faced with suppressed rage at the time, so she hadn't looked quite so well, but still.

Any nineteenth-century princedom in Europe would have

36

snatched her up in a moment, rage or not. She had been like an exquisite racehorse: quivering with nerves, beauty and breeding.

No, Bess vowed, determined to do right by both her daughter and herself on this important occasion, Amy would be done up and that was it. Couldn't Amy see? It was important to Bess that her beloved daughter be as beautiful as Edward's daughter and nieces.

'Do that thing with the eyebrows, the darkening and winging it out thing that's all the rage,' Bess ordered, having seen the look in the hairdressers when she was having her roots touched up to hide the grey.

'I'm not sure it suits her colouring,' insisted the make-up artist, who was so over the eyebrow thing.

'Look, just do it,' Bess said crossly, ignoring her daughter.

Amy said nothing.

In work when mentoring women, Bess had always pointed out that you had to say what you thought. Nobody would ever get by in business with slight glances at each other. How had she missed these vital steps with her own daughter? If Amy didn't like the make-up, all she had to do was speak!

'In marrying Edward, I have gained a wonderful family, chief among them my two beautiful stepchildren, Jojo and Paul. I also have a fabulous son-in-law, the handsome Hugh, and lovely stepdaughter-in-law, Lena, and best of all, the most darling step-grandchild named Heidi. Here's a photo from the wedding.'

Heidi was fourteen months old and was a darling. Bess had adored holding her, hugging her and thinking that, at last, she had her own grandchild, even if she was truly Lottie's grandchild, but still. Having Heidi at the wedding helped no end, particularly at the photographs, because there was always a diversion in saying, 'Look at the camera, Heidi!' in a loud, happy voice to divert attention from the fact that one segment of the wedding party was displaying a cold front towards the other. It was the Cold War in fancy clothes with music.

The photograph Bess had sent out with her Christmas missive had taken an age to choose. Despite there being scores of wedding photographs, Bess wanted one where Jojo wasn't standing as far away from her new stepmother as possible so that it wasn't instantly obvious that Jojo loathed being at her father's wedding a mere two and a half years after her mother had died.

At least Jojo had come to the wedding – Bess had Edward's sister-in-law, Nora, to thank for that. Nora had convinced her, apparently.

'Paul has come round to the idea of it all, he says I should be happy. Jojo will get to that stage too, darling,' Edward said, but Bess had the strangest feeling that he either wasn't telling the truth – or was hoping that if he said it often enough, it would become the truth.

Edward was a successful businessman because he had drive and ambition, like Bess herself. But in this case, Bess wondered if he was trying very hard to convince himself that his daughter would be reconciled to this wedding, and ignoring all the evidence to the contrary.

For all that men were supposed to be strong, Bess found that sometimes they couldn't face reality.

Paul was a different case entirely when it came to his father's wedding. He was a son. He'd adored his mother but he had a life, a wife and toddler, and he lived in another country. All entirely different.

Everybody knew that girls adored their fathers – look at poor Amy and the absent Dennis – and Bess had certainly loved her own.

But Jojo was an adult. Didn't that make a difference?

Bess had resolutely not done any research into blending her family into Edward's. She didn't hold with such mumbo jumbo. People had to get on with things. But she knew girls took fathers remarrying differently than sons. Daddy's little princess and all that. It would blow over.

But it hadn't, not at the wedding, anyhow.

The perfect wedding photo had been captured finally because the photographer, whom Bess had warned in advance, had positioned the family group in a tiny floral bower so that everyone *had* to stand close, whether they liked it or not.

Jojo was beside her father, leaving a very anxious Amy in her Vera Wang to stand next to her, with Paul beside Bess, his new stepmother. Paul's wife, Lena, holding the gorgeous Heidi, stood beside Paul, and Hugh – Jojo's lovely husband – stood on the other side of Amy, looking more relaxed than any of the rest of them.

Amy looked as well as she ever had, but despite the dress, the make-up, the eyebrows, even the diet Bess had forced her on, nothing could dim Jojo's spectacular beauty.

An almost Scandinavian blonde like her departed mother, Jojo was lean, willowy and standing in Bess's way.

Jojo needed to know: Bess would win this battle.

And yet, it wasn't easy. With his daughter present, Edward was infinitesimally different with Bess. At the wedding itself, there was less hand-holding and kissing even when Jojo wasn't around, and when she was, there was almost no hand-holding at all, no touch of Edward's lips on her collarbone, his favourite place on her body, he murmured.

Time, Bess hoped. Time would fix it...?

She looked at the few invitations for Edward's birthday that still lay on her desk. Everyone would have the invitations by now. She'd spent ages choosing them. Not too expensive-looking, she'd decided. Simple cream card with gold lettering:

Edward and Bess Brannigan invite you to celebrate
Edward's seventieth birthday party in the glorious surroundings
of Lisowen Castle, Co. Kerry on the weekend of 25th March.
We would be delighted if you would be our guests for
a weekend of celebration.

There followed details of the Friday night dinner (semi-casual) and then the grand black-tie dinner on Saturday, where Bess had decided not to mention, on paper, that there would be a band and dancing, and vintage champagne.

To make too much of it all on the invitation might raise too much ire. She felt as if she'd been judged enough by the Brannigan family as it was and she didn't want Edward's birthday to turn into an event about herself instead of about her husband.

Because she did love him, very much, despite what some people thought. Only a fool or a masochist would marry a man for his money when his beloved wife was dead a mere two and a half years, a wife whom everyone treated as if she were Mother Theresa and Audrey Hepburn rolled into one perfect package. And Bess was no fool.

If she hadn't loved Edward, she would have taken one look at the Brannigan family with all their cabals and tribal alignments and run as far as she could. But she did love him. And that was that.

She thought of Jojo and her naked hatred. Bess had had people hate her before, people in business who might not have expected her to be so scrupulously honest, so determined to stick to the letter of the law.

It wasn't a nice feeling being hated. But it happened.

Having Edward's seventieth in the hotel beside the old family home, where all of them, Edward's dead wife included, had come from was certainly a risk, yes. But why not. She was doing it for her husband. She adored him and he adored her back.

Didn't that trump everything?

Three

SECRETS OF A HAPPY MARRIAGE #1

Perfect true love exists only in fairytales. In real life,
tempers get frayed, princes forget birthdays and princesses
somehow end up doing more of the housework! Take the
fairytale out of the equation and things will improve.

Jojo Hennessy sat in the small office-cum-stockroom in the clothes shop, looking at the order book, and compared what she and her business partner, Elaine, had ordered in Paris with what had actually turned up in their boxes, and felt a paralysing headache coming on.

The headache was not from the small room, which was painted a tasteful warm grey with white woodwork, and which was perfectly organised by Elaine, Jojo's business partner in I'll Take It, the mid-sized, mid-priced boutique in Silver Bay that Jojo and Elaine had been running successfully for the past six years.

The stockroom was tidier than most people's houses, certainly tidier than Jojo's bedroom, which she would be ashamed to show to anyone other than Hugh, her husband.

Jojo, despite looking supremely, coolly organised on the outside, had a certain chaos attached to her when it came to her own possessions, bits of paper, and things in the fridge that needed to have been used a week ago and might now poison somebody should they dare to eat them.

She spent a lot of life saying to Hugh: 'I'm going to sort out the fridge, honey, and don't mind the pile of clothes on the spare room bed. I need to go through them for the charity shop...' And then being too busy to get round to it.

Hugh, who had fair ruffled hair that was receding, the kindest

41

heart, and adored Jojo, agreed, and then sorted out the fridge himself because he hated mess. A corporate lawyer, one of his best friends in the office was a family lawyer and you couldn't hear that many stories of vitriolic divorces that had started innocently over who was always leaving the toilet seat up or who never filled the dishwasher correctly without realising that sweating the small stuff did not lead to happy marriages.

'Dunno how you put up with me,' Jojo would say when she'd open a pristine fridge where all the about-to-become-alive fluffy things had been put in the compost bin and a cut-up lemon had soaked up the bad smells.

'Because I love you,' Hugh said, and Jojo thanked her lucky stars for both Hugh and his mother, a wise woman who'd sent all her kids off into the world with coping skills, including the ability to cook, clean and use the washing machine.

In the shop, Jojo's partner Elaine anxiously admitted that she was hovering around the edges of mild obsessive compulsive disorder.

'I'm not imprisoned by it, thankfully, but I'm certainly on the spectrum,' she liked to say. 'Although why did they call it OCD? If you have OCD, the placement of the letters is beyond annoying. I alphabetise my *Vogue*s. It should be CDO, as per the alphabet.'

Jojo's headache that morning was coming from what was emerging from the big cardboard box that had been delivered earlier, one of the later of the deliveries of their spring collection.

She and Elaine had been in Paris in January to pick up some new stock because the early stuff had sold so well another trip had been necessary.

Running a shop like theirs did not mean meeting posh designers in the Plaza Athenée or sitting in the frow at Paris Fashion Week – it involved wearing out shoe leather traipsing up and down Paris's garment districts and ordering direct from small warehouse shops or ateliers, in certain cases.

Today's box was from Mimi le Peu Mitzou, a little whole-salers in their usual haunt in Le Sentier. It had piles of fake fur stuff in one window and some lovely knitwear in the other. They'd never bought from Mimi le Peu Mitzou, hadn't remembered seeing the shop before, but as they'd walked past Elaine had spotted the knitwear in the window.

'Shall we?'

'We don't know them,' Jojo said, ever cautious, consulting her list of wholesalers.

Despite her untidiness, she was the sensible one of the pair when it came to buying. Elaine was so in love with fashion that she couldn't help but take the odd risk. Jojo was her father's daughter business-wise. They could only afford so many risks per season.

Buying wholesale meant instant payment, no credit, so they were careful about what they bought and who they bought it from, but Elaine had spotted some old rose and dusty turquoise knits in a lovely merino wool and she'd felt they might sell well for spring.

They'd gone in, ordered and had spent an hour working out what sizes, colours and how many of each piece of knitwear they wanted. It was a slow process, slowed down by all the other boutique owners there doing exactly the same thing. Job done, they'd gone off to buy more things and had returned three hours later to find their stuff packed up in sealed boxes and ready to be paid for and shipped later. Years ago, the women had brought huge suitcases and taken their clothes haul home with them on the plane but that had been a nightmare, so these days they paid extra for the clothes to be couriered.

Now, in the giant box with everything packed into separate cellophane bags that slithered through her hands like plastic fish, Jojo could see creams and blacks, nothing in marl grey, which was always a fabulous seller, and no old rose or dusty turquoise, either.

The true source of her headache were the six long beaded

evening gowns that had been carefully tissue-papered and packed in and as she pulled the last one out, she didn't know whether to curse or cry. The dresses were exquisite.

But their shop in Silver Bay was not the place where women went to get Oscar-worthy dresses. It was, instead, a shop where ordinary women found comfortable yet modern clothes, clever simple things that you just threw on and forgot about, a shirt they could wear to work with a simple, on-trend skirt or dress up with heels for night.

Jojo and Elaine had built their shop up on the basis of being a spot where both clothes-addicts and those uninterested in clothes could rush in, find a capsule wardrobe and then jazz it all up with one of Elaine's mad buys, like the lipstick-pink trenchcoats that had sold out in a week, or the matte sequinned navy bomber jackets that everyone from thirty to seventy wanted. These six Oscar dresses were wrong, wrong, wrong and Jojo knew that she hadn't ordered them.

She'd heard of wholesalers who did this to customers who weren't regulars or who might not be back: inserted something crazy and took out the easily sold garments, meaning that the shop in question would either have to ship the wrong things back, at great expense, or just take the hit and try to sell them – even though they weren't right for their market. Why had she tried a new supplier instead of sticking with her old friends? This had never happened to her before. She'd bet it was a new shop and would be gone if she went back. Someone who was messing up business for all the professionals in the Parisian garment district.

The dresses weren't listed on the invoice, so by checking her iPad for the code to understand the complicated pricing on the list of figures on the garments, Jojo worked out that the dresses had cost 200 euros each wholesale. If she applied the basic shop principle of mark-up, she'd have to charge at least 560 euros for each dress. Nothing in the shop, not even the expensive leather knee boots in Spanish leather that everyone was lusting after, cost anything near that.

Damn. This was what happened when they went off-track with buying and went to unknown wholesalers. They ran the shop on a tight margin and couldn't afford a hit like this.

She looked at the evening gowns and sighed again.

Her smartphone shoved into her jeans pocket buzzed and seeing it was her Aunt Nora, who was as close as a mother these days now that her own darling Mum was gone, Jojo answered.

'Hello, pet, are you working hard? You work too hard, you know.'

Jojo smiled into the phone.

Nora always started conversations this way. It was comforting, and sad too. Jojo's own mother would never say those things to her again, although Lottie used to say, 'Get out of that stockroom, darling, and come and meet me for a coffee! You'll get neck strain from dragging boxes around.'

'I don't work too hard, Nora,' said Jojo, trying to wipe her eyes without entirely ruining her eye make-up. In the first year after her mother had died, Jojo had worn very little make-up because she routinely scrubbed it off and she finally discovered why people liked those eye drops so much. Not that she cared about having red eyes but the sight of them made people put sympathetic hands on her and say, 'How are you feeling?' which made Jojo want to stab them.

'How do you think I am feeling?' she wanted to demand.

Sick, desperate, hollow, frozen, as if I will never be happy again!

And who wanted that conversation?

The death of a parent was such a huge void in a person's life and when the parent was as close to her child as Lottie had been to Jojo, it was more than a void: it was an abyss that kept looking back grimly.

The abyss had been made worse by her father marrying again.

That was the betrayal from which Jojo could not recover.

It was as if, in one swift move, he'd made her childhood home and love mean nothing because how could he ever have loved her mother if he could marry again so quickly?

'I bet you're in that stockroom hauling things around,' Nora said.

'Crystal ball out again?' joked Jojo, thinking that this must be progress if she could joke.

'Educated guess. Your mother always said you spent more time in that room than on the floor, figuring out what had sold, what was a mistake, trying to analyse it all.'

'Yeah, she did,' said Jojo.

That was the other great thing about Nora – she talked about Jojo's mother, didn't avoid the subject as if Lottie Brannigan had never existed and they'd all be better if they just forgot about her.

Did people think that helped you deal with death? Ignore it, like a giant elephant in the room that everybody carefully avoided mentioning.

Jojo's father, Edward, didn't talk about his dead wife. Not any more. Not since he'd married that bitch, Bess.

'A pot of tea? I'm just around the corner?' said Nora, who must indeed have a crystal ball, so quickly did she move the conversation on. 'Elaine's in today, isn't she?'

'Yes, she is and I'd love to see you,' Jojo said.

They arranged to meet and Jojo hung up. From outside on the floor, she could hear Elaine trying to sell something/ anything to one of those customers who came in, tried on everything in the shop, and then said they'd go home 'to think about it'.

'They're bored, they don't want to buy.' Jojo shrugged. She had seen it all before and no longer got irritated by such behaviour.

Elaine took this as a challenge.

'When they make me find every size possible and locate

long-lost scarves to accessorise, and have to have shoes and jewellery, and then march off to say they'll think about it, I go insane! I want them to buy *something*. Even a bracelet!'

Jojo finished her tidy-up of the stockroom and came out to find Elaine vacuuming the already-spotless shop floor with a certain degree of rage.

'Not even a bracelet, huh?' said Jojo, when Elaine had banged the vacuum's 'off' button with her heel.

'She tried on the most expensive thing in the shop—'

'The navy silk dress?'

'The navy silk,' confirmed Elaine, 'and it suited her, actually, the old cow, and then, once she'd sweated all over it for half an hour and I had found five pairs of shoes and three jackets to try different looks, says she "would think about it …" As if that woman has enough brain cells to think? Can't I put my Most Wanted poster list on the door?'

Jojo laughed. Elaine's latest plan was to hang a facsimile of the FBI Most Wanted poster with the most serial offenders of the 'trying everything on and buy nothing' photos on it on the door. These women were to be denied access to the shop on the grounds of sheer irritation. Or on the grounds that they were trying everything on to then go home and order it cheaper on the internet.

'We would be out of business in a day, honey,' Jojo said. 'Lots of people come in, try stuff on and leave. That's how shops work. We can't stop the internet-checker-outers, either.'

'These cows never buy anything! You know they don't. Imagine the sheer the pleasure of barring them—' said Elaine, lost in the daydream. 'A woman came in looking for a necklace while Madam was in the changing room and I had to race to serve her, and I'm sure she'd have tried some stuff on if that old cow hadn't been hogging my attention.'

'When we write our memoirs,' Jojo said soothingly, 'we can include them all.'

'The ones who insist they're a size six when they're not and

47

tell us all our clothes must be cheap junk with the wrong sizes on them?'

'Those ones too,' Jojo said. 'I'm dropping out for a coffee with Nora. Can you manage? Not kill anyone by strangling them with the vacuum hose?'

Elaine laughed. She was, at thirty-three, one year younger than Jojo, but Jojo was convinced that these days her friend looked ten years younger somehow. This was partly due to Elaine's pixie face with huge dark eyes and dark hair cut in a complicated style that looked as if it needed four hairstylists at it every morning, but which Jojo knew – from sharing a room on their buying trips – Elaine styled by simply running her hands through it with a bit of styling wax.

Jojo's hair needed fixing every morning because she woke looking as if she'd been electrocuted as she slept, while Elaine's looked cutting edge with a mere hand rubbed idly through it.

'It's nothing to do with me, I just have obedient hair,' Elaine said, when Jojo went at her frizz with the hair straighteners for a good fifteen minutes.

They made a good team: Jojo was the tall, cool one and Elaine was the sparky one, the life and soul of every party, the person doing tequila shots and organising dancing when everyone else was thinking about getting taxis home.

People assumed Jojo was the organised one too and she was when it came to money and stock control, but otherwise Elaine ruled the roost.

'You look cool and calm,' Elaine said, 'which is entirely misleading since you can't hold on to your mobile phone for five minutes and you're a cauldron of wild passion, while I look like the "mad" one. It's the blonde hair. If my hair was straight and blonde, decent, sensible men would ask me out instead of all the lunatics who seem to make a beeline for me.'

'I only wish my hair was naturally straight,' Jojo pointed out, 'and besides, you like lunatics.'

'I'm thirty-three now,' said Elaine. 'You can only go out with

48

crazy, "let's-drive-to-Belfast-tonight-just-for-the-hell-of-it-because-my-friend's-band's-playing" men for so long. I want to settle down, stop going out with musicians or people writing avant-garde plays that nobody wants to put on. I want my own version of Hugh: kind, sensible, gorgeous and in love with the woman he married. Can't you have him cloned for me?'

'The two of you are far too organised to ever be together,' Jojo said, laughing. 'It works between us because I drop my coat on the newel post and Hugh takes it upstairs and hangs it up. With you, you'd be fighting over who got to hang things up and arguing over who had control of the kitchen pot scrubber. No, you need a nice chaotic man who wouldn't recognise a pot scrubber if it bit him.'

'The world's full of them,' Elaine said gloomily, 'although I feel as if I've gone out with them all already. All I need is for a fresh batch to be released from prison with abs of steel and prison ink tattoos to say who they've killed and which white supremacist gang they like best, and I'll probably fall for them despite myself and my liberal, anti-racist views. You need to save me from my hopeless taste in men. Not keep recommending mad ones.'

They'd known each other since college, although Jojo felt she was ageing far faster than the one-year gap implied. Elaine's skin was unlined while hers – well, if you could have Photoshop for your daily life, she'd have signed up for it.

Particularly now.

The menopause was hard on the skin, even when you were thirty-four. Even if it was a fake menopause caused by fertility treatment. In fact, especially then. Because surely normal menopause came when you were ready for it, had – hopefully – had your chance for children, had done zillions of cycles of menstruation, were expecting what was euphemistically called 'the change'.

But being forced into an unnatural menopause so that the infertility people could be in total charge of her cycle, *that*

49

played havoc with everything: skin, mood, anxiety, a desire to scream at people, crying bouts. Worse, she had no mother to tell about it all. The only people who knew were herself, her husband, Hugh, and her cousin, Cari, without whom Jojo might currently be in jail where she could get her own prison ink: a teardrop on her cheek signifying how many people she'd killed. She'd only need one, for Bess.

Only Cari knew how angry and upset Jojo really was by her father marrying that bitch; only Cari knew how betrayed Jojo felt; and because telling Nora, Cari's mother, about the infertility would remind her too much of how she'd never been able to tell her own mother, only Cari knew about that too.

Her younger brother Paul wouldn't understand – Paul had got married and had a baby within a twelve-month time frame. He would say something anodyne like 'Give it time, Jojo,' and she'd have to hop on a plane to Manhattan and kick him in the shins the way she used to when they were kids and he'd annoyed her.

No. He couldn't know. Nobody could.

Nobody could know that Jojo and Hugh were currently on their third course of infertility treatment, treatment that meant daily injections for Jojo to regulate her cycle, injections that had transformed her into a woman suffering from triple grief: the grief of childlessness, the grief of her mother's death and the grief that came with being on a third IVF cycle because the other two had failed so spectacularly. She'd thought it would work first time. That getting pregnant would be her gift from the heavens for losing her mother: a trade-off. What an idiot she had been.

She was no psychologist, although she and Hugh had to see one before each cycle to see how well they were coping with the whole thing, but Jojo knew that secrets, infertility and grief were not good for a person's psyche.

She had been a different person once: happy, funny, able to laugh at herself and take joy in other people's happiness.

But the triad of pain over the past few years had hit her like a hurricane.

Her mother's illness and death, her own infertility, and now Bess, attempting to fill an altogether unfillable gap in all their lives, had all made Jojo into someone else, someone angry with the world, someone she didn't like very much.

The fun, passionate woman Hugh had fallen in love with had gone and Jojo mourned her too.

'Mum is gone and I can't talk to her about any of this,' Jojo sobbed to her cousin Cari during that first hideous IVF treatment, when she hadn't known what to expect and her hormones and mood had joined forces and gone to the depths of the Mariana Trench.

Cari, who was clever, wise and the sort of friend who said the right thing and not what you wanted to hear, had delivered tough love: 'Yes, Auntie Lottie is gone, Jojo, honey, but hating Bess will not bring her back. You can't do two things at once – hate her and keep enough love in you to have a baby. This rage and anxiety is not the way to prepare to be pregnant. What's the point of having soothing lavender baths and burning calming essential oils morning noon and night if you're consumed with rage? I bet you never said any of this to the psychologist at the pre-treatment sessions.'

'No,' said Jojo. Blasted Cari, always hitting the nail on the head. 'But that's not the point—'

'It *is* the point,' insisted Cari. 'You can't control what your dad does, Jojo. Let it go. Let him be married and—'

'Mum's dead and he got married again to someone who is her complete opposite. He said he'd love Mum for ever! He was lying!' Jojo raged.

'People lie,' Cari said flatly, thinking of Barney, and then amended it to: 'Your father adored your mother, Jojo, and you know it. Adored her. But men move on. Life moves on. You need your life to move on. What do you want more – a baby or a sign on your headstone saying: "Childless but, wow, she sure made her stepmother's life hell?"'

Even Jojo had to laugh at that. 'Have you ever considered psychiatric stand-up? You could make them laugh and diagnose all illnesses as well.'

Cari grinned. 'I have read a lot of self-help books in the past three years. Some of them are even quite good, except for the ones that suggest having one single square of dark chocolate if you need sugar. One square? Who can eat just one square? Anyway, I did not get over bloody Barney and Traci by raging mentally over them day and night. OK, I did at first,' she admitted, 'because I dreamed up scenarios about how I'd either kill them both or just kill Traci and have Barney all to myself. But then, I had to move on, Jojo, or I'd be sitting somewhere in a haze of booze and tranquillisers staring at the wall and saying "poor me". Look, I know this is different – you adored your mother and she was taken too early. Add that to this desperation to have a baby, and then what you feel is your dad betraying you, and you will never get pregnant. Your body is under too much stress. All that cortisol and stuff, it wreaks havoc with your system.'

'I know,' agreed Jojo, anything to get Cari to stop with the truth and the honesty.

So she'd tried to get over Bess, she really had, but then Bess had wanted to overhaul Tanglewood, Jojo and Paul's old home, and all the rage had come back.

She left the shop to meet her aunt, wishing she was able to tell dear Elaine about the infertility treatment because Elaine would have to be a blind, deaf mute not to notice how up and down her moods were, but then Elaine would drive her nuts every day asking about how she was, how the injections had gone, did she feel *different*? How about adoption, fostering, getting a dog?

Elaine wasn't in the slightest bit motherly and had no interest in children, although she did talk of getting a cat.

'Something unusual so I wouldn't look like a mad cat lady.
One of those sweet hairless sphinxes, perhaps, so it could have
clothes, poor little mite. They have pink mohair cat sweaters
with hearts on the front in the pet shop, you know?'

Nora was already sitting in the café at a window table when
Jojo reached the other side of the road to the café. As she
waited for the traffic to pass, she could see Nora clearly, the
paper open at the crossword and a pot of tea, probably Earl
Grey, in front of her. Seeing her there, short grey hair standing
up like a brush, undoubtedly not a jot of make-up on her lined
face, tiny glasses perched on the end of her nose and wearing
what looked from a distance like some sort of misshapen and
oft-washed sweater in an unattractive concrete colour, Jojo felt
a passionate love for her aunt. Nora was family.

She and Jojo's mother had been the closest of friends, both
married to brothers and at ease with the long history of the
Brannigan family, which included tales of old Granny Brannigan, their grandmother (a tyrant) and Rose Brannigan (a
saint), who'd adored her three sons and their families.

At the great and frequent family parties, Nora and Lottie
would tease Edward Brannigan about the days before Brannigan Engineering had become a big company, when he'd been
thrown out of the small school in Lisowen with great force by
the teacher one day for not bringing his sod of turf to heat
the fire.

'He was lucky the master didn't kill him, he was a violent
man,' protested Nora's husband, Mick. 'It wasn't funny. He
scared the hell out of me.'

'Edward would have turned and showed him how bullies are
treated if he'd felt scared or if he'd ever really threatened you or
Kit,' said Lottie proudly, kissing her husband's forehead. 'He's
never been afraid of anyone, have you, love?'

'Except for you, pet,' Edward said, laughing.

'Why did they call the teacher "master"?' a young Jojo wanted to know.

'Total control,' Lottie would say. 'They went in for that type of control in school in those days. God forbid you tried any independent thinking. School was for having facts beaten into you and independent thinking beaten out of you.'

'Now, Fáinne was a great one for independent thinking,' Mick said, and there was a silence, one of those 'little pitchers have big ears' silences.

'Who's Fáinne?' asked Jojo, who knew it was the Irish word for ring but had never heard a person called such a name and had never heard any mention of a Fáinne before.

'Oh, a girl from the past,' Nora said easily, and somehow, the conversation would get wildly boring about how dreadful it had all been back then, and the cousins would stop listening because who wanted to hear long stories about polio and tuberculosis and emigration?

But the name Fáinne had had a strange fascination for the young Jojo – this person from the past that she clearly wasn't to know about. Why not?

Yet, the talk would move on, an adult would put a stop to all questioning and games had to be played.

Nora and Lottie would stare over their children's heads at each other and think of Fáinne and how tragically it had all played out. How it would be different now but the chance was gone, long gone. Fáinne was just a memory in their lives, a place at the table in their hearts.

Proof that a person could just disappear.

Jojo and Cari – Nora and Mick's elder daughter – were the oldest and they ruled the roost over the other four.

There was Jojo's little brother, Paul, two years younger than Cari and Jojo, who were exactly the same age. By promising introductions to all sorts of girls, they'd had fabulous power over poor Paul for most of their teenage years.

'Claudia really likes you,' they'd fib, watching poor Paul turn pink, then puce, then white at the thought of his current teenage crush actually returning his feelings.

It was, Nora thought, a miracle Paul even spoke to his older sister and his cousin now, given the torture they'd put him through when he was a girl-obsessed teenager with acne and a tendency to lose the ability to speak when around any female other than his cousins.

Maggie – Nora's second daughter – and her partner in crime, Trina, who was Kit and Helen's daughter, were another kettle of fish altogether.

Maggie was a total minx and tortured all around her, including her parents and her cousins.

And Trina, who as daughter of the not-very-beloved Aunt Helen could have been left on the sidelines, was a Brannigan girl through and through, ready for all scrapes and escapades, not in the slightest bit afraid of her mother's sharp tongue, and devoted to her cousins.

Lottie and Nora had been kind to their other sister-in-law, Helen, but they'd both known closeness wasn't possible with Helen, who was a woman caught in the deadly triad of jealousy, bitterness and mistrust. She was jealous at Edward Brannigan's great success and full of bitterness that her husband, Kit, hadn't managed so well. She was also jealous of Lottie's beauty and entirely natural style, and subsequently, never wore the same dress twice to a family gathering. She mistrusted any attempts at closeness and eventually Lottie and Nora had left her alone.

'We can't be friends with the whole world, Lottie,' Nora had said. 'Not everyone wants friends.'

'But she's lonely – you know she is,' Lottie protested.

Lottie had believed in peace, love, kindness and stopping by the side of the road if she saw a run-over animal. More than one injured creature had been carried to the vet on the passenger seat of Lottie's old mini, bleeding everywhere and whimpering.

Lottie would drive and pet the animal, crooning reassurance, strong in the face of disaster.

She'd been so strong, Nora remembered. Even when she'd been diagnosed.

'How could that first scan have said she was cancer-free when she wasn't?' raged Edward, when the mistake was discovered, three months after that first, mistaken all-clear.

'These things happen,' Lottie had said, endlessly, as Edward had raged in pain and bewilderment for a long time. Edward had wanted people fired, consequences for the misdiagnosis... Someone should pay.

Lottie and Nora knew that there was no exact science in medicine and that fighting with the people who were trying to save you wasted time, and there was so little time left: 'There's no point crying over that – let's see what we can do now, let's move on.'

There had been no moving on, though. Not much choice for stage four breast cancer apart from a last-ditch attempt at chemotherapy, which would only buy Lottie time: nauseated, weak, ill time at that, as drugs and cancer raged through her body.

The doctors, kind and compassionate, were honest about how much extra time the drugs might give her but that it would not be easy. The decision was hers.

'If the treatment would give me years, I'd take it in a flash,' she'd told them all. 'But it won't. It will be a month or two at the most and I will be too sick with it to actually be present with all of you. Let's enjoy what I have left and then, bring on the palliative drugs so I'm going into the next world in a haze of soft-focus meds and enough painkillers to kill an ox.'

When the cancer reached her bones, the pain was agonising. An old friend, who'd once been addicted to and then miraculously escaped the clutches of heroin, had come to Nora sobbing: 'Why don't they just shoot her up with heroin. Numb the heck out of the bloody pain, stop making her suffer. We don't do this to dogs, do we?'

Nora hugged her: everyone had an opinion on how Lottie should die but it was Lottie's choice, nobody else's.

Lottie was dead at sixty and the world was a sadder, less golden place without her.

Nora wiped her eyes with her napkin and spotted her niece crossing the road.

Blast.

She dropped the napkin and pretended to be studying her crossword again.

The café door slammed and Nora watched Jojo wend her way through the tightly packed tables. Jojo was too thin, had been since her mother's illness, which had initially hit the family like a lightning bolt over three years ago.

Life could throw so many terrible things into the world, Nora thought, remembering a time when their worries had been smaller.

Nora could remember Cari and Jojo as teenagers, sitting in Cari's bedroom painting their toenails and discussing did puppy fat go or did you need to actually do something about it?

'I am giving up cheese,' Jojo announced firmly. 'Giving up cheese gives you cheekbones, you know. I read it in a magazine. Dairy is bad for you. I read that too.'

'I could live forever without cheese,' Cari replied sadly. 'It's chocolate with me. I love it and it loves me back. Although that's dairy too, the fabulous side of dairy.'

And great sighs would be heard and then, when lunch was ready and it was toasted cheese sandwiches with a home-made chocolate brownie for afters, everyone ate and nobody rushed off to the loo to vomit it up.

Nora and Lottie would silently smile at each other. Their daughters were beautiful and were thankfully not caught up in any unhealthy relationships with food. No bulimia, no anorexia – they both blessed themselves at this – and no body dysmorphia. They had much to be grateful for.

Their children had health, happiness and, so far, no sadness. It would all work out.

And it had, Nora thought – until Cari's disastrous wedding day, which had been catastrophe one, and until Lottie had been diagnosed, catastrophe two, which had shown Nora what a real catastrophe was, because at least Cari *could* recover, but Lottie wouldn't.

Life: forever throwing that curveball, Nora thought sadly. She wished with all her heart that she could make it all better but she couldn't. Nobody could.

She couldn't fix that cold, hard place that had grown in Cari's heart since the wedding day and she couldn't fix the pain she saw on Jojo's face since both her mother's death and her father's subsequent remarriage.

'Nora.'

Jojo leaned in for a hug with her aunt, then sat and looked at the menu, although Nora knew she'd order what she always did: plain black coffee, no milk or sugar.

'Hello, Jojo, like the dress,' said Nora, and they both laughed because Jojo was wearing an asymmetric navy felted wool dress with an orange perspex necklace, and Nora was well known for caring absolutely nothing about clothes except as things to keep her warm.

'It would totally suit you, Nora,' Jojo teased. 'I have it in winter white too, perfect for your colouring.'

'I'd look like I'd just escaped from some maximum security home,' Nora said, 'and you know it.'

A waitress came by and to Nora's utter astonishment, her niece ordered tea and a muffin.

'What?' said Jojo, going slightly pink under Nora's scrutiny. 'I felt hungry.' The injections were making her ravenous. Who knew that being menopausal meant constant eating?

'Make that two muffins,' said Nora, delighted.

They chatted idly about this and that as they waited for the food. Cari had been in London the day before for an editorial meeting of the publishing company, Cambridge, where she worked as a senior editor.

Just a day trip, Nora said. Cari was hoping for a big promotion and possibly a move to London, which would break her parents' hearts but it might help her. It was long since time to move on from Barney. Nora was pretty sure that although Cari had had a few dates since her wedding, she had never been even vaguely serious about any of them.

Nora doubted if any of the said dates had even got as far as kissing Cari, much less got to put a foot inside her apartment. The wedding disaster had broken something inside her and Cari was hiding it with toughness.

Of course, Cari would be equally shattered by the information Nora was about to impart about Edward's birthday party because, odds on, Barney and Traci would be there, but one shattered girl at a time, she decided: she'd deal with that whenever Cari phoned, which she would. Cari wouldn't open the envelope. She'd assume it was a wedding invitation and she had, understandably, sworn off weddings for life. Nora, dear Lord, would have to break the news to her.

A Brannigan family affair would include *all* of the family, including the distant cousins and possibly – because Bess would hardly have a clue not to put him on the list – the one-time love of Cari's life.

Nora, who never baulked at a challenge, hated the thought of hurting her daughter by having to tell her about it all.

He would be there, source of catastrophe number one, along with Traci, a daughter of a distant Brannigan cousin, and a total bitch.

Nora looked at the women at the next table who were gossiping happily after some party they'd been at where the hostess had had a raging fight with her husband in the kitchen, while most of the guests listened.

'I always thought they were so happy,' said the first woman.

'Ah, they've always been like that,' said the second woman. 'It's called passionate arguing. It's very good for relationships, you know: I read that in a magazine. If you don't argue like cats and dogs, now *then* you're in trouble. And the sex—' The woman lowered her voice. 'Supposed to be amazing, making-up sex after a passionate row.'

Nora hid a grin and then it vanished, Lottie too close to her mind. She and Lottie used to love listening in to other people when they met up. Now, Nora had nobody to share such simple pleasures with.

'Take care of Jojo and Paul for me, will you, Nora?' Lottie had said at the end, before the 'making her comfortable' morphine had really kicked in and she could barely speak.

'Edward is strong, he will survive, and Paul has Lena. But Jojo is so fragile. I know nobody else sees it, but you and I do. Please...'

Nora had often wondered why Lena, Lottie's daughter-in-law, was seen as strong enough to take care of the soon-to-be-bereaved Paul when Hugh, Jojo's husband was not.

Something she didn't know? Or just Lottie's feeling that women had such inner strength, a lioness protecting whomever she had to protect. Lena could do that. Hugh, sweet and kind though he was, could not. At least, Nora hoped that's all it was.

She waited until Jojo had actually eaten a good portion of her orange and chocolate muffin before attacking the subject.

'You know it's your dad's seventieth soon,' she said.

Jojo looked up.

'Ye-es.' The one syllable was drawn out slowly.

Nora took a deep breath: bad news was best delivered quickly. 'Bess has sent out invitations to a grand birthday party, in

Lisowen Castle...' She had the invitation in her bag, ready to bring it out.

For a brief moment, Jojo was mute, her hand in mid-air with a few muffin crumbs in it.

'Lisowen was where Mum and Dad celebrated their silver wedding anniversary,' she said.

'Yes.'

Nora looked down at her empty plate. She always gulped her food when she was nervous.

Edward was such a moron. It was one thing for his new wife to suggest a big birthday party in a hotel near where he'd grown up, another entirely to say yes to it when he'd celebrated twenty-five years of marriage to his previous wife there. A wife who was mother to his two adult children, one of whom loathed said new wife. So, the wedding anniversary had been nine or ten years ago, but still.

He was a complete idiot. It was the only way to explain it. Either that, or Bess had some spectacular technique in bed which made his brain freeze over so she could bend him to her will. Something with ping pong balls or— Nora's imagination went at this point. She did not want to imagine any of this. Damned Bess!

'Here.' Nora put the invitation on the table in front of her niece. Jojo had to see it.

Who knew how Edward would deliver Jojo's invitation? He might phone Jojo to invite her and Hugh rather than send a cold card.

Jojo stared for a long moment at the words on the lovely cream card as if she were unable to read and could make no sense of them. Then, she abruptly jumped out of her seat, grabbing her handbag.

'Nora, sorry, I can't stay. I, I—'

Jojo couldn't find the words. Her father's wedding had been bad enough but this?

Without even hugging her aunt, Jojo crashed out of the café

after banging into half of the small tables. Tears were streaming down her face.

Her parents' silver wedding, nine years ago, had been so lovely. Before the party, Mum had gone with Jojo to Paris, a trip that had made Jojo even more determined to open her own shop one day, and they'd taken blissful trips into Galeries Lafayette, Colette and Hausmann, trying on fabulous evening gowns fit for a woman who was married twenty-five years.

'It's all so hideously expensive,' Lottie had said, looking at price tags with horror. She liked nice clothes but not wildly expensive ones. Not when there were tiny babies starving in the world, the ice caps were melting and pandas were dying out.

'Mum, please?' Jojo had begged. 'Just this once. I know you hate waste but this is special.'

The dress had been Balmain, a dusty rose around the curving shoulder line, the colour of the fabric merging from rose into the dark pink camellia colour of the wedding bouquet Lottie O'Brien had carried twenty-five years previously when she'd married the oldest Brannigan brother.

Jojo still had the dress, in acid-free paper, in an archival garment box. She now had almost all of her mother's clothes because her father hadn't been able to throw them out initially, and then he'd met Bess and once Jojo had heard of her – 'You'll love her, Jojo, she's a wonderful person!' – Jojo had raced round to her parents' house in a frenzy and had ripped every personal item of her mother's from the place.

That Balmain dress, still beautiful, stood for everything her mother had been: timeless, lovely and she'd looked like a golden angel in it. How could her father sully her mother's memory by letting that bitch organise his birthday in the same hotel?

Jojo didn't run back to the shop. Instead, she made for her car, sat in it and hit her brother's number on speed dial. She needed someone who'd understand.

New York

Paul didn't have time for the call but the phone identified the caller as his sister, Jojo, so he picked it up anyway. It was eight-thirty in New York, he was racing into a meeting and neither he nor his wife, Lena, had spotted that his tie was decorated with their little daughter's eggy breakfast as he was leaving the apartment.

Heidi might only be fourteen months old, but she was a clever little bunny and had already worked out that Dada spent more time at home if she messed up his clothes in the morning.

'Either that's a new look or you've food on your necktie,' said one of the laconic receptionists at FitzgeraldProject Inc., the cutting edge ad agency where he worked.

Breakfast on people's clothes at Fitzgerald's was something a creative person might just get away with because the dress code was fluid to say the least, but today Paul's team were making a pre-presentation to a group of Big Diet Drink people who were very corporate and would be suited, booted and unhappy at any sign of Jimi Hendrix T-shirts, urban modern hair, too many facial piercings or dirty ties.

Paul pulled the egged tie off, while simultaneously answering the phone to his sister and beginning to search frantically in his desk drawer for an emergency tie-thing.

'Yo, sis, what's up?' he said, about to follow this jokey hello with 'I'm sort of rushing here so can I phone you back—?'

But Jojo wasn't listening.

'*That bitch* is having Dad's seventieth birthday party next month in Lisowen, Paul. Lisowen! I will kill her, I swear I will.'

Paul sat down in his chair.

Big Diet Drinks or not, his beloved big sister was his beloved big sister.

'I haven't seen any invitations – are you sure?'

'Nora told me about fifteen minutes ago. She brought hers with her. It's going to be a "gala evening, black tie…" I hate that woman! Does she ever think about us, about Mum? How can Dad let her do this type of thing?'

Paul wondered the same thing and thought that while it was great that his father had found someone else after their mother's death, he seemed to have had his sensitivity radar surgically removed at the same time as his second marriage.

Dad had to have known the venue would drive Jojo insane.

Paul looked at the photos of Lena and Heidi on his desk.

His mother hadn't seen Heidi, hadn't known of her existence because Lena had become pregnant after his mother's death, and that was hard because Paul had been close to Lottie, she'd been a wonderful mother: kind, loving and yet tough when it was required.

And yet, what could he do?

People died, even parents you adored. You had to move on.

He loved Dad and Jojo, loved his cousins too, loved them all, but he had Lena and Heidi now: they were his family. Strange how a new family somehow shifted the balance of the old one. The allegiance, the 'I will kill to protect these people', moved.

Jojo and Hugh didn't have that. He often wanted to say it to Jojo but he was afraid she was too fragile to hear it: that if she had her own child, she might come to terms with their mother's death in the way that new life allowed people to move on.

He was going to say it, soon. Just not now.

'Have you talked to Dad?' he asked.

'No. If he's stupid enough to let her do this, then I won't stop them but I won't go either.'

'What does Hugh think?'

'I haven't told him yet.'

She sounded as if she'd been crying for some time.

'Jojo,' said Paul, looking at his watch. He was now officially late. 'I have to go, it's important or I wouldn't hang up. I'll phone you in about two hours, OK,' and because he had to keep his job as there were now two people entirely dependent on him, Paul Brannigan said 'I love you,' to his sister, hung up and wondered had his new stepmother ever stopped for one moment to consider that marrying a widower with children might require some vague hint of sensitivity.

In the offices of McConnells and Balcon, Hugh Hennessy sat in his high-ceilinged Georgian office and listened to his colleague and oldest college friend, Elizabeth Ryan, as she sat with her head back, massaging an aching neck, and telling him how she was sorry she'd ever gone into family law in the first place.

'It's one of those horrible cases, ones where nobody wins, where they started proceedings for the judicial separation in the heat of the moment, where everyone's bewildered by pain and where you really want to tell them to go away to Italy for a week, make love in the sun and forget about it all.'

'George McConnell would stab you if you told any paying client to go to Italy for a week to forget about the case,' said Hugh, trying to make her laugh.

'What? With his Mont Blanc fountain pen?' asked Elizabeth, and they both managed to laugh at the notion of the fastidious senior partner doing anything as déclassé as stabbing anyone. 'Dear George, he only raises his voice above a whisper if he thinks your billing is down,' Elizabeth went on.

'Bad morning, then?' said Hugh. His hadn't been any better. His speciality was commercial law and the brightest spot in the morning had been when the coffee machine had finally broken for good and Finola, the assistant he shared, had gone to the café across the road and brought back proper espressos instead of the watery battery acid the machine had been hissing out for a month. For Jojo's sake, Hugh was staying off coffee at home. He was also off wine, anything that she shouldn't eat, and was going slightly insane making healthy smoothies and vegetable juices in case she fancied one because he worried about her health.

'The worst morning,' Elizabeth sighed. 'Nobody knows other people's marriages, but you have a damn good view in my job and this couple were not ready for it, not by a long shot. Hugh, you have no idea how many clients ask me am I married, and you can tell they're hoping I say I'm divorced, so I know what they're going through.'

'You don't have to tell them,' said Hugh.

'Listen, apart from the rare hard-as-nails types, they all look like dogs who've been kicked in the ribs and I can't snap that it's not germane to the business at hand to tell them whether I'm married or not. When I say I am, they either look as if they want to cry or else tell me I must be mad and that the spouse will cheat or disappoint me in some way at some point and then I'll understand.'

'Tell them you're on your second marriage,' Hugh said. 'That shows them you understand and that there's always a second chance.'

'I should say "It's complicated", like they do on Facebook,' Elizabeth said gloomily. 'Wolfie is still in Berlin trying to get a gallery to exhibit his work, will be for another few months. I'd get a dog if I was ever home long enough to take care of it.'

Hugh's private mobile vibrated in his suit jacket breast pocket.

'Hugh,' said Jojo.

'Darling,' he replied, happy to hear her voice. But he got no further.

'Bloody Bess is having Daddy's seventieth at Lisowen Castle. It's where he and Mum had their twenty-fifth wedding anniversary!'

Hugh's eyes caught Elizabeth's and she stood up, waved goodbye and left the office.

He thought briefly of those times when he and Jojo had double dated with Elizabeth and Wolfgang, and the fun they'd had. Nights out at the cinema, followed by larky dinners in cheap restaurants where they'd talked non-stop and sometimes dancing later, because Jojo and Elizabeth loved dancing and were always keeping an ear out for clubs that played music for what they called 'oldies' like themselves.

Now Wolfgang was away a lot in Germany calling on old contacts to try to get his art career re-energised, because the market for white canvases with the odd navy blob on them wasn't as good as it had been in the heady years of the late nineties, and Jojo didn't want to go out with anyone, ever. She didn't want to explain to people at dinners why she didn't want even a teeny glass of wine or have anyone ask her how she was getting on since her mother had died, and wasn't it lovely that her father had found love again, or, worst of all, bump into the endless stream of thoughtless people who liked to ask: 'Any sign of babies, yet?' with all the gravity of a person asking a physicist to explain string theory.

'Honey, I have a gap in an hour,' Hugh said, consulting his diary. 'Could you get in to town to meet me for a coffee – sorry, herbal tea?'

'I can't,' sobbed Jojo. 'I have to go back to the shop and we got all these expensive dresses we didn't order and oh, Hugh, I feel so miserable. I'm sorry, I'm always whining, always phoning you like this at work—'

'It's fine, darling. I love you,' said Hugh, and then he had to go because Finola put her head round the door to tell him his next client was there.

Somehow, he put his work face on: the calm, confident face of Hugh Hennessy, the tall, well-built former rowing champion who'd run marathons for charity, who'd always made everyone in his life proud of him and who felt utterly hopeless because he couldn't get his wife pregnant or comfort her about all the pain in her life.

Four

'Remember that sometimes not getting what
you want is a wonderful stroke of luck.'
Dalai Lama

Edward Brannigan had a bronze relief plaque on his office wall: '*Ancora imparo*', which meant 'I am still learning.'

It was a quote by Leonardo da Vinci and Lottie had given it to him as part of a Christmas or a birthday present once. He couldn't remember which one, a thought which made him smile wryly at the notion of the palaver surrounding the perfect gift for various occasions.

Soap, socks, ties with Santas on them – he had collections of them all and yet the presents that he remembered were unusual ones that lasted, even if he couldn't remember when he'd received them. Like Lottie's plaque because it was a quote he'd often repeated.

'We'll never know it all, will we?' Lottie had said to him when he'd told her he'd hung it on his office wall the day before, and he could remember, very clearly, how he'd given her a quick hug and said 'no', and then gone off out to get his clubs ready for his Saturday golf match, yelling back that he should be in by seven but might have dinner with the lads at the club, and would she mind?

Lottie had never minded but when she was dead, and he was alone in the sprawling bungalow, listening to nothing but his own breathing because every radio or television show had something in it to make him cry and he couldn't bear to cry any more, Edward had wished she had minded.

Or that he hadn't been so selfish as to leave her.

Why play all that golf when they had so little time left together? He hadn't known then, not when she'd given him the little da Vinci plaque. But he should have known. Damn it, he was supposed to be clever and yet he hadn't seen any of the signs, hadn't ever thought that one day Lottie might be taken from him and he'd be alone.

Women were the ones who were supposed to live longest. She was supposed to outlive him, not the other way round.

He, Mick, Nora and Lottie would joke about this on nights out. Before.

'Lottie and I shall get ourselves toyboys,' Nora might say, when Mick and Edward had got stuck into a cul-de-sac of an unwinnable conversation about football or hurling or the merits of one politician over another, and were oblivious to all around them, and Nora would decide to knock them off their perches and drag them back into the world.

'Oh, toyboys, yes,' Lottie would agree. 'The nice man who packs my bags in the market, he'd be lovely.'

'He's a bit old,' Nora might say, sounding scandalised. 'A toyboy has to be at least twenty-five years younger or he's no good to you, past his prime . . .'

And they'd laugh at the notion of it all and Mick and Edward would raise their eyes to heaven, and Edward might demand what the two women would say if he and Mick started discussing some young girl on the checkout counter, where-upon Lottie would gaze at him, so beautiful with those blue eyes, and say: 'I know you wouldn't.'

And he wouldn't. Hadn't. Had never so much as looked at another woman during his marriage.

There had been one woman after Lottie's death – a disaster of an encounter abroad when longing for the touch of another human body had brought him to a woman's room after a conference, and he'd nearly gone through with it. She'd been half-naked, his hands on her breasts and suddenly, in a flashback,

Edward could see the frailness of Lottie at the end, and the breasts that had killed her, and any desire in him had died.

'I'm sorry,' he'd said, pushing himself off the hotel bed, feeling both stupid and embarrassed. 'My wife—' he began.

'Too soon, huh?' said the woman, covering herself up with a pillow and looking as defeated as he felt.

'I'm sorry,' he said again, like a broken record.

'Me too,' she said and Edward saw she was about to cry.

He bent down and kissed her gently on the temple. 'You're beautiful and any man would be a fool not to want you but you're right, it is too soon for me. If it had been anyone, I wish it had been you.'

Loneliness seemed to be his future, until that night he'd met Bess. Love and actual desire had flooded him.

He'd barely been able to concentrate on the food or the conversation around him – all he'd thought of was this beautiful woman who wasn't flirting with him, but was merely talking, and fascinating him.

He had thought of Lottie afterwards, when he went home and worked out how to see Bess again, and he knew Lottie would have approved.

White roses, she'd have said. Not red ones. Red is so obvious. Lottie had had such amazing taste. She'd taught him so much – how to be classy with his money, to give to charity without fanfare and how to keep his wealth out of the gossip columns, staying under the radar instead of becoming a byword for the nouveau riche.

Was it desperation to imagine that she would have liked Bess Reynolds, even though they were entirely different in every way?

His son Paul had liked Bess too but not Jojo, who couldn't bear to be in the same room as her.

He'd talk to Nora about it, he thought: if anyone could fix this impasse between Jojo and Bess, it was his sister-in-law.

Paul had FaceTimed Edward from New York that lunchtime when it was morning in New York and, as usual, it had lifted Edward's spirits.

Heidi was growing all the time, and the impish smile on her tiny face reminded him of Jojo at a similar age.

'See!' she said loudly into the camera, thrusting a purple velour giraffe with orange spots at him. 'Schaff!'

'Yes, giraffe,' said Edward, feeling his heart contract at the sight of that little sparkling smile, and the blonde fluffy hair in two haphazard bunches on either side of her head.

'Morning, Edward, let me tell you, your granddaughter is into *everything*,' Lena said, coming into focus on the camera and waving at her father-in-law. 'She is a one-small-person demolition squad. Since she started toddling round the apartment, nothing is safe. But every corner is safety-covered, every plug socket has a safety plug and the blinds are unusable in case she gets one stuck around her neck...'

Edward could see Lena shudder at the thought, that bone-deep parental fear that the bogeyman of life would get your child.

'I understand, honey. All parents think the worst but it will be all right,' he said, assuming the figure of paterfamilias since Lena's own father was not the sort of man to care much about sharp corners on things. Lena had been in school with Paul, and Lottie and Edward had known her family well. They had been so different as parents from Lottie and him: very drinky, out with their pals for wild weekends and happy for their kids to meander along whatever.

In a way, he could see that New York was an escape for Lena from the chaos of her family but it meant that he wasn't getting to see his beloved Heidi. He and Bess had discussed a trip to New York once his birthday was over – a week of spending time with the family, maybe taking in a show. Another honeymoon with Bess, and with time spent with Paul, Lena and dear

Heidi thrown in for good measure. He was sure Lena's family hadn't been over once since Paul and Lena had moved, and yet they'd made it to the Canaries at least twice a year. Never mind, he would never let them down.

'Dad,' said Paul, moving the iPad away from Heidi, who shrieked with rage as if she was in mortal peril at having her other favourite toy removed, 'Jojo is pretty cut up about your party.'

Edward sighed. They were always your kids – even when they were thirty-four and married themselves like Jojo. 'I know, son, but what can I do? I thought it would get better with time …'

'It hasn't, not really. And the venue of Lisowen is what's really killing her because it's where you and Mum had your twenty-fifth wedding anniversary.'

Edward loosened the buttons on the charcoal shirt that Bess had said, only that morning, made him look very handsome. Edward has kissed her on the lips and only the fact that they both had meetings to attend to meant he hadn't dragged her upstairs to bed again.

'Bess is having it there because it means so much to me,' Edward said sharply, 'in the same way your mother realised that.'

His son would probably never understand how it felt to be one of the peasants, poor beyond belief, denied education beyond the age of fifteen and forced to work on the small family farm. To have come this far from such a beginning was something Edward could not enunciate and yet both Lottie and Bess had understood it perfectly.

It would have been far handier for Bess to have the party in Dublin, handier because she wouldn't have had to take two day-trip return plane rides to Kerry to go over endless details, to make sure it was all perfect. But she was doing it for him.

'Your sister will come round, Paul,' he said now, determined, sure of himself. He had fought all battles in his life and won, except the battle for Lottie's life and in the end, it had been one of the few battles he couldn't fight – he'd been there holding Lottie's hand, sobbing, as she'd dealt with her cancer by letting go with grace.

'I'll talk to Jojo,' he added, and the feelings of nervousness, so unaccustomed, began to creep in. Lottie had been the one for all sorts of tricky conversations in their house and how did a man explain to his daughter that he needed another woman after her mother? That he'd been lonely, that he couldn't cope with being alone and then he'd found the right person. Because wasn't there supposed to be only one right person?

When he'd met Bess, had seen her that night in the dinner, formally dressed and clearly used to holding herself back, he'd recognised a kindred spirit and yet one he was extremely attracted to. Bess had been nothing like Lottie, nothing.

Lottie was fey, normally dressed as if she was fleeing the scene of a crime and had thrown on the first clothes to hand, and yet always looked beautiful, exotic, more lovely than any other woman he knew. She'd the most genuinely kind heart: was a mother warrior and the kindest human being he'd ever met.

Bess was shorter, curvier, a delicate pony to Lottie's thoroughbred racehorse, yet Bess had fire in her eyes and he could see she was a sensual woman from the very way she moved. Edward, who had only had that one failed sexual encounter since Lottie died, had been shocked to feel that old desire stir in him when he'd spotted Bess at the dinner: she'd been wearing a formal black trouser suit, yet her blouse, a silky cream thing he was astonished to find himself fantasising about removing, was revealing. It was new, she'd finally told him weeks later: new and untested. She'd spent the evening wishing the buttonholes were tighter because the buttons, too small, kept escaping the holes and showing off hints of skin and full breast imprisoned in a white bra.

So many women had been throwing themselves at him since

73

Lottie died, something he considered distasteful. Even Helen, his own sister-in-law, never his favourite person, had been flicking her lacquered blonde helmet of hair in his direction and saying archly, 'We must find you a little friend, Edward,' as if he needed a pet poodle that Helen herself would keep on a leash.

'She means well,' said Kit, his brother, and Edward had nodded but he was annoyed.

Nora wasn't coming up with prospective dates like a pimp, was she? Nora had loved Lottie. Nora understood that he needed to grieve. But then he'd met Bess and meeting her hadn't made him forget Lottie – nothing on earth could do that – but she had healed something inside him that he'd thought was gone for ever.

His sense of being a man, his sense of being desired again.

After one date, he'd known that he was considering what some might imagine the unthinkable – of finding someone else to love.

'Men aren't made to live alone,' he'd told Mick, his younger brother one evening, when they sat on the big couch in Tanglewood where Edward had spent many a lonely evening, watching footie on the TV. 'I've met someone else. I know you loved Lottie: I adored her, Mick, you know that, but this woman is funny and clever and I need that. Companionship, love, being with a woman, sharing life...'

His voice had trailed away because he'd half-expected Mick to storm out but then Mick had always been thoughtful, and after all, he was married to the most emotionally intelligent woman on the planet.

'Nora said you'd need to marry again,' Mick said gently. 'She said all that, the stuff you said now. Said women can manage on their own but us lot, we need them. I'm glad for you, Ed, and Nora will be glad for you too. Who the heck are we to tell you to live alone when I have Nora and she has me? Neither of us have time for that sort of hypocrisy. You go and find your happiness. Lottie wanted that and, God knows, you've had enough pain.'

'Thank you,' said Edward, exhaling slowly, realising only then that he'd been holding his breath. 'There's nobody like Nora, is there?' he added, feeling a wash of huge love for the sister-in-law who'd been best friends with Lottie yet still understood that Edward needed a life after her death.

Paul had understood too, Paul who was so happy in New York with his beloved Lena.

'Go for it, Dad,' Paul had said gruffly. 'Mum would hate you sad, would hate any of us to be sad.'

But Jojo had been a different story.

Stupidly, Edward had thought she would feel the same. Now he had his brother's blessing, and Paul's, and Nora's, Lottie's closest friend, he'd thought his darling daughter would get it, understand his loneliness.

But she hadn't.

'How could you?' was all she could say, and then she'd raged against Bess, totally shocking Edward.

He could have called the whole thing off when Jojo had become so vehemently opposed to it and for a brief moment, he almost had.

He'd thought about going round to Bess's apartment – Edward was never a coward, he would deliver the hard news in person, always – and tell her it was over. If his daughter couldn't accept Bess into his life, then it would have to end. He'd picked up the phone and suddenly, he couldn't do it.

He wanted Bess Reynolds in his life; wanted her warmth, her sharp humour, the softness she'd kept hidden for so many years. He'd wanted to curl up in bed with her at night and be soothed by her presence as she read books and he rattled the newspaper, peace stealing up on him at her presence.

So he'd chosen Bess and Jojo would not forgive him.

She would in time, he hoped. Time was a great healer, people said.

And then he thought of how time had made the cancer spread in Lottie, and he felt a chill.

In the Starbucks on her way home from work in Met-Ro, Amy Reynolds watched the barista squirt cream on top of her hot chocolate. He was cute. Dark-skinned, late twenties, a purring South American accent when he'd asked if she wanted the cream or not.

Amy didn't know which country his accent was from, which made her feel as if she was guilty of racism in some way. She should know, not just label him as South American. It was a continent and saying he was South American was like saying she was European, too vague.

He had long hair tied up in one of those man buns that almost nobody but the exquisitely manly could pull off and a complicated tattoo on one brown, muscled forearm. Imagine that arm around her, holding her, muscles flexed as he purred at her in Spanish or Portuguese or...

Amy quickly looked away from the guy. She had got to stop reading romantic novels where the unexpected romance was a speciality.

Someone like the dark-skinned barista would never so much as look at her as anything other than as a customer waiting in line. Even when she'd been younger, his age. Especially not now she was thirty-two.

Other women were married at her age, had children, or careers, or something.

Amy could almost hear her mother's voice, heavy with exasperation: 'Amy, you have to settle down at something. You know at your age, I had you and was separated, and you don't want to end up alone...'

Which was the point at which Amy tuned out. A person could only take so much of their mother reminding them that biological clocks pinged inexorably. Her mother reminding her that she might end up alone was a new variation on the theme.

New since her mother had met Edward Brannigan and turned from tough cookie with a single daughter into a different woman entirely. Now Bess Reynolds, well, Mrs Bess Brannigan, was like one of those girls who'd stomped around on campus with placards declaiming men, until they met the right guy – often entirely the wrong guy – and became loved-up creatures with blissful expressions on their faces from lots of sex, a warm body round them at night and someone to goofily admire them as they put their clothes on.

Bess Brannigan never mentioned how useless men were any more, not since she had met Edward who was, even Amy had to admit, a good-looking old guy in a sort of movie star way: that craggy face with a perpetual tan no matter the weather, and hazel eyes that shone with intelligence and interest in everything, and the silver hair that fell into place without a hint of any metrosexual grooming stuff.

It wasn't as if her mother hadn't met plenty of good-looking men before – she'd just jettisoned them before they got close because she Had No Time For Men. This was code for Amy's Father Had Ruined It For Her.

And which Amy – who had done a module on psychology in her arts degree – knew was really code for how Granny Maura Sharkey, the toughest cookie ever to walk the planet, had been widowed young and had brought Bess up to believe that nobody could ever do it better than her and a man would definitely ruin it all.

It was quite amazing how the bitterness of one woman could screw up two generations so successfully.

Amy had once thought of writing a paper on this in college but hadn't because she might have ended up in psychology, and her mother would have read her thesis and imagine that?

Poor Mum had meant well. Bess had never been given anything, had worked so hard to get where she was, while Amy had had all the best chances and yet... How could she explain to her mother that self-confidence was the one thing money/advice/hectoring couldn't supply?

The things Amy wanted to do with her life weren't even on Bess Reynolds's, sorry Bess *Brannigan*'s, mental radar. That Amy had a rich inner life that might one day change everything but, then again, might not.

Because she wasn't smart enough and she must have been mad to think that she could do this incredible job she wanted because so many people wanted it and she wasn't special enough, was she? Never had been special enough.

Not special enough for a man to want to stay with her. Not special enough for her father to want to stay. Not even special enough for her mother to be proud of her, even though her mother said she was.

This unwelcome and oft-trodden pathway had the usual effect: Amy's desire for sugar-laden caramel sprinkles on her coffee lit up the neurons in her brain like fireworks.

Sugar eased the pain, although she still had the guilt of her addiction. Some people were addicted to sex, others to drugs – trust her to be addicted to sugar. She wondered if she could order a pistachio brownie too ... but then, she'd have to race home to eat it in her tiny apartment in Delaney Gardens where the acid-green buds on a sycamore tree were beginning to open just beside her bedroom window. Her home was the place where she could cook and eat what she wanted in privacy.

Starbucks, on the other hand, was public. Someone might see her and report back to her mother.

Amy had never been skinny and during her school years it had been her mother's mission to change this. The house had been full of low-fat foods. Bess herself had eaten a diet modelled on one Granny Maura had copied from Jackie Kennedy's White House diet – a staggeringly low eight hundred calories a day – but in the White House, it had been made by chefs, and whenever Amy had grown more Rubensesque, Bess had watched her daughter like a hawk to see that she kept to this unkeepable-to regime.

When she'd been a schoolgirl, it felt as if her mother had friends the way some countries had secret spy agencies. This network of spies managed to watch every move Amy made. Particularly every move that included food.

'Oh, I heard from Gloria that you were in the ice cream shop in Glasthule having an ice cream sundae.'

'Miriam spotted you and your pals in the waffle place. Do you know how many calories there are in one of those waffles with syrup?'

At sixteen, Amy had not been the tiny-waisted and slender-legged beauty of the historical novels she loved to read. She'd had no discernible waist and her breasts spilled out of her bras. Bess felt it was character-building not to buy a new, bigger bra for her daughter or a larger school skirt.

If Bess stopped fitting into a skirt, she cut out things she liked for a month: ruthlessly. She'd gone from taking sugar in her tea to taking none in just one move.

'All it takes is discipline,' she'd said, patting her flat stomach.

Why couldn't Amy do the same? Then there would be no need of a new bra or new whatever.

It was simple, really, Bess said with earnestness.

And horribly, Amy knew that her mother wasn't just saying this bitchily – she believed it to be true. If you wanted to stop eating sugar/take over the world/get an A-plus in higher level maths, all you had to do was simply work harder at it.

Nobody had handed her mother anything in life and she'd had to work so hard at everything to keep their life going when Amy's father had left. Amy knew all this but it had made her mother tough, and Amy was the exact opposite of tough: she loved living in the world of her imagination and that world did not fit in with her mother's vision of how to get a good, pensionable job or succeed in life.

When she'd been a teenager, Amy and her partners in crime, Tiana and Nola, discussed spy satellites and how parents knew what you were doing almost in real time.

'My mother asks me every day if I met boys and if so, *what did we do?* It's like the Salem witch trials,' Tiana reported.

Her mother read the Bible with zeal, wore her knees out saying the rosary every night and had her own seat in the church where she went for nine o'clock Mass every single morning of her life.

Tiana's problem was not a surfeit of sugar – it was a surfeit of Bible quotes for every happening and war breaking out if she missed the family rosary, said at eight every evening.

Tiana was the sole girl in a family of three boys and her mother was hoping, *praying*, that Tiana would have a vocation to be a nun.

'Possibly one of those ones who get locked away and can't see people except from behind a metal grille,' Tiana said grimly. 'That's what she'd like. So I could be locked in praying and not be out in the world sinning with boys. Why is it that Catholic religious people, who are not supposed to think about sex, spend all their bloody lives thinking about it and trying to put the kybosh on it?'

Her real name was Emerentiana, after the female saint on whose feast day she was born in January. Even Tiana's mother couldn't get people to wrap their tongues around Emerentiana, so Tiana had stuck her heels in and insisted her name be a bit more pronounceable.

'My mother would be delighted if I met a boy,' Nola said. 'She's hoping someone falls in love with me for my mind and my sense of humour and my curves!'

Nola was big, beautiful and sexy with it, just like her mother. Everyone loved Nola's mother and it was to Nola's house that the trio gravitated after school and at weekends.

There, nobody hassled them for eating too much or for

smiling in a way that implied sluttish, non-C[...]
immediately-to-helldom.

After college, Tiana became engaged to D[...]
firefighter who was a Buddhist – 'I love him [...]
he's into Buddhism and not Catholicism, if [...]
Tiana had told her friends, who both said it mad[...]
sense.

Amy said she was mildly surprised Tiana hadn't located a
Satanist cult to take up with and that Dean was far too lovely
and normal to upset Tiana's mother sufficiently.

'In my more bitter years, I did think of finding a nice tat-
tooed bloke with a nose ring, a few eyebrow rings, a skinhead
and a Prince Albert, but they're not as easy to find as you'd
think.'

Nola and Amy giggled.

'We could have helped you look,' they'd said, all thrilled at
the thought of introducing said boyfriend to Tiana's mother,
who said she would not countenance a marriage between her
daughter, a good Catholic, and Dean, whom she called 'that
heathen'.

Tiana, even though she said she should have known what
would happen, was ridiculously devastated at her mother's
intractability.

'We could have found someone in a heavy metal band?' said
Nola, to drag humour back into it.

'We could have hired an actor,' said Amy. 'Drawn a penta-
gram in magic marker on his forehead and hung a few weird
animal bones on him, given him a pack of Tarot to flash
around...?'

'I always loved hearing your essays read out in English,' said
Tiana wistfully, close to tears. 'You're so inventive. I don't know
why you didn't go into creative writing instead of window
dressing. No, Dean it is. Even if my mother hates him and me.'

Tiana and Dean got married without her mother present
and then moved to New Zealand. Her Facebook posts were

her beloved young children, work, Dean and pot-luck ners with gorgeous new New Zealand friends. It all sounded wonderful. She had entirely turned her back on religion and even Buddhism had taken a hit.

'I'm potty-training Brandon – I don't have time for meditation!'

Nola was larger than ever and had a successful business in London on how to be fabulous and feel it.

Amy glowed with pride when she saw the adverts on the internet: 'Own your Big Beauty!'

Big Beauty specialised in makeovers for women who'd felt marginalised all their lives for being larger. One look at Nola – size twenty-two, sexy and able to rock leather trousers and red lipstick – and women threw away tent dresses like nobody's business and went looking for their own leather trousers.

She was happy, she told Amy, and while she wasn't sure about settling down yet, there was no shortage of Mr Right Nows in her life.

And Amy felt left behind.

Her two closest friends had moved on and she felt stagnant.

Even her mother – who had sworn off love for ever – was enjoying a blissful second marriage.

And Amy couldn't help but think that her mother was comparing her to Edward's daughter, Jojo.

Jojo was stunning and look how desperately Bess had tried to doll Amy up for the wedding. Why else would she do that unless she felt that Amy would look terrible beside her new, exquisite stepdaughter?

Despite all the make-up and the expensive dress, Amy had not outshone Jojo at her mother's wedding to Edward Brannigan – well, who could? Jojo was gorgeous. So gorgeous, she made Amy feel shy, and she clearly hated Amy's mother, although she'd been polite to Amy, which had been a huge relief.

Jojo, Cari and Paul had great jobs. Careers.

Amy had wanted to talk to Edward's niece, Cari, about publishing but had felt too shy: Cari was so glamorous, like the vision of a career woman from a magazine, all long legs and heels with that silky dark hair, and glossy lips, forever joking and laughing.

Amy worked in the window design department of a discount chain of shops. She was not rearranging elegant mannequins draped in Pucci and Gucci. She was dressing very cheap dummies in 4.99-euro sweatsuits and 1.99-euro-for-five knickers alongside lawnmowers and angle grinders. It was not what she wanted to do with her life but it was experience, seeing things, and she needed to pay for her apartment and eat.

Her apartment was tiny, although she loved it, mainly because it was on the corner of Delaney Gardens, which was so pretty and had such a sense of community that it didn't matter that she had an hour's commute to work.

She was still overweight – not by normal people's standards, but by her mother's. She wasn't large enough to be noticed, the way dear Nola could never, ever blend into the background. People noticed Nola, what with the fabulous clothes, the red lippie and the over-the-top gestures that made men love her.

But nobody noticed Amy, for all that the hairdressers were always saying she had 'beautiful hair and skin and could be so pretty...' which was code, she knew, for 'You'd be prettier if you were thinner or tried harder.'

Amy didn't want to be thinner.

She wanted to be happy.

Sometimes, when he had time and came over, she was beyond happy. When he was in bed with her, telling her how beautiful she was, Amy felt gloriously happy. But she couldn't boast about her man on Facebook or post photos of them out enjoying dinners or walking along beaches. Because Clive, gorgeous Clive, was married.

Five

'Experience is the hardest kind of teacher. It gives
you the test first, and the lesson afterward.'
Oscar Wilde

Maggie Brannigan worked in an insurance firm run by a close
friend of her uncle's. It was not the job from heaven but it was
better than working for her Uncle Edward, who had always
seemed to be a pussycat during her childhood, but whom, it
transpired, magically turned into a cold-eyed automaton at
work and expected all his commands to be carried out almost
before the words had left his mouth.

Maggie's year after college, being trained up to be a secre-
tarial assistant in Brannigan's Engineering, was not filled with
memories of fabulousness.

'Uncle Eddie expects the family to work even harder than
anyone else in the place,' her big sister, Cari, had explained
when Maggie had put forward the notion that their uncle had
been eaten by pod people and replaced by an alien as soon as
his Lexus pulled into the office car park. 'He's a high achiever,
he expects the same of everyone and more so of us.'

'Why?' demanded Maggie, who'd thought she'd scored a nice
number in the family business when it turned out that her
liberal arts degree had somehow not been translatable into
actual employment, other than in the fast-food business.

'We're Brannigans,' said Cari, as if that explained it all.

Fine for Cari to say that, Maggie thought crossly. Cari had
been born with determination, brains and all that other businessy stuff in her veins. Cari was all for careers and breaking
glass ceilings.

84

But what if you wanted a job where you started at nine, left at five, got paid well and had no real responsibility?

Maggie was in her twenties! This was the decade for fun, letting loose, drifting through the world like a free spirit, going on fabulous holidays with gorgeous men!

Her mother, Nora, the kindest woman on the planet and the most maternal, was – unfortunately – not impressed when Maggie was, reluctantly, let go from the family firm.

'I think it's the best thing for her, Nora,' Uncle Edward said on the phone. 'She's immature, nothing like Cari. If we keep her, she'll think she doesn't have to work. I'll find her something.'

'Thanks, Ed, for being so honest with me,' Nora replied, knowing he was right. Blood, like lava, boiled up inside her, and when Maggie arrived home – obviously, she hadn't managed to move out of the family house yet, because rent was so high and it was hard to combine actual rent and partying – she found her mother waiting for her.

'Your Uncle Edward phoned with the news,' she said, knowing that Maggie was a good kid and yet wondering what the heck she, as a mother, had done wrong? At Maggie's age, Nora had a job and a child, and still put dinner on the table for Mick every night.

'You are clever, Maggie Brannigan. You did brilliantly in your exams in school and yet in college you did nothing. Nothing! It's a miracle you got any degree at all.'

'Mum, the office was dreadful. All these old biddies glaring at me if I left the desk to go to the loo. And in college, come on, I was finding out who I wanted to be. Everyone does that, it's like, practically a rite of passage,' said Maggie, twirling a bit of hair and wondering if she ought to dye her dark hair blonde because the last two guys she'd dated had moved on to platinum blondes, and she'd really liked one of the guys, and therefore, her look might be wrong—

'Maggie, I love you and I will always love you, but if you

think you are going to become a boomerang kid, racing back home when you're thirty because you've screwed up a job, I will shave that lovely head of yours and your eyebrows, and throw you out on the streets, kiddo. Tough love!'

'Jeez, Mum—' began Maggie.

'Don't take the Lord's name in vain in front of me!' snapped her mother. 'We are the poor Brannigans, your father has a decent job and I'm only part-time in the school. So forget any trust fund dreams. It took a lot of effort to send you to college. I know damn well your Uncle Edward would give us any amount of money if we asked but your father and I are not like that. We make our own way.'

'I'm sorry...'

Maggie burst into tears, looking, at twenty-five, much like she'd looked when she was five. Big blue eyes wobbling, dark hair a mess, lips wobbling.

The tough love thing was over, Nora thought, and pulled her younger daughter into her arms. Why couldn't she have a little medium in her life – she had one over-achieving daughter who had – understandably – no time for men in her life, and another who viewed over-achievers as lunatics. Did one child automatically want to be the polar opposite of the other? She should have had a third – it might have balanced the whole thing out.

'We are invited to a party,' Maggie messaged her cousin Trina on Friday morning, in neither of their break times. 'Two posh invitations arrived in the post. I opened yours too.'

Maggie, who now worked in We'll Be There For You insurance, said she had perfected the art of pretending to be on her computer on office business when she was really on her smartphone, tap tapping away as she discussed things with Trina like the dress she'd seen online that she might get, should she try pink streaks in her hair, or Trina's latest boyfriend – 'He is so hairy, it's like dating Cromagnon man,' Trina said, 'but it's sort of sexy – does that make me strange?'

They now shared an apartment but found that, weirdly, despite seeing each other blearily over their toast every morning and over wine, box sets, pizzas or emergency there's-nothing-in-the-place-to-eat cereal meals at night, there just wasn't enough time in the day to talk about all the things they needed to talk about, hence all the work calls, WhatsApps and messaging.

Trina worked in a very off-beat shoe shop in a cool, tourist trap part of Dublin city and there were vast periods when nobody came in or out of the shop, so she could generally tweet/text/WhatsApp or phone anyone she felt like whenever she felt like it. The market for perilous brocade shoes that looked like something Louis XVI might have worn was shaky at best. They did much better on the biker boots.

'Why sell biker boots *and* those weird dressing-up sort of shoes?' Jojo had asked once. 'Why not one or the other, the more profitable one?'

'Dunno.' Trina shrugged. She had no interest in the actual business as long as she got her wages every Friday lunchtime.

Like Maggie, Trina saw work as a means to an end.

They worked to be able to afford their apartment and a fun lifestyle – the former currently a bit messy and requiring a clean, but they were both too busy. Everyone thought the pair were sisters instead of cousins. While Jojo was the Scandi-looking one of the Brannigan girl cousins, Maggie, Trina and Cari were the dark ones with the fabulous blue/green eyes.

Cari's hair was short and stylish, while Maggie's was long with the recent addition of purple streaks. She wore a slender tattoo in Chinese that climbed elegantly around her wrist. Their mother still wasn't used to the tattoo.

'What does it say?' asked Nora.

'I forget – something about good fortune…' Maggie said,

wondering where she'd put the bit of paper with the actual translation.

Their cousin Trina's hair was equally long but more glossy and she was a dab hand at making gentle curls with her hair straighteners.

Out together, the flatmates looked like a hip Manga girl and her posh, hair-flicking sister.

When Trina got the message, the shop was empty and she hit speed dial for Maggie.

'A party?' squealed Trina. 'Whose party?'

'Nothing thrilling, Uncle Edward's seventieth.'

'Oh.' The single syllable made it clear how deeply un-fascinating this type of family event was to Trina.

Family parties were fine when they were kids and the three families had done so much together but now – ugh.

'The parents will make us go,' Maggie reminded her. 'Although it'll probably just be all of us and unless we try inbreeding, there won't be anyone exciting to meet,' she added.

'But—' Trina's voice held a grin in it. 'It's in Lisowen Castle. A whole weekend, and I betcha it's all expenses paid.'

Maggie matched that grin. 'OMG, I betcha you're right! Spa treatments! Holy freaking shit!' she said, far too loudly.

The words just slipped out and immediately, Maggie hid behind her computer monitor. That had come out louder than she planned. Unless a wholly unexpected storm had wiped out half the western seaboard, nobody said things like 'holy freaking shit' in We'll Be There For You insurance.

Because the whole email complaint section had been badly hacked twice, it was currently closed. Therefore, the staff had all reluctantly been trained in how to say things like: 'I'll look into that for you; I'll put it onto somebody in senior management; we take this type of thing very seriously, indeed', all of which were code for 'I don't really care as it's nearly five o'clock and I have a date with a guy from Claims, but still, you are a cus-tomer and, hey, nobody wants you to phone the papers/radio/

go online bitching about us, so your name will be added to our lengthy complaints list for whatever sap is working Complaints this week. We will get back to you, like, whenever.'

'Holy freaking shit' had not been on any of the training modules.

'I better let you go,' Trina muttered, as Maggie whispered 'shit' again, much more quietly.

Trina hung up, thinking of what she'd wear to Lisowen Castle. She couldn't tap her mother for more money – Ma was getting bad-tempered about money lately. Said it wasn't fair they were always broke and bloody Edward was married now, so no hope he was going to leave them shedloads of cash when he died.

Sometimes Trina worried about her mother's future in the karmic sense – not that Trina was into the whole heaven or hell concept, but surely it was bad karma to even be thinking about Uncle Ed's death, wasn't it?

With practised ease, she flipped back to thinking about the hotel. Maggie had mentioned spa treatments. Was there a spa – *of course* there was a spa! All those posh places had spas now. She'd look it up online in a minute.

What could she have done? Total body massage, mani and pedi, obvs. That would be covered too, surely? Uncle Edward wasn't a cheapskate, whatever else you said about him and even Bess, the recently installed Aunt Bess, with a white gold engagement ring with a diamond solitaire the size of a golf ball on her bony finger, wasn't mean. Conniving, possibly, and definitely vulgar, as Trina's mother insisted, but not mean.

Friday was Jojo's late morning when Elaine opened up the shop, so she could have a late breakfast. Late meant a luxurious nine, which gave her time to have a long shower and do her hair afterwards because it was always a busy day. That morning, the radio in the kitchen was blaring out the news – miserable

– while the kettle was boiling with its 'I-am-a-rocket-about-to-take-off' noise.

She looked at her breakfast: spelt toast, a banana, low-fat spread and low-sugar marmalade ready to go.

Low everything.

Health was vital. You couldn't make a baby with the appliance of science if you drank, smoked or partied.

During her wild college years, Jojo had tried ultra hard not to have a baby.

She'd had the morning-after pill (made her sick), taken the contraceptive pill (made her put on weight) *and* made boyfriends use condoms, and had still spent a handful of fearful mornings staring into the toilet bowl, wishing it would turn red.

It always had. Lucky, lucky! she'd thought then. Lucky never to have become pregnant after a fling with some guy she wouldn't want to date longer than a month, never mind have a child with.

But with hideous irony, at the ancient age of thirty-two, married, having recently lost her mother and *ready* to be a mother, it turned out that she couldn't have a baby after all. She and Hugh had begun a battery of tests a year ago which proved that Hugh's sperm could win Olympic medals in the freestyle swimming events and that Jojo's insides looked as bumpy as the dark side of the moon – she'd seen the laparoscopy DVD – with endometriosis.

Two failed cycles of IVF later, she was wondering if irony was a speciality of whoever was in charge of the planet.

Unwanted babies cried in foreign orphanages, tiny children in sub-Saharan countries died from having nothing to drink but dirty water, and Jojo had not managed that magic second line on the pregnancy testing kit.

Worse, there were babies everywhere.

She'd stopped going on Facebook because all her school friends put up endless photos of their adorable children; clients of the shop she co-owned came in shimmering with delight and wondering might they fit into a large sweater 'Because it's early days and I can still wear my jeans! Although my sister – who has three kids – says I won't once I hit four months. That's when you really need the pregnancy stuff on your first pregnancy. On your second, you need it straight off. It's the stomach muscles, apparently…'

Jojo controlled the urge to slap said pregnant people, and discovered an urgent call she had to make, asking Elaine to take over.

Infertility played hell with your social life too – either people gave her knowing looks when she said she wasn't going to have a celebratory glass of wine: 'Are you expecting?' they might whisper, with all the quiet of a pantomime dame.

Or they'd be happily married with a carload of children and ask, when were she and Hugh going to stop partying and settle down to have kids?

'You don't know what you're missing!' they'd roar, so that the people in the cheap seats could hear too.

Just once, Jojo longed to be able to say: 'We don't want kids. I hate them. I'm keeping all the money we'd be spending on them to buy a yacht in the Caribbean. It's combining luxury with population control…' Just to see the look on their faces.

'Doesn't anyone ever *think* before they open their mouths?' she'd rage to Hugh on the way home in the car.

'No, love,' said Hugh sadly, and then she'd feel guilty because Hugh wanted children too. He didn't have endometriosis. Every part of him was in perfect working order. Plus, he had two older brothers, they both had children and Hugh made the best uncle ever.

Jojo's sisters-in-law were nice women but, seriously, neither of them had the slightest clue when it came to discussing all things baby in her presence. Surely they must have put two and two together and figured out that a couple together as long as she and Hugh were childless because something wasn't working? Or perhaps not.

Family parties were the worst.

'Oh, Hugh, hold little Tallulah… she's so cute. Look, she's smiling at you! She only smiles for us! You have a gift with children!'

Teeth gritted, Jojo would slip out of the room and text Cari: 'Send bail money – am going to kill someone.'

At least Jojo didn't have to compete with Cari when it came to kids.

Barney's stunt at the altar had put paid to all Cari's thoughts in that direction. Cari's sister, Maggie, six years younger, thought kids were cute from a distance – like from Outer Mongolia, maybe – but didn't really want one of her own.

'It's like guys,' said Maggie thoughtfully. 'If they annoy you, you can send them off to their own place and look for a better one. You can't do that with kids, can you?'

'Not without social services getting involved,' Jojo agreed.

These days, Hugh and Jojo's house was health central. There was no booze in the house, Jojo had sworn off the fake tan and she'd even bought organic make-up remover, *just in case*.

Hugh had arrived home one evening the month before with a giant red juicer machine.

'Is this a theme,' Jojo teased her husband. 'Red coffee maker, red food mixer, red toaster. Red sports car next?'

'I wish.' He grinned at her. 'Think of how healthy we'll be – it could help,' he'd added, large frame and huge hands hugging her much smaller body in a hello kiss. They fit together beautifully: a dance of ten years' practice.

A week of drinking green sludge had merely made Jojo intimately acquainted with the loo in the shop. Not a good option at the times when she was there on her own and had to actually lock up before she made a dash into the back.

'You'll have to be a superhero drinking green juice on your own, honey,' she told him at the end of the week. 'Either I've picked up a tropical disease that cleans your intestines out – or else I'm allergic to vegetables.'

'Coward.'

'No, it's just that a juice cleanse is cleansing me a bit too much. I like my food to stop briefly inside me before it reaches the escape hatch. Yes, Too Much Information! Sorry!'

'I'll make you fruit ones instead,' said Hugh kindly.

At weekends, she watched as Hugh carefully cut up a cucumber into precise, even shapes, although the machine was supposed to make mincemeat of even the hardest of veggies. He prepped for stir fries the same way.

'*Exacting*,' was the word, Jojo thought. She loved that about her husband: his precision and organisation.

They were total opposites. She was messy, couldn't help trailing books and make-up around their room, and abandoned half-read magazines with corners turned down on the couch at night.

Her home desk – where she did the shop's accounts, kept records of orders and inputted stock-taking details – was cluttered. The inevitable 'a clean desk is the sign of a sick mind' sign was stuck at a corner of her computer. But despite the mess, she was her father's child – the accounts were flawless, even if the desk itself was chaotic.

Hugh's home desk – sleek and grey – was always empty unless he was working on it, when his work laptop and an OCD-level desk organiser were set at right angles to the desk side. And even his pens – he liked pale blue ones – were set at the correct angle.

She could see him as a father: sitting at a table doing homework with their child.

She wasn't greedy – one was enough.

It was a lovely picture: his large frame bent over their small child, fair hair flopping forward, his hands impatiently hauling it back as he drew graphs and maps, with coloured pens for capital cities, highlighters on important facts...

The pain grabbed her: visceral, somewhere – ironically – in her belly. A clenching fist that told her it would never happen. That what happened to other people who went the IVF route would not happen to her. That she would never hold her own baby in her arms. Her early hopefulness had been dashed by that first negative pregnancy test. Then, the second negative test.

'I am asking for help,' she muttered softly, then loudly. 'I am asking for help.'

'The universe helps,' her cousin, Maggie – fan of crystals, psychics and angel cards – insisted when she wanted something.

But then Maggie had been asking the universe for a BMW and a hunky rich boyfriend for years now and no joy, so who knew?

Toast finished, Jojo shoved her dishes in the dishwasher, noticing Hugh's glass with remnants of green sludge already there. He made his juice the night before: 'Cold press juicer,' he'd said, having investigated the whole thing beforehand. 'You can leave it overnight because it hasn't been heated by centrifugal force.' He drank it as breakfast at half six just before he left for work. Corporate law waited for no man.

The shop could wait for one of its owners to come in because today was one of Elaine's early days. Fridays were always busy in the shop with women deciding they had *nothing* to wear for weekend nights out.

'You should have called it Nothing To Wear,' pointed out her other cousin, Trina, the first time she'd helped out by working behind the till, her being broke coinciding neatly with Elaine being off sick with gastric flu one weekend. 'That's what everyone seems to say when they arrive. Honestly, all they do is buy clothes – how come they have nothing to wear?'

Trina, being permanently broke, lived in Primark and bought the cheapest things she could online. Jojo helped her and

94

Maggie out by giving them things at cost or for free and giving them shifts in the shop when they had maxed out their credit cards, which was just about every month.

'Pot meet kettle,' laughed Jojo. 'You're always in the shops.'

'Yeah, but I buy tops for a tenner,' said Trina.

'That's down to disposable income,' Jojo said. 'If you earned more you'd spend it. Women love clothes – society tells us we need loads of them. Plus, if they didn't come in here, I'd have no business and since Maggie has done quite a few shifts for me, and I've given her clothes for you too, you and Maggie would half the wardrobes you already have.'

'Yeah, fair enough,' Trina said equably.

'You guys have to learn how to budget,' Jojo added. 'I saw your credit card bill last time I was over. Have you bought a foreign country and not told us?'

'You shouldn't have looked,' said Trina, not even slightly upset.

'It was on the couch and I was sitting on it,' Jojo said with a grin. 'Your filing system is worse than mine. But you guys have got to get your finances sorted. The partying gets boring, you know. You need to think about the future and getting settled—'

'Yeah, that's what Cari says too,' agreed Trina cheerfully, her face saying 'Yeah, whatevs', and raced off to help a customer who'd already said she didn't need any help.

Breakfast finished, Jojo went upstairs to shower and do her hair and make-up. In the bathroom mirror, she didn't see her face or body any more. She saw instead the slight curve of her belly despite the thinness of the rest of her. Menopausal belly and menopausal breasts? she wondered. It had been the same the first two times too – her breasts had felt strange during what the doctors called the down regulation part of the process.

The second part of the process, where she had to inject herself daily to grow what they called 'follicles' and what she and Hugh, after seeing them on-screen during one of the many vaginal scans, called eggs, meant she had the weirdest feeling inside her. As if she was a creature working hard to grow these precious eggs.

'It's like being a simple life form, a mammal, growing my babies,' she said to Hugh as they sat curled up on the couch each evening, stroking her belly, willing the eggs to grow.

'Those scans are amazing,' Hugh said, his long strong fingers gentle. 'It's like you've another world inside you, a world of strange ghostly shapes and then these little buds of happiness.'

Seven of the buds of happiness had been harvested and the two best embryos, after life in their petri dish with Hugh's sperm, had been transferred. After the embryo transfer, when Jojo had felt as if jewels had been put inside her as the two precious embryos were carefully placed in her uterus, she had touched her breasts constantly and looked at them, willing the signs of pregnancy.

'Do you think I look pregnant?' she'd ask Hugh constantly, turning this way and that, examining her slenderness to see if there was any sign. 'My breasts feel different, I'm sure of it.'

They'd had to wait sixteen days after the transfer to do a pregnancy test. Each day had felt like years to Jojo.

She'd been torn two ways – that she was pregnant, that it had worked because they wanted it so much. The ache that Jojo felt inside her to hold her own baby couldn't be called what sociologists described as Baby Hunger– it was a wild, animal need to have her own child. A fierceness that she hadn't known existed until they'd begun this painful journey.

The second feeling was that she wasn't pregnant – that it would never happen. Her mother had died, how could any-thing good now happen? If only they'd really started earlier, hadn't kept putting off going to a specialist when they were first married because they were young and healthy, because they'd been sure she'd get pregnant naturally, right? And then putting off going to a specialist because Lottie was sick and

Jojo had buried her need deep inside herself in order to help her mother through a terminal cancer diagnosis.

On the sixteenth day that first time, her hands had been shaking as she'd done the test. Whatever the result, she needed to go into the fertility clinic later for a blood test.

When she'd peed on the stick, she and Hugh had sat on the bathroom floor, the stick back in the packet, him holding her close, almost too tightly as if afraid she would fall apart if the result was negative.

'We have to be prepared for whatever happens,' he said.

His face was taut, an expression on it that Jojo hadn't known until they'd started the treatment. He was a serious-looking man but he so rarely looked serious when he was looking at Jojo: he had what Cari called 'his Jojo face' that Cari insisted was charming and romantic and said that this clever man with two degrees – law and economics – could scarcely believe his luck in having found someone as wonderful as Jojo.

'Hugh, I am prepared, you know that,' said Jojo.

She was lying through her teeth. She wasn't prepared: had never felt so untethered in her life. Her hands shook as she held on to Hugh. She loved him so much, they'd been together so long, since she was twenty-four and yet she felt utterly alone.

This procedure, this whole infertility system, did more than just transform her body into a supposedly fertile ground for embryos – it ripped a couple in two. The clinic psychologist had warned them but she hadn't believed it at the time. Now she knew it to be the truth. Infertility might turn some couples into even stronger units – it had turned Jojo and Hugh into islands drifting on the same sea.

If there was no baby, Jojo wanted to be alone. She couldn't bear to see her husband because this pain would feel like hers and only hers. He would not understand. Nobody would.

How had she ever been optimistic about it all?

Hugh's phone alarm finally sounded the three minutes.

They looked at the little white stick. A piece of plastic standing in for the Oracle at Delphi.

There was only one line in the tiny window.

Even as she looked at it, Jojo curled in on herself, bending over so that the half-retching, half-crying noises were made as she curled herself into a human ball.

'No! no!' she sobbed.

Nothing had ever felt like this.

'Please, Hugh, go away,' she'd begged. And he had.

Six

'And yet it moves...'

*As whispered by Galileo after the Inquisition made him
recant his statement that the Sun did not move,
the Earth moved around it.*

Hugh Hennessy rolled over in the big bed and reached out to Jojo's side. The sheets were cold, the duvet pulled back. He angled himself up enough to see the fat cube clock he'd had since before phones had alarms, a thing that could wake the dead if you didn't hit the 'off' button within five seconds. He didn't need it any more: somehow, he woke at five to six every morning, even at weekends. Years at college and then work had trained him. But today was Saturday, there had been no need to leave the cosy nest at six this morning, no need to move now – except.

It was just after seven. Four minutes after, to be precise. A lie-in, he thought gratefully.

But his wife was up. Up and undoubtedly worrying.

Sighing, Hugh buried his head in his pillow and tried to doze again but it was no good: the sleep cycle was broken and his mind was a racing minefield of worries about Jojo, the infertility treatment, her father, her stepmother... this damn seventieth birthday.

If it was possible, Hugh would like to airlift Jojo and himself to a remote land for six months so she could get away from family, work, parties, grief and the ache he saw on his wife's face every day.

They had talked about what infertility treatment meant, they had seen a counsellor connected with the clinic and they

99

thought they were ready for what the counsellor described as a 'rollercoaster of emotions'.

Rollercoaster? It was more like being strapped onto the outside of a rocket heading for Mars: rollercoaster could not do justice to the highs and lows of each part of the procedure, and Hugh wasn't even the one who was being pumped with drugs that played havoc with your hormones.

He was naturally optimistic, he believed it would work. So had Jojo.

Therefore they'd been excited and full of anticipation at the early trips in and out of the clinic.

Science could do anything!

Then had come the talk about ovarian hyper-stimulation and how women had died from this. They must be on the alert for the symptoms: lungs could fill with fluid, serious anti-stroke meds needed to be injected instantly.

They'd both stared at each other in horror.

'Are we mad to be doing this?' Hugh had asked in the car on the way home.

'No,' cried Jojo fiercely. 'I want a baby, Hugh: it's the only way. It's my body that's letting us down. This is a risk but we're ready for it, aren't we?'

What turned out to be the riskiest of all was the gradual disintegration of their relationship.

When the first treatment had failed, Jojo had been devastated but slowly and eventually determined. 'We'll try again,' she'd said.

With the second negative test, she'd turned in on herself.

She was still there physically, still able to smile, but it was a smile that never reached her eyes.

Hugh felt as if he'd lost her.

'We've got to talk, Jojo,' he'd tried to say. 'Please, talk to me.'

But she wouldn't.

And then she'd wanted, been determined, to go through with another round of treatment when the three months after the last one was up, which was when they were allowed by the clinic to go through another cycle.

'We're not ready for it,' he'd said flatly to her. 'I'm going to tell the psychologist you're not over the last one. Not every couple are right for this – it's huge pressure. We can try adoption—'

Jojo, but not a Jojo he recognised, had turned on him, almost snarling as she interrupted, 'We are doing it, you are not saying anything like that, you are not! Do it for me, Hugh, for me.'

Shaken, he'd tried again, making her sit beside him at the kitchen table, holding her arm, an arm that had grown so thin. 'Please, lovie—'

'I need this, Hugh!'

He felt like such a coward for not fighting her.

Instead, he'd gone with her to see the psychologist without whose agreement they wouldn't be accepted for another cycle.

'We're fine,' he'd lied, Jojo's hand gripping his so tightly under the table that it hurt.

And here they were again: just another week till Jojo had another transfer, a frozen one this time, where the five remaining embryos, which had been frozen last time, would be defrosted to see if they could survive to the next stage, ready for two to be implanted.

Jojo was adamant that nobody could know apart from Cari, and she hadn't told Cari the exact dates this time. Last time, Cari had texted not long after they'd done the pregnancy test, and Hugh had had to answer it. Jojo hadn't been able.

'Yeah, fine, let's tell nobody then, if that's what you want,' Hugh had agreed when it came to this secrecy. He was sure this was a mistake: people needed support when they were having infertility treatment – OK, not everyone they knew, but still, a few people to support them. Now Jojo had Cari and he had no one.

He rubbed his hand across his eyes. He was awake. A run

might help. He dragged himself out of bed and went into the bathroom. Ten miles, no fifteen. Make it hurt. Sometimes that helped.

There were pluses and minus to living alone, Cari knew. Plus meant there was nobody to take control of the zapper and mutter that they really wanted to watch the whole series of *Breaking Bad again* when you were starting onto the second series of *The Bridge*.

Another plus was the ability to repaint the entire second-floor flat of the Georgian house a gleaming white, so that it resembled a home magazine shoot when tidy – or a post-burglary scene from a crime show when not. Men – well, Barney or He Who Should Never Be Named Apart From Scumbag – thought that all-white was a bit girlie.

Cari liked her gleaming floorboards, and being able to have a pretty white distressed antique-style cabinet on one side of her living room with crystal perfume bottles, which she picked up at junk sales. She liked her big posters of Georgia O'Keeffe flowers without any man staring at them in horror and saying: 'Is that... er... a... you know, woman's...?'

She liked lots of cushions and throws, which were man ar-senic; she liked soft rugs on the floor and walking round in her slippers all the time. Most of all, she liked her bedroom which was a shrine to white lace, also purchased for next to nothing at antique fairs and sewn onto white linen cushions. Men hated that type of thing, thought it was all girlie, and since men never got to set foot in Cari's house, which was about a mile along the main Silver Bay road from Jojo and Hugh's rather more modern, Scandi-themed townhouse, no man ever had to look at it and wonder how Cari Brannigan, tough cookie extraordinaire, should live in such a romantic bower.

Minuses of living alone included talking to yourself to the point that you forgot and kept it up when you were out in public, and the fact that when there was a scrabbling in the kitchen cupboards, you could either phone the pest control people or peer, gingerly, into said cupboards early on a Saturday morning, when you should be sinking into bed with coffee and a book you didn't have to read for work.

'Damn torch.' Her torch had passed away without her knowing and Cari shook it to rattle the batteries a bit as she tried to stare in at the back of the under the sink cupboard past the bleach, industrial-strength cleaner and packets of kitchen wipes, looking for mousy evidence.

Her mother went for the environmentally friendly approach to kitchen cleaning – Nora reckoned you could clean anything with either vinegar, washing-up liquid, lemon juice or a paste made of bread soda.

'It's better for the planet,' Nora said with the pride of a woman whose family home gleamed with wood polished with actual beeswax and was scented with home-made candles, aromatherapy oils and dried lavender from her own garden.

'What has the planet done for me lately?' Cari liked to tease.

'Helped you breathe in oxygen instead of carbon dioxide,' her mother would chide, unable to help herself. 'For every two breaths you take, one comes from the ocean, which is being slowly poisoned because we don't think enough about it – consider that next time you use toxic chemicals that you then wash down the drain.'

'Hippie,' Cari would reply, grinning.

'How have I raised such a pair of philistines? You and Maggie are just the same,' her mother would say, throwing her arms up. 'Go on, wreck the planet, don't come running to me when it breaks.'

Her mother would no doubt have some plan to relocate the mice to another, more mouse-friendly home or free them into the countryside to have happy, fulfilled mousy lives, Cari thought grimly as she searched amid all her wildly toxic cleaning products for mice poo.

'What do I do with mice?' she asked her mother on the phone, when the evidence had been found.

It was only eight but Nora rose early all the time.

'Sauté or oven cook with root veg,' Nora suggested. 'Have you found droppings?'

'Little tiny black bits?' Cari said, squashing the phone into the curve of her neck and washing her hands again.

'Yes, they're droppings. I'll send your father over with mouse traps.'

'No,' wailed Cari. 'I don't want mouse corpses in my kitchen – I want them to eat something poisonous and die horribly a long, long way from me.'

There was a pause. Cari could imagine her mother at her usual Saturday routine: up early to walk the dogs, detour to pick up the papers, freshly made bread for breakfast with the last of the apple jelly from the previous autumn's crop of their own apples.

Nora and Mick Brannigan's 1950s semi-detached house with its long back garden might have sat just two miles from the city centre, but it could have been in the countryside from the bounty Nora coaxed out of it. She'd grown fruit and vegetables all her life, and Cari could remember wishing her mother was more like other modern mums in school instead of a throwback to a country farmer's wife with short, unfashionably cut hair and weird felted skirts which she wore with handknitted sweaters. Then, Cari had thought the vegetable-growing and unchanging and unfashionable clothes were a choice: now, she knew it had been necessity. Mick Brannigan worked in a garage as chief mechanic. He could have worked for his brother, a fact Maggie, in particular, brought up again and again.

'Then we'd be rich!' Maggie said.

'Then we'd be spongers,' her father would say, chucking his younger daughter under the chin. Her father didn't approve of family working for family, having seen how badly it had worked out for his brother, Kit.

At Aunt Helen's insistence, Uncle Kit had tried to work with Uncle Edward but it had not gone well. Kit wasn't mechanically minded and he was laid-back, too laid-back for Edward. Kit had got out while they were still friends. Helen still wasn't over it, Nora could tell, and was jealous of how Edward and Lottie had become rich while the Kit Brannigan side of the family were not.

Nora had managed to keep Edward's involvement in Maggie's career from her husband on the grounds that Maggie was different and without some help she'd be living in her own childhood bedroom until she was ninety, still coming downstairs sheepishly looking for a loan to tide her over till payday.

'Cari,' Nora informed her daughter now, 'mice do not helpfully clamber onto buses to go miles away and die: they die behind your cupboards or under your floorboards and stink for ages.' There was a pause. 'Visitors won't like it.'

Cari knew her mother had been about to say 'boyfriends won't like it' but had controlled the urge.

Among her mother's fondness for all things environmental was a fondness for the pairing up of the species, a bit like Noah but without the flood.

'I'm avoiding those sort of visitors until I get my gun licence back,' Cari said.

On the other end of the phone, Nora sighed. 'I thank the Lord daily that this country has such tough laws on weapons, Cari.'

'I have my baseball bat,' Cari replied cheerfully.

'I would suggest anger management classes but I know you are joking. You *are* joking, right?' Nora ploughed on. 'So you got the invitation to Eddie's party, then? I thought you'd ring me when you saw the card.'

It was Cari's turn to pause. 'Yeah, I got it. Opened it by mistake when I was on my way to the airport in London yesterday. I nearly puked. Do you think *he'll* be there?'

'I don't know. Traci's sure to be asked. Eddie will want

everyone there and Bess doesn't really know the history. If Lottie was still around, she'd insist they weren't there so as not to hurt you but with Bess...'

'Yeah, I know. Doesn't know, doesn't care.'

'She doesn't understand our family yet,' Nora said diplomatically. 'I could talk to her—'

'No! The invitations will have gone out already. That would be even more embarrassing. I just won't go, simple,' said Cari.

'Did you get the invitation?' Mick said, lying down on Cari's kitchen floor and beginning to do something that sounded as if he was pulling the back of the cupboard out.

'Yes. What are you doing, Dad?' demanded Cari, trying to look but not wanting to get too close in case a battalion of mice made a dash for freedom. 'If you take the back of the cupboard off, they just have a bigger door to climb through. Should I get a neon sign too, saying: "Hey, mice: free food – this way! Run around my bedroom while you're at it and climb on me when I'm asleep!"'

'I'm putting the traps back here,' her father said mildly. 'In these old houses, fitted kitchens don't really fit. There's often a gap and mice love a gap. You've no idea how tiny a hole they can fit through.'

'I don't want to know,' wailed Cari, tough in the boardroom, a wimp when it came to rodents.

'I'll put the back of the cupboard on and come during the week to check them,' continued her father. 'Now, we have to set some in other places.'

'Yeuch.'

'You should get a cat.'

'I would then become a cat woman,' said Cari.

'What's a cat woman? Like Michelle Pfeiffer in *Batman*?'

Mick stood up, pleased with his work. There was something very satisfying about helping his daughter out. But it shouldn't be him doing this. It should be a husband, no matter how much Cari banged on about how she was independent, thank you very much.

Cari gave him a patient look. 'No, being a cat woman almost never implies black PVC catsuits. It means I have no life except Tiddles, he will be the only creature to sleep on my bed, ever, the place will be knee-deep in scratching boards and cat toys, and I will sign all cards "With love Cari and Tiddles".'

Mick Brannigan looked at her calmly. 'As your mother has been teaching me in the language of texting, that stuff about PVC catsuits and people in your bed is TMI, Too Much Information, thank you very much,' he said.

'You. Are. Amazing.' Clive slithered over her until his breath was tickling the back of Amy's neck and his hands were curved around her full breasts.

Amy burrowed into her sheets – freshly changed for this precise reason – and sighed with pleasure. There was nothing on the planet to compare with having a man in your bed, holding you, saying nice things, murmuring words of love. Even if it was all wrong.

But she was lonely and when Clive had texted her, saying he had a few free hours on Saturday afternoon, she'd rushed into action and changed the sheets. This was wrong, she'd told herself, even as she sprayed a burst of perfume onto the sheets.

And then he'd called at her door, carrying flowers, wine and fresh fruit, and she simply hadn't the heart to turn him away. The weekends were the loneliest of all, two days stretching ahead of her and nobody to share them with. And now here Clive was, making time for her.

Clive was like none of the few boyfriends Amy had had over the years. He was dark-haired, really good-looking, with all his own hair and a good job. He seemed to like her body, which Amy adored but couldn't quite understand because he could have had anyone and couldn't he see her flaws?

He was also her boss, which made it wrong on many levels.

And, worst of all, he was married, which made it wrong on so many other moral levels that, once he was gone, Amy always finished off the rest of the bottle of wine he'd brought in a state of desperate guilt and got down on her knees and prayed with a fervour that Tiana's mother would have approved of.

'I am sorry, I won't do it again, please help me not to do it again. Please let him and Suzanne work it out so that they have properly separate lives and do not have to live together while waiting for the separation decree.' If only divorce proceedings were quicker in Ireland.

Amy never asked Clive to come to her little apartment, she never said anything to him in work apart from discussing actual work issues, and she had never so much as touched him fleetingly in a teasing way.

She was not that sort of girl, she told herself. But when he turned up at her door – always randomly, always after a discreet text some five minutes before – she could never bear to turn him away.

He was a light in her world and all the guilt couldn't make her say, 'No, Clive, it's wrong, go home. You and Suzanne have to be properly living apart.'

'But we are, darling – it's only finances keeping us in the same house. I can't move out for a few more months, not until I get a raise, and then, it's you and me and you will love the children, I know you will.'

'Of course I will: they're your children,' she'd say earnestly. She loved children, wanted her own, wanted her own full life with Clive and his little ones in it, and their little ones and no more sneaking around because Clive said it was tricky until the legal things were finalised …

His touch upon her skin felt like the only kindness in the world and lonely Amy couldn't turn her back on it. Her mother was so loved up with Edward that it felt impossible to be with them because she felt like an interloper: they were always touching. Edward would brush his lips against her mother's forehead as he handed her a cup of coffee, Bess would stroke her husband's shoulder lovingly as he read the paper and she reached over him for the business supplement.

'Come up to us, have dinner with us at the weekend. It's just me and Edward,' her mother sometimes said on Fridays, which was her mother's way of both including Amy – and finding out if her was daughter seeing anyone, did she have friends, was there a date planned for either Friday or Saturday night?

Amy could see through this spying rigmarole. Imagine if Bess found out about Clive? She'd probably go round to the office and lacerate him with words, accuse him of taking advantage of an employee, which he honestly wasn't. Or she'd find his address and she and Edward – they went everywhere as a team now – would march round and confront him, wife and all. There would be no way to explain that the Clive-and-his-wife marriage was complicated to explain. Older people didn't understand that sort of thing.

'Myself and the pottery girls are going out,' Amy would say when her mother asked her to dinner now. The pottery class had lasted eight weeks and Amy had loved it but she hadn't really stayed in touch with the other people.

Her grandmother had always told her she was 'too shy. You want to come out of yourself, girl, or nobody will talk to you at all!' Unlike lessons about flood plains, cloud formations and the cosine rule in school, those words had stuck in Amy's mind like glue. She was shy, not good with people. She'd really liked the girls at the pottery class but she was sure they hadn't liked her. She'd only done the course because she'd realised that apart from work, Clive's always unexpected visits, and the time she spent on her laptop, she never really did anything.

So to cover up both her lack of friends apart from Nola, who lived in the UK, and Tiana, who lived on the other side of the world, and the reality of who her lover was, she said things like, 'The gang in the store and myself are all going to the cinema.'

All lies, of course. Bess would kill her daughter if she knew that Amy was waiting for that rare Saturday text when Clive was supposed to be out doing grocery shopping or dropping into the office or whatever else it was that husbands did at weekends, when he rolled up at her place for an hour, sometimes less. They would get into bed almost immediately, and Amy, who knew of foreplay only from books because her two previous boyfriends had not been gifted in that department, would be so overcome with desire and gratefulness that she didn't mind this ripping off of clothes, and her loneliness helped her overlook this sense that her bedroom was a hotel that charged by the hour.

Her mother would never have let a man treat her like that.

Amy wasn't stupid – she was always scared that Clive was coming to her simply for sex but she kept hoping that it was more, because how could a man say those things if it was just sex? He wouldn't, she knew it.

It had started nearly a year before when Amy had begun working for Met-Ro, a German company whose cut-price stores were growing around Europe at high speed. Amy had been hired as part of the window dressing team, which her mother had told her was a ridiculous job with no prospects.

'Edward will give you a job in his company. It's not charity, you're family now. Well, almost. A few more months to the wedding—'

Her mother had smiled in that distant way she did now, a way that made Amy think she was dreaming of Edward and their life together. Mother had never smiled like that about Dad, Amy thought sadly. Dad had not fitted the bill for perfect husband material.

Amy's new job was the same – too flash-in-the-pan, not career-woman enough.

Yet the job had given her Clive, boss of the whole Irish operation, so high up that she was astonished he'd even noticed her.

He'd brushed against her hand that first day.

'Welcome to the club,' he'd said, the hideous overhead lights glinting on his mahogany hair and making him look like a knight from the Arthurian legends, complete with startlingly blue eyes. He was tall and large, not overweight large, but strong large like those heroes in her novels. The ones who were dukes and rescued feisty ladies and took them to bed where people fractured into orgasm, which was something Amy was fascinated by. How could you fracture into orgasm? Or splinter? Amy desperately wanted to know, to feel it. She was truly hopeless, missing out on one of life's great joys, if she couldn't achieve this.

Later, Amy had overheard someone say that Clive was 'dangerous – a real ladykiller', but they just didn't know him the way she did.

His marriage was a phoney.

'Suzanne is a lovely woman but we never should have got married,' he'd told her, his face sad, his eyes weary at what all this pain meant for the woman he respected and their beloved children. 'We both know it now but finances' – he shrugged, as if embarrassed to be having this conversation – 'mean we must live together until we have enough money to sell the house and buy two separate places. It's economic necessity that keeps us together. But,' he'd added, 'she is truly a wonderful woman who deserves happiness in her future.'

Amy loved that he had such respect for his wife. She would have not been able to be with him if he'd said dreadful things about Suzanne, but this, this liking and respect, made it bearable.

'We're too similar. She's a career woman through and through. You'd think that company would fall apart if she wasn't in it.'

What Clive wanted, he told Amy that first time was 'someone gentle, kind, loving. Like – like you, Amy.'

He'd touched her face and said he was sorry.

'I can't promise you anything but love right now, my darling,' he'd said, playing with her hair, marvelling at its auburn and strawberry highlights and the way it turned a rich burnished copper under certain lights. 'Never cut your hair.'

She would never have gone to bed with him that first time if he hadn't seemed so torn about it: 'This damn situation! I love you, Amy ... this is heartbreaking ...'

'We don't have to,' said Amy, knowing he was right and hating that he was married, even when he'd explained it all to her. 'We can wait until you and Suzanne live separately, that would work. I can wait, darling?'

'You're right, we should ... but when I see you like this ...'

One large hand had touched the buttons on her long, flowy shirt, because Amy never wore tight-fitting things because they showed off her figure, the breasts she tried so hard to hide.

Then his hands were on her breasts and she knew that he and she were beyond conversation now.

He loved her breasts, and she thought of all the years her mother had forced her into too-small bras, and now, here was this man adoring those same heavy breasts and her creamy shoulders. She had a waist now too, although she was hopeless at showing it off. Clive had told her what she should do, his hands spanning its width, his voice hoarse.

'Wear clingy little sweaters and fifties skirts: that would suit you, my darling,' he'd said, 'and stockings, like girls from the fifties – just not at work or I'd never be able to stop myself pouncing on you!'

Amy, longing for love and not able to imagine anyone ever wanting to pounce on her, had flushed at the very notion of Clive thinking about her at work.

Of course, she couldn't tell anyone. Not Nola, who would kill her for being with a man who lived with his wife, no matter what the circumstances. Not Tiana via email or Skype, who would say she was nuts, it was going nowhere because he was married, and she ought to dump him sharpish. They didn't know Clive, they didn't see how much he meant all the things he said, they didn't understand how it pained him waiting for the day until they could be together.

And certainly not her mother, who could easily march round to Clive's house and ask to speak to Suzanne to verify it all.

So it was Amy's secret. Everyone was entitled to them, weren't they?

Bess almost didn't recognise the woman standing in the expensive lingerie shop changing room. This woman was all curves and sensuality, all highlighted by a dusky rose-pink silk bra and French knickers, with a matching wrap.

'Pale pink will wash you out,' the sales lady, an imposing woman with an equally imposing bosom and a tape measure round her neck, had explained from the start.

She'd sent Bess into the room, measured her briskly, then arrived back with a few armfuls of silks and lace. 'Us older ladies need structure but you don't have to look like you're going in for the shotput in the Olympics, either,' she'd said, with a brief glance at Bess's plain bra, white as snow, just as pure, and with a bra strap at least three-quarters of an inch in width.

Bess, who knew her way round most situations, felt entirely out of her depth here. She'd bought what she thought was 'good' lingerie for her wedding. Good meant sensible, lasting a long time. Bess had never had enough money for frivolity when it came to undergarments, and besides, in her previous incarnation, Before Edward, who was going to see them?

She'd never held with that 'wear your red knickers and matching bra to work on a difficult day' shenanigans. Her strength in work came from her head, not from the colour of her bra.

But the other night, she and Edward had been lying on the couch, curled up like a couple of teenagers, and there had been a love scene in the film they were watching.

The actress had been clad in silk: expensive stuff, Bess surmised, all frou frou and lace, the type of thing Bess knew cost a fortune. And yet Edward had turned to her, murmuring gently: 'That would suit you, darling. Well, suit you long enough for me to rip it off.'

And she'd felt that rippling of excitement low in her belly that this man desired her and said so.

'If I paid for that, I'd kill you for ripping it!' said Bess in her teasing voice, but when Edward laughed and said: 'My darling sensible wife,' she'd thought again. What if her 'good' things weren't good enough? What if good really meant boring and unsexy, and Edward wanted to see her in silks and lace?

She'd taken a long lunch break the next day and ended up in The Boudoir, where a quick glance at the price tag on a garter belt had nearly sent her out again, but she'd stayed.

She had been buying sensible things for forty years now – that must be money in the bank saved up for this moment.

'These suit you,' said the sales lady, admiring a balconette bra in a honeyed gold that transformed Bess in a way her white sensible stuff never had. 'You've been wearing the wrong size for years: mind you, everybody does. You simply wouldn't credit the number of woman who come in here wearing the wrong-sized bra.'

Bess thought with a pang of guilt of those years when Amy had needed a bigger bra and Bess had piously insisted it was just fat, and if only Amy was slimmer she'd be able to fit into her old bras.

How insensitive had she been?

It was repeating what she'd been taught, she knew: her own mother had not been the warm and fuzzy kind of parent. But that didn't mean Bess had to go out and recreate the pattern. Just because she was trying to keep food on the table as a single mother didn't mean she had to be so hard on her only daughter.

She thought, too, of how much Edward loved his two

children – even though one of those children was the source of great trauma to Bess – she loved that about him. She could never have been with a man who didn't care about his kids. A man like Dennis, for example, who cared for neither Bess nor Amy.

Bess had rung Amy earlier, asking if she'd come up to dinner with them that night but Amy was going out with her 'gang'. Bess was suspicious of this. Amy had always been quite a shy girl and this gang stuff didn't sound like her... But then if Amy was blossoming and spreading her wings, how wonderful. It eased Bess's guilt a little.

'Do you want to try anything else?' said the saleswoman, who'd gone back out for more stuff, seeing as she had a willing customer in the dressing room.

'What other colours do you have this in?' Bess asked.

Tonight, she would surprise Edward with this, she decided. She could never have envisaged a time in her life when she'd be this happy. It would work out, it had to. The alternative was too devastating.

Seven

*Compromise saves marriages. The thing is, compromise
works two ways. If one person is always making the
compromises, the relationship is not in balance ...*

Cari waited till the weekend was over before she phoned John
Steele.

'Don't phone John Steele – he's my author now,' had been
the brusque email from Gavin Watson that awaited her when
she arrived in work on Monday morning. Jeff, lugubrious in his
office and with his beard not shaved, gave her a glance which
seemed to say the same thing.

'Baby not sleeping or a late one?' Cari said, putting her head
round the door. Jeff had married a few years ago, and now had
a small daughter, a three-month-old baby named Jasmine and
a permanent look of total exhaustion on his face.

'Yeah, wild party. Went on till four—' said Jeff, taking a swig
of the energy drink that gave Cari heart palpitations when
she drank it. 'No, of course it wasn't a late one: the baby's not
sleeping. Babies do not appear to sleep. Why do people say, "I
slept like a baby?" to imply otherwise? It just means you wake
up crying every hour.'

'Which is why I am childless,' said Cari sweetly.

Jeff did look like hell.

'He'd be gorgeous if he smiled,' had been Jojo's summation
of him after they'd met.

'He does smile,' Cari said. 'I think you intimidate him, that's
all.'

'And you don't? With those five-inch heels?'

116

'He knows me.'

Jeff had come from sales to head the Cambridge Ireland company and had steered it through difficult times with skill. He was great with people, kind to all the (small) junior team and always encouraging the three sales reps as they trailed around the country in company cars, suffering with bad backs from so long behind the wheel and not getting overtime for rolling up at book events or launches.

He threw a decent Christmas party every year, fought for their bonuses, and let the editorial team (Cari and her second-in-command, Declan) run with the books they knew would sell.

Compared to bosses who bullied and fought with editors without ever having been one themselves, it was a joy.

Now Cari shut the door of Jeff's office quietly, because to slam it would have everyone in the small outer office looking up in astonishment, and threw herself into the chair in front of his desk. She was miserable on every level, not least because she'd bought the biggest Toblerone in the airport and had spent Friday night miserably eating it, before she'd gone out on Saturday after her father had left and bought fudge brownie ice cream, also now long gone. Her hair was greasy because she simply hadn't the heart to wash it that morning at seven o'clock and her favourite trousers were too tight, so she was working the hair bobbin round the button to lengthen it. Life and everything else sucked.

'How are you doing?' asked Jeff, his face kind, sympathy in the brown eyes, and when he steepled his fingers and looked at Cari over the tips of his nails, Cari had to control the urge to say, 'Really?'

'I take it you heard,' she said, instead. No point alienating all her superiors in the company.

'They told me just before the meeting,' he said. 'Edwin expressly forbade me to warn you and I put it to him firmly that you would be humiliated by the whole thing, that you work on my team and you should have been told beforehand. Letting it happen in front of Gavin Watson was uncalled for. I don't know why bloody John Steele's agent couldn't have told you. That would have been politic, kind, decent!'

'Gavin Watson doesn't do decent. He certainly couldn't spell it!' Cari said, picking up one of the many doodads that sat on Jeff's desk and idly wondering did the Voodoo dolly thing work. Most of the doodads were mini sculptures by Jeff's wife's nephews and were of weird little creatures made with plasticine. Cari could make a wax dolly of Gavin and then she could stick pins in it. Someone was bound to have published a book on this – there were books on everything.

'Now I want you to listen to me, Cari.'

Something in her boss's tone made Cari look at him instead of glumly at the desk. Jeff had never gone in for internet TED-style encouraging speeches before, but he looked as if he was gearing up for one now.

'If you hadn't hared off ahead of all of us to Heathrow, I'd have been able to say this to you in person, but I can now. Gavin Watson can't edit. You know it and I do too. He made mincemeat out of that Evelyn Walker book he took over.'

They both nodded. Gavin's early attempts to do really hands-on editing had failed miserably with one of the imprint's big names, a *grande dame* thriller writer who had a CBE, a high-three-figure IQ and a well-known lack of patience with fools.

Three weeks of being edited by Gavin when her existing editor had fallen ill with pneumonia had sent her shrieking insults down the phone to all and sundry, including the company's chairman – and necessitated a scrabble through ancient actual phonebooks for an old editor of hers she'd liked years ago, who'd had to be coaxed out of retirement to assist.

'He will screw this up,' Jeff continued. 'I would bet money on it. Plus, you know he won't stay long with Xenon. Edwin Miller is keeping Gavin close so he can keep an eye on him but you can bet your bottom dollar that our Gav gets shunted off to another imprint within the group in a couple of years where he can leap up another step of the ladder and make someone else's life hell. He'll still be under Edwin, essentially, but he'll have another boss to annoy. In the meantime, you have to pretend you don't care.'

'You sound like Dr Phil,' grumbled Cari.

'Dr Phil is often right.'

'Not in this case. I *do* care. I made John Steele. He had the raw talent but he had no self-belief, Jeff, remember?' Cari begged. 'He didn't think he could do it but I made him believe in himself, I coaxed the edit of the first book out of him. I coaxed the second one out too.'

The third and fourth had been easier because, by then, John Steele, resident of a small fishing village, a genius with a lathe, was world famous, if uncomfortable with this new-found fame. The money – not so uncomfortable with that.

It turned out that John, once a socialist to his toenails, loved filthy lucre and had lost his head so far as to buy a Ferrari – a vehicle entirely unsuitable for narrow country roads with grass ridges in the middle, given that the Ferrari's racing chassis was about seven inches off the ground.

Still, Cari hadn't cared. The book sales were stratospheric, she'd received a huge bonus for both finding and nurturing him, she'd won Editor of the Year at the prestigious Bookseller Awards and she had become the company's golden girl for it all. A move to London to inhabit a corner office with a view could only be months away – and now this.

'Find another John Steele!' said Jeff, and sat back, looking satisfied.

'Is that it? The pep talk? There aren't many of them out there, Jeff, in case you hadn't noticed: people who can tell a story so that you can barely turn the pages fast enough.'

'Anna asked me if you wanted to come to dinner to us at the

weekend, Friday?' Jeff added, with the rapid change of subject she was used to.

The TED talk was over, they were moving on. 'It's a sort of cheer-you-up type of thing. My brother, Conal, is home from Paris. He's finally moved back.'

Cari had heard all about this brother, a year or two younger than Jeff, who was a scientist, something medical, sounded equally decent, kind and probably equally hangdoggy. He'd worked in some part of the charity industry, she thought, which probably meant he wore awful clothes and had no conversation apart from how wasteful the western world was. She wasn't sure if she was supposed to launch said brother back into Irish society or if he was to be her date on the grounds that she was in the depths of misery. Either way, she didn't need the pity or the blind date with Father Teresa.

'Say a huge thanks to Anna for me, Jeff,' she said, 'but I have a family thing on Friday.'

She didn't but she'd come up with an imaginary one.

'No you don't,' said Jeff. 'Just one dinner. You'd like my brother. He used to be a bit of a nerd but Paris has loosened him up. Unless you have really filled that apartment full of cats and have to stay at home to change litter trays.'

'What's wrong with cats?' demanded Cari, forgetting that she'd dissed felines to her father the other day. 'Cats are cool and cuddly and don't rip up the house when you're gone, like my mother's old dog, Frantic, who ate cushions like his life depended on it.'

Jeff laughed. 'Does that mean that if your porn name is based on your first pet's name, you're Frantic...?'

'You. Are. Sick,' Cari said. 'I am an employee and that's sexual harassment.'

Jeff raised his arms in apology and Cari got a blast of unwashed armpits. 'I apologise. Margins are tight, we can't afford an inquiry.'

'Don't do it again, moron,' she said. 'What if I was a junior.'

'I wouldn't do it to a junior,' said Jeff, horrified. 'You're, you know – unshockable, spiky. That's part of your charm.'

'That and my brains,' said Cari smartly.

'We all know you have brains to burn, Cari, just use them when it comes to dealing with John Steele and Gavin-the-author-stealer from now on.'

She left the office where the scent of exhausted, unshaved man lingered unpleasantly. It was nearly nine and Jeff had a sales meeting this morning, she remembered. Unshaven, smelly boss, even one with a small baby, was not a good message for the troops.

She stuck her head back into Jeff's office. 'Stick on some aftershave, will you? You smell like a polecat,' she said, one friend to another.

'I thought I was sexually harassing you?' said Jeff.

'You couldn't sexually harass a hamster,' she snapped back fondly.

'Don't call John Steele,' repeated Jeff, in the same friendship vein. 'Call Freddie and rip him a new one if you really want to, but not John. He wants to stay out of it. You know the drill: do not upset the author at all costs. Pissing off agents isn't a good idea either but I know you want to kill something…'

Cari waited till the sales meeting was under way with half the office closeted with Jeff, then shut her office door, pulled down her rarely used office blinds and phoned John Steele. Yes, she could have phoned his agent and, oh boy, she would, but first she had to speak to the man she'd honestly considered a friend for the past four years.

After dialling John's mobile number, she wondered if he would answer: after all, he knew the office's Dublin phone number and was used to calls from them. It would not take a rocket scientist to figure out that an early morning call could be from her and he might easily let the call go to voicemail and check later.

So she was surprised when he answered on the first ring, that gritty Sheffield accent undiminished despite twenty years in Ireland and marriage to an Irish woman.

'Hello, John Steele.'

'John.'

'Cari. I wanted to phone you—'

All the clever things Cari had been practising in her head all weekend just vanished. She was left with the dumb, deeply unclever: 'Why didn't you?'

'I chickened out.'

This honesty removed the final bits of Cari's sparkling repertoire.

'If I was doing something wrong, you could have told me,' she said, speaking as a wounded friend to another friend, instead of as a professional to someone who'd just skewered her. 'Given me a chance, John. And to go to Gavin Watson—' She snorted with disgust. 'I hate him, you know that. I even told you all about the debacle when he took over Evelyn Walker's editing job. He's not a good editor, he'll wreck your confidence—'

She paused and berated herself mentally. Stupid cow – she'd let her mouth run off on her again. What had she been thinking?

She was not the Cari of old talking to her dear friend, John, on the phone, laughing about their days and the people they'd met. That collegial relationship was over.

He was an important author and she was his former editor.

Who knew what damage she could do to her already damaged career now if she slagged off Gavin to his new author.

'Forget I said that,' she said crisply. 'I wish you the best with Gavin, I'm sure it will be good for both of you. Just tell me one thing: why did you want to move? If I'm that bad an editor, I need to hear it from you because we worked well together, I thought I had helped your career, and if I've lost my editing mojo or something, I need to know. I still need this job, John.'

Cari stopped before her voice broke.

Damn. She wished she'd stolen some of Jeff's cache of energy drinks. She could do with a blast of energetic heartbeating instead of the empty, betrayed feeling she was experiencing now.

There was silence on the other end of the phone.

John Steele was thoughtful, slow to answer things. It was why he'd never been keen on publicity and hated to do television shows. Pondering questions did not go down well on quick-fire TV slots where a seven-minute time slot was considered hugely long. Pondering an answer could take up valuable time, made for bad TV and meant the author was never booked again.

Finally, John answered: 'Freddie told me that working with Gavin would be good for my career. That I needed an editor in London, at the heart of things and Gavin is that.'

'Oh.' Cari swivelled in her chair so she could look out of the window.

The Cambridge Ireland offices were on the edge of a modern industrial estate, sheets of glass and steel facing fields on one side, fields that would one day, no doubt, be populated with more gleaming office buildings. But for now, Cari could see a line of sycamore trees and a horse on the other side: piebald, the type the gypsies favoured, with a small grey donkey to keep him company. They were swishing their tails and contentedly looking over their field.

Right now, she wished she was with the horse and the donkey – she might swap places with them. Her career couldn't be any worse with a piebald horse doing her job.

It all came down to location, location, location. Just when she'd been planning to move, too. Talk about fabulous timing.

'Also—'

Cari tuned in again.

'I didn't know how to tell you.'

'You could have picked up the phone and said it,' she replied.

'How many things have we talked about over the past few years, John? Everything and anything.'

Some things she shuddered to think of. She'd discussed her failed attempt at getting married and they'd managed to laugh about it, in his house, with his wife, Mags, laughing with them as they ate beautiful local West Cork cheeses, and drank fabulous red wine. That had been healing. Sharing her pain with friends. Now, it felt like an open sore again.

They had not been friends. They had been workmates and she had made the fatal, career-shattering mistake of confusing the two.

'I am godmother to your son, John. Did I not cut the mustard there either?'

'I'm sorry. So sorry.'

There was a noise at his end of the phone and Mags, his wife, came on.

'Cari, oh Cari, I am so, so sorry.' It sounded as if Mags was crying but Cari was getting sick of this 'sorry, sorry' chant.

'I wanted to tell you, told Bozo here not to be a coward and to tell you but blasted Freddie insisted he'd handle it, said you'd understand, but I knew you wouldn't and it's for John's career, and we have to think of the kids now that I'm pregnant again...'

'It's OK, Mags,' said Cari gently. She had to cut this off, couldn't take any more of it.

What had she been doing, thinking John and Mags were her friends? She worked with him, for him really. She'd made the mistake of thinking that people she worked with were friends.

In exactly the same way as she'd made the mistake of thinking that a man she loved had actually loved her in return.

For a smart woman, she really was dumb.

Was there a spectrum for that? A clever woman with zero emotional intelligence? Why was nobody doing research on that one? She might ask Jeff's nerdy scientific brother that question.

'Mags, I have to go. I've another call waiting,' Cari lied. She hated using such a cheap ruse but she needed to get off the phone.

She wouldn't phone John's agent, Freddie, either. What was the point?

This all hurt too much.

Monday morning's post was late but when she got it and opened the invitation, Helen Brannigan inhaled deeply and put a shaky hand on the hall table, which rattled the pollen on the stargazer lilies she had in her hall at all times.

She marched into her husband's study with the invitation, with her mouth – already thin with its daily application of Elizabeth Arden Bold Red – in a very thin line.

Kit's study was the perfect microcosm of an old English study complete with panelled wooden walls and old books, and Kit himself looked like a perfect Wodehousian English gentleman except for the fact that he came from a smallholding in County Kerry like his brothers and there had been no study in the farmhouse in Lisowen where they'd grown up.

A huge old black range where their mother cooked giant meals, yes.

A sheepdog under the big kitchen table and a line of ancient workmen's boots at the back door alongside tattered waterproof coats, also yes.

Wooden panelling, no.

Helen, who'd come from two miles down the road from a smaller farm with a father who put all their money into the pub or on the horses, in that order, didn't even have the sheepdog. There was nothing for it to round up. Anything saleable, like a sheep, was always sold come race day so her father had a few pounds for the tote. But both Kit and Helen liked to forget their beginnings and, normally, they managed it.

They'd called their home Green Lawns. Helen spoke as if Jane Austen had put the words in her mouth and had once gone so far as to discuss her dear father as if he'd been a country vicar instead of a man barred from every pub both sides of Killarney. Even when Trina – born when Helen was thirty-one, a very late baby indeed for the era, so late she'd been indulged too much – went off the rails and had to be rescued from some scrape, Helen carried on as if such larks were part and parcel of the gentry born.

'Trina's having so much fun!' Helen would say happily to the relatives, as if fun was the aim of life and Trina might be heading off on a Grand Tour of Europe soon with a coming-out ball at the Crillion along with a line of exquisite Russian billionaire daughters and impoverished royalty instead of having just survived not getting arrested after a water charges protest.

Helen had determinedly forgotten that not too many generations ago, their ancestors had written X on the census as a sign that they were alive: present but illiterate. Helen had no interest in celebrating the past – she wanted to wipe it clean away and rebrand the family as if they'd all come from a different mould.

You could change your life, Helen had long ago decided: all it took was determination to forget the past utterly, to reinvent.

'Yes, love,' said Kit, looking up from his paper as he heard his wife approach. From the expression on Helen's face, he could see trouble arriving and wondered if he could ward it off. All Kit wanted was an easy life – was that too much to ask?

'Did you know about this?' she demanded.

'*This*' was a piece of cream paper and Helen brandished it with the same revulsion as if it were a stapled centrefold from *Playboy*, a pneumatic girl who had hair extensions down to her bum and liked long hot bubble baths and water skiing.

'Bess,' – the name was spat out – 'is giving Edward a seventieth birthday party in Lisowen Castle in March. We are all invited, the whole clan, and on the Saturday night, it's to be a spectacular gala evening, with guests. Black tie.'

Kit knew what this meant: a new dress. An expensive new dress, something to 'take Bess's eye out…'

When his older brother had married Bess, Helen's clothes bill from a posh boutique on the other side of the city had made someone from the bank ring to check the credit card hadn't been stolen.

'No,' Kit had said, only the faintest wobble to his voice. 'More's the pity.'

'Pet,' he said now, wheedling, 'we can't go over the top with clothes this time. The bank were onto me the other day about the overdraft—'

He got a glare in return.

Helen was a handsome woman of fifty-nine with fewer lines than other women her age, which was down to her facials, she told Kit. She had pencilled-in eyebrows above dark eyes that didn't gleam with warmth and, today, glittered like agate.

'If you think I'm turning up at a five-star hotel with anything less than a new, five-star wardrobe, then you're mistaken, Christopher,' hissed his wife, who only called him Christopher when she was vexed. Her accent had gone back to its Kerry roots too, which only happened when she was very angry or had too many glasses of wine, an event which almost never happened. As the daughter of a man who lost control every time he so much as set eyes on a bottle of hard liquor, Helen kept herself in firm check.

'Just because Nora will roll up in some old black dress she's had since Cari was in primary school doesn't mean I'm going to! And Bess will be in something very exclusive, I'm sure! That wedding outfit she had came from the US, I know that for a fact!'

Helen deposited the cream invitation on her husband's lap and swept out of the room, expensive scent and bad humour trailing after her.

Kit Brannigan picked up the invitation and looked at it in wonder. Seventy. His older brother would soon be seventy; he was just two years behind. Mick, the youngest brother, was sixty-six. And Fáinne, little Fáinne would be over sixty – but she had vanished off the face of the earth, a fact to which Kit had long since reconciled himself. Life was strange. You never knew where the twists and turns would take you next: he knew that better than anyone.

But as he looked at the invitation he wondered, where had the years gone?

One day, they'd been young lads on the farm talking about life, girls and cars, and the next, they were old men with wives, children, and a grandchild in Edward's case. There was no sign of Trina producing anything other than crises, but then she'd been a late baby, when he and Helen had given up hope in that regard.

Kit suspected his dear Trina viewed becoming a mother with the same horror as her own mother viewed turning up at a party in a previously seen dress. He laid the invitation down and went back to the paper.

Eight

'Fashion is the armour to survive
the reality of everyday life.'
Photographer Bill Cunningham

It was ten to eight and the lights were only just going on all over the store as Faenia walked through the four fashion and shoe floors of Schiffer's to get a feel for anything new that had come in and to see if there was anything different to add to the rails for her clients that she'd already set up in her office. She'd been doing it since she'd first started in retail thirty years ago.

'Know ze clothes,' said Beáta, the Hungarian chief personal shopper at Bloomberg's, the Manhattan store where Faenia had made her start. 'If you know what is on ze rails, zen you can master zis business. You have ze style – ze rest iz easy, apart from ze people, no?'

As Faenia walked quickly in her Lanvin flats past a rail of boxy, short-bodied jackets that would tax all but a supermodel, she came upon a rail newly stocked with a cotton pique shirt that would suit her afternoon client, a tall woman who liked business-wear for work and a slightly more laid-back version of it for home.

Slipping a couple of shirts over one arm, Faenia lingered by the sweaters for a moment, then headed up to the high-end of the store where she was hoping the new pants by Mizrahi had come in.

Her morning client was a new one and that always meant a tough day because new clients came in with more than just shopping in their heads: they wanted a whole new look, a whole new *them*. With a new person, even when Faenia had their sizing details in her book, she didn't know what sort of six or eight or twelve they were: curvy, straight, long-bodied, short-bodied, with hips, without, with big breasts or nothing that a Calvin Klein bralette couldn't cope with, if they liked heels or walked fast, if they wanted a look for a life they didn't have, if they thought their body was hideous and desperately wanted to tent it.

A good personal shopper was half fashion stylist, half psychologist and sometimes Faenia felt too old for this job. Like today, when yesterday had gone by without a word from Nic and she felt the sadness ripple through her. She would not let it destroy her, though.

Instead, she had bought expensive out-of-season gardenias at the flower shop at the bottom of her street and let the intense, heady scent of the beautiful white flowers waft through the house, and had played Etta James's honeyed voice loudly so that as she walked around, she could smell gardenia and hear Etta's delicious growl telling her she'd get over it. Because you did, Faenia knew that. She'd also taken off the Claddagh ring and had put it in her jewellery box, the old tiny walnut one she'd brought from home which held the few treasures she'd owned then: a gilded bird brooch with flaking blue wings; a tiny cat on a slender chain reaching for a pearlescent ball and a little St Christopher's medal that she used to wear all the time.

The Claddagh ring was in the past too, apparently. She would not revisit it.

But Ireland . . . perhaps she might revisit that.

Her new client was in at half nine, delivered to the door by a limo and greeted by Faenia.

The woman was tiny, perhaps forty, wearing head-to-toe Chanel like armour, as if she needed protection. Her hair was shoulder length, blonde and no doubt blown out by a stylist at eight in her home, the same stylist who'd probably fixed her make-up which was a little old for her.

Faenia wanted to hug her, feed her hot chocolate and get her out of the Chanel and into something that would make her no longer look like a wealthy San Francisco matron twenty years older than she really was.

'Blair Winston,' said the blonde, putting forward a small hand with an enormous princess-cut diamond on it.

'Faenia Lennox,' said Faenia, smiling at the doorman, Theo, as he held open the vast metallic door and taking little Blair into her kingdom.

After half an hour of walking the store, Faenia had loosened her new client up, found that she had married into money, did a lot for charity, had two little girls at school, and was scared of elegant clothes so worked on the same principle as with a bottle of wine: if it was expensive and people recognised the name, it must be good. This was not a good principle on which to base dressing.

In Faenia's suite of dressing rooms where her office was located, she'd made green tea for them both and extracted the Chanel jacket from Blair. It was a thing of great beauty, exquisitely made, but the wrong shape for Blair, the wrong colour for her, the wrong everything.

'I choose wine depending on how pretty the picture on the label is,' confided Faenia, which always made people laugh. 'Really. Doesn't always work but I think it's probably as good a way of working out as the price rating.'

'My husband has a wine collection,' said Blair.

I bet he does, thought Faenia, then chided herself. Marvin had loved wine, while Chuck had been a beer man. She wondered how he was. She must phone him and Denise, catch up, see how their grandkids were doing.

She turned to her new client.

'With clothes, it isn't about what they cost or what the label is. For sure, a pair of pants beautifully designed and perfectly crafted by a brilliant pattern cutter will fit better than a mass market cheap pair for fifteen dollars, but spending money doesn't always guarantee anything. We could dress you with cashmeres and simple knits that cost a fortune, and find that simple Gap jeans are the best for your shape. Better than anything more expensive because you are slim and don't need any new technology to hold in your thighs. The Gap ones will always look best on you and you'll feel your best in them. That's what we're going to find out. What works for you. What your ideal wardrobe should look like. It's not about racking up zeroes on your credit card. It's about finding out what you like and what looks good on you.'

Blair sat forward in her chair, diamonds winking in the overhead light.

'Thank you,' she said earnestly. 'I thought this was going to be scary but my mother-in-law told me you're the best and I should have the best, and—'

'It's not about the best,' interrupted Faenia gently, thinking that she could be this girl's mother. 'It's about finding out what suits you and makes you happy. People who say clothes don't matter don't understand how dressing feels to women, how it lifts us and gives us strength. How we can't break down because when we got up this morning, we put on our favourite shoes and lipstick, chose a bag we earned with our own money, how we survived long enough to do that and will survive to do it again. Strong women wear what they love, not what they think other people will love.'

Blair's little face lit up.

'That's so clever,' she said.

'A clever woman taught it all to me when I was much younger than you,' said Faenia. She didn't add, 'When I had no hope whatsoever and wondered what I was going to do with the rest of my life.'

When she'd met Beáta, Faenia had been been married to Chuck and living in a four-up, one and a half-bedroom apartment with the bath in the kitchen, a huge and hopeless air conditioning machine vibrating through the walls all summer, and a tiny bit of fire escape upon which Faenia often sat and cried because it had all gone so wrong. The irony of her life hurt so much.

She loved Chuck, he loved her and yet—

She couldn't give him what he wanted and all that pain was crippling their marriage, creating a barrier neither of them could cross.

1969 The Bronx, New York

Isobel's aunt opened the door to Fáinne and with one look at the drenched Irish teenager in front of her, and another quick look at the porches of the other houses around, pulled her in quickly.

'Better if people don't know our business,' said Mary-Kate, who was twenty years older than Fáinne's best friend, Isobel, back in Lisowen and had apparently provided solace for more than a few Irish girls in trouble over the years.

'Thank you, thank you,' said Fáinne, standing shaking, both from the cold and from nerves.

'Here, I'll take you into the back room and you can strip off those wet clothes. I'll boil the kettle if you're up to a drop of tea.'

'Thank you,' said Fáinne, which was all she seemed able to say.

She was here, in New York, safe from what the scandal would do to her family.

The journey had been something of a nightmare. First, the bus journey to Shannon, which had meant three separate buses, first the local one where the driver, a man named Micilín, considered it an insult if you didn't converse with him during the entire ride.

Fáinne's morning sickness, which she and Isobel had diagnosed with horror from the lack of her period, was not confined to morning and as Micilín chattered on, expecting answers and an equal amount of gossip, Fáinne had just about managed not to be sick or even look ill as she sat on the seat closest to the driver and pretended to have a cough to explain her sweating, white face.

'A dose of cold, is it?' said Micilín eventually.

Fáinne nodded.

'Bad when you're off to the town.' Micilín looked cryptically at her small suitcase.

'I'm going to see Edward in London,' Fáinne lied, her heart breaking at the thought. Her big brother would have helped her, she was sure of it, but how? How could he get her out of this? There were ways to stop women being pregnant but she wouldn't involve darling Edward in this, couldn't bear the thought of the disgust in his face.

No, Isobel had told her she needed to go far away and then, and only then, she could deal with this.

American people were often coming to take Irish orphans away but the mothers were sent to places where no woman should ever be.

'Magdalene laundries,' whispered Isobel. 'The nuns run them and the Church look over them. You're there for ever, beaten and forced to work. Nobody ever gets out of them, Fáinne, all because you got pregnant.'

'What about the man who got you pregnant?' whispered Fáinne. 'I wasn't alone.'

She thought of how much she'd loved Peadar and how she'd thought – how could she *ever* have thought it – that if only she'd make love with him the way he'd wanted to for so many months, then he wouldn't leave Lisowen to marry the rich, older woman further up the county, a woman with a farm. Peadar, last of four, would have no farm, no prospects, except building site work in Britain. Work on the lump, he called it, where men worked themselves to the bone and sent home a few pounds every week. It was not a life with prospects.

'I have to go, Fáinne,' Peader had said afterwards, when they

134

lay on the hay bales, sated and skin damp with lovemaking. 'I wish it was different...'

'But it is, now!' she'd said happily. 'We've made love, we have to get married now.'

'A ghrá.' He used the old Irish word for love. 'It doesn't work like that,' Peadar said with great sadness, stroking her lovely eighteen-year-old face and touching the freckles that no amount of buttermilk would ever remove.

Peadar had packed his bags and gone and even though all the Brannigans had been invited to the wedding, none had gone.

'He wasn't good enough for you,' said Mick loyally.

Mam was sick then, thin as a rail and trying to keep it all together. Bad enough that her daughter had nailed her colours to the mast for a man who'd gone off to marry another woman, it would be worse in this small conservative place to have that same daughter pregnant and alone.

Being pregnant and unmarried in small town Ireland in 1969 was a crime like no other, a crime that spoke of a girl with no morals, a *family* with no morals.

If she stayed, and Fáinne knew her mother loved her enough to ignore the people with the rosaries and the harsh words, they would all be tainted.

No, leaving was the only way. She would not go into one of these hated homes. She would not destroy her beloved family.

Isobel had an aunt in New York: 'She's gone a long time. Has never forgotten us, still sends home the American boxes, though,' Isobel said fondly, thinking of the cherished parcels that relatives in the US sent home with old clothes and shoes that were probably worn out to the US owners but were more beautiful and bright than anything new in the small Irish towns to which they were delivered.

'Mam won't tell me anything about Mary-Kate, which means there's a lot to tell. I know, though I'm not supposed to, that she went pregnant. Went on the boat to save the scandal. Went with a man but he left her and there's no talk since of any baby.'

Both girls had been quiet, thinking about how much worse it must have been in the fifties to have taken a boat to America to hide the scandal.

'Why is having a baby and not being married so bad?' said Fáinne. 'The priest visits that man whom we all know beat his wife to death and prays with him, like he's a good man. But have a baby without a husband and you are lower than low, far lower than a man who beats his wife to death. Why?'

Isobel put her arms around her friend. 'They have a weird way of working out what's bad in the world. If you're a man, you can do what you want.'

Fáinne nodded.

'Peadar shouldn't have left,' said Isobel in a rush.

Fáinne shook her head. 'I should have known better.'

'You could tell him you're pregnant.'

'No, he's married now.'

Fáinne wasn't stupid. She had been but not any more. Peadar had made his choice. 'That dream is over. I'll go. But I'll miss you.'

They hugged, two teenagers who'd spent so much of their lives together, and now reality had come crashing into it.

'But you'll come back?'

'Of course.'

Nine

'There are years that ask questions,
and years that answer.'
Zora Neale Hurston

He spent too much time at his desk, Edward Brannigan thought ruefully, as he sat scrolling through the profits on-screen for the past month, and felt the dual surge of pleasure and power when he thought of all he'd achieved in his life. Few people knew what a battle it had all been: Eddie looked so urbane and self-assured. People were sure he'd been born with a silver spoon in his mouth and the best of education – in fact, Eddie had left school at fifteen to work on the meagre Kerry farm, a smallholding without much hope of supporting himself and three brothers. He'd emigrated at twenty to London and in his six years there he'd gone to night classes and had finished his education. When he'd returned to Ireland, and married the beautiful Charlotte Harrington, who'd been just a schoolgirl when he'd left, he'd seen the gap in the market for an engineering firm dealing with fine machinery parts. Nobody would give him a loan for the business.

'You must be stone mad looking for a loan,' Kit had said. 'Who'd give out money to the likes of us?'

'I'd help if I could,' Mick had said sorrowfully, 'but we haven't a shilling to spare, Ed, or you'd have it, you know that.'

Edward knew he needed more capital, so he'd worked night and day, doing two jobs, to come up with it. He'd gone back to London to work on the building sites, doing the dangerous jobs for cash, risking it all for his dream. He'd worked in pubs, in a nice one in Chalford St Giles, where he'd found a better class of drunk along with nice people who tipped well. He'd worked in the electrical factory at nights for six months, nothing but nights so that when it was all over, he was white as the driven snow from never having seen the sun for that six months. But he had the money he needed. And finally, Brannigan Engineering had been born.

Sometimes Eddie thought that young people didn't understand work the way his generation did: they'd come from nothing, had little education and had had to fight for every chance and every penny. Bess understood this about him in a way few other people did now.

'Mrs Brannigan on line one for you, Eddie.'

Patricia Glasson didn't call him Mr Brannigan. Eddie had no time for that sort of rubbish. She'd been with him for over thirty-five years, answering phones, typing, doing all jobs in the early days. A widow with young children when she'd started, Patricia was no stranger to hard work herself.

She could recall when he'd arrive into the office with his lunch in his briefcase, a wax-paper-wrapped ham and cheese sandwich made by Lottie because he had neither the time nor the money to go to the pub for lunch.

Patricia had heard him flatter a client on the phone, put it down, the earnest smile still on his face after saying, 'Ah, next time, think of us, will you?' and then curse because Brannigan Engineering had lost the business to a bigger competitor.

She'd heard him dissolve into tears, had been calmly there with the tissues, when Lottie had phoned, shocked, from the hospital to say the mammogram wasn't turning out to be straightforward, a needle biopsy was needed and would he come in?

'Hello, Bess, my darling, how are you?' said Eddie now to his new bride.

The second Mrs Brannigan wasn't one of those women who liked endearments, Patricia had thought at first. She was nobody's 'pet', nobody's 'honey'. Woe betide the person in the business who tried the over-friendly approach with her. But incredibly, she let Edward say these things to her. Patricia didn't need to listen in on the phone – she wouldn't, anyway. She could hear it all from outside the office, the walls of which were not as soundproof as Edward seemed to think but she had no interest in Eddie's love life as long as he was happy, because he was a good boss, had been good to her.

Patricia went back to her computer and left the Brannigans to their lovey-dovey-ness. Her own husband had been dead so long, she only thought of him at the family get-togethers when the children talked about him. The notion of marrying again had simply never occurred to her but then, she knew, men and women were different.

Women could survive on their own and men needed a woman in their life.

'I'm fine,' Bess said to her husband. Formalities over, she got straight to the point because if she stopped, she might cry: 'Edward, the replies are racing in for your birthday but—'

Edward tensed in his seat. He had a feeling about the 'but'. Knew what it would be.

'Jojo hasn't replied.'

Jojo was both the image of his darling, dead Lottie and a woman who would be forever his little girl – though he would never say such a thing to Bess, not if he didn't want his heart mounted on the brocade gallery wall in the hall beside the art Bess loved and which he, he had to be honest, hated. He liked modern stuff and Bess had gone for some mad thing with animals and jungle. But live and let live was his motto.

'Edward, did you hear me?'

Bess waited for no man. But now that he loved her and had married her Edward knew that the Bess she showed to the outside world was very different from the loving woman she was on the inside. He'd broken down Bess's carapace and he was so proud of that, like someone who'd tamed a wild cat at the zoo.

'Give her time,' was what Edward wanted to say. Lottie had been dead for three years now. It had been so fast: four months in total from the hideous diagnosis that undetected breast cancer, missed in a first, scheduled mammogram, had already metastasised to her liver, kidneys and bones.

Instead, he said none of this. All his marriage he'd held firm to the maxim of: do you want to be right or do you want to be happy? Happy was infinitely easier.

'I'll phone her later,' he said, adding a hint of cheerfulness to his voice, a sense of 'I'll sort this out, don't you worry,' when in fact, he knew nothing of the sort.

'Good. Now, catering. I know you aren't interested, Edward,' Bess went on, managing to hide the anxiety in her voice with the minutiae of catering 'but I think the squid in risotto with scallops is perfect for one of the starters.'

'I love that stuff and yes, I am interested,' he protested. 'I'd eat that every day of the week.'

'You'd have black teeth,' laughed Bess and Eddie laughed too.

'Listen to us – talking about squid ink risotto,' he said fondly.

'My mother would have been the first to say, "It's far from squid ink you were reared, Bess!"' Bess said.

They laughed again.

The tricky bit was over.

Bess and his daughter, Jojo, were like oil and water and so far Edward's attempts to mix them had failed. So too had Bess's and that was worse.

Because Bess did not like to fail. She wanted Jojo to know that she loved Edward, adored him.

Eddie was a complex, clever man when it came to business. But he was clever enough to know that he was not a genius when it came to emotional intelligence or dealing with human frailties.

Lottie had looked after all that with their two children. She'd been there for parent-teacher meetings for Jojo and Paul. Wise, funny and motherly to the nth degree, she'd known how to negotiate the teenage years, how to back off when the hormones raged, how to hug when hugs were required, how to be stern when they were in danger of going off the rails.

Eddie had sometimes envied his youngest brother, Mick, who had an amazing relationship with his two kids, *well*, grown-ups. Cari and Maggie were adults now, but still, they were always your kids, no matter how old they were.

Cari and Maggie thought the sun shone out of Mick's rear end. But then, Mick hadn't seen his wife die, hadn't found someone else to love.

That made things different.

Eddie tried to console himself with a glance round his modern office with its wall full of awards, the honorary doctorate he was inordinately proud of because of his charity work and photos of himself with the rich and famous of Irish society at various events. Today, none of the bounties of his work helped.

He stared at the phone glumly. He'd rather phone anyone right now than Jojo.

At lunchtime.

Lunchtime he'd phone. Beg Jojo to come. When all else failed, a bit of begging might work.

Bess looked at her lists with an unseeing eye. Despite her best efforts, anger surged up in her. She knew she should love her husband's children. It made sense – you loved a man and you loved that he loved his children and then you loved them … but that simple theoretical maths did not work out so simply in real, non-theoretical life. Paul was easy to love: funny, happy, good-natured like his father but Jojo …

Jojo had grown up with two parents she loved, not like Bess's poor Amy, who'd had to make do with just Bess and the odd contact with her father. Jojo had gone to the best schools, had a mother at home every evening to tend to all of her needs, not like Amy who'd gone home to her grandmother or alone when she was legally old enough and refused, in a rare act of defiance, to let Maura take care of her.

Yes, Jojo had suffered hugely by having her beloved mother taken from her – sometimes, in Bess's darkest moments, she felt the curdle of jealousy towards Lottie and then felt the equal curdle of self-disgust of even thinking of such a thing because Lottie had died.

Everyone had loved Lottie Brannigan. Everyone.

Bess was not trying to be her, was not trying to be a mother. She was trying to be Edward Brannigan's wife and he deserved that, *she* deserved that.

Except Jojo didn't think so.

The ungratefulness of Jojo Brannigan made the red mist of anger cloud everything in Bess's head.

This party would be glorious: a celebration of the man she loved, a man who'd come from nothing to run this highly successful company and who had, when heart attacks and all sorts of illnesses had decimated so many others, made it to seventy.

He deserved the celebration, he would have it.

Bess had shunned the services of a planning company: she'd run her own very profitable business for long enough and one weekend – albeit one with a large guest list – would hardly tax her.

She had tasted squid ink risotto, asparagus wrapped in parma ham, gravadlax with rocket salad, lamb, *boeuf en croute*, sole off the bone. She had reserved rooms, discussed flowers, queried the possibility of having dahlias – and oh, how she hated dahlias – on the main table because Edward's mother had grown them and this was about him, and he still smiled whenever he saw a dahlia.

And that little cow was going to ruin it all.

Anger was inappropriate in most of life: Bess had learned this the hard way. Anger was something one felt in private, when it could be stared down, made small and manageable. Clever women did not give in to anger in public or especially in the business arena where it would look as if they were 'hysterical'.

Clever women did not rage against husbands because they were hopeless at buying Christmas gifts – they knew to buy it themselves, get the shop to wrap it and hand it to the husband in question, smiling.

That would have been Bess's motto if her first husband had stayed around long enough or had had the money to buy anything and she had no time for women who thought otherwise.

A woman who wanted the perfect gift should buy it herself and not waste time wondering angrily why another human being didn't understand her great need for it.

And yet the anger in this case overwhelmed all of her legendarily fierce self-control.

Bess swept the papers off her desk in a motion so uncharacteristic it would have startled her daughter.

Bess had done her very best and yet her stepdaughter, an idiotic blonde woman, apparently thought her father should sit shiva for ever over his dead wife.

If Jojo truly loved Edward, why didn't she understand that he needed a woman in his life. Not just any woman: Bess.

What Bess wanted most of all was for Jojo to see that Edward loved Bess, that she was not second best, that she could exist alongside the memory of Lottie.

Elaine and Jojo were celebrating: a low-key little celebration involving cupcakes from the café, Earl Grey for Jojo and a skinny flatté for Elaine.

A customer who'd lost three stone, dejunked her closet, and resold some of her old gems, had come in to restock.

'I never thought I'd fit into anything like this,' Carol said, twirling happily in a short fitted cream dress that both Jojo and Elaine had done their best to prevent her taking into the dressing room.

It was a dress that required either a Pilates-hard body inside it or else two pairs of Spanx and no food for a week.

There were women in Silver Bay who could get away with it – but not Carol.

The shop owners had shared a complicit gaze. They could not let lovely Carol leave the premises in a dress she would either never wear again or else would wear once and then never wear again on the grounds that it showed off every single line of the body, including the elastic waistline of her tights. Clothes that made you feel bad had a strange, magical power: both Elaine and Jojo agreed. One look at yourself in a strangely ugly outfit could cast a spell and ruin your week, your day, the rest of your life.

As Elaine put it: 'You could cure the worst illnesses on the planet and you'd spend time saying, "But I looked horrible in that dress on the news..." Yes, even the scientific, serious women feel it – we all feel it!'

Elaine gave Jojo the raised eyebrow look that implied: will you? Or will I?

Jojo took over.

'It looks amazing, Carol,' Jojo said, 'so let's put it on the "possible" rail. Cream does suit you and this' – she produced a far more elegant dress – 'could also work.'

An hour later, Carol left – without the unflattering dress – and with some beautiful items that would form what Elaine lovingly referred to as a capsule wardrobe.

'Everything has to work with everything else,' she said to all comers, which was why they had so many loyal customers.

Of course, nobody but fashion stylists could ever successfully work a capsule wardrobe, so they had to keep coming back wondering why this random top they'd bought on their holidays had looked lovely in Portugal or glorious in the half-price sales in town but hideous back home.

Jojo was licking cupcake crumbs off her fingers, thinking that she was definitely going to put on weight with this latest treatment cycle, when her mobile rang.

Her father.

Wiping her sticky fingers on a napkin, she took the call and went into the back room.

'Hi, Dad.'

She knew what this was about.

'Hello, Joanne, lovie,' said her father. 'Am I interrupting?' He was the only one who ever occasionally called her Joanne, which was lovely and different, except it was what the hated Bess now called her too.

'A celebration, we're finished, though.'

'Celebrating what?'

'Oh, just a customer bought quite a few things and it's been a good month for us—' Jojo stopped. Her father's version of a good month financially and hers were quite different. Since he'd married Bess, he'd been making noises about investing in the shop. 'Helping you and Elaine to have an empire,' he'd said gruffly.

Trying to bribe his new wife's way into their lives, more like.

Dad had wanted to be involved in the shop six years ago but her mother had always been very firm about how the Brannigan kids would not be ruined by not understanding how to work for a living.

'We're not raising trust fund brats, Eddie,' she'd always said. 'Paul and Jojo are clever enough to earn their own livings.'

They'd always both had summer jobs: Jojo in clothes retail so she could learn the trade and Paul in a bar during college so he could buy the motorbike that made their mother pale when she saw it for the first time.

At least that nauseous stepmother could never accuse Jojo of hanging onto her father's coat-tails for money.

'Hugh well?' said Dad.

'Fine,' said Jojo. *Not that we're talking because he hates me doing another cycle of infertility treatment.*

'And you, lovie?'

'Happy as a clam,' she said. *A clam that feels as if it's sinking too deeply into the ocean where the clam-eating monsters live.*

'OK.'

It was awkward silence time.

There had never been awkward silences in the Brannigan household before but now life was full of them.

Like the classic moment when Edward had told his daughter: 'I am going to marry Bess, Jojo, and I want you to be happy for me.' *Cue biggest awkward silence on the planet.*

'The thing is,' Edward went on stiffly, 'this party for me, I want you and Hugh to come and Bess says you haven't replied.'

Cari had edited a business book once that said you should wait a beat before replying to tricky things.

'Don't feel the need to fill the silence,' Cari had explained the details.

Jojo was sure that her cousin was an expert in not filling in silences but Jojo wasn't built that way.

Lottie had raced into all silences, smiling, chatting, putting her arm round people and drawing them into conversation if they were shy. Jojo had inherited it all: the talking to strangers on trains and handing out coins or take-away cups of tea to homeless people.

'Dad, I don't know why she's having it in Lisowen, that's all. You and Mum had your anniversary there – it's . . .'

Jojo blindly searched for a word that didn't have an expletive attached. 'It's hard to imagine us all there without Mum and you with someone else. OK?'

'Pease, Jojo, for me? Please make an effort, come up to the house and talk to Bess. She's doing it for me, you know.'

And because Jojo was emotional and because her father's voice made her think of other times, she found herself agreeing to drop in to her old home that night. Tanglewood. Her old home, where she'd shared the loveliest and happiest of childhoods with Paul and Dad, all thanks to her darling mum, who made it a haven for them all.

On the way home from work, Edward phoned Bess.

'Jojo's dropping in this evening,' he said, trying to sound cheerful and not quite managing it.

'Right,' Bess said, unnerved. She'd just parked outside the house and looked at it as her stepdaughter would see it: changed utterly.

Jojo had not visited once since the renovations. She had accompanied Hugh, Paul, Lena and Heidi to a couple of meals with her father and Bess when Paul had been home from New York, and that was it, apart from the wedding.

In some ways, Bess would be perfectly happy if Jojo had no part in her or Edward's life but she was his daughter and he loved her.

She wanted to say, 'Jojo should grow up! Nothing in life is easy!' She wanted to say so many things but none of them would be helpful. If she'd had a retinue of female friends to call, then life might have been easier, but she didn't. The mothers she met when Amy was at school had not been her friends, scared as they were of her stealing their damn husbands, which was laughable. Bess had been trying to cope with single parent-hood, not fend off bored married men.

At work, she'd had to be utterly professional, and besides, she'd nearly always been in a far higher position than most of the other female staff in all the companies for which she'd worked: a woman apart because, at that time, there were far fewer female CPAs, and she'd known she'd lower her power base if she went to lunch with the assistants and receptionists, even though she'd yearned for female company. No wonder women in business were seen as such tough cookies: they'd had to be to survive.

So Bess had cut herself off and now here she was: couldn't get her daughter to come up and have dinner with her, and with no women friends to talk to.

She went into the house and found her husband's old address

book, found Nora Brannigan's number and dialled it before she chickened out.

Nora's soft warm voice came on the line.

'Nora, it's Bess here, Bess Brannigan.'

Cool, calm and collected Nora took a breath.

'Bess,' she said finally, 'lovely to talk to you. We got the invitations,' she went on, as if it was obvious that this was what Bess was phoning about.

'You're coming?'

'Wouldn't miss it for the world. It's not going to be too dressy, is it?' Nora asked. 'I'm not much of a woman for dressing up.'

'Wear what you want,' said Bess, smiling. She really liked this woman. Nora had the courage of her convictions in the most fabulous way. You couldn't help but admire her. 'Nora, perhaps we could have coffee or lunch during the week?' she went on. 'I ... I wanted to talk to you about something.'

With the calm of an agent handler in Moscow discussing a wild change of plans with a double agent, Nora took it all in her stride.

'Of course, Bess. What day suits?'

'How about now?' Bess wanted to say, but controlled herself. 'Friday?'

'Friday it is.'

'I could come to Silver Bay – there's that nice café near you, isn't there, the one with the coffee buns?' Bess said because she'd met Amy there once. Odd that Amy lived so near to Nora, in that quirky square with the beautiful old trees and the pretty houses.

'The Death By Coffee ones with the hard coffee icing and a health warning with them? They're fabulous but they go straight onto my hips,' sighed Nora. 'See you there at one.'

Jojo parked the car in the driveway of Tanglewood, noticing with pain that her mother's crappy old Mini had gone. Mum had loved that car. Its suspension had been a thing of distant memory and too many encounters with shopping centre car park pillars meant it had been dented so many times it almost resembled a piece of modern art. Squash it a smidge more and it could have stood as an outdoor installation for a Manhattan gallery with a card under it: '*Battered, bashed, still working: a symbol of modern life.*'

'Why doesn't your mum have a swanky car?' her younger cousin, Trina had asked once idly. Jojo knew that if Trina had access to any sum of money at all, she'd spend it at once on designer clothes, partying and on renting a fabulous apartment. She would spend like a lottery winner until it all ran out and be ripe for one of those TV shows on ex-lottery-millionaires who had spent wildly and wanted to speak out about how it had all gone wrong and they were looking for a cleaning job and had had to give up the fags.

But wanting a swanky car was merely Trina repeating what she'd learned as a kid. It was like listening to Aunt Helen speaking. Helen would have had a brand new Range Rover or a Bentley blocking the drive if she'd been married to the rich one of the three Brannigan brothers. Not one car: no, *two*. Two Bentleys.

'Mum doesn't care about things like cars,' Jojo had explained.

She hadn't entirely understood this herself when she was fourteen and her mother would roll up at school to collect her on wet afternoons.

Then, Jojo had been in the throes of teenage hormones and was embarrassed by the Mini's decrepitude.

'Ugh, I hate this crappy old car,' she'd say sulkily, flinging herself into the front seat and shoving Noodle, a grey half-poodle, half-many other things into the back. Noodle had existed in the years before clever dog breeding had created no shedding Labradoodles.

Thanks to Noodle's wildly mixed-up parentage, she shed hair

like a four-week-old Christmas tree shed pine needles. The car was covered in it, the back of Jojo's navy school uniform was instantly covered in hair as soon as she'd sat down and with Noodle half on her, deliriously trying to wash her face, the front of Jojo's uniform would soon be covered in grey dog hair too.

'You love it, really,' Mum would say, smiling. 'Keeps you in touch with the real world.'

'I got an E in my maths homework today and Miss Harrison read me the riot act. That's enough real world for me,' Jojo muttered. 'Dad will go mental.'

'Never mind your father,' Lottie said cheerfully. 'Not everyone is a maths head. We'll get it into his skull one of these days that you aren't going to college to study engineering. Now, I know you've probably got enough homework to keep you going for ten years but will we stop in Santina's for a quick coffee? We can sit outside under an umbrella, have Noodle with us and share a piece of cake?'

Much later, at college with people from all over the country and all different backgrounds, Jojo finally understood how marvellous it was her mother didn't care about stuff. She'd found that too many people measured themselves and others by what they owned rather than by who they were.

Jojo's mum didn't need to show off her family's wealth to anyone. Family, love and kindness meant all to her. When she said she wanted her children to be happy, it wasn't a platitude: she meant it.

Be the happiest roadsweeper in the world rather than the most miserable brain surgeon was her motto.

The car was gone. So too was the statue of the Venus de Milo that Lottie had bought for half nothing and had set about carefully 'ageing' by painting it with yogurt one summer.

'I read that yogurt helps mould grow on stone so it looks

older,' she'd said, painting earnestly, in her gardening clothes with her blonde hair tied up with what might or might not have been an old duster. She'd proudly placed the statue in a prominent place on the right-hand side of the drive where they could all view its beauty.

Sadly, Venus had merely looked as if she'd been badly white-washed for about three months until one day Dad had run back into the house shouting, 'Girls! Paul! Come quick. Venus has been transformed! The Louvre restorers or else helpful elves have come overnight!'

Laughing, delighted, they'd run outside to the drive to see that the white-washed look had been miraculously replaced with a genuinely old mossy effect on the stone, making the bargain basement statue look like a priceless antique unearthed from a lost Mediterranean garden.

Mum had cried. 'I'm going to yogurt everything!' she said, wiping her eyes.

'Stay out of my room,' Paul had joked.

'Yours is already a shrine to penicillin,' his mother joked back. Paul liked to take mugs of tea upstairs to drink while studying, and didn't bring them back down. Quarter-full mugs, ripe with green and white mould which bloomed out of all his vessels when they were gathered up.

Paul should have been here with her, Jojo thought miserably, getting out of her own car and looking around at the garden of Tanglewood to see what else had changed. Set on a hill overlooking the Irish Sea, the house was one level and had always had a hint of 1970s bungalow about it. All that had changed.

In the months since Jojo had been to her old home, Tangle-wood had been entirely transformed. The 1970s vibe was gone. In its place was a modernist architect's vision of how a single-storey old house might look when the entire front wall had been replaced by a sheet of plate glass revealing the sort of millennial house where something as bourgeois as curtains weren't allowed.

The porch was now a little glacier to the left and without stepping foot inside, Jojo could see everything. A dormer upstairs had been added, with stairs that curved, and the wall where the family's TV used to sit now appeared to be a blank concrete space with a piece of huge modern art, less Kandinsky and more the work of Coco the Clown, Jojo thought viciously, assuming her new stepmother had bought it.

'Jojo! I'm so glad you're here!'

Her father, a great bear of a man, enveloped her in a hug. Jojo hadn't even heard him emerge from the house and he smelled like his old self, even with that familiar cologne he always wore. Something from the Burren Perfumery that her mother had always bought him. Heathery with a hint of lemon, and sea spray and something that was from the barks and lichens of the Burren, apparently. His hair was silver and he wore the same clothes he always wore after work: tonight, a soft grey sweater, a check shirt peeking out from the top and faded charcoal corduroys from about a million years ago.

'Dad.'

She allowed herself to sink against him, wishing – wishing it was years ago, that her mother wasn't gone, that she wasn't trying to do the most difficult thing of her life without her beloved mother by her side.

'Don't you just love the place?' her father moved so that they were both facing the new house and all Jojo's heartfelt longing was skewered. How could a man this intelligent be so dumb?

New house, new wife – did he not think any of this might be hard for his children to take?

'It's certainly different,' she said caustically. 'I hardly recognise it.'

He seemed oblivious to her tone.

'Jojo, you're going to love it. You should have brought Hugh. The architect – well, Bess found him. He's a genius. He said why had we these beautiful views when we couldn't see them with the puny little windows we had before.'

Because Mum used to have picnics on the lawn with our teddy bears – that's how we saw the views, Jojo wanted to cry out, but she knew Bess was inside waiting for her and she'd break down if she thought about her mother too much. She would not cry in front of Bess.

In all of those fairytales about the wicked stepmother, they'd got it bang on, Jojo thought grimly.

Bess stood in the small alcove off the hall, one of the few places in the front room that wasn't visible from outside, and found that she was summoning up courage to go out and greet her stepdaughter.

Bess loved the house, the very unexpectedness of it all in the middle of the pretty country-style garden.

One wall in the huge front room was pure concrete, so modern when paired with that giant modern painting Edward loved.

'Lottie hated this type of thing,' he'd said the day they went to look at the giant canvas.

Bess had put her head to one side, examining. She was not artistic: had not an arty bone in her body, they'd said at school. She could do colour for clothes but she wasn't good at clothes, either. Her only colour leanings were in flowers, and she loved the wild vibrancy of richly pink orchids with extravagant darker spots dappling the petals even though the orchid purists only liked the white ones, it seemed.

'I don't know if I like it but I don't dislike it,' she said to Edward, gazing at the picture. 'I think we should have it.'

'Lottie would have never said that,' Edward whispered quietly to her.

Bess felt her teeth grind and the corresponding pain in her ear reminded her that she hadn't worn her night-time retainer for a long time.

Marrying a widow was like slipping into someone else's clothes, wearing their slippers, sipping from their cups. It was hard to prove to a husband, long accustomed to one way, that a new wife, a new woman, saw things differently.

'I am not Lottie, honey,' she reminded him, determinedly light. 'Let's buy it. While I like—' She looked around for something she fancied, spotted a picture of exotic flowers with a tiger hidden behind them, all in a wildly realistic style. Probably something so deeply unartistic that it was just a hair's breath away from being painted on velvet. Lottie, who appeared to have had enough artistic sense for ten people, would undoubtedly have turned her nose up at it, and Jojo, who had gone to fashion college, would undoubtedly vomit if she ever saw it but Bess would not trouble herself with their views. 'That. I would like *that*.'

Once she'd started on this ironic, insane painting purchasing fit, Bess could barely stop. Some inner demon meant she was still looking for an oil of Elvis in his Hawaii comeback suit, and when she got it she was going to hang it up in the subtle old gold and beige granite of the cloakroom and let everyone think it was trailer park chic or whatever. She didn't care.

This was her home now, hers and Edward's.

Tanglewood was a different house from when Lottie had lived there. It was about time people realised this, Jojo in particular.

Edward had apparently wanted to rip half of it down for years.

'I hate bungalows but the views were so good and the kids were small. Plus we had no money to do it up and when we did have the money, Lottie didn't want to: said she loved it all.'

Bess found the easiest way was to reply as if she and Dennis had had such similar discussions, even though Dennis had been gone from her life for many years. It made her feel equal, as if she had lost a life-long love instead of got rid of the most hopeless husband ever many moons ago.

'Dennis was like that too,' she'd say idly, 'keen on the status quo.'

'Whereas we, my love, like change,' Edward said, hugging her.

Bess leaned in to him. 'Yes,' she said, 'we do.'

Now Tanglewood was a sleek modern home, and Jojo would hate it. Not for any architectural reasons but because it was different. This was her first trip to her old family home since she'd gone there months ago to beg Edward not to marry Bess. Edward had, unwisely, phoned Bess afterwards and spilled out each word.

'She was so angry.' He was almost unable to speak, so upset, so close to the verge of tears. 'The names she called you, honey, I can't bear this. Why can't it be simple – why?' His voice had become croaky and Bess knew he was crying and, just as unwisely, had been unable to stop herself saying, 'What did she say about me?'

'She said you were a slut, after my money and I said, Jojo, it's not like that, Bess has her own business, her own money. But she cried and said how could I, with her mum just a couple of years dead.'

There was a gap while he searched for his pocket hand-kerchief. Bess knew the sound, loved a man who used a genuine handkerchief. 'I loved Lottie, Bess, you know I did, but a man has to live, life has to go on.'

Flattening down her rage against Jojo and determined to comfort Edward, who deserved better, Bess had hopped into her car that night – a little runaround because she could never see the point of spending money on cars – and had driven up to Edward's and spent the night.

Beforehand, Edward had been too anxious in case the kids

– Jojo mainly, as Paul, his son, lived in New York – turned up out of the blue.

But now, Bess thought with grim rage, now that 'the slut' was official, she might as well complete her slutdom and move in.

The renovations had been quick because Edward had moved into Bess's apartment while they were being done. They would move into the renovated house together after the wedding.

Bess had never seen such work completed so quickly – her new fiancé was a hard taskmaster – and the luxury: marble on bathroom floors, granite on the kitchen surfaces, under-floor heating, glass panels that turned opaque at the touch of a switch, wallpapers that cost three figures a roll, handmade couches.

She'd grown up in a three-bedrooms-and-a-boxroom red-brick off the North Circular Road where her mother collected good china, like Belleek, and lovingly admired it in the front room, a room Bess and her father were only allowed into when there were guests.

'She thinks we're like bulls in a china shop – will wreck all her folderols,' Dad would laugh.

'When I grow up, I am going to have no things just for good, just things we can use all the time,' Bess insisted. The family drank juice out of old marmalade jars that could be used as glasses and every tea cup in the kitchen was cracked and needed scrubbing with bread soda paste to get the stain of tannin from the bottom, while glasses of crystal and gleaming plates sat in state in the good room, pristine and unused.

Dad never fought with her mother about things like the 'good room' or even about her ruling the roost with a rod of iron. Bess supposed nobody had ever fought with Maura Sharkey, although as *she* went through her teenage years, she fought back.

Poor Dad had never had a hope. He was funny, gentle, the

opposite of the alpha male. Dead of a heart attack at forty-eight, leaving Maura forever locked in Greek tragedy. With her husband dead, Maura had gone back to work in a lesser job than her pre-marriage one in the civil service, a job she'd had to leave when she was married due to an archaic Irish system known as 'the marriage bar', which meant that as soon as they got married, women had to leave civil service jobs in order to leave them open to men.

Bess had feminism running through her veins at a young age hearing her mother railing against this 'bar'.

'Men have it all and they shouldn't,' Maura would say, leaving nobody in any doubt as to which sex she considered the stronger.

Bess heard her husband and his daughter walking on the gravel, coming towards the house.

Stronger? She wasn't sure she felt strong right now. Irritated, yes. Anxious, for sure. She'd picked that damn hotel for one reason and one reason alone: because Edward loved it.

Lisowen Castle had been the ravaged home of the gentry when he and his brothers, part of the peasant class, had grown up in the town and to be able to return to the now luxury hotel as a famous, wealthy son of the place – it was his dream. It was undoubtedly why Lottie – sometimes Bess felt like wincing at her name because Lottie hung over everything she did like a ghost – had arranged for the twenty-fifth wedding anniversary party to be held there. It was why Bess, who'd have preferred anywhere else, had arranged for the same thing.

But Maura Sharkey hadn't reared a quitter.

Bess stepped out of the front door and smiled, the best smile she could manage under the circumstances.

'Joanne, hello,' she said, thinking that 'Welcome home' might induce total rage.

'Bess.' Jojo spoke in a clipped tone. 'The house is different—'

Bess could see her stepdaughter was about to cry from the faint reddening around her eyes and she wanted to shout, 'Oh grow up!' She knew it was her mother speaking, the tough Maura who saw a tear and said, 'Stop crying or I'll give you something to cry about!' but she couldn't help it. What was it about her stepdaughter that turned her into this harpie?

'But it's lovely,' Edward said, wheedling. 'Wait till you see what we've done with it: and your room is always there for you.'

That had been a battle royal during the renovations – 'She's married, in her thirties and has her own home: what does she want her own room in our house for?' Bess had demanded during the meeting with the architect when Edward had insisted that his kids still have rooms in their old home.

'So she has somewhere if she needs it...'

'Did your mother keep a room in your house for you once you'd left?' asked Bess, knowing this was madness but unable to stop herself.

The architect shuffled his papers about, muttered something about going to get a cup of tea and scarpered. He was undoubtedly used to couples engaged in warfare over house design. There was probably a college module on it. 'Leave; make tea. Don't go back until the shrieking has stopped.'

'We lived in a cottage, Bess,' said Edward tiredly. 'My bedroom was tiny and shared with Mick and Kit. They just had more space in the room when I left.'

'And after?' pressed Bess. 'After you were all gone?'

'No,' admitted Edward. 'My mother kept it as a guest room but there was so little space, she kept her old winter coats in there. Things that had been in the family since the year dot. It always smelled of damp and mothballs afterwards.'

The old stone house in Kerry was just a wreck now: too far gone to be restored. Edward had taken Bess to see it early in their courtship so she could see where he'd come from, how proud he was of his humble roots.

They'd stayed in the majestic and newly restored Lisowen

Castle Hotel then – a glorious five-star establishment much favoured by wealthy tourists, people tracking down Irish roots and movie stars on honeymoon.

'But that's not the point, Bess. It was different then. The kids need that, I want it.'

Bess had felt humbled then: of course he wanted it. How could she deny him that? Why was she being such a bitch?

'Your old room is pretty much the way it always was,' Bess said to Jojo, trying to be conciliatory. 'A lot is different but not that. And Paul's is the same. We kept the garden at the back the same way your mother had it—'

She got no further before Jojo turned on her, eyes blazing.

'But it's all different out the front and where's her statue, the old Venus? And the car? I wanted that car!'

'It was a wreck,' began Bess unwisely.

'It was hers!'

'I'm sorry,' said Bess formally and then instantly regretted having apologised. She was fed up with this. She was married to Edward, for God's sake. Their marriage, their happiness could not depend on this young woman. At Jojo's age, Bess was married, as good as divorced, and had a young daughter to take care of. What did this little madam have? A shop, no doubt paid for by Edward, though he said otherwise, and no sign of chick or child. Worse, she was poking her privileged little nose into Bess's business.

Like the deadly volcano Krakatoa in the sixth century, Bess blew.

'It was a dangerous heap of rust, shouldn't have been on the road, and if you wanted it that badly, you should have come to get it before now. This is my home now. Not yours, despite the bedroom. You're a grown-up with a husband, start behaving like one. If you had children of your own, you'd understand that all you want is for your children to be happy, which is why your poor father keeps pandering to you.'

'Bess, stop,' said Eddie frantically.

'No!' Bess held up the hand that had stopped board meetings in their tracks and could silence her own daughter in an instant.

'He wants you to be happy and because I love him – yes, I *love* him – I want that too. But you cannot think that you have the ultimate power over our lives.'

She stopped suddenly. What had she done?

Jojo was white in the face: not just pale but a deathly colour as if some unseen force had exsanguinated all her blood.

'I understand,' she whispered. 'I understand.'

'Jojo!'

Edward reached for her but Jojo slipped from his grasp, ran out of the iceberg hall and to her car.

They stood and listened to the screeching of tyres as she roared down the drive.

'You shouldn't have said those things,' said Edward in a tone of voice that made Bess feel frightened. What if she had gone too far? She had no filter, her mother always said, which was rich coming from Maura, whose tactlessness was known far and wide.

'I didn't mean to hurt her but we—'

'We don't want anyone with ultimate power over our lives,' Edward dully repeated his wife's words. 'I know, Bess. I agree. I married you when I knew Jojo didn't want me to but there was no need for the things you said. No need at all. She's my daughter and I love her. We knew it would take time. I lost my little sister a long time ago, I can't lose my daughter now.'

Bess bit her lip. Edward had told her of Fáinne, the little sister who'd vanished because she was pregnant.

He'd seen the note in her lovely handwriting, the language eloquent because the nuns had always said Fáinne would go far.

She had gone because she didn't want to be a problem, a scandal. Edward had never forgiven himself for not being there for her because nothing would have stopped him caring for

Fáinne, pregnancy or not. His darling Jojo had eyes just like his sister's; she reminded him so much of Fáinne: a sensitive person who loved too deeply. He was afraid that if he lost Jojo now, he would never have her again. Love was so fragile, like Fáinne had been fragile and Jojo, too. He could see his daughter crumbling in front of his eyes and Bess was making it all worse.

He turned, grabbed his car keys from the console table in the hall.

'Are you going after her?'

'I don't think there's any point. I'm going back to the office.' Edward looked at her straight on. 'People there listen to me. I don't know how you could be so cruel to Jojo, so callous. I didn't know you had that in you. It's like—' He seemed to be casting about wildly for the words. 'It's like there's another person in you, one you've hidden up till now, someone vicious.'

Bess watched him leave, thinking how could a marriage survive when there were so many people in it, all clamouring for love? How could it survive when one party had seen the other give full vent to their rage? She should not be battling Edward's daughter for his love and yet that's just what she had done, time after time. This time, worst of all.

When he'd driven away, she went into the kitchen and poured herself a glass of wine. She'd never been much of a drinker but Edward had such a great cellar and there was always some nice white wine in the fridge. When Amy had been young, there hadn't been money for luxuries like wine. Bess had been too scared of losing control that way, of numbing any pain or loneliness via the bottle. Who would look after Amy then?

It had been tough: she had had to be tough. Amy had suffered, no doubt about it.

In this lovely kitchen with wine inside her and the pain unquenched, Bess could admit it. She had been a tough-love mother to her daughter, in much the same way as her own mother had practised tough love on her.

She'd hated it as a child, having a tough mother, and yet she'd still repeated the pattern with Amy.

There had been no other way, she'd told herself. She was alone, husbandless, living just within her means. It had been frightening and that fear had made her hard.

Alone in her gleaming new kitchen with its hand-painted wooden doors and a black granite worktop, with every mod con available, Bess let the tears fall, finished the first glass of wine and poured another.

And then she thought of her mother's cautionary tales all those years ago, when she'd first thrown Dennis out.

'Don't turn into a drunk,' Maura had advised briskly, as if she was advising on a hat to wear at the races. 'I'm not raising Amy for you. I have my own life. You've made your bed, now lie in it and not with a bottle of gin.'

Bess shoved the glass of wine away from her and it fell on the table, the fine glass shattering and wine slopping everywhere. The old marmalade glasses wouldn't have broken, she thought.

If only her dad was still around: she'd loved him, had felt close to him. Until Edward had come along, there had been nobody on earth Bess had ever felt closer to. Not even Amy, the small voice in her head taunted her. Because she'd been so busy making sure Amy had a roof over her head and had a future, that the love part had been secondary.

She had no close female friends now: was that sad? Nobody to phone and sob her eyes out to. Bess wanted someone kind to talk to, someone, anyone.

Her mother had had no female friends, either. Maura Sharkey had not been the sort of woman for coffee morning conferences or gentle discussions over garden walls. Somehow, by osmosis, Bess had picked up on this and she had been happy with it, content, until now.

But no woman was an island – she could see it truly now.

She needed help and she thought of the one person who could give it to her, the one person who might not turn her away with distaste.

Jojo drove down the drive at speed, barely missing some of the beautifully placed stones along the edge of it.

'Fucking stones,' she swore as she swerved.

There had been no stones in her mother's day: Lottie had had railway sleepers, ancient things that had somehow fitted in with the garden and had been slippery to walk on and sometimes Lottie had said she was going to get them replaced. But she never had, they were part and parcel of the house. Like the Venus statue and the old Mini…

Jojo could feel the tears clouding her eyes and she knew she shouldn't really be driving, but she didn't care. The urge to do something self-destructive was so powerful. How could her father have married that woman? How could her father have thought so little of her mother, that mere years after her mother's death, he'd marry someone else, someone nothing like Lottie Brannigan? That was the nub of the question.

Yes, Jojo knew that men often married sooner after being widowed than women did. Women lived longer and are able to survive on their own, while men needed someone else there. But two and a half years?

That was *nothing*. It was an insult to Jojo's mother's memory. And Paul – what about Paul? She pulled in on the side of the road, not really the safest place to stop on that stretch of road, but she didn't care. Let someone bang into her and let her father grieve over that.

Would he go out and adopt a new daughter after two years? Probably.

Knowing that her feelings were juvenile to say the least, she fought against them, but she couldn't help it. She felt so angry, so hurt, so like … so like a child.

Maybe that was why she couldn't have a child – she still

was one, she thought with bitterness. And for that bitch to say that if she had children of her own, she'd understand? That hurt most of all: a piece of barbed wire twisted in an open wound.

When she'd first stopped, she had picked up her mobile phone to call her brother in New York, but she knew it was stupid. Paul would be at work and he wouldn't be able to talk. Then if she waited until he was at home, he'd be talking to Lena or playing with Heidi. The beautiful baby, so beautiful it almost hurt Jojo to look at her.

Jojo leaned her head against the steering wheel. What sort of a horrible person have I become, she thought. The image of my beautiful baby niece gives me pain, because she is proof that my brother and his wife have a baby and I can't, what sort of horrible cow am I?

She scrubbed her eyes dry and started the car again. She'd drive home to Hugh and maybe he'd be able to fix it, fix her.

Hugh was at home, tidying out the fridge, which was partly for practical reasons and partly because he knew Jojo was up in Edward and Bess's house and he knew she'd come home in a towering rage, so fridge-tidying gave him something to calm his mind.

His mother was a real fan of men being able to do things around the house, and all of his previous girlfriends before Jojo had always been astonished at this, as if he were the veritable monkey typing out the works of Shakespeare on an old typewriter.

'What's so weird about a guy cleaning out a fridge?' Hugh would say.

'We're not used to it,' the various girlfriends had all said.

'Proof of how fabulous the Hennessy men are,' Hugh's mother, Daphne, would say proudly.

Her three sons were self-sufficient, all able to cook meals, wash clothes, iron clothes, put up shelves.

Daphne was a very self-sufficient sort of woman and she wanted to send her kids out into the world with the same abilities. Sometimes, Hugh got the feeling that his mother was going off Jojo.

It was very subtle, but over the past year, he'd sensed it: the feeling that Daphne had run out of patience for Jojo and her wild grief over her mother. If only he had been able to tell her about the infertility, but Jojo had been adamant that it was their battle and their battle alone.

'Nobody else must know,' she said fervently.

And he knew that was because her own mother hadn't known, therefore it felt like a betrayal from Jojo's point of view that anyone else would know. But Lottie Brannigan was dead, she was never going to know that they were trying desperately for a baby, never going to know about the pain and the grief and the trauma, the sense of failure, the pain every time Hugh looked at another colleague with a swelling baby belly or a father on his way to the park with a couple of kids.

Sometimes he wondered if Jojo thought it only affected her, because it didn't, it affected both of them. He knew it would feel like a betrayal of Jojo to do it, but he wanted to tell his mum, wanted to tell his brothers, wanted to have people on his side that he could discuss this with. Because infertility was always seen as the woman's issue. No matter whose 'fault' it was that a baby was not being gifted to a couple, the main person to receive sympathy always seemed to be the woman, as if only women longed for children, as if men had no biological clock, no desire to hold their own baby in their arms.

Hugh carefully put the last cartons of milk back in the fridge, their bottoms carefully wiped. It was sparkling now. Not that Jojo would notice, she wasn't noticing much of anything at the moment. He'd give it another week and then he'd talk to his mum, one of his brothers, someone: he needed to tell someone, just not to feel so alone.

*

Jojo shut the door carefully when she came in. She didn't want to storm into the house. She would try to be grown-up, try to be with her husband and accept his loving and kindness.

Hugh was in the kitchen, wearing an apron.

'Hello,' he said warily, as if he expected a full-on explosion.

Jojo couldn't take her eyes off the apron. Hugh had known she was going to visit Bess and her father and in some childish part of her brain, she wanted him to be waiting for her, medieval torture implement in hand, ready to go up to Tanglewood and slay some dragons (Bess) for her.

Instead, he was wearing a red and white gingham apron, holding a cloth and looked mildly anxious at her return.

'How did you get on?' he asked.

Jojo did not know why, and she cursed herself as soon as she'd said them, but the first words out of her mouth were bitchy: 'All tickety-boo. You're really rocking that Martha Stewart look,' she said.

Hugh flushed and ripped the apron off.

'Someone has to clean the fridge,' he snapped.

'Lucky I've got a house husband to do it,' Jojo snapped back.

Hugh considered this for a moment. 'Lucky you've got a husband at all,' he said quietly and he left the room, brushing past her. 'I'm going for a run. Don't wait up.'

Alone in the kitchen, Jojo began to cry. Why had she picked on poor Hugh? What was wrong with her? She was falling to pieces and taking the people she loved with her.

Ten

Tuesday was Mick's traditional night out with the lads. It was more of a two-pints-in-the pub than an actual night out because all the lads were in their sixties now, and the days of long sessions with someone taking out a bodhrán or a fiddle to play traditional Irish music were no more, but still, it was his night out. Nora went to things on Wednesday night – it used to be her keep-fit classes, then step aerobics, now she and Sherry from across the road did Bums and Tums in the church hall on a Monday at seven, and every few Wednesdays a gang of women would pick a film.

The criteria for the film was trickier.

Sherry only wanted films where nice men got their shirts off.

'We just need a loop of *Magic Mike* for you, Sherry,' everyone teased her.

Millicent had always had a fondness for anything foreign language, especially French, which had been her subject at university and which she'd taught in secondary school for thirty years.

Clare couldn't bear anything with violence in it, and since Agatha had got divorced, she refused to see anything love story-ish.

'That leaves us with French non-violent thrillers with attractive men who undress occasionally, and with a jaundiced view of love where nobody ends up happily ever after,' Nora said, in summation. 'Is that a genre?'

'Astonishingly, not yet,' Millicent joked.

Compromise had been reached and tomorrow night, they were going to see a Greek comedy about a big family wedding.

'Bound to have all that palaver about how true love changes everything in it,' Agatha said miserably.

'You can put your hands over your eyes for any kissing, swearing of eternal love or marriage vows where they intend to keep them,' Nora said. 'Just don't boo at the romantic bits.'

'There's definitely romantic bits in it, then?' Agatha asked.

'Listen,' said Nora, 'it's a wedding comedy: there will be a mix-up at the hen night, some divorced parents will meet up and decide they don't want to be divorced any more but love each other and need to dump their new spouses, and at least one hopelessly uncoordinated cousin will discover she can dance if it's with the right person when she meets up with her childhood friend who has always been in love with her, right? So yes, there will be some romance. But it will be funny. Humour will take away the pain of the lovey-dovey bits.'

'As long as I'm prepared,' Agatha said.

'As long as there's tanned male skin, preferably muscular,' added Sherry.

Clare laughed and Millicent patted Sherry's knee. 'Girls,' she said, 'it's set in Greece. In summer. Someone with the body of a Greek god is bound to have his shirt off.'

Nora was taking advantage of Mick's absence to catch up on the ironing and watch her soaps, smiling while thinking about herself and the girls' nights out. None of them were girls any more, of course, all of them were at least in their sixties, except for Sherry, who was fifty-nine and dreading being sixty, and over the years of living in Silver Bay, they'd been friends through all sorts of crises. She didn't know what she'd have done without the girls over the years – when Lottie had been sick, they'd been there and listened to her sobbing when she knew she couldn't sob in front of her beloved sister-in-law.

When Cari had been stood up at the altar by – Nora paused because she didn't swear often but she had only one name for him – that *bastard* – they'd been there to talk her out of going round to his house and stabbing him with her garden shears.

'You don't mean it,' they'd said. 'Cari needs you here, not in prison without bail, which is what will happen if you get at him with the shears.'

'Besides, Cari's better off knowing,' said Millicent, always wise. 'What would be the point of marrying someone who doesn't really love you.'

'Better to find out now that he's a cheating son of a bitch than later,' Agatha had pointed out darkly, because she knew what she was talking about.

The men didn't talk with the same depth when they had their nights out, the girls had often surmised. They discussed football, politics and the price of the pint, Millicent thought. Not worry over grown-up kids or breast lumps or if their husbands were depressed and how to get a depressed husband to the doctor to ask for help.

Nora didn't care what the men talked about: all she knew was that friendship for men worked in the same basic way it did for women: made people feel part of something bigger, less alone. So men couldn't talk about feelings or anxieties, but having each other seemed to be enough.

Nora finished ironing another one of Mick's shirts and hung it up.

The kitchen was cosy. The dogs were conked out in their bed, worn out after a big walk that morning. Being retired was wonderful, Nora often thought. She got up early and walked the two dogs along the strand on Silver Bay itself. In the early mornings, there were plenty of people taking advantage of the tides in the giant curve that was Dublin Bay. The dogs loved it and were well behaved – well, Copper, a nervy brindle greyhound who shied away from everyone, was well behaved. Prancer, a bouncing golden retriever, was less well behaved,

169

despite the training classes. Prancer had never met another dog whose bottom he didn't want to sniff energetically. He often did it to people, which shocked the non-dog-owning people running.

Prancer's snores fought with the sound of the TV, and Nora smiled as she ironed. She loved those two daft dogs. Loved how Copper shivered a long anxious nose into her mistress's hand and loved how Prancer poked his under her elbow when she had her breakfast, a combination of 'Hurry up, I want to walk' and 'Can I have some of your food, I've finished mine and astonishingly I'm still hungry?'

At that precise moment, the doorbell rang.

Longford Terrace was a friendly place and Nora was used to people coming to and fro during the day, but not so much in the evening. She checked her watch. Nearly eight. Either charity collectors or, neighbour-wise, it could be Jen next door looking for some emergency item – Jen worked, had three children and was a firm believer in home-cooked meals. Nora was never sure how she managed it but those kids ate home-made everything. The last time Jen had arrived, she'd been full of apologies but had run out of yeast to make home-made pizza dough and did Nora have any?

At the time, Nora had found herself comparing Jen with her own daughter, Cari, and thinking sadly that they were the same age, thirty-three, and there was no sign of Cari ever needing yeast to make pizza dough for her kids. If Cari wanted pizza, she called out to the pizza place down the road. If she wanted kids – well, she was hiding it very well.

The dogs followed Nora to the door and Prancer, doing his only bit of vaguely good behaviour, stood back when she told him to so she could open it.

For the first time ever, her new sister-in-law stood on the doorstep, dressed as if for the office in a grey skirt suit, cream silk shirt, with pearl earrings and her dark hair beautifully styled around those handsome dark eyes.

Nora was so surprised at the sight of Bess that she couldn't speak momentarily.

'I know, I'm sorry for dropping in unannounced but I needed to speak to someone now, not next week. I totally understand if you're busy—' said Bess hesitantly.

Nora found the hesitancy even more startling than Bess turning up in the first place. In the times she'd met her new sister-in-law, there had never before been any sense that Bess wasn't entirely sure of what she wanted or where she was going in life. Earlier, Nora had been stunned at Bess's phone call asking for a coffee. And now here she stood at Nora's door, looking devastated, asking for help.

It was a watershed moment.

But Bess was beyond feeling such things. All the emotions she'd clamped down for years had been freeing themselves gleefully since she'd met Edward and a deeply unhappy bunch coalesced in her head, turning on the rarely-before-felt water-fall of tears. Unable to stop them, Bess let them out, a flood of emotion streaming down her face.

'I feel as if I'm screwing everything up,' Bess sobbed.

Tears were Nora's speciality, Lottie used to say.

'You could calm people after an earthquake,' she'd remark kindly, when Nora had soothed everyone's ruffled feathers and the argument or bitter, never-to-be-forgotten fight was over.

Nora felt that tears needed a hug. There were few things in life that couldn't be helped a little with a hug, even the desperate things like terminal cancer. She'd hugged Lottie so many times those last months, gently as time went on, as Lottie got thinner and the cancer reached her poor bones, but Lottie had still smiled afterwards. Hugs didn't cure cancer but they had helped Lottie.

Even though she'd only ever shaken Bess's hand and given her a peck on the cheek on the day of Bess and Edward's wedding, Nora now pulled Bess into the small house and held her.

'You've come to the right place,' she said. 'I have a special offer on sorting things out – twenty per cent off.'

Somehow, Bess managed to laugh and she unattached herself from Nora, as if embarrassed to be held in an embrace in the first place.

'You must think I'm stupid but I have nobody else to talk to and—'

'Let's forget about explanations for a moment and have some tea,' Nora said.

As she led Bess past the hall with wallpaper Mick had been meaning to replace for a few years and down into the cosy but undeniably shabby kitchen, she reflected that her home was nothing like the elegantly refurbished Tanglewood, which had been transformed and where Bess and Edward had held a small dinner party not that long ago.

The guest list had consisted of just the brothers and their wives, and Helen had been spitting with rage and envy at the sight of the newly decorated and architect-designed house, which had made Nora feel sadder than ever because she could imagine herself and Lottie exchanging glances throughout the meal, the way they used to when Helen was in one of her moods.

They'd have tried to cheer her up, remind her that her own home was lovely and ask her about her new dress, which was always a tried and trusted method for making Helen happier.

But of course, Lottie was gone and this new woman, the one responsible for all this grandeur and now standing in Nora's modest home, was her replacement.

There had been moments, though, at that dinner, when she'd seen Bess's eyes on her, twinkling in a way that implied she understood Helen's jealousy.

Compared to Tanglewood, the family home on Longford Terrace was a humble place indeed. It was, however, pretty, clean and neat, with the scent of Nora's lavender oil wafting into the air from the little aromatherapy burner she had placed on the window sill.

Nora's beloved cookbooks took up most of the bookshelves and the walls were covered in a wallpaper decorated with poppies and wild flowers. The garden was inside as well as out, Mick liked to joke.

It was snug with its space for a couch and two armchairs, with the TV in a nook, where the family had always sat in the evenings. In winter, they lit the log stove and the dogs threw themselves in front of it with joy.

'Do sit down, in that chair,' Nora directed. 'It's the one the dogs are forbidden to get into.'

And, as Prancer had clearly decided to get to know Bess better with his goosing, she ordered him back to his bed sharply.

'It's fine, I like dogs,' said Bess, stroking the soft blond doggy head.

'You do?' Nora was utterly surprised. It shocked her that buttoned-up Bess like animals.

'We were never able to have a dog when I was growing up,' Bess said. 'My mother wouldn't have stood all that dog hair and when I was married, it seemed like another burden—'

She paused, as if aware she'd said too much about the Dennis years.

'Tea – builders' or herbal?'

Nora was not one for offering guests wine or strong drink. Tea and home-made fruit cake or biscuits when she hadn't been baking were what they got in her house.

'Builders'.'

Nora made tea, quickly coming to the conclusion that this must be about Jojo – what else could have Bess Brannigan here in her house at eight at night, unannounced?

'Home-made?' said Bess, holding up a shortbread biscuit.

'Shop bought, as we used to say when I was a child,' Nora

173

said, grinning. 'Shop bought was both the height of luxury and excitement then. And now it's the reverse.'

'My mother bought everything,' Bess said, adding a hint of milk to her tea. 'Our Friday night treat was chips and smoked cod from the chipper down the street. She worked, you see – had no time for homemaking.'

'I never knew that,' said Nora, assessing her guest.

This appeared to be confidante time but Nora was wary of giving too much away yet.

'Tell me, what are you "screwing up" and what do you think I can help with?'

'Joanne. She hates me,' said Bess and laid down the biscuit perilously close to Prancer's drooling face. 'She came up to the house earlier, the first time she's been there since the wedding.'

Nora noticed that Bess didn't say the word 'home', even though Tanglewood had been Jojo's home since she was a baby.

'She wouldn't respond to the invitations for Eddie's seventieth and I got Eddie to phone her, so she came up to see us and it didn't go well.'

'What happened?' said Nora slowly, thinking of what it must be like for Jojo to go to Tanglewood for the first time in a long time.

Bess looked into the middle distance and Pancer took advantage of her absentmindedness to use his long pink tongue to lean in and snaffle her biscuit. He munched happily and no jury would ever convict him because he looked the picture of innocence. Nora said nothing. There was a time to discuss her dog's bad behaviour and this wasn't it.

'She hates me,' said Bess simply. 'She just hates me and there is nothing I can do about it. She also hates that we are having the anniversary party in Lisowen Castle because it's special to her parents but I simply arranged to have the party there because Edward wants it there. I just didn't think it would cause so much trouble. All I do is cause trouble when I'm trying not to, when I'm trying to be her friend.' Bess paused.

Was she trying to be Jojo's friend – was that an honest state-ment? There was something about Nora's presence that made honesty a prerequisite.

'At least, I'm not trying to be her mother. I'm not stupid.'

Bess kept stroking Prancer's head gently and Nora sipped her tea. It was strange, this, having Bess in her kitchen asking for her advice when Bess's predecessor had been her best friend.

Nora sent a prayer up to heaven where Lottie was certainly looking down on them, probably with great fascination. Lottie had always been interested in other people's problems and this was certainly interesting. Her best friend and her husband's new wife – you couldn't get more thrilling than that.

'The thing is,' Bess said, 'you knew Lottie and you know Joanne—'

'Jojo,' said Nora. 'Her name is Jojo. First bit of advice: don't call her Joanne. Nobody calls her Joanne.'

'Sorry, Jojo. She hates me and she was always going to hate whoever took her mother's place, but I wasn't there when her mother was alive, I came along when her mother was gone, when her father needed somebody. Why can't she be a grown-up and understand that?'

'Because when it comes to your parents, it takes a long time to become a grown-up and I don't think Jojo has fully grieved over her mother's death yet,' Nora said. 'It probably wouldn't matter who her father married, but it may make it harder that you are so different to her mother.'

Bess looked at Nora wearily. 'And would it have been easier if I had been one of your friends, someone who'd help comfort Edward when Lottie was dying or someone who'd stepped into the breach because he was the rich Brannigan brother? Would that have made it easier? Or else someone who was just like her mother, artistic, fey and beautiful? Would that have made it any easier?' Bess asked. 'No, it wouldn't matter who I was or what I looked like or what I did, Jojo was going to hate me, and I have tried so hard and I love him…'

Nora was astonished to see the tears begin to fall again down Bess's face. It was strange, seeing this always-in-control woman sobbing again and she felt huge guilt for initially assuming that Bess had married Edward for his money or for convenience.

Because she suddenly realised that sitting there in front of her, in her cosy kitchen, petting Prancer who was now practically sitting on top of Bess as he always tried to take care of people who were upset, was a woman who loved Edward Brannigan.

Nora grabbed the small stool she kept beside the fire, pulled it over to Bess's chair and sat on it. She understood that Bess wasn't into affectionate gestures but she needed to be close to say this and she needed to grab Bess's hands.

'Go on, Prancer, get out of the way,' she said, giving her big, beautiful dog an affectionate shove.

Dismissed after all his helpfulness, Prancer stomped sulkily back to his bed where Copper nuzzled him as if he had been away for a week.

'Now, listen,' said Nora, holding on to Bess's hands, 'I'm sorry, I didn't realise how much you loved Edward.'

'You thought I had married him for his money,' said Bess bitterly. 'That's what everyone thinks. What is it about me that makes people think I'd be the sort of woman to marry into a big clan and take on all of this, stepchildren, brothers, sisters-in-law, you name it, for *money*. I have money. I have worked very bloody hard my whole life for my own damn money and I have enough, I didn't need any of this. I didn't need this hatred. Jojo hates me and that bloody Helen hates me too.'

'Helen hates everyone,' said Nora simply. 'She's got an inferiority complex due to a tricky childhood and it manifests itself in disliking everyone on the planet because she thinks everyone is looking down on her. Take her out of the equation. This is about you, Edward and Jojo. I'll do my best to help, but it might help if Jojo understood that you are not having the party in Lisowen Castle just to spite her or just to make a point about her mother's memory. It might help if she understood that you are doing it purely for her father's sake, because it's important for him to remember where he and Lottie grew up: where we all grew up.'

Bess nodded but said nothing. She pulled one of her hands away from Nora's and ineffectually tried to wipe the tears off her face.

'OK,' she said.

'First, let's look at why it's important to Edward to have the party there. When we grew up in Lisowen,' began Nora, thinking back to those days, 'nobody had a ha'penny. We were poor, there was no other word for it. Poor and with no prospects. There was nothing there for any of us but farming small bits of land, and none of the lads wanted to be farmers because it was backbreaking work and none of us had any sort of good land. The old history of the farms breaking up when sons married had been going on for so long, that if you got a bit of land, it was a few acres and what could you do with that?' Nora explained.

Bess nodded. She knew all this, more or less. Edward had told her but she also knew that Nora would give her a woman's perspective on it, the more unvarnished truth with emotional detail, the way Edward couldn't.

'Lottie was there then but she was a lot younger than us and to be honest, Ed didn't meet her until much later. There was a gang of us.'

Nora's voice trailed off, thinking of one other person in the gang who was no longer with them, but she recovered. 'There was a gang of us,' she began again, 'and we hung around together, went to dances, helped out with haymaking, stood beside each other in the church, all the while talking about the time when we'd be out of Lisowen, because when you grew up in one of those small towns in those days, you did want to be out of it. We never thought of riches: we wanted to survive and the boys not to have to tip their caps to the gentry. The people who owned Lisowen Castle, they were the gentry, make

177

no mistake about it. We might have been a republic, but the class system was there, Bess. We didn't want to be them, no. Apart from Ed. He used to say, "Why can't we be like them?"'

Bess could imagine her strong, fierce husband looking at people who'd had land and prosperity thrust upon them through inheritance and thinking he could achieve their wealth too.

'For the rest of us, it was like reaching for the moon. Not for Ed,' sighed Nora. 'That's why Lisowen Castle has always meant so much to him. It signified everything he hadn't been born with, and I don't mean that he was obsessed with the people who owned it, or that he wanted to be like them, no. It's just that when the family lost it and it became a hotel, you could see something in his eyes, some dream of going back there now that he was the big man. Having the party there for his and Lottie's anniversary meant so much to him and going back there for his seventieth would mean something to him again. And—'

Nora paused. 'It's tied up with Fáinne too. She just vanished, left a note but not a mention of where she was going. Sent a letter when their mother died, said she couldn't come back now to bring them more scandal. Edward searched for her but it was like she disappeared into thin air. All that family and love and loss are connected with Lisowen, along with it fuelling his dreams, and it's why it's so important to him.'

'But why doesn't he say any of that to Jojo?' Bess said.

'Because it doesn't occur to him that he has to say it to her. Because he thinks that she knows that he came from poverty and that he's so proud that he achieved all he has in his life. That's what's important and Lottie is mixed up with that too.'

'If he told Jojo all this, would she be able to like me?' asked Bess finally.

'I don't know,' Nora sighed. 'Second marriages are never going to be easy. The children, whether they're young or grown-up, are always going to feel they have to side with one parent or the other, and when one is dead – well, you can see that Jojo idolised her mother and can't bear the thought of anyone replacing her.

'Helen had these dinner parties for Edward when Lottie died: ostensibly to keep him from being lonely, but she kept dragging along eligible women and I can tell you, Jojo went mad about it. I did too, to be honest. He was grieving, he wasn't ready to be exchanging bon mots with women over the pudding. But you know Helen, hasn't a clue.'

Bess nodded. She felt included now in the analysis of Helen: she understood her new sister-in-law better.

'Jojo was very close to Lottie—'

'I never say her name, you know,' interrupted Bess. '*Lottie*. Like it's an evil talisman. Is that horrible of me?'

'Just jealous,' said Nora, 'which is, let's face it, entirely normal.'

Bess nodded. Just jealous.

'She was amazing, my best friend and I miss her so much but I'm happy to see Edward happy now. She wouldn't have wanted him to be alone,' went on Nora. 'If Helen dropped dead tomorrow, she'd want Kit to grieve for ever and wear black until he died, but not Lottie. She wanted the people in her life to move on.'

'So why can't they?' said Bess, petting Prancer, who had returned sneakily.

'Knowing what you should do and being able to do it are entirely different things.'

'I have never tried to fill Lottie's shoes,' said Bess fiercely. 'I am too old for that. I tried to be me and let people know I loved Edward. And now I'm going crazy with grief and misery – well, maybe I haven't gone totally to Crazyland but I can certainly see it from here.'

Nora laughed, a deep throaty laugh.

'You're funny,' she said. 'Lottie was funny too. If I tell you something, don't be freaked out by it but you would have liked Lottie and she would have liked you. You think she was this perfect woman but everyone is perfect when they die. All our faults are forgiven. She wasn't perfect but she was special, wonderful, loving, kind. A brilliant mother when Ed was off out empire-building. And my best friend.'

'I'm sorry. I can go if you like,' said Bess, feeling stupid at all she'd said to Lottie's best friend. Why had she come here?

Nora waved a hand dismissively. 'Don't be ridiculous. There are no high horses here, Bess, so don't try to climb onto one. Listen, and this is important, Lottie wanted Edward to be happy again,' she continued. 'She was the most practical woman I know, despite her arty ways. She was a realist. She should have said as much to Jojo but she did to Edward: "Find someone else, don't be lonely," she said. I know because she told me. If only she'd told Jojo. To be honest, I thought she was going to but she was too sick and she mustn't have.'

'Lottie told Edward to find someone else?' Bess stared at Nora. 'He never told me, never. Why hasn't he told Jojo? Could you tell her now?' begged Bess, and Nora looked at her sorrowfully.

'No, I think her father has to do that and he's not good at the emotional stuff. You can't do it and I can't either. You love him, she'll see that, eventually.'

'Eventually.' Bess sounded bitter. 'At one of our funerals, perhaps, when we are dead and have become perfect in the way the dead are? I can't wait that long.'

'This is a long game,' Nora advised, 'and you know more than you did earlier. You have to wait it out, take the hits, there is no other way. Plus—' she paused. 'There is something else going on with Jojo and I wish I knew what it was, grief, sorrow, her marriage, I don't know. I met her for coffee the other day and she looked haunted, and it's not just over her mother—'

She stopped, already feeling guilty that she had said too much about her niece. Jojo deserved her privacy.

And then she thought of one more thing she had to talk

about, Traci and Barney and what their coming to the great party would mean to her own daughter.

'This is another matter entirely, but are Traci O' Reilly and her husband Barney on the seventieth party guest list? It's a long story, but first, are they coming?'

Bess put her head to one side and thought.

Nora could see how Edward would fall in love with someone like Bess: she was so clever. Watching her mentally scanning her guest list was like watching Edward thinking about something. Lottie hadn't been anything like that. She was bright all right: bright as hell. But she didn't have that business brain the way Bess and Edward did, the analytical one always running down the numbers or the angles.

'Yes,' she said slowly. 'Edward wanted to invite people who hadn't come to the wedding because we kept it so small, and his cousin Owen was on the list, and Traci's Owen's daughter. I am almost sure they're all coming. Why?'

Nora sighed. 'You couldn't be expected to know and it would be difficult for Edward not to invite them, but Barney was engaged to my daughter, Cari.'

Bess breathed in. 'This is ringing some bells in my head,' she said slowly.

'Bells of doom,' said Nora grimly. 'They weren't just engaged: they were ready to be married, as in Cari was at the altar when Barney suddenly turned to her and said sorry, that he couldn't do it. And he left with Traci.'

'Oh good Lord,' said Bess before she could stop herself. 'That's just terrible. I mean, why? Not why did he break it off with her – people fall out of love, but why then? Why not even the day before, anything to save her that humiliation?'

Nora absently patted Prancer's soft head. 'I don't know,' she said.

Eleven

'When people show you who they are,
believe them the first time.'
Maya Angelou

Three years before

Nora stared at the flowers as the Appassionata people delivered them: Cari had wanted unweddingy flowers – pretty tumbling posies of peonies, tightly budded, not yet full bodied, and also trails of meadow flowers added in as if this wedding had happened a thousand years ago when the Irish wild flowers would have decorated the wedding maiden. There were tiny white wood anemones, the elegant blue of periwinkles, the velvety white stems of lady's tresses, and lesser celandines, as well as delicate cornflowers with their shocking amethyst centres. She had stems of rosemary and lavender for their heady scent, and a bough of rowan for the luck of the Lady. The bouquet, a mass of colours and greenery, was all held together with silken ribbons plaited as if for a Celtic maiden handfasting her vows in the rowan groves…

Barney's poor mother was dealing with the stress of the wedding badly, Nora thought. Yvonne was a ditherer and a worrier of Olympian standards. Nora didn't entirely agree with medicating worry because she'd found that two hours in the garden was a great way to calm one's nerves, yet she felt that poor Yvonne would benefit greatly from the help of some sort of relaxing pharmaceutical. Unless she was already on a relaxing pharmaceutical, in which case, God help her, because it wasn't working or else her dosage needed to be upped.

Yvonne was small, skinny, clearly lived on her nerves and was anxious about everything: the speed of the wedding which had been planned in a mere three months; whether March was a good time to get married in the first place, what with the threat of rain; and finally, about Cari's slender ivory dress and plans for her bouquet and headdress, like something from a fairy story about forest maeneds. Where were the lilies, the tiara, the plans for fake-tan application so that Cari would look like a bronzed South American showgirl before she went on her honeymoon, a look that Yvonne felt was necessary?

'Is it weddingy enough?' she'd worried, when Cari showed her the dress. 'You could carry off a full skirt, you know. Girls lose weight before the wedding.'

Cari's jaw clenched.

Yvonne worried about the bridesmaids' outfits too.

Cari had chosen an unusual colour green, a pale sage-green silk to tie in with her forest faery look, and the church flowers would all have sage-green ribbons trailing down from them, as would Cari's own bouquet.

'Isn't green unlucky in weddings?' Yvonne fretted. 'Plus, it's not a colour that suits everybody,' she'd said. 'I'm in pink – that could look strange. Pink totally doesn't go with green and it might look as if I'm not happy with the wedding theme and I'd hate anyone to think *that* because I love you, Cari. I mean, I don't like the green but—'

'Ma, it will be lovely,' said Jacinta, Barney's sister, who was a rock of sense from coping with her mother's nerves all her life.

But Yvonne's wedding anxiety was well beyond being handled by her own daughter and would probably – and Cari was only guessing – need a fleet of psychiatrists to sort it out.

'Cari, you know I love the colour of the wedding, don't you?' said Yvonne anxiously.

'You handle her, Mum,' Cari had begged Nora on the quiet. 'I know she means well but I cannot cope with neurotic people. I'm busy at work, so's Barney, and we're planning a wedding not Middle Eastern Peace Talks.'

'If I'm in pink, it will look so different,' Yvonne was still repeating plaintively with high notes of anxiety. 'So out of step compared to the rest of you. What do you think people will say?'

Cari didn't care particularly what people said. Neither did Barney for that matter. But Yvonne worried endlessly about what people would say: would people like the meal choices, would people think it was acceptable that the wedding was being held in March instead of what she considered to be the more normal wedding time of May or June, should she change her wedding outfit because the shop might take it back but green wasn't her colour and she looked like she had gastroenteritis when she wore it…

'People get married all year round,' Nora had said, trying to calm Yvonne, but that wasn't good enough.

'Please, Mum,' said Cari again, 'will you look after her, I'm busy at work and I can't keep her calm. I don't know how Barney has been able to cope with her all these years. And then I think, she's going to be my mother-in-law now and I'm going to have her round for dinner – it's frightening.'

Nora laughed heartily. 'That's one of the problems of getting married,' she said, smiling. 'You don't just marry a man, you marry his family. His father's very relaxed – ying and yang time.'

'Obviously out of necessity,' muttered Cari.

Barney's father, Owen, was the exact opposite of his wife: calm and easy-going. He hadn't minded the speed at which the wedding plans had taken place, had seemed to have understood that once Cari and Barney decided to get married, that they wanted to get married now. So while Yvonne was anxious about the whole notion of a very short engagement, Owen was laid-back about it. There was no secret to it all, no second blue line in a pregnancy testing kit that had pushed them forward. Barney and Cari had simply decided that they wanted to get married after living together for a year.

The day was approaching fast. Cari was no Bridezilla. In the same way that she organised everything at work, she and her mother had organised everything. Bridesmaids dresses: check; menu for the wedding: check; flowers: check. Barney was looking after the honeymoon and he wanted it to be a secret.

'Come on, you have got to tell me where we are going, I need to pack, you know,' Cari had said.

Barney had grinned and dragged her into his arms.

Cari was a tall woman in her heels and one of the many things she loved about Barney was that he was taller and stronger, so that when he pulled her into his arms, it felt good.

'Look, you controlling minx,' he said, 'for once in your life let me organise something and just relax.'

'Relaxing is not what I do best,' said Cari, but she was smiling.

Marriage was special, different: it would be thrilling to start this new life by letting go of some of her control. Besides, and she would never admit this to anyone apart from Jojo, there was something incredibly exciting about going on a honeymoon when she didn't know where she was going.

'Don't ever tell anyone I said this, but it's sort of sexy not knowing where we're going,' she said to her cousin on the phone.

'Sexy?' teased Jojo. 'I thought you didn't do the duke and his girlfriend novels.'

'Yeah, yeah, laugh all you want,' Cari said, laughing herself. 'I know – very anachronistic of me to be turned on by this but I am. Nobody ever organises anything for me because *I* organise it. But Barney put his foot down about this: said he wanted a traditional honeymoon where I knew nothing about it. Nothing's a secret about the wedding night any more: we all know everything, we've all lived with each other before we get married now. This brings back a thrill...'

'You old crazy romantic, you,' Jojo said.

Cari sighed. 'Yeah, that's me.'

Everyone at work knew about the honeymoon secret – they all talked about it.

'It's so romantic,' sighed Mo from sales.

Even Declan, Cari's new junior editor, loved the idea, 'I'd quite like to be whisked away somewhere exotic not knowing where I was going,' he said with a wistful hint.

Cari hoped he had someone in his life to do some whisking but she'd felt they didn't know each other well enough for her to ask.

Only Jeff, company MD, had any concerns at all. 'I don't know how you are going along with this, Cari,' he'd said, almost grumpily. 'It's so unlike you to let someone else decide things.'

Cari had immediately felt defensive: 'It's just something Barney and I agreed on. And we'd probably have killed each other trying to figure out what to do for the honeymoon, and this way, the choice is made.'

'Be sure and take plenty of books in case you hate it,' said Jeff, sounding like Eeyore after a bad day in The Hundred Acre Wood.

'I will,' said Cari brightly, slightly annoyed that Jeff, who had been her mentor and her friend for so long, didn't seem to approve of this part of the wedding, but then for some other weird reason Jeff didn't really approve of Barney either.

Oh, he kept it well hidden, but Cari knew Jeff and Barney didn't like each other, which was strange and odd, because everyone loved Barney and everyone loved Jeff. They were two entirely lovable people and yet they could barely disguise their dislike for each other.

Barney called Jeff 'that big dope who runs your office', which annoyed her no end.

Jeff didn't call Barney anything but she was sure if she'd asked – not that she wanted to – she'd hear something she didn't like.

She discussed the whole thing with Jojo who advised her not to worry about it.

'For heaven's sake, who cares if they get on or not, it's not as if you are going to be living in each other's pockets. Men can be territorial.'

'That's probably it,' agreed Cari.

Yet what were they being territorial about?

On the morning of the wedding, it wasn't the gloriously sunny day that every bride dreamed about. There was a faint March drizzle and a definite sense of coolness in the air. No matter, Cari thought, as she stood outside the back door in her parents' house and tried to get a feel for the temperature. She had a beautiful crocheted shawl to wear over her dress, a garment that looked like fine lace if fine lace was the soft cream of antique threads dipped in tea, then decorated with hints of olive- and sage-green embroidery, with a few silken tassels thrown in for good luck.

Along with her meadowflower bouquet, and the faery look of her dress, not to mention the crown of flowers in her hair, it was full of all sorts of other hippyish things that she completely loved, and which she knew poor Yvonne hated. Cari had seen Yvonne's outfit, which was a bright pink coat and sleeveless dress, classic mother-of-the-bride, with a bit of a feathery hat thing that Yvonne called a fascinator and which Cari's father, Mick, was naughtily calling a 'fornicator', a joke that made him giggle like an irrascible schoolboy each time he said it.

Mick appeared at the back door with two mugs of tea.

'Tea for the condemned woman,' he said, holding out a mug.

'Thanks, Dad,' said Cari, 'you are a sweetheart.'

'You know,' her father said, 'I think the sun might be peeking out behind those clouds. You might get a bit of sun for your wedding, after all.'

Cari had smiled up at him. He was so good and kind, and she was looking forward to seeing his proud face as he walked her down the aisle. 'I don't need sun for my wedding,' she said, 'the sun will come from the inside, that's where all the best glows come from,' she said happily.

'You have to keep that sort of philosophical stuff to a minimum,' said Mick gruffly, 'or else I will cry, and I will never be able to hold my head up in the pub again.'

By eleven o'clock, the house on Longford Terrace was full of people, with laughter and giggling and the clinking of glasses coming from every room.

'Will somebody help me with my corsage,' roared Maggie. 'I just can't seem to get it right and I'm afraid I'm going to rip the silk on this blasted dress.'

'Here, let me,' said Jacinta, Barney's sister, who had proven herself to be a remarkably helpful bridesmaid.

She was definitely more like Barney than her mother, Cari decided: kind, clever, and the silken sage-green dress suited her beautifully, went gloriously with her slightly mousy curls, despite her mother's anxious wailing that the colour would drown her and make the rest of them look like plague victims.

Mick had opened some champagne and Nora was cautioning against people drinking too much.

'Just half a glass,' she said to everyone and then spent the next hour trying to get them to eat a sandwich. 'I don't want you all plastered before we get to the church, half a glass is all.'

'Don't worry, Nora,' said Lottie, Jojo's mum. 'Nobody is going to be plastered.'

Lottie was sick then, but nothing was going to stop her being in the house on Longford Terrace for the day of Cari's wedding. She was pale and her beautiful face was rounded from the steroids but she was still smiling, putting a very brave face on it.

Nora kept looking at her dearest friend and worrying that it wouldn't be long now. None of the girls seemed to be aware of it, not Jojo that was for sure. Not even Paul, who was back from New York with his new wife, Lena, and should have seen the huge decline in his mother since he'd seen her last just a few weeks before, seemed to have the slightest notion that Lottie was dying.

It was strange, Nora thought, that doctors could talk gravely to families about their beloved relatives living with cancer and how they were doing the best they could, and how it didn't seem to sink in. Perhaps it was because Lottie was so full of life, had such a life force within herself, that nobody believed that she could actually cease to exist.

And soon, Nora thought sadly, soon that would be the case.

Her beloved Lottie would be gone and what would they all do then?

'Ma,' came a roar from upstairs. 'Will you come and help me with my flowers?'

'They're perfect,' said the hairdresser's voice just as loudly and with a hint of irritation in it.

'I just want my mum to have a look at them,' said Cari.

The hairdresser was probably used to being second-guessed on all things bridal. It must be tough working on weddings, Nora thought.

She raced up the stairs again. There would be no problem getting in her 10,000 steps today – she must have done 10,000 already, what with running around the house, making sandwiches, trying to press them on people, opening and closing the front door as half of Longford Terrace arrived to say Happy Wedding Day to them all, and making sure the dogs didn't get out onto the road because Prancer, in particular, was madly keen to see what was going on out on the road and were there any bins he could knock over and attack. Nora was looking forward to it all so much, knew she'd cry when Cari and Barney said their vows, but she was exhausted.

Perhaps that was the secret to a good wedding: concentrating on the aftermath glow?

When Cari was ready, she stared at herself in her old bedroom mirror, a bedroom she hadn't slept in for a very long time until the night before, and looked at a woman that was both her and not her.

The bridal make-up was subtle because Cari hadn't wanted her normal, businessy look today, and the simple flick of a cat's eye on each eyelid and a hint of pink lip gloss only emphasised her delicate features. Her dark hair was twisted and twirled into a riot of curls with a coronet of little white flowers around her head. She looked different, like the faery she wanted to be for her wedding day.

During the planning of it all, Barney had teased her for wanting such a romantic wedding.

'Here you are having a romantic dress and a romantic wedding, and you've always insisted you're not a romantic at all,' he'd said.

'I know,' Cari said, feeling a tiny bit foolish. 'But I have always sort of dreamed of something Celtic and different... does that make me a silly old thing?'

'No, makes me love you,' Barney had said.

Thinking about that moment reignited the ember of unease that resided within Cari's heart. Barney didn't say things like that any more, not for the last month at least and it worried her.

She had said as much to him once: was everything all right? Was he happy, did he want to go ahead with it all?

He had almost snapped her head off.

'Of course everything is all right, work is just difficult, that's all. Cari, the world doesn't end just because we are getting married you know.'

'OK, OK.' She had held her hands up. 'Fine I get it, work, busy – yes. I get it, totally, so go off and kill some dinosaurs, He-Man.'

But the niggle wouldn't go away. He had been distant at the rehearsal dinner the night before, as if his mind was on a different planet altogether.

It wasn't just with her, she'd noticed: it was with other people too. Barney was always very kind to his mother and Cari had noticed that he'd snapped her head off a couple of times at the dinner, so much so that Cari had intervened and said: 'Barney, don't be such a pig, apologise to your mother. I know you have got a lot on your plate, but really.'

'Thank you,' sniffed Yvonne, who had had two glasses of wine and was tearful.

'You look beautiful, darling,' said her mother now, coming into the room quietly. And Cari automatically smiled back at her mother's reflection in the mirror.

'Thank you,' she said. 'It's all make-up and artifice, you know that.'

'No, it's you, my darling daughter, and I love you. Your father and I are so proud of you today,' Nora said. 'All days, actually.'

Finally, it was just Cari and Mick waiting to go to the church. Maggie had gone at last, after one huge hug, crying because she always was emotional, but Cari hadn't cried.

She felt too wound up and worried. That weird feeling was still there and she picked up her mobile phone and looked at its blank screen with irritation before throwing it into her tiny wedding handbag. There were no messages, no last minute things from Barney saying, 'sorry about last night, I was just a bit stressed, nothing. Can't wait to marry you.'

That was the sort of thing he used to do – but not any more. Maybe weddings stressed men too?

'Are you ready, me darling girl?' said Dad, standing at the door.

Mick Brannigan wasn't built for a tuxedo, not like his brothers, Kit and Edward. Kit looked as if he had been born into one, a sort of silver-haired James Bond character. And as for Edward, he had the most expensive of dress suits, made abroad and tailored to fit him perfectly. But at that moment Cari thought that her father, who had never had much money in his life and was wearing a beautiful dress suit hired from the shop down the road, looked better than he ever had and better by far than either of his brothers.

She beamed up at him. 'I'm ready, Pa,' she said.

The Star of the Sea Church in Silver Bay was one of the prettiest churches Cari had ever been in. Today, it looked positively beautiful, with the much anticipated sun finally gleaming on it and the promise of all the flowers inside, along with the people she loved – not to mention the man she adored standing waiting for her.

They weren't late. Cari didn't really hold with the whole bride rolling up half an hour late shenanigans at weddings. She had been about to say it to Barney the night before and thought better of it. Maybe his being off with her was just nerves and that would make it worse.

But how could he have any nerves, how could he think she wouldn't come? Wasn't that why men got nervous before their weddings – at the thought that their bride-to-be wouldn't turn up in the church and that they'd be left standing there looking like fools in front of their friends and relatives?

That was not happening today. Today, Cari would stand beside the love of her life and marry him.

Inside, the church was a flurry of activity. Her mother was waiting, dressed in a flowery ensemble that Cari knew full well Lottie had helped her pick out.

Nora was not one of life's beautiful dressers and, without help, might have turned up in one of her old dresses in exasperation with the world of clothes shopping. Jojo looked like something out of a fairytale, as usual, with her beautiful blonde hair curled up onto her head with the same tiny flowers as in Cari's hair entwined through it. Maggie and Trina were waiting, in their roles as bridesmaids, looking for all the world like delectable sugared almonds in their sage-green silken frocks.

'I can't believe you're getting married, darling sis,' said

Maggie, wiping away a tear and hugging Cari carefully in case she squashed some bit of the bridal ensemble.

Someone came down from the front of the church: it was Stevie, Barney's best man.

'The priest wants to know if you are ready?' he said.

Then with a quick glance at Cari, he said, with an air of duty: 'You look beautiful on your wedding day, Cari: a beautiful bride.'

Cari, Maggie, Trina and Jojo giggled. Dear Stevie. Cari did look fabulous but Stevie had clearly swallowed a wedding etiquette manual and was determined to do it all by the book. The best man's speech would not be filled with rude jokes and inappropriate comments about bridesmaids, that was for sure.

'He is a sweetie,' said Cari, as Stevie legged it back up the aisle again.

'Not my type,' said Maggie.

'Nor mine,' added Trina. 'Second groomsman on the left . . . he's mine tonight.'

'Meanie,' teased Maggie. 'I fancy him.'

The music started.

'I think that's my cue to sit down,' said Nora and, planting a heartfelt kiss on her daughter's cheek, made her own way back up the church.

Mick looked at his daughter. 'That's our song,' he said.

Jojo grabbed Trina and Maggie, told them to calm down on the giggling and shushed them up the aisle. Cari watched them, smiling. She could still see both of the girls' shoulders shaking as they walked, a sure sign that they were laughing. She loved that they were laughing: today was a day of fun, laughter and absolutely no rules. Because today, she, Cari Brannigan, was marrying the man of her dreams.

'Ready?' asked Jojo, turning back.

'As I'll ever be,' Cari replied.

Jojo turned and glided up the church, a Viking princess in

her gown. Cari could see Hugh up the top of the church staring with love and admiration at his beautiful wife.

Aunt Helen's hat, a giant thing the size of a UFO, made seeing other people tricky.

'Is she trying to get radio signals from Moscow?' Maggie had asked earlier, out of Trina's earshot.

Cari could see Lottie beside Uncle Edward now, him stately and elegant in his black coat, Lottie wearing what Cari knew was an old dress of hers, something ethereal in cool lavender. Lottie wasn't feeling well enough right now to go shopping, she'd said to Cari lightly, but this was a dress she loved and she'd wanted to wear something special, something with meaning, for Cari's wedding.

'OK?' said her father.

'OK.'

And then it was Mick and Cari following at a stately pace that Cari found quite difficult to keep to despite practising. She was so used to striding around everywhere at speed and her gold bridal shoes were tight, so now they felt painful. Plus, they were not made for striding or even standing, for that matter. They were too flimsy, too delicate a leather and there was the sense that they would disintegrate if she did any stomping around in them at all. Still, it was a small price to pay for their beauty. She was definitely going to go barefoot later, though.

As she walked up the aisle slowly, she looked at the beautiful flowers hung carefully on the end of the pews and at the smiling faces of friends and relatives beaming as they saw her and her father. Truly, getting married was the most glorious thing. How had she ever thought it was better to be modern and just live together for ever, forsaking that piece of paper because, who needed it?

At the altar stood Barney, waiting for her.

When Cari had first met him, she had been slightly surprised that he had noticed her. Not that she thought that she was a boot or anything like that, because she and Jojo both knew they were hardly the worst-looking girls on the planet. People looked at the Brannigan girls, all of them – from Jojo's blonde Viking beauty to the other three's dark elegance with their amazing blue eyes with the emerald chips.

But Barney had always been in a different league, a sort of very young George Clooney but, astonishingly, with better hair.

Women looked at him when they were out together, longing looks at him and envious ones at Cari.

He was an advertising executive in a big firm, an old pal of Paul's, her cousin. He was very clever, going places everyone said, but that didn't mention the sheer sculpted beauty of him both in and out of his clothes. Barney wasn't vain but he spent plenty of time in the gym honing those same muscles that gave Cari such pleasure in bed.

Cari grinned up at him as she finally arrived at his side, thinking how naughty she was to be imagining her groom without his clothes as they stood in a church with the priest in front of them.

And she was just wondering if she could possibly murmur this thought into his ear, her eyes sparkling at the deliciousness of it all, when Barney leaned low and said, 'Cari, I can't do this, I'm really sorry I just can't.'

'What?'

Her heart realised the meaning of his words before her mind had. It began to thump loudly, forcefully, beating out of her chest. She stared at him, wondering, was this a joke? If it was, it was a poorly thought out one at that. She would kill him for teasing her so at the altar.

Nobody else could hear, everyone else was still listening to the final strains of the music, a string quartet Uncle Ed had insisted they'd have to have, which was to be one of his wedding presents to them. Along with the quartet had come a lady soprano with an exquisite voice that reached into the vaulted ceiling of the Star of the Sea and was making everyone tearful with its beauty.

'What do you mean you can't go through with this?' whispered Cari.

'I'm really sorry, I'm sorry to do it now, but I can't. I meant to talk to you about it all but...'

Barney, god-like in his dark suit, looked down at her with such a look of pain and yearning on his face.

Still not understanding, not able to compute this, Cari reached out and touched his cheek.

Later when she thought about it, she wanted to cut off her own hand for having touched him so tenderly and not belted him halfway across the church, but he was her darling Barney and he looked so distraught that she had to do something.

He pulled her hand away roughly. 'Don't,' he said huskily. 'I can't do this, it's not fair to you.'

And then he muttered sorry again and turned and strode down the church on those long legs, out of Cari's life for ever.

Twelve

Resentment increases at a rate faster than compound interest.
That tiny thing you resented two years ago? It's a giant woolly-
mammoth-sized resentment now. Get it out into the open early
before the compound interest resentment equation gets at it.

'The big party for Edward's seventieth is going to be a party the likes
of which Lisowen has never seen before,' wrote Isobel to Faenia.

'All the flower shops in the area have gone into overdrive searching out orchids and black lilies because old Mrs Brannigan loved lilies and had those black ones in the garden, remember? They were said to only bloom once every seven years.'

Isobel paused. She didn't want to lay it on too thick.

'I hear that there's practically an orchestra coming, which is lovely, because Edward deserves it after how he's built up his empire from nothing. Lord knows, none of you had a ha'penny in those days, pet. His new wife is a much tougher cookie than poor Lottie was but from what I hear up at the castle, she wants it to be right for him – not for her.'

Isobel's fingers, now arthritic and with the nodes of inflammation on the joints, needed stretching, so she stopped, paused. She wanted Faenia to come home, just this one time, because if she didn't come now, she'd be coming home for one of her brothers' funerals and that was no way to come back: to stand at the grave of someone you hadn't seen for forty years and watch cold earth being shovelled onto their coffin.

'We are all invited. Yes, I knew I'd shock you. My invitation came for the big Saturday night gala. The Friday night is dinner for the family, but I am thrilled we're all going.
 Won't you come?'

Isobel wiped her eyes. It had been over forty years since she'd seen Faenia, for all that air travel was fabulous and fast, and she wanted to see her now. She didn't want to say that Edward, Kit and Mick weren't getting any younger, or that neither was she. She didn't say that it was time for Faenia to come home, time to leave the past in the past.

Faenia felt as if she'd spent half of the day in the stockroom. She had an assistant who could do it for her but Faenia liked the order of the stockroom and the treasures it sometimes threw up. Like the adorable beach sandals that looked as if they'd been made with Hawaii in mind, and were a riot of colours and textures, sure to make everyone's toes look as if they'd just been bathing in an azure pool.

Scooping every size she could find, she got her assistant, Annette, to carry them up to their dressing room.

'These are just darling,' Faenia said.

'Very retro,' said Annette, who had a good eye.

'I had sandals just like these ones,' Faenia said when they got up to the dressing room, putting one on a small, pale foot and examining it from a distance.

And then she remembered the truth: her memory was playing tricks on her. She had never had these sandals – she'd seen ones like them in movies in the old theatre house, The Graham on Whitney Avenue in Brooklyn, where they used to play old movies for Saturday matinees and she sat with her popcorn in the dark and cried over her marriage to Chuck.

Mary-Kate got her a job.

'Waitressing,' she said. 'You can do that, can't you?'

'I was raised on a farm,' said Fáinne with spirit. 'If I can help make the hay and bring in the turf, I can fill a few coffee cups.'

It was a different sort of work but just as backbreaking. The shifts were often ten-hour ones and while the tips were good once Fáinne got over her shyness, she was exhausted when she got home at night.

The diner was like ones Fáinne had only ever seen in movies: voluptuous red booths, chrome fittings and an actual uniform with a gingham dress and an apron.

She was three and a half months' pregnant now but with a bit of letting out of seams, she got into the uniform.

'You can't tell?' she said twirling round in the only room in the small house with a long mirror.

'Not now but you will soon enough, honey.'

Mary-Kate was kind to her but realistic.

Her own child had been born in a shared room in Brooklyn, no drugs, no doctor, nothing. Just the landlady screaming that no kids were allowed as Mary-Kate's son had slid, painfully, into the world. Mary-Kate had tried not to fall in love with his beautiful face and had signed the adoption papers quickly, in floods of tears.

'You didn't want to keep him?' said Fáinne, this new world and her new life giving her the confidence to ask questions she might never have asked at home.

'The father had gone,' said Mary-Kate bluntly. 'There was no marriage, no happy ever after. What could I do? I had nothing to offer a child, Fáinne. Nothing. I gave him the best gift I could.

'What are you going to do when the baby's born?' she asked, dishing up the meat loaf for dinner. She'd taught Fáinne how to make it. 'If you're going to live here, you need to learn American dishes,' Mary-Kate said. 'No pining for potato cakes, soda bread and barley soup.'

'Keep him or her.'

'At least you never considered an abortion.' Mary-Kate crossed herself. 'It's the worst sin.'

'And keeping pregnant women in slave labour in Magdalene houses in Ireland isn't a sin?' snapped back Fáinne. 'Sin is balanced out in a very convenient way, isn't it? Who works it out, because it's not very kind to women?'

Mary-Kate, who went to morning Mass and saved money to send to the missions to convert poor folks who'd never heard of the Bible, crossed herself again.

'You can't say things like that.'

Fáinne dug her fork into her dinner mutinously. She would say what she liked: this big new country had given her that right.

Chuck was a regular visitor to the diner. He was like the Americans Fáinne had seen in the movies: big and kind, with a slow drawl to his voice that he said meant he came from Texas, the Lone Star State. He had a way of calling her 'ma'am' that made her flush in a way she hadn't since Peadar.

'Miss Fae... Miss Fay...' Her name was on a badge over her left breast and just about nobody who worked in the diner could pronounce it.

'Faynea.'

'Hey, we can't say it either,' roared the short-order cook.

'Faynea's a nice way to say it,' Fáinne said, fed up with trying to get the sense of the Irish *fáda* and its emphasis on a word into everyone. The only person in her new world who could say her name was Mary-Kate. 'How would you spell that?'

Blushing, Chuck took a notebook and a small propelling pencil out of one pocket.

'Hey, Irish, hurry up, coffee over here!' said a customer. 'I don't care what you're called, as long as you're quick.'

Fáinne rushed off with the ever-ready coffee pot and by the time she was back to Chuck, he had a few versions of her name written down in neat handwriting.

Fáinne's finger stopped at one that started *Fae*, which Chuck had actually crossed off.

'Doesn't make sense,' Chuck said.

'No, I like it.'

Fáinne took the pencil from him and wrote it down fully: Faenia.

It wasn't Fáinne, not by a long shot, but she had a new home now: she could have a new name. She beamed at Chuck. 'Can you say that?'

'Faenia,' he said, pronouncing it the way it looked 'Fay-nea.'

'My new name,' she said, 'for my new home.'

Chuck began to wait for her shifts to finish so he could escort her home.

The first night, Faenia let him: she was tired, her feet and lower back hurt and she wasn't thinking straight.

He'd helped her onto the bus and paid her fare.

'You don't have to,' Faenia said, alarmed now.

'I'm a Texan, ma'am,' said Chuck. 'That's what we do.'

At her front door, he shook her hand formally and headed back down the street.

'Have you gone out of your mind, girl?' said Mary-Kate, as soon as Faenia shut the door behind her.

'He asked to walk me home and—'

'You can't encourage men like that.'

'I didn't encourage him,' shot back Faenia, stung.

'Something encouraged him. Have you an invisible friend now, who flirts with strange men?'

*

Next day at work, Chuck came in minutes before Faenia was due on her break and she realised that he noticed her breaks, was waiting for some time alone with her.

'I might stretch my legs,' she said to him, which was a lie, as her legs were tired – who knew standing all day was so exhausting? But it would get her alone with Chuck, who needed to be told the truth.

There was a tiny park near the diner and they found a free bench.

Faenia didn't waste any time. She had changed a lot in these weeks in New York: she had a different life now and even though she was still young, she had to be savvy.

'Chuck, it was lovely of you to walk me home last night but it can't happen again.'

'Whyever not, Faenia?' he said.

'Because I'm four months' pregnant, Chuck, an unmarried pregnant girl and this—' She cast around for the words she needed. 'This relationship has nowhere to go. You're a kind person but I can't offer you anything else.'

There. She'd done it. She got up to go but Chuck laid a gentle hand on her arm.

'I know, honey. I can tell, could tell from the get-go. I grew up on a cattle ranch. That doesn't matter.'

Faenia sat down again. To the expert eye, pregnant women and cows obviously had more in common than she'd thought, which was not flattering.

'Chuck, were you not listening? I am pregnant with another man's child and I don't know what that's like in small-town Texas, but it's a pretty big deal, and not a good deal, in small-town Ireland. So—'

'My pop didn't hang around either,' Chuck said. 'I have feelings for you, Faenia. I'd like to be there for you, marry you. Be a daddy to your baby.'

Her mouth fell open. 'Don't be daft. I can't marry you.'

'Whyever not?'

It was a slow courtship, and a strange one. Mary-Kate was convinced it was all doomed to failure and she glared at Chuck every time he came into the house but he never deviated in his mannerly way with her.

He'd left Texas to work in New York for an oil company, but he planned on going back there, he told Faenia.

'I hope that's good with you, honey,' he said. 'I could never live here.' He gestured to the city blocks as if he was stifled from being away from the large blue skies and landscapes that stretched on for ever.

Faenia, who was slowly falling in love with this gentle giant, didn't mind.

'Better get used to dry heat, lots of cattle and men with guns,' Mary-Kate said grimly.

'I don't care about any heat in the future,' said Faenia, because the baby was sticking a knee or something into her bladder and she needed the bathroom. 'Plenty of guns at home and cattle too, just not enough in my family. Just rocky land that only sheep like.'

Faenia kept working her shifts in the diner but she insisted that there would be no wedding until after the baby was born.

'Why not, honey?' demanded Chuck, the closest Faenia had ever seen him come to anger.

'Because you say now that you love me and you love this baby but—' She cradled her belly. 'Let's see how you feel when the baby is born. I made a big rash decision once – not again. I love you, Chuck,' she said, and she felt joy that she meant it.

This big kind man had brought so much to her life: laughter, acceptance, love. It wasn't the wild, childish passion she'd had with Peadar. This was more real, the careful slow love of a woman who knew this man cared for her and her child. She valued his love and kindness. But she still wouldn't marry him yet.

'Let's just wait.'

Chuck bought her an engagement ring and she wore it proudly. She knew it hurt him that she wouldn't marry him before the baby was born but it was a risk Faenia couldn't take. She had to take care of this baby, not rely on anyone else, even someone as special as Chuck.

One night, after a long, hard shift, at six months' pregnant, Faenia had come home alone because Chuck had to work late. Mary-Kate was at a church fundraiser and, for once, Faenia had the house to herself.

She was in the small kitchen, sitting at the blue Formica table with the metallic edge, imagining a time when she might have her own table and a modern top-loader washing machine instead of handwashing and using the launderette with the big stuff. She'd make curtains better than the ones Mary-Kate had.

Mary-Kate was a sweetheart, a little prickly sometimes, but a kind woman and yet style wasn't on her agenda. For all that she was stuck in large pregnancy clothes now, Faenia found she liked clothes, loved looking at the old fashion magazines people sometimes left in the diner, loved watching professional women coming in and out, elegant in their little suits and hats, those fabulous shirred stockings making their legs look endless. She watched one woman in particular: she was small, dark, with deep-set eyes and an exotic accent and yet her clothes... Faenia didn't know, couldn't tell if they were expensive or not, not like some of the women she'd seen in New York or in the magazines, but this woman had style. She favoured a white shirt, always crisp, a bangle on one wrist, an unusual necklace around her neck and plain dark pants from which elegant ankles emerged in what looked like little ballet shoes.

She brought style into the diner and Faenia followed her with her eyes.

When Faenia had had her darling baby, she was going to buy white shirts and dark pants, and little ballet flats... she was just dreaming

And then the pain ripped through her, suddenly, like the worst cramps she'd ever felt but it was worse, so much worse. She gripped the metal edge of the table with both hands and gasped with the pain, felt the flood of water between her legs and knew her waters had broken. But this was early. Too early.

Thirteen

'Everyone has a chapter
they don't read out loud.'
Anonymous

In the weeks since Jojo had come to Tanglewood and ripped a hole in their marriage, Bess knew that her relationship with Edward had plummeted. Even though she now had an ally in Nora, someone she felt that she could talk to, Edward was still cutting her out as if he were somehow trying to make things better with his daughter by not speaking to his new wife. As a strategy for marital harmony, it was completely hopeless.

Bess still had her own chartered accountancy firm, but she had a partner now and she had cut back on her hours when she married Edward. Not that he'd cut back on his hours, but there was something about being a new bride that made her think she wanted to be there more, there to help their love and their relationship grow.

It was a strange sensation for Bess, a woman who had been brought up to know that she and only she could bring home the bacon.

Edward had encouraged her cutting back on work too.

'You've worked so hard all your life, darling,' he'd said. 'Why don't you cut back a bit, take your foot off the pedal just a little. Don't kill me for saying that.'

And he'd laughed and she'd laughed.

With any other man, she might have shot him a fierce glare for such misogynistic comments, but with Edward it had been lovely, a sign that he cared about her, that someone loved her enough to worry about her working herself into the ground the way she had for so many years.

Consequently, she did a lot of the cooking around the place, a role that she had found herself settling into with remarkable ease. Because she'd lived alone in her apartment for so many years, she'd got into the habit of eating sparingly and easily: salads and quickly prepared stir-frys and the other light meals that she'd enjoyed. The single, working woman's diet.

But now she enjoyed making beautiful meals for herself and her husband. She'd light candles mid-week for no reason, use cloth napkins, put on music they both liked. And they'd talk – about anything and everything. It had been bliss. Had been. Past tense.

Since the confrontation with Jojo, all the joy and love had gone out of those dinners.

If she was home before Edward and started cooking, she'd listen for the sound of his key in the door and be full of anticipation, hoping that this evening was the one where they rekindled what they'd had before.

Then he'd come into the kitchen and say, politely but still quite formal, 'Hello, how was your day? What are we having tonight?'

The words weren't the problem – it was the way he said them.

As if he was talking to a housekeeper, not her, not Bess.

'I'm doing beef stroganoff,' she'd say, checking the casserole in the oven, lifting the lid to let the glorious scent out even more. It was the sort of thing she'd never have cooked before but Edward loved his meaty dishes.

'How was your day?' she'd ask, hating herself for sounding just as formal.

It was impossible to lean against him and beg for it all to go back to the way it had been before: all she could do was steel herself for this coolness and hope, pray, it would end.

'Fine, fine,' he'd reply, 'a bit busy but nothing much. I'll just go up and change out of my suit.'

And that would be it. No hug, no kiss, no him leaning over and peering at what she was doing on the stove with one arm around her, and his face taking a slight detour into her neck to plant a gentle, loving kiss there. That was all gone.

Bess was heartbroken because she missed it so much.

Before Edward, she hadn't known that sort of love existed. Now it was gone, it left a gaping hole inside her. She had messed up and yet she had no tools for fixing it. She was too old to try to fix it. Too old to change her leopard's spots. Perhaps her mother was right and she should have just got used to being alone, because, as Maura used to say: 'We all die alone.'

Charming and cheerful. That was her mother.

It was too late to resist all the conditioning now.

Worse, growing away inside her like a canker was the knowledge, via Nora, that Lottie had told Edward that he needed to find someone else when she was gone. She had given him permission to find another woman, had encouraged him too.

Yet he had never said that to her.

Had never explained it to Jojo, which would have made all their lives so much easier. With that information, perhaps Jojo mightn't have hated her. Perhaps there would have been hope for their marriage.

Bess decided sadly that there could be only one explanation for this – Edward still wasn't sure if he wanted to truly be with Bess for the rest of his life, so he was keeping his cards close to his chest. And that Bess couldn't forgive.

'How are things?' Nora asked on the telephone.

Bess didn't regret seeking her sister-in-law out for help but she was beginning to wonder if it was all beyond help now.

'We're not talking much,' she said to Nora.

'You have to talk to Jojo,' Nora went on. That was her main

point: sit down and talk to Jojo and get some of this out into the open, yet Bess was damned if she was going to tell Jojo that her dying mother had urged her father to find someone new. That had been Edward's job and he hadn't done it. He had not made it easy for Bess, and that was pushing her out of his life.

'Plus, you and Edward have to talk about the past, talk about Lottie and how her death affected Jojo. They were very close and he needs to sit down with Jojo and discuss all of that. She's hurting really badly, and there is something else there...' Nora had said.

Nora said she didn't know what it was, but she sensed a great unhappiness in her niece, an unhappiness that was coming from more than just her mother's death.

'Edward doesn't talk to me, Nora,' said Bess angrily. 'I can't cope with it much longer, being second best, waiting...'

'Hold in there,' Nora advised. 'It will come right. I know it will.'

Bess had to believe her. But the secrets Edward was keeping from her and Jojo – why did people get married and keep secrets? What hope was there for marriage without honesty?

'Don't leave him, Bess,' said Nora. 'He needs you.'

Bess had hung up, wanting to cry. She knew that Nora was wise about people and their emotional states in a way that she, Bess, had never been.

Look at her relationship with Amy, another example of where her once-orderly life was falling apart.

She had been trying so hard lately but Amy was definitely holding her at a distance.

Bess was no coward. She was able to look back with a cold eye and she knew that she hadn't tried as hard as she could with her daughter. She had focused on the material things, on keeping a roof over their heads and food on the table – all those sorts of things, and hadn't realised that Amy was nothing like her, that Amy needed a different sort of love, a gentler love, one that Bess probably wasn't suited to giving her.

All of which brought Bess round in a horrible circle to where she was now: married to a man who was working late in the evening, every evening and all because his daughter hated Bess. Worse, her own daughter, Amy, barely rang and had sent an actual text message to say: 'Party sounds great, thanks, would love to come.'

There had been no phone call, no cosy conversation along the lines of: 'Will we go shopping for clothes together or do you need any help with the arrangements?'

None of that. Just one brisk little text message from a daughter who knew that Bess was perfectly capable of organising a presidential visit never mind a seventieth birthday party with no help whatsoever.

She thought of how removed Amy had been from Bess and Edward's wedding, and how she'd never realised it might be hard for Amy to see her mother marry another man. The thought simply hadn't occurred to her. Amy was an adult and Dennis wasn't part of either of their lives. And yet…

Bess had not wanted a hen night for her second wedding.

'I couldn't think of anything worse,' she had said to Edward.

'You must do something to celebrate the end of your single years,' he replied, teasing her.

He was going out with his son Paul, his son-in-law Hugh and his two brothers. It wasn't going to be a wild rampaging night through the town, but they were going out to dinner and then possibly to a pub for a few more drinks.

'Not a late one,' Edward had said. He had a few cigars with him, even though none of them smoked. Bess figured it was some male bonding behaviour and had smiled at the thought of her dear Edward and the others standing outside a pub, smoking and coughing because cigars were part of it all, weren't they?

In lieu of a proper hen night, Bess and Amy had gone out to dinner the night before the wedding. Even then Bess had known there was absolutely no point in inviting her soon-to-be stepdaughter to come out with her.

Edward had suggested it, muttering how perhaps she could ask Jojo...? Deftly, Bess had steered him away from this.

'No,' she said, 'I feel terribly guilty I haven't being spending any time with Amy and us being alone together tonight is very important to me,' she said. It was all true: she hadn't been spending very much time for Amy, because Amy had weirdly absented herself from the whole wedding process. Bess guiltily knew this was her fault, her fault for desperately wanting her daughter to fit in with the beautiful Brannigan girls. It was her fault for making Amy endure three testing make-up sessions: it was her fault for not being there for Amy so much of her life. Surrounded by the evidence of Lottie's huge love for her children, a love that Edward could talk about so easily, not knowing that when he did so it wounded Bess, that self-evident love made Bess realise she hadn't been that sort of mother. She'd have to be different, she knew that. But it didn't make it any easier, and now the guilt had set in. Bess wanted to change it all but was it too late?

She and Amy had gone to a very simple restaurant they used to go to years ago when they hadn't had any money at all. It was cheap and cheerful and Amy used to love it.

'Brilliant idea, Mum,' she said, when they met there.

As usual, Amy had insisted on meeting her mother there and not meeting up in advance and then going to the restaurant together. It was one of those weird things that Bess didn't understand.

Why was Amy always pushing her away, insisting they meet in the restaurant? Bess had only been inside Amy's new apartment in Delaney Gardens a couple of times, not that it was anything to write home about, and then Bess remembered criticising it and looking at the couch and saying something about how impractical a colour it was because really, a cream couch? How would you get any stains out?

'It's IKEA,' Amy had said flatly. 'The cover is washable.'

Thinking about it made Bess cringe. Weren't you supposed to get wiser as you got older and not make more cretinious mistakes than ever?

'I thought we deserved to come here now that we have enough money to have a starter, a main course and dessert,' Bess said, recovering, and she put her arm through Amy's as they went in.

She could feel Amy stiffen slightly but she held on.

It was never too late, never too late at all. And Amy was hers, the deepest part of her, and tomorrow – well, Bess was anxious about tomorrow for all that she was marrying Edward whom she adored.

Because with Edward came Jojo and Jojo hated her. Bess tried to bring the conversation round to the wedding a couple of times, but Amy seemed to be avoiding it.

'What do you think of Jojo?' Bess asked, trying to sound bright.

Amy gave her a shrewd look. 'She seems nice but she doesn't like you, does she?'

'No.' Bess seemed to sink in on herself, her normally upright bearing deserting her at this moment. 'I think she hates me. I've dealt with people who didn't like my methods in business and didn't like that I was a tough woman in quite a male dominated business and yet this...' She rubbed the bridge of her nose feeling a tension headache start. 'This hatred is just awful.'

'Has she ever said anything specifically to you?' Amy asked.

'No,' admitted Bess, 'but she glares at me and it's freaky. And when her father told her that we were getting married, she went crazy. Not exactly the recipe for a dream wedding.'

'It's her issue to deal with,' Amy said calmly. 'You can't live other people's lives for them.'

Bess looked at her daughter in astonishment. How wise.

'That's very deep, Amy,' she said.

'I can be deep, Mum,' Amy replied, laughing, 'you just normally never give me a chance to let you see that side of me.'

'Sorry,' said Bess, humbled. She was hopeless with people, hopeless.

'I hope you enjoy tomorrow,' Bess added. 'I know weddings aren't really your cup of tea and I know the whole getting your make-up done three times and everything was awful, it's just that Jojo is so stunning—'

'And I'm not,' snapped Amy. 'You know, it was hard enough growing up with the fact that you believed that I was overweight and needed to be monitored like an escapee from fat camp, but I'm a grown-up now and it's frankly upsetting and demeaning to have my own mother treat me like that.'

'Well,' stammered Bess, 'I'm sorry but you should have said something.'

'I'm saying it now,' said Amy. 'You know what, I'm not really in the mood for this. Let's just have a main course and go.'

'But we can have everything: three courses, wine,' pleaded Bess.

Amy looked at her almost pityingly. 'Mum, it's fine, one course is fine. I don't cry if I don't get dessert any more.'

Now, Bess thought of that night before her wedding with a heavy heart. She, Bess, had made it that way. She had, without meaning to, treated Amy precisely the way her mother had treated her: like a creature to be trained and then sent off into the world.

Maura had told her men were hopeless, that women should rule the world, that no sane woman relied on a man for anything. Maura had taught her to be hard and Bess had never wondered if these were the right lessons to be learning, or the right lessons to pass along to her only child.

How could she try to be a good wife at this stage in her life when she'd been a cool, unemotional mother who had hated her daughter's weight gain as a symbol of everything that was wrong with their small family? Amy had just been a kid with puppy fat and she was right, Bess had policed her when it came to food.

She had failed, Bess thought miserably, failed at everything. Failed at marrying that first time. Failed with Amy. And now she was failing with Edward because his daughter hated her and she wasn't warm or kind enough to make Jojo love her. Edward should have married someone like Lottie: a fey, sweet woman who loved stray animals. Jojo could have cared for that woman, or learned to like her at least.

Bess loved Edward but there was no point staying married to him if this was what their future was going to be.

She had gone into their marriage with her eyes open, hoping for a full loving relationship and now this battle royale with Jojo was there like a splinter between them and it wasn't going away.

She didn't know how to deal with it, *he* didn't know how to deal with it. What hope was there for them?

All Bess could think was that if she left it till after the party, then she might know what to do. Just a few weeks to go till the grand event in Lisowen. If Edward was still vacillating then, there would be no place for him in Bess's life. She might not be a genius when it came to decoding people's emotions but she knew when to get out.

And then...? Then she might see if she had any relationship with her daughter that was worth repairing.

Amy had lost four whole pounds. It had been an absolute nightmare because she hated diets, they reminded her of all those years when her mother watched her calorific intake like a jailer watches a prisoner. But she had done it. She had loaded her plate with vegetables, emptied her cupboards of nice things and gone for three-mile brisk walks every evening, although her walking had been slightly impeded by the fact that she had kept looking at her phone every few steps in case Clive had texted her. That was the problem with going out with a married man: you kept waiting for him to ring or text or do something to say he was there, that he was thinking about you.

Sometimes Clive dropped in with only a tiny bit of notice, so she couldn't very well walk too far. What if he arrived at hers and she was gone?

She solved that problem by walking around the small park near her apartment twice. It was a full three miles and it meant that she was never too far from home. Everyone in Met-Ro had noticed the weight loss.

'Look at you, babe,' said Seanie, one of the guys from the buying team. 'You look fabulous.'

'How did you do it?' everyone else wanted to know.

'Weight Watchers, Slimming World, replacement meals, what was it exactly?'

'Hard work,' Amy informed them, shimmering in the compliments and the new-found confidence.

She had been working on her hair too. She'd bought this special new spray-on stuff that made her hair glossier and sheenier so that when she blow-dried it in the morning, it fell about her face in beautiful auburn waves.

She'd had her eye make-up done in a department store, the type of thing her mother had being trying to get her to do for years. It was incredible the difference that putting on your eyeliner in a different way made.

Apparently she had been doing it in a really old-fashioned way for years and she thought that worked, but the make-up artist – who looked about twenty – had given her a slightly scathing glance and said: 'Seriously, you are still wearing that? It's very hard to do a smoky eye like that, especially at your age, especially if you're not a professional. Don't you have YouTube? They have demos on there.'

Amy had felt about a hundred at the time, but now, four pounds down with her hair glossy and her new make-up on, and a few YouTube make-up demos up, she felt fantastic. Love was the ultimate makeover tip.

She bumped into Clive in the elevator at work. It was one of those magical moments when suddenly they were both in it on their own, and she almost couldn't breathe. It was like being in *Grey's Anatomy*, with McDreamy in the same elevator as Meredith, and she waited for Clive to do something, the way McDreamy would do. Say something cute, grab her as if he wanted to haul her off to the doctor's on-call room… Instead he grunted.

'Hi,' he said. 'What're you up to?'

'Er, just trying to get windows done. I'm going to the Drumcondra store in half an hour and then I'm home this evening.'

She said it eagerly, hoping he'd pick up on what she was saying. She was home every evening, but she didn't want to appear too needy, too much like a woman waiting for her married lover to see her. Not that he was properly married, because he had explained that he and Suzanne shared a marriage of convenience, they were waiting for the kids to be a bit older. It was complicated…

'Yeah, right,' muttered Clive, looking down at the figures on the iPad in front of him. 'The Drumcondra store is coming on well. Just, you know, do your best work.'

The lift hit his floor and he got out. Amy should have got out too, but she stood there silently, still a little stunned, as the doors shut noiselessly.

Was that it? Was that all he had to say to her? 'Do your best work?' Not caring about the new make-up or anyone seeing her, Amy started to cry.

Edward Brannigan sat in the traffic on the way home from the office and tried to concentrate but it was hard. His mind felt, bizarrely, as it had during that maelstrom of emotion he'd gone through when Lottie was dying. At that time, his mind had refused to work the clear-cut way it always had in the past: instead, it was muddied and dull and it felt as if nothing was right.

Now, in the midst of all this trauma, he thought about that blissful time when he had been with Bess first of all, when he felt happy, so happy after the pain of losing Lottie.

It had been glorious to be in love again, to feel loved, to have another body beside him in the bed at night, not a body that he watched disintegrate with the enormous grief that had accompanied Lottie's passing.

Nobody could prepare you for that: the death of your beautiful wife.

No talks with doctors, no kindness from hospice nurses, nothing.

When the person you had adored for so long was being taken away from you by bloody cancer, there was no comfort. Edward had never thought he'd be whole again because it felt as if a part of him was dying too. And he couldn't explain this to anyone.

Jojo, Paul, Mick, Nora, Kit: they had all tried so hard to be there for him and they were there.

Nora particularly. Nora and Mick.

He didn't know what he'd have done without them at that time because Jojo had done her best to be strong, but she had been so close to her mother and she had fallen apart with Lottie's illness.

But Nora and Mick... Despite himself and his pain, Edward smiled. They were amazing, the most incredibly together couple he knew, the perfect definition of a happy marriage.

He and Lottie had had a happy marriage, for sure.

They were very different: Lottie had been artistic, prone to wild enthusiasms for various projects, like her funny old Venus statue in the garden. He could remember her pure joy when the yogurt painting had transformed the statue into something covered in delicate green moss that made it look hundreds of years old.

That was Lottie in all her glory and fun and humour.

She had kept their home and their family together for so long and he knew he hadn't been one of those men who took it all for granted: oh no. He'd thanked her, loved her, appreciated her.

Nobody could ever say that Edward Brannigan hadn't appreciated his wife. No doubt about it, he'd been caught up with work sometimes and he hadn't always been brilliant at being home on time, or even, probably, saying the right thing at the sight of the beautifully cooked meal she had on the table for him no matter what time he came in at.

But she'd flick her apron at him, often an apron covered with oil paint from a recent painting, and say, 'Oi, Captain of Industry, the slaves need thanking!' and he'd laugh, and say, 'Sorry, really sorry. My mind was elsewhere, my love,' and then he'd hug her, and his mind would still be halfway elsewhere but Lottie could cope with that. Total distance was what she would never have stood for but their love, complex and real, had allowed his mind and hers to race off in different directions to what fascinated each of them.

She had understood his drive to make Brannigan Engineering a big successful firm and she'd supported him all the way, the way he supported her art and her gardening, and any moment of madness in between.

And then, suddenly, she was gone. There was nothing to prepare a person for that. Not the priest at the funeral talking about how all the worries of the world were now gone from Lottie's shoulders: how time, the thing everyone worried about most, didn't matter to her now that she was at God's side.

Edward had wanted to stand up at that moment during the funeral service and scream at the priest and say, 'Time was not the biggest worry in Lottie's life: worrying about her family had been the biggest thing, thinking of them, caring for them had been the important things, and just because she wasn't there, if there was any after-world at all, she'd still be worrying about them.'

That was a problem with funeral services, certainly Catholic ones. Men who had never married or had children were expected to officiate over and understand the loss of a mother and wife to a husband and family, and deliver a sermon that made sense of that loss. These men had mothers and fathers, brothers and sisters, but not children, not wives, not husbands.

Edward had raged internally against the funeral service but Nora and Mick had understood that, both of them had come to him after the funeral and laid a hand on him. It wasn't Father John's fault: 'He's a good man, he was just trying to say the right thing,' Mick said gently.

Nora stood beside Mick, her hand soft on her brother-in-law's arm in its dark suit and he felt comforted.

It was strange, Edward often thought, how he envied his younger brother Mick so much. Mick was a mechanic and had never earned big money. Edward had wanted to give him money over the years but Mick had stood firm. 'If we need it we'll ask,' he'd say. 'I am honoured by your kindness, Ed, but Nora and I like to do it our own way. Thank you, we appreciate it and if we need it, of course we'll come to you.'

Nora was a woman in a million.

Bess, he knew, was a woman in a million too.

He had been so lucky to find her because he'd never thought he'd find any happiness after Lottie's death and then she'd come along and he'd been able to laugh again.

He'd clutched at that with both hands, because he wanted to laugh, wanted to be happy, didn't want to go home every night to a lonely house that reeked of the memories of other happier times.

If only Jojo understood that but it seemed she couldn't.

Paul seemed to understand. Paul often phoned from New

York and said: 'Dad, I know it's hard on Jojo but stay with Bess. She's good for you, you need that. Jojo will come round.'

Yet Edward didn't think Jojo would come round.

It was as if his marrying another woman was a betrayal too far and his beloved daughter could not cope with it. She couldn't cope with the concept that life moved on and people were desperate to be loved, to feel comfort, to feel happiness – all the things that Bess brought him.

He loved Bess and he'd loved Lottie: what was wrong with that?

Was he supposed to choose between his daughter and his wife?

He didn't know. It wasn't a choice he could make and yet, if he had to, could he hurt Jojo any more than she'd already been?

Fourteen

'Learn how to see. Realise that everything
connects to everything else.'
Leonardo da Vinci

Declan, twenty-four, sweet and green-behind-the-ears editor,
swung himself into the chair in front of Cari's desk and beamed
at her.

'So, what's the story, Cars?'

He was the only person able to call her 'Cars' and get away
with it. Partly because he was a delight to work with, eager
to do anything no matter how boring, and partly because he
insisted that people of his generation shortened all names and
only boring old farts had a problem with it.

'We're texters. We say "gr8",' he pointed out. 'You can't be
Cari, you've got to be Cars.'

'Like James Joyce is JimJoy?' said Cari.

'Yeah, exactly.'

'Heathen,' shouted Cari, putting her hands over her ears.

Today, Declan – 'call me Dec' – was wearing a lilac dress
shirt, purple tartan bow tie and a pair of beige jeans so skinny
that Cari feared for his circulation. On his beanpole body, it
all looked fine, though. Dapper, almost.

In his hands, he carried the latest slushpile: the unsolicited
manuscripts that people sent in. Unlike many other publishers,
Cambridge Ireland had a policy of accepting unsolicited ones
and there were many people who'd set their hearts on becoming a writer, so that some weeks, the office received as many
as twenty manuscripts.

In most publishers, different departments took different

types of book but in a small publishing house like the office in Ireland, the editors coped with all genres.

He arranged the piles on her desk.

'OK, I've divided them according to my tried and tested system,' he said. 'This pile' – he indicated two – 'are the ones where the writers use random capitals, say they are a cross between Scott Fitzgerald/ Maya Angelou/Beckett and say they don't want to be edited because it's all perfect.'

'Only two?' said Cari sarcastically. Sometimes in a month they got as many as ten people who felt that their work was already at such a high standard that the only thing required was for the publisher to print it up, jam any old cover on it, and 'Hello, Booker Prize'.

'This one is special,' Dec added, pulling the top one off and handing it to Cari. 'The lady is Irish, has never set foot in the US, isn't a person of colour – important point, that – and yet she feels that her novel about a family living through racism in the Deep South during the Jim Crow years really works on an emotional level. Oh yeah, and she doesn't read, either, which she thinks will help as she won't be stealing anyone else's ideas. Or "Ideas" as she puts it herself.'

'Lovely!' said Cari with insincerity. She never ceased to be astonished by the number of people who wanted to write books without having actually read any and who were wildly proud of the fact.

Cari glanced down the letter. 'She can't use the spell-check on her computer, either,' she added, skimming. She put the letter back. 'Definitely send those to Gloria.'

Gloria was their best reader, a retired editor who said she no longer had the energy to edit, and yet could always write charming notes to the more delusional of the would-be authors. Cari simply couldn't do it any more because the people often wrote back, full of outrage, to tell her she was passing up the chance of publishing an award-winning, fabulous, bestseller!

Plus, what did she know, anyway? Oh, and a plague on all her houses, while they were at it.

'It might be a work of towering genius,' Cari sighed. 'Who knows?'

'I did skim the first chapter and er, perhaps not,' Dec said. 'Zora Neale Hurston it ain't.'

'Now these' – he pointed to the middle pile – 'all sound intelligent and promising, many genres, all can use spell-check, and several of them awkwardly say they aren't sure are they mad or not to be sending a book in at all.'

'Give me that half of that pile,' said Cari, reaching.

She loved letters where the author had anxiety about their work: it was the true sign of something that might be special, she thought. The people who couldn't write for toffee and only had a passing acquaintance with the possessive case were always the ones who thought they were geniuses, deigning to send their book in before whisking it off to Hollywood where Steven Spielberg would be begging them for film rights, you wait and see.

'This pile is crime.' Dec paused. 'I, er didn't know if you wanted to see any crime because . . .'

'Because John Steele dumped me like a hot potato?' said Cari cynically.

Seeing Dec's stricken face, she apologised. 'Sorry. I'm just blowing off steam and you're very kind. I love crime, always will. Give me that pile too.'

'Which leaves me with the mummy porn,' said Dec sadly, 'and one fantasy/sci-fi thing, which is the first of a series, apparently.'

The last pile of scripts was enormous. The number of people desperately trying to recreate the success of the Fifty Shades series was exponential and Dec and Cari took turns in trundling through red rooms, purple rooms and nipple clamps, until Dec said he was never going to eat a mussel again because he couldn't bear to think of what had been done to one in *The Billionaire's Purple Bedchamber*.

'OK, deal,' said Cari, relenting. 'Let's split the crime and the mummy porn, and you do the fantasy as I'm the only non-*Game of Thrones* person on the planet.'

'That's not fantasy,' said Dec, shocked. R.R. Martin was his absolute hero. 'It's, it's ...' Words failed him. He simply could not describe R.R. Martin's genius.

'Whatevs, as you young people say. If you're not keen on something, pass it along to Gloria, and if you are keen, pass it along to me, right?'

When Dec was gone, Cari arranged the pile of manuscripts and took five to take home that night. Some editors hated reading unsoliticted manuscripts but Cari didn't. There was that buzz, a ripple that ran through you when you found the perfect one. Her mind ran, unbidden, to the time she'd first read John Steele's first manuscript. The thrill, the sense of the hairs standing up on the back of her neck...

One editor she knew swore she felt almost orgasmic when she found a good book, a story the editor had subsequently blamed on all the wine that had been consumed at the conference when she'd told everyone.

'I never meant it like that—' she'd said, puce with mortification.

'We know you didn't,' everyone else said, smirking.

Cari turned to her emails, flipped past ones she could delay until the next day, replied to one setting up a phone call with a writer who was struggling with a deadline – surprise, surprise – and then saw one from Gavin. Marked both urgent and with one of the little red arrows that indicated that it needed to be done immediately, if not sooner.

Sighing, Cari opened it.

'Cari,
Can you send me editorial notes on last two John Steele books.
I need them.
    Gavin.'

Briefly, Cari decided that Gavin was just messing with her – he wanted all the evidence of her work erased from the planet. If he could, he would recall all of John Steele's books and have them pulped, just so he could remove the acknowledgement: 'The best editor and friend in the world: Cari Brannigan, who believed in me when nobody else did.'

Typical Gavin: now that he had won, he was determined to rub her nose in it.

Caffeine might help.

She shoved back her chair and went to the tiny kitchenette, idly exchanging chat with Mo from sales who was there too, and looked grey in the face from three country trips in a row.

'Decaff or full-blown caffeine alert?' asked Cari, reaching for the cafetière as she knew that Mo liked French press coffee the way she did.

'Full blown with nuclear capabilities,' Mo answered. 'Or is speed legal?'

'Nah,' said Cari. 'Highly addictive, bad for you but apparently makes you thin, though, as well as keeping you awake for a looong time.'

'So I can't ask for it on my health insurance?' Mo asked, wagging her mug.

'No. But instead you can have number five blend, ultra strong French diner coffee instead. Guaranteed to keep you awake until at least lunchtime.'

'Fine.'

Back in her office, with a cup of black-as-midnight coffee in front of her, the colour only vaguely softened by the application of milk, Cari took a sip and looked at Gavin's email again.

What could she write?

'Dear Gavin, No, you scum-sucking bottom-feeder, you may not have my email editorial notes because you will have to work out your own plan with John Steele. If you can.'

Or, better.

> 'Gavin, did you not receive the Voodoo curse dolls, the sheep's skull and the chicken blood in the post? I bubble-wrapped it twice so you could pop the bubbles if you are having a stressy day in the office. The smell's not so bad – the lady who gave it to me said you get used to it. The curse only lasts one calendar year. Serious gris gris lasts longer but I am too broke for a lifelong curse. Toodles!'

Grinning evilly, Cari decided that laughing really was the best medicine.

'Gavin,' she wrote.

> 'Don't have the notes any more. Deleted them all when John was removed from my list of writers. Sure you understand.
> Cari.'

It was childish, yes. Unprofessional, probably. But it felt good.

In West Cork, John Steele came out of his study with his hair standing on end and a look on his face that his wife, Mags, hadn't seen for a long time.

'You OK, honey?' she asked, knowing damn well that he wasn't anywhere near all right. He looked both miserable and defeated, not a tricky combination to pull off.

'No,' muttered her husband, heading for the window where he stared blankly into the garden where a team of workers were landscaping the entire acre and a half at a phenomenal cost.

Mags decided to keep his mind off what was worrying him by pointing out all the lovely new things the landscapers were doing.

Up until now, John hadn't thought about the money it was costing: hadn't thought much about money for a long time apart from his and Mags's late-night ruminating on how lucky they had been. They'd gone through near bankruptcy years before, when the bottom had fallen out of expensive, hand-crafted kitchens, and suddenly, when all else seemed doomed, John's obsession with his writing had succeeded where everything else had failed. Thanks to massive book sales all over the world, particularly in the US, they were rich. *Sunday Times*, *Sydney Morning Herald* and *New York Times* bestseller lists had all fallen to John Steele's particular brilliance and his current book was still number two in New York.

But this book… this book was floundering like a fish that had found itself on a river bank, too far away to wriggle back into the water. Worse, his new editor, Gavin, seemed entirely clueless when it came to helping him.

Gavin had turned up in West Cork for a 'brainstorming and editing session', which was apparently Gavin's code for drinking plenty of the nice claret he'd brought as he polished off Mags's wild mushroom quiche and salad.

Instead of discussing plot issues, he'd wanted to talk about territories yet to be conquered, the touring schedule, and what did John feel about doing three events in one day and then flying out early the next morning to another location? It was gruelling but it worked. First Hong Kong, New Zealand, Australia, then the US.

'They wanted business class for you, John, but I said "for my author, it's got to be first class!" Good, right?'

Gavin beamed.

'We need to talk about where the book is going,' John said firmly.

'That was in the early days,' Gavin said airily. 'We trust you, John. You know how to do it. You supply the genius without any pesky editor niggling at you. I know Cari Brannigan likes to think she's something special in the editing business, but you're a pro, now. I loved that last draft of the first half, by the way. Loved it.'

And John Steele, who would always feel he was only faking

it being a world-class author and was really a carpenter in disguise, felt the anxiety clutch about him but said nothing.

Yes, he was the author, not Cari not Gavin. It was up to him to get it right. It had always been up to him. Freddie had said editors have different styles and some held back, while some did hand-holding. Gavin was obviously one of the holding-back type and if John wasn't OK with that, then it was his fault.

He was to blame.

Plus, he'd moved on from Cari – lovely, clever, wise Cari – to Gavin and he could hardly go back now. If he needed someone to discuss the finer plot points with, then he was just being unprofessional and was being a carpenter, not a writer. It was all up to him.

Mags put a hand on her husband's arm as she admired the work going on in the garden.

'Do you think we could do an indoor pool afterwards?' she asked idly. 'Only I was thinking how nice it would be…'

John thought of the half-unwritten book on his computer and felt indigestion or something acidic rattle around in his stomach.

'Yeah, perhaps,' he muttered.

The apartment was blissfully quiet. No sound of little mousy feet running around anywhere. Her father had come round the night before and checked the traps. He'd taken away all but two of them and, as requested, had not showed Cari what was in this batch or any of the previous hauls.

'I thought you were tough,' Mick teased his older daughter.

'Tough in some ways but I draw the line at mice. They were mice right?' She started at him with big anxious eyes. 'Not rats?'

'Little mice, micelets almost, they were so small,' he consoled her, 'and none tonight.'

After her father had gone, Cari fixed herself some dinner.

That was one of the nice things about being on her own, she told herself.

She'd spent a lot of time since Barney had gone thinking about all the positives of living on her own: like being able to eat whatever she wanted or watch whatever she wanted or go out to a yoga class if she felt like it, or, even, set up her yoga mat in the middle of the floor in front of the television and do a full workout.

Not, Cari thought with a certain grimness, that she actually did do any yoga workouts. In fact, in the three years since Barney had left – it was easier to think of Barney leaving than remembering what had really happened – she hadn't really done much yoga at all. Yoga was too contemplative.

She certainly ate what she want. No full meals with meat and major carbs and red meat three times a week. None of that stuff. She ate salads, quinoa, things Barney would have hated. But she also made use of the supermarket ready-meals. Far too much use.

She had also changed the apartment totally since he'd lived there. She'd sold a lot of the furniture and painted the flat white. It was literally a white canvas for her to begin again and she'd picked up bits and bobs all over the place, sometimes planning to repaint furniture herself to make it pretty and unusual ... but she had never got around to that, either.

Apart from the mounds of books, and manuscripts, and plants – because Cari, like her mother, loved plants – the apartment was a bit on the naked side. She opened the freezer, took out a low-cal microwaveable meal and jammed it in the microwave, then she made herself some green tea because Cambridge had recently published a book saying that green tea was the answer to all ills, and sat down at the kitchen table with her manuscripts.

Reading manuscripts was a very important part of an editor's job and it was a part that Cari loved. Sometimes she could tell really quickly if the writer had promise or if they were simply writing with dollar signs in their eyes. There were people who read a successful book and thought that if they just recreated the story with different characters in a vaguely different plot, then they were onto a winner. Publishing didn't really work like that.

Sure, when a certain type of book was successful, there were many similar books produced as publishers tried to leap on the bandwagon, because, after all, they were in business. But the follow-up books had to have merit, had to work within the genre, had to have *something*.

Some people wrote in with novels that had been lingering in drawers, novels that didn't really have any merit and were quite unpublishable. There were always those would-be authors who felt that commas, full stops and spellings were for the editors to put in and certainly not for the actual authors to include.

Cari had once worked under a wonderfully eccentric but brilliant editor who called these people the 'Leona Helmsley authors' – ones who thought grammar was for the little people, in the same way that the famous New York socialite and businesswoman had thought tax was for the little people.

'The Leonas should not be allowed publish books,' Ivanka had said, flicking a white hair back into her purple, velvet turban with one deep carmine nail and drinking the Virgin Mary she kept at her desk from nine to noon. At noon, it was transformed into a Bloody Mary – apart from the enormous consumption of tomato juice, Ivanka liked to say that celery was the only vegetable she ate.

'Oh, and olives in my Martinis,' she might add naughtily.

Of course, those had been different times but fun times, Cari thought, wistfully. She missed Ivanka, who had been fun and would have told all the Random Capitals, jumping-on-the-latest-bandwagon and I-don't-want-my-book-edited-at-all people to get stuffed. In that precise language.

Now she turned to the first manuscript. Whoever had sent it

in had clearly followed all the publishing rules perfectly. It was neatly and beautifully printed on one side of A4 paper, double spaced in a decent-sized typeface.

A good start, Cari thought approvingly. She'd get the first few pages read as her dinner cooked.

She started to read but the microwave pinging, telling her that her meal was ready, went unheeded, because Cari Brannigan was lost in the world of another person's mind. In this world, she was reading about a seventy-year-old woman looking back at a life full of events, and yet – due to something still hidden from the reader – she was still wondering what was the point of it all, and Cari felt the same thrill of excitement, the same sensation of the hairs standing up on the back of her neck, as she had when she read John Steele's first novel.

She flicked back to the accompanying letter.

A.J. Sharkey was the name of the author. The letter didn't imply whether the person was male or female, but Cari was sure this was written by a woman and she was just as sure that she was reading something very, very special.

It was the night of the dreaded dinner party at Jeff's, so she could tell him tonight she decided.

She wondered should she wash her hair – she felt too tired to do so, but maybe she'd make a bit of an effort.

It would be rude not to.

At seven, Cari glumly rang the doorbell at Jeff and Anna's house. She'd prefer to be going hang-gliding or even parachuting without a parachute at this exact moment. All she could think about was that she hated blind dates more than anything – with the possible exception of dates in general. She didn't need a man. No woman did and why they thought they did ...

The door opened at that moment and instead of it being Jeff with his normal hangdog, exhausted expression on his face, it was someone who looked absolutely nothing like Jeff. This door-opener dude was different and, Cari had to admit, hot.

While Jeff was tall and might have once been called rangy before he put on weight from too many energy drinks and chocolate bars in work to help him stay awake because of baby-induced sleep deprivation, this tall guy was rangy and positively sexy. He had stubble on a lean face that wasn't metrosexual designer stubble; he looked as if his jeans were worn in all the right places because he'd worn them in rather than because some fashion shop had sold them to him that way; and he had slanting, assessing eyes that were taking every inch of her in with frank appreciation.

Cari felt momentarily jolted and wondered if she had come to the wrong house.

'This is Jeff's, isn't it?' she said almost rudely, thinking that Jeff could have moved and not mentioned it because he talked of nothing else but the baby. A burst water main or a gas explosion might have demolished his row of terraced houses, and Jeff might easily have forgotten to mention it what with the discussion over sleeping schedules and how an extra half an hour had somehow been added on to the baby's sleep.

'Yeah, this is Jeff's,' said the hunk in a deep voice that was not unlike Jeff's but held more promise, more interest. 'You must be Cari?'

He smiled a smile that she was sure normally worked magic and had women falling over to divest themselves of all their clothes, earrings and morals, but Cari was so not in the mood for any of his male hotness.

She had done the men thing. Men were shits. One had just messed up her career and one had left her at the altar.

She gave him her deadly glittering smile that said: 'Watch it, sucker.'

If Jojo had been around, she would have recognised the smile. So would Cari's boss, Jeff, but Mr Hotness merely smiled back, not realising for a moment the danger he was in.

'Lovely to finally meet you,' he said. 'I'm Conal.'

Yup, Jeff's brother. The allegedly nerdy scientist one. Jeff really had got that one wrong.

Cari decided it was time to let Mr Hot know there would be no games, morals-dropping or, indeed, clothes-dropping, going on around here. Despite all that, she was glad she'd washed her hair after all. She wasn't dead.

'I'm Cari, the work colleague who is supposed to take pity on you and show you around the sites of Dublin since you've been gone so long,' she said, icily sarcastic.

'Hello, lovely Cari,' Conal said, opening the door wider and letting her in. 'It's lovely to meet new people and be insulted,' he added, without a hint of having been insulted.

He sounded amused, to Cari's utter annoyance. Why had she washed her hair? 'I'm sorry we haven't met before. I can't account for that,' he said.

'I can,' said Cari chirpily. 'Jeff did keep saying he had this loser brother and I haven't being dying to meet you, so that's why we haven't met before. I ran out of excuses ...'

Jeff's brother laughed and Cari scowled, finding it hard to hide how weirdly jolted she was by the sight of this extremely attractive man. She hadn't liked the look of a man for years. Three to be exact.

And yet this ... this flirtbag had grabbed her attention.

It was pure animal lust, she decided.

A woman's needs and all that. And those needs must be kept under control.

Yet, she liked the way he wore his jeans and how his shirt fitted across broad shoulders. She even liked the way he'd batted her own rudeness nicely back to her and how he was still admiring her, despite her rudeness.

She mentally shook her head, told herself that all men were lying cheating scum and she must have lost control of her senses for a moment. Plus, he was Jeff's brother and dating the boss's siblings was probably on some 'do not do' list somewhere.

*

233

Jeff appeared with baby sick on his sweater shoulder, arms outstretched, a smile on his face and bags under his eyes.

'You two have met, fabulous,' he said. 'Sorry I didn't get the door but Jasmine was crying.'

'Yes,' said Cari gravely. 'Conal and I have met and have taken full account of each other—'

'And you were right, bro,' said Conal. 'She is fantastically marvellous and spiky and I'm not going to mention the fact that she was recently shafted at work.'

Jeff went puce, but Cari laughed. Mr Flirty didn't disappoint.

'I sort of like your brother already,' she said to her boss. 'He's sort of like you but with a sharper, bitchier edge. Pity he's not so good-looking, though, and such a loser as well as a nerd. I mean, blind dating...? Really? I thought the only reason Irish guys went to Paris was in order to have exquisite French chicks surgically attached to them.'

She thought she heard Conal snort as they all moved into the kitchen, him close behind her. Finally, he bent down and murmured into her ear. 'I didn't come here to be insulted, you know,' he said in a voice that said so much more.

'Oh no?' whispered Cari back. 'Where do you normally go to be insulted?'

'I'll show you later if you really want to know,' Conal murmured. 'My place. I'm still moving in but I've got a king-size bed so it's a fabulous place for insults to be thrown.'

'Hell will freeze over,' murmured Cari back, still smiling at Jeff. 'I assume the king-size bed is for the king-sized ego? Plus, I only date clever guys who read actual books instead of stare at petri dishes all day.'

'You could make an exception for me,' Conal said. 'I'm house-trained.' The slanting, assessing eyes were laughing now.

'You big nerdy boys all say you're house-trained, but you're not,' Cari shot back. 'It's simply not possible. Not enough brain cells directed towards the real world.'

'I have missed this country,' Conal said loudly. 'The banter, the fun—'

'The hand-to-hand combat,' Cari said.

Somehow they got through dinner, Cari increasingly jolted by this good-looking, charming, witty man who turned out to be a doctor with a marvellous career in immunology, was just as clever as Jeff, had joined a cancer research lab in Dublin after what appeared to have been a stellar career in France and did not have baby sick on any part of him. It was clear that he loved the baby and when Anna brought the little mite back down after a tiny snooze – a gurgling and adorable creature called Jasmine – even Cari allowed herself to melt enough to hold the baby in her arms and croon little murmuring noises into that little squashed-up face.

'I didn't think you'd be good with children,' whispered Conal. 'I thought you'd be more of the put-them-in-a-pot-and-boil-them-and-eat-them type.'

'I only do that on Tuesdays,' said Cari sweetly. 'The weekends I save for putting people on the rack, general torture, inquisition sort of stuff. Have you seen my shoes, for example? I trample on people with them.'

She lifted out a foot shod in her favourite new shoes, leather weapons of purple and black with a spike heel so nutcrackingly sharp that it would frighten any other man. Conal's dark eyebrows raised. His eyes were a steely grey, she realised. Not unfathomable at all, indecently glittering at her, implying all the wicked things he'd like to do to her. Cari swallowed. She must stop this. It was the mummy porn – she should have given all of those ones to Declan. There had to be some benefits to being the senior editor.

She nuzzled baby Jasmine, adoring the scent of baby and telling herself that this life wasn't for her but oh, there was something about Jasmine's soft cheeks and the way her tiny pink, almost translucent, fingers clung to Cari's index finger that made her want to well up inside.

She could live without a man – had done. But this? She spent so little time with small children because none of her friends had babies – or was it that she didn't spend time with friends who had babies on purpose? Briefly she allowed herself to understand the savage hunger in Jojo for her own child. Then she put that to the back of her mind. Nearly a quarter of people lived alone – she could handle that. She liked cats. She would get one or two. Rescue cats. Rescued from life, like her.

She looked up to find Conal watching her, eyes hooded, assessing and sexy. The lizard part of Cari's brain leapt from baby to baby-maker in a second.

Why this, why now?

'You like the shoes, then?' she said to cover up her confusion, still holding Jasmine tightly but angling her foot so the pointy end of the spike looked at its most lethal. Shoes, she often felt, were women's way of projecting their power. A weapon by any other name, they said: 'I can be as tall as you with these on and if you annoy me, I will step all over your carcass in these shoes.'

'I like them very much,' said Conal. 'But it would be rude for me to rip them off and caress your ankles flirtatiously at my brother and sister-in-law's table.'

'You call this flirting?' Cari asked in fake surprise, handing Jasmine over to him in a sneaky move.

Babies always separated the men from the boys, she found. So many pretend-macho men fell apart when faced with a small child because they were scared the baby would be sick on them or require a nappy change, all anathema to men who did Iron Men competitions, swam fast miles in dirty water and cycled hundreds of kilometres in their own sweat every weekend.

To her amazement, Conal took the baby expertly, cuddling her against his shoulder, holding her precious little head perfectly so it wouldn't fall back.

'You look good like that,' she said, suddenly not joking at all. Hundreds of thousands of years of evolution and a human

236

desire to populate the earth hit her over the head like a cave-man wielding a club.

'I like children and I love this little darling,' he said and he wasn't joking either.

And it was that moment, which wasn't laden with teasing or joking or flirting, that made Cari Brannigan think she might be falling in serious lust with Jeff's brother. How exactly had that happened? She had sealed her heart over in case any man might slip through when Barney dumped her. Now this guy seemed to be worming his way in in spite of her best efforts to repel him. Worse, he was holding a baby and the combination of man and baby was making her breathe faster.

'Wine.' She held out her glass and startled Jeff.

'Thought you'd driven and weren't drinking.'

'Changed my mind,' said Cari, because she could hardly say bringing the car had simply been an excuse to leave early. 'The car's just outside. I'll pick it up tomorrow.'

The night flew. Jeff and Conal had clearly not spent enough time together since he'd come back to Ireland and Jeff was madly keen to talk to his brother, even though Conal wanted to talk to Cari.

'Jeff, you're monopolising Conal,' said Anna in exasperation, when she came back from putting Jasmine up to bed again to find the same discussion going on, and Cari beginning to tidy up.

'I agree,' said Conal. 'Why don't you two sit and relax while myself and Cari wash up.'

'Good idea,' said Cari before realising that it wasn't – Jeff had a long galley kitchen which would not accommodate herself and this large, disturbing man. She had to save herself from sheer lust.

'Actually, you sit and talk to Anna and Conal and I'll tidy,' she contradicted herself.

'No, sweetums,' Conal said quietly, 'I need you all to myself. The blind dates must talk or else it insults their hosts who set the whole thing up.'

'I might be a bad washer upper,' said Cari.

'I wash, you dry.'

'No, mister: I wash, you dry. I hate drying.'

'I hate washing,' Conal said, 'unless it's in the bath—'

'You have such a one-track mind,' Cari said. 'What did you say you were researching a cure to?' she added sweetly. 'Sexually transmitted diseases?'

She heard Anna laugh out loud.

'You did say she was funny,' Conal said to his sister-in-law. 'Sexually transmitted diseases are on the rise.' Then, in a quieter voice to Cari, he said: 'If I did have syphilis or some other STD, and I don't, thankfully, we would need to be doing more than washing up for you to contract it. But we could manage, if I put you down on this countertop,' he said thoughtfully, grabbing her waist with both strong arms and gazing at her as if he were thinking of picking her up—

'Let me go—' she growled.

'Only teasing, buttercup,' he said.

'Don't call me buttercup!'

He let her go reluctantly and she began to fill the sink with water. 'Sorry about the crack about STDs, it was in bad taste.'

'You washing or drying?' he said.

Cari sighed. 'Since you'll probably have to wash your hands ten times before we can start as if you're scrubbing in for an appendectomy, you might as well wash.'

'I don't do appendectomies,' he said with a filthy grin, 'but I know exactly where it is and I could show you later.'

'Bet you played doctors and nurses will all the little girls,' Cari grumbled.

'Only the ones I liked.'

For once, Jasmine slept, and, taking advantage of that fact, Anna and Jeff were asleep on the couch by the time Cari and Conal emerged from the kitchen. Jeff was open-mouthed and snoring.

'Poor things. I'll go,' whispered Cari. 'I can hail a taxi on the street or use an App.'

'I'll drive you,' said Conal. 'I brought my car too, so no booze.'

They shut the front door quietly behind them, and Conal locked the second lock from a set of keys on his keyring. Cari wondered how many places he had keys to and then berated herself for such a thought. He was just the sort of man to spend his time in Paris with women superglued to him. He was sexy, funny and clever, despite her taunting. Far too sexy, funny and clever. She needed to get away from him.

Then he led her to a car parked halfway down the street: a low-slung vintage thing in a fiery red with a long, low bonnet and fat wheels.

Cari liked it but didn't want to admit it. Her seven-year-old white Mistubishi, parked four cars up, looked very tame in comparison.

The steering wheel was on the other side, which must have made it tricky to drive in Ireland, Cari figured.

'Couldn't afford a new one?' she teased, as he unlocked the passenger door, 'Or are you just in love with old things? Do you bring out the original Twister for dates?'

'I do like older, classic things,' he said, grinning, 'That's why I like you, otherwise I'd be like most thirty-seven-year-old men and be dating a twenty-five-year-old.'

'Twenty-five-year-olds don't like American muscle cars,' she snapped back.

He slipped into the low-slung seat beside her, his seat shoved back to accommodate his long legs. 'You do know what it is,' he said, impressed.

'Did a book on them once. Seventies Corvette?'

'Stingray L82,' he said with a certain reverence.

'Now I know why you go on blind dates: you're a car nerd,' Cari groaned, as he fired up the car and she tried not to be impressed by what sounded like a rocket engine under the bonnet.

'The V-8 rumble,' he said proudly.

'You brought it over from France?'

'Yeah, the left-hand drive was fine there but I may have to give up on it here.'

He sounded genuinely sad and Cari thought of Jeff telling her that his brother had been a bit of a nerd. She'd been a book nerd and could understand how being obsessed with something, obviously science in his case, could isolate you. Maybe dreaming about cool cars had been his release.

'How fast does it go?' she asked. 'And no lengthy discussions on horse power or cylinders or any of that crap.'

'Very fast,' he said, shifting a hand onto the gear stick. 'Like me.'

'Fast, are you? Has that line ever worked in the whole history of corny chat-up lines?'

'Not always. Do you know, the NASA boys drove these cars when they were working on the space programme – imagine, astronauts riding to work in this to go into space.'

'You are a small boy,' she said, grinning at him.

For the first time that evening, his face wasn't amused or smiling. 'Yeah, small boy, that's me,' he said grimly.

Realising she'd touched some nerve, Cari did a conversational swerve.

'So you are actually curing cancer.'

'Part of a vast worldwide team who are trying to,' he said, concentrating on the road. 'Our lab is doing specific research but the results are important to all research labs.'

'Wow. I've never been with a doctor before,' said Cari, then quickly amended it to 'I've never been out with a doctor before.'

'First answer stands,' he murmured. 'Being a medic is handy as I can tell you what bit I'm touching as I touch it but I'm in the lab permanently these days, not a clinician.'

'Most guys have a limited triangular area of expertise: kissing, hands on boobs, then straight to procreation central,' said Cari idly, 'so medical science is not required.'

'Tell me,' he said, one big hand on the gearstick. 'Have the guys you've gone out with always done the triangular area of expertise? Kissing, breasts and, er, the procreation area?'

Cari knew she shouldn't have said that. The downside of not having dated in so long – she had no idea how to behave and her filter was permanently switched to off.

'Well... it's classic male, isn't it?' she stammered.

'Not this classic male,' he said, and she could have sworn his voice slipped from baritone into a lower register. 'People who study anatomy see the body as an exquisite instrument and it needs to be treated as such.'

Cari knew this was all her fault and she had to change the conversation soon.

'Sorry, let's change the subject. That previous conversation was just an occupational hazard: myself and Declan, the other editor, are always reviewing mummy porn from the slush pile and you get so bored with it, you forget that everyone doesn't talk about sex like some people discuss shopping lists. We have to divide it up and send it off if it's any good – there are different divisions: serious bondage, semi-serious bondage, phone-the-police-because-these-people-are-clearly-nuts, you know...' She realised she was babbling and this was getting worse.

They had topped at a red light and Conal stared at her. 'What is this mummy porn?' he said, fascinated.

'Oh, come on, seriously,' said Cari. 'Everyone knows.'

'I don't,' he said. 'I mean, do you know what Pembrolizumab is?' he asked.

'A new capital city? One of Saturn's rings?'

'It's an immuotherapy drug, pretty ground-breaking. Developing immunotherapy treatment is what I do. So mummy porn, utterly fascinating as it sounds, is not on my mental radar. Jeff calls me a nerd and he's right – I am obsessed with what I do. I think all scientists are. You are going to hate me for saying this but I am not a reader unless it's about science. But, I could change that with the … er … mummy porn stuff …?'

And then, as the lights turned green, he looked at her with a look so hot that Cari giggled. The car made its loud rumbling sound.

'It's an entire new genre of hot books where thirty-something billionaires with dark secrets and possible psychological issues that might need medicating tie up virginal twenty-year-olds and hit them with riding crops.'

She watched his face to see his reaction.

'Really?'

She was gratified to see that he looked astonished. 'Why twenty-year-olds? And what's with the riding crops?'

Cari felt a wild desire to throw herself onto his lap. A normal man who made her feel good for the first time in three years and didn't want a riding crop. Due to not actually having a relationship with a real man in three years, she'd fallen into the trap of assuming that all men wanted the televisual and mummy porn standard of virginal twenty-somethings and not used up and dried-out women of thirty-four.

'Twenty-year-olds in books have never had sex – apparently.'

'I don't believe that for a moment.' Conal was scathing.

'Exactly!' she said. 'I'm fed up with reading about all these virgins. The office hasn't room for all the manuscripts that keep pouring in. Can't they be older and have hot sex without whips and handcuffs?'

'Ah, you never mentioned handcuffs,' Conal teased, almost in a growl. 'Pink furry ones … I could go for that.'

'Pervert. Take a left here,' she directed.

'Or a blindfold …'

Cari could not say how utterly enticing the notion of playing with a blindfold with Conal was, only he'd be wearing it.

'We're here,' she said as the car turned into her road.

'I might have to come in and have a cold shower.'

'Oh please, you really are a pervert,' she said again, and was about to hop out of the car but one strong arm across her lap stopped her.

'Can we have a date and continue this fascinating conversation,' he said, mouth close to hers.

'Only if we don't talk about this stuff,' she said, feeling a flush of embarrassment. What sort of woman would he think she was? The sort who hadn't had a date in three years and read too much mummy porn, that's what. And Cari was not that sort of woman. He'd merely got her on a bad day when she was hormonal and deprived and had a man who gave off the sexual heat of two normal men.

'We could see something in the concert hall, a classical recital,' she said desperately, determined to regain lost ground and show her cultural interests.

'Great,' he beamed. 'Or opera.' Now he sounded really excited.

How lovely, a man who liked opera.

'Not *Madame Butterfly*,' she said suddenly. 'Always makes me want to cry.'

'But I'd comfort you,' said Conal gently.

'Nobody can comfort you after *Madame Butterfly*,' Cari said bleakly. 'It cuts to the bone.' And she'd clambered out of the car, with the feeling that Conal was dangerous and exciting and bad for her nerves.

Love hurt, she wasn't risking it again.

No dates for him. She was going in to read a crime novel: nothing like dead bodies, bad guys and a forensic pathologist weighing up dead people's brains to stifle any sexual urges.

Barney listened to the water cooler chat about the weekend.

Someone from new advertising accounts, one of the newbies, was wittering on about a match they'd been to: in Paris. Stade de France, the buzz, a few drinks beforehand and a glorious celebratory dinner in the Marais near their hotel when Munster won.

243

'Ten points,' the newbie was saying. 'We hammered them!'

'You all look like death microwaved up. Did every single one of you get hammered too, with booze this time?' asked another newbie, this one a woman, the girl with the long black hair who reminded him of Cari every time he saw her. Her name was Saskia and she was tall too, strode along in her advertising copy-writer standard gear of skinny jeans, cool shoes and a fashionable top, lean legs eating up the miles of corridors in Bentleys DB4. She was going places too. Not cut from the same cloth as many of the new hires who'd all got relatives in the business and had got in through the back door.

Saskia was possibly the first in her family to go to college, he remembered, and she made mincemeat of the art college boys with the old school ties, taking no prisoners.

The newbie guy backtracked: Saskia was gorgeous, not Cari gorgeous but still pretty damn good-looking, and Barney was sure there was a secret bet going to see who could get a date with her first. Sexual harassment law had not reached advertising as hard as it had reached other businesses. He had a pal in a bank who'd have been canned if he so much as winked at a female colleague.

Traci phoned him as he walked back to the office he shared with another lawyer. The photo on his phone changed to their wedding photo. Every time Barney changed it to a different picture for when she called, she nabbed his phone and changed it back. As if she never wanted him to forget that day.

'We need to talk,' she said.

Barney often thought he'd compile a list of the most-hated phrases in the world and 'We need to talk' would come quite high up on it. 'I have something to tell you,' would feature highly too. Traci liked both of these phrases.

'Talk about what?' he said.

He was at work: she knew he couldn't chat at work, even on his mobile phone. Bentleys DB4 carried no passengers.

'Edward Brannigan's having a seventieth and we're invited.'

Barney couldn't help himself. He drew a long deep breath in and exhaled for even longer. It calmed his heart a little. Breathing was good for you, or so he'd heard.

'We're invited?'

'Yup.'

'We can't go. Obviously.'

'Why not?' Traci said, with a hint of petulance. 'All my family are going. I've replied anyway. Said we were going.'

Barney rubbed his eyes. 'Fine,' he said. 'You go but I won't.'

'Oh, Barney, everyone's over it now but you. Cari's got on with her life. Nobody blames you, why can't we just go?'

Barney paused, not really knowing how to explain.

'Traci, there's another call coming in that I've got to take, sorry.'

Barney lied and hung up on his wife, then watched as the leggy Saskia stalked past his office. She reminded him so much of Cari: the same fierce intelligence, the same spark in her eyes. A spark he'd put out that horrible day three years ago.

How could Traci possibly think he'd want to go to a birthday party when Cari was there, when he'd ruined her life, publicly. Sometimes, Traci just didn't think. Of course, sometimes she thought so much that she rang rings around him. As he'd learned to his cost.

He wondered how Paul, his old pal, was doing in New York. Paul and he had been friends through work, which was how he'd come into the Brannigan family orbit, how he'd met up with and fallen in love with Cari, and then how he'd met Traci.

One night at an award ceremony with Traci had been all it had taken to screw up his life spectacularly. If only he could do it all again, he'd do it differently. He'd be with Cari and not Traci, never Traci.

Fifteen

SECRETS OF A HAPPY MARRIAGE #4

Long-time married love is different from first-few-dates love. Less
adrenaline, less movie dates, more time on the couch discussing the
children, the finances or should you get the bathroom retiled. But
don't lose that love from the beginning. It's special.

Hugh tried to take Jojo's hand as they walked into the clinic.
'Are you OK, honey?'

She pulled away from him. She didn't want to hold his hand:
she didn't want to hold anyone's hand or touch anyone. It was
as if she felt better in this little isolated chamber of just being
Jojo.

'Yes and no,' she said with false brightness. 'I'll be fine, let's
get in, we don't want to be late.'

Their appointment was for ten, it was twenty to ten.

There was no way they were going to be late, but Hugh
didn't say anything. He just smiled anxiously back at his wife,
the way he had been smiling ever since they started this long
journey of infertility.

They checked in at the clinic front desk and sat and waited
in the waiting room, while Hugh flicked through old copies
of *Time* and *National Geographic*, and Jojo sat with copies of
women's magazines on her lap and stared at them, unseeing.

How often had she sat here? How often had she waited
for blood tests or scans, that horrible vaginal scanner that she
hated, that poked around at her ovaries and found so many
follicles dangling on the end like little jewels in a necklace all
tangled up?

Before tests, she felt nervous and there were so many tests

246

during cycles. Tests to determine if the dosages were right, tests to determine the level of her follicle stimulating hormone. Once, Jojo had been nervous about having blood taken: now she just proferred an arm and barely flinched when the needle went in.

Same as with the vaginal scanner. She went into the little scan room, happy that the waiting was over and slipped off the lower half of her clothes, lying on the bed at high speed with a towel covering her from waist to knee.

Get it done, tell me the news – that was all she wanted. News, good news. No matter the pain from the scanner as it was angled painfully around inside her, no matter how gently the nurses worked. Pain didn't touch her if the test results or the scan results were positive.

Today was transfer day – the most important day in the whole schedule as far as Jojo was concerned, apart from that hideous day when she had to do a pregnancy test.

Today might still not happen if the embryos were not of good enough quality, if the embryologists said they couldn't go through with it, that a new cycle would be needed and it could only start after another three months.

Jojo had read of people who'd been down this route for years. This was her third cycle of IVF but she felt so fragile, as if she didn't have anything left in her for another go. Third time lucky?

Today she was having two embryos transferred into her and she felt absolutely terrified, as if it was destined for failure from the very start. How could she say any of this to Hugh? You couldn't say something like that. This was his life and these were his dreams and his hopes too. So she pretended to be happy despite all the churning emotions inside her.

Their names were called and they went through the doors to the inner sanctum which was the theatre area, to the charming Dr Stevens who had accompanied them on the journey so often. Dr Stevens was smiling and talking and hopeful, everyone in the theatre was hopeful. They always were kind and gentle and ... Jojo could hardly bear it. The kindness, their understanding of her pain and anxiety made her fragility come closer to the surface. She would not cry, not now.

In the theatre she was helped onto the operating table: this was a surgical procedure. Her legs were put in the stirrups and she had to wait. She had been here before, her legs in stirrups while the follicles were collected and her legs in stirrups while embryos were put back in the first time. And every time she saw the stirrups, she wondered would there ever be a time when she'd be a woman in hospital with her legs in stirrups having a baby?

Did all women who went through infertility treatment think this? Did they all wonder would it ever work out?

Incredibly, the transfer didn't hurt and the doctor played music while they did it.

'What would you like to listen to?' said Rosie, one of the nurses that Jojo had come to love.

'Oh anything,' said Jojo. 'Anything.'

Rosie fiddled around with a CD player that seemed weirdly old compared to the up-to-the-minute technology of the theatre. 'Strauss? I think classical helps,' said Rosie.

Hugh stood at Jojo's head, holding her hand tightly.

I must always remember this moment, Jojo told herself. This could be the moment when my child first comes into my body. She listened to the rise and fall of the music, tried to identify the waltz.

'Comfy?' asked Dr Stevens.

'Fine,' said Jojo tightly.

Dr Stevens talked to the people in the embryology lab as they checked, double-checked and triple-checked that the embryos that were being inserted into her body were indeed hers and Hugh's.

It was a lengthy procedure and she waited, legs aloft

throughout, trying to smile despite feeling a deep ache in her heart. How could this ever work?

She kept her eyes open, even when Dr Stevens came with the long needle to insert the embryos. There was a brief moment of discomfort but that was all.

Stay and become babies, Jojo whispered in her heart. Please stay with me. Please.

When it was over she and Hugh walked slowly from the clinic. She was supposed to go home and rest, and she kept thinking of all those stories of women who had got pregnant by lying up against walls with their legs straight up in the air after sex to ensure that the precious sperm swam into the ovum. Such things sounded like fairytales to her now. Fairytales didn't really happen for people like her, a woman for whom the very concept of having babies was all about tubes, petri dishes, frozen cycles, down regulation and hoping. Massive amounts of hoping.

Hugh kept holding her hand even as they drove home. By mutual consent, they had talk radio on so they didn't have to actually speak to one another. He knew her so well she thought sadly, even though she could barely reach out to him because of her pain. He knew she was in that dark place.

'I love you, you know that, no matter what happens,' he said as they pulled into the drive.

'I know,' said Jojo quietly. It was the best she could do under the circumstances.

Nora loved her morning walks with Copper and Prancer. She usually went out at half eight, come rain or shine, down Longford Terrace first, waving at various neighbours along the way and chatting to other dog owners as she did the loop that went past Delaney Gardens and down to the sea front.

She liked to stop on the way home at Mrs Glynn's house and say hello, because Mrs Glynn was an elderly widow with no family left and Nora felt that if the neighbours didn't make an effort, poor Mrs Glynn would wither away inside her pretty, old-fashioned little house where she still had the antimacassars on the armchairs. But that was on the way home – Prancer would never stand for any chatting at the start of his walk: he was an adventuring dog and eager to get on with it, the careful investigation of each pillar, close examination of bins and joyful reunions with his doggy friends as if he hadn't seen them for years instead of, possibly, the day before.

All the dog walkers knew each other although they mightn't always know each other's names. They were 'the lady with the poodle' or 'the man with the two collies'. But they always knew the name of their dogs.

'Hello, Flora, hello, Lollipop,' said Nora when she came upon a harassed young mother with a pushchair, a small child, and a straining terrier who wanted to be set free *now*, and was fed up with this on-the-lead business. 'How are you, Jen?' she said to the young mother.

'Fine,' said Jen, then remembered she was talking to Nora, with whom honesty was perfectly fine, and amended it to: 'Worn out. Flora's teething, aren't you, honey?' she said to the red-cheeked little poppet in the pushchair who glared at Nora as if she'd never set eyes on her before and was consigning her features to memory for *Crimewatch*.

'Oh, you don't look like a happy bunny, do you?' said Nora, getting down to Flora's level.

Flora decided she did remember Nora after all, and made a great gulping sob of misery, huge blue eyes filling instantly with tears.

Nora leaned in and stroked the red cheeks tenderly. The little girl snuffled and rested her face on Nora's hand.

'She loves you,' said Jen.

'And I love her,' crooned Nora. 'Poor little darling: teething's so hard for them.'

'Not so much fun for me,' sniffled Jen, who looked as if she might cry too.

'Why don't you drop in to me after the walk and you can sit down and have tea, and I'll amuse Her Ladyship.'

'Ah, no,' said Jen.

'Honestly, I'd love it,' said Nora. 'She loves my place and we can stick the dogs in the garden and let them dig up things, while Flora rolls around on the floor. It's bad enough being in pain but at least we can amuse her.'

Jen grabbed the opportunity with both hands.

'Thank you, Nora,' she said fervently.

'I'll be back by half ten and I'll have the kettle boiling,' Nora said, and, with one last stroke of poor Flora's soft cheeks, she headed off, wishing she didn't feel this big gap of a grandchild inside her.

Maggie was too young still but Cari...

She didn't know if Barney and Traci were idiotic and thoughtless enough to come to Ed's seventieth birthday party but she sincerely hoped they wouldn't. Nora was a great fan of forgiving people for things but when she thought of her darling Cari, trying so hard to get on with her life after being dumped, and when she thought of the old family crib up in the attic, she wanted to slap both Barney and Traci very hard across the face.

Cari couldn't help it – all she could think about was Conal. She was even dreaming about him: dreaming about having sex with him in his car. In the dream, they were somewhere in the American Southern states, somewhere with a lake and trees where all the local teenagers parked to have sex, which was utterly unlike where people went in Silver Bay when they were teenagers because nobody had cars and they were all terrified to have sex in case they got pregnant.

She'd woken up the morning after meeting him, and she'd

had this hot dream for the first time and she felt both exhilarated and scared.

Exhilarated because she felt that she was finally over Barney – and scared because she had no idea how to have a relationship any more. She hadn't done the 'crazy get him out of my system' dating when Barney had gone. Instead, she'd isolated herself into becoming a cool career girl. A girl with a career in trouble.

Conal had phoned the morning after: she'd known it was his number because she didn't recognise it, but she felt too anxious to answer it.

She'd made all those stupid comments about mummy porn and he'd think she was nothing but a hot tamale who had a headboard like an antique Medici carving with all the conquest notches in it. So she didn't answer it or reply to his text message: 'Would you like lunch?' which was probably code for 'Come round to my place and tell me more about the whips and the handcuffs.'

No, she needed to concentrate on her career. She wasn't ready for this – she was scared. A woman who'd been left at the altar was obviously hopeless at relationships and making emotional choices, so the best bet was to choose nothing at all.

Jojo was her closest friend but she couldn't talk about any of this with Jojo, not now. Besides, Jojo's problems made her own recede. Worrying about whether to date a man or not after so long an enforced celibacy was not a real worry at all compared to Jojo's problems.

Cari would concentrate on the rest of her life instead.

Her beloved cousin was in the depths of misery – it had been plainly obvious to Cari for ages but she didn't know who she should say anything to. She could hardly tell Hugh because he was going through the same thing. But who? Nobody else knew about the infertility treatment at all ...

This secret-keeping business was unhealthy, Cari thought.

She knew about the infertility treatment although nobody else did, not anyone from Hugh's family, which seemed unfair on him.

Hugh was a complex man, not the sort who only needed a beer and the footie to solve his emotional needs. He cared about things, he adored Jojo, he was suffering through this the same as Jojo, just in a slightly different way.

Sure, he wasn't the one being pumped full of hormones, which meant he had to *watch* her undergoing treatment, and see her pain, and yet – on Jojo's instructions – not talk to anyone about it.

The couple had just had their latest IVF transfer and they were in the waiting period to find out if Jojo was pregnant, although Jojo wasn't saying when the date for the pregnancy test should be.

'I don't want to build it up to a big thing, like last time,' Jojo had said on the phone. 'That backfired on me last time,' she added, with a little laugh that wasn't a laugh at all.

'Fine,' said Cari easily, as if she was happy with whatever Jojo decided.

It should be an exciting although nerve-racking time for both of them and yet Jojo's mood was strangely dark, as if she could already see a negative test, and Cari was worried about what this instinctive negativity in her cousin meant.

She toyed with the idea of talking it over with her mum. Nora had hinted a long time ago that Lottie, Jojo's mum, had suffered from depression. Was this it? Was this what it was like? This slow sadness that seemed to shift across Jojo's face when they were talking face to face.

Infertility was a nightmare, Cari knew that. Marriages split up over it.

But maybe there was something more going on than just the trauma of being treated for infertility, maybe there was something sadder affecting her cousin.

Cari hadn't even been able to ask about the waiting period,

which was what she had done the last time, saying things like 'only four more days, only three more days, promise you'll phone me whatever happens', hoping she was being helpful and hoping she wasn't being the most annoying person on the planet.

But she had been one of the few people who had actually known, apart from the doctors and nurses in the clinic, so she'd had to say something.

Cari fretted. Should she talk to Hugh? Should she talk to her mother for advice?

Cari, so efficient and in control in work, just didn't know. This wasn't her secret to tell but she was worried.

Hugh had got out of the habit of going for drinks after work. In the office, there were always a few hardy (younger) souls ready to drown their sorrows after a bad day with a few beers or some wine, but Hugh had long since stopped being one of them.

Today, though, when one of his long-time mates, Rob, stuck his head over the top of Hugh's computer and said, 'Fancy a pint?' Hugh decided that he did absolutely fancy a pint.

Just to delay going home to where Jojo would be sitting, waiting – oh yes, she might be pretending to watch TV or cooking but she was still waiting, the seconds ticking away till The Day.

Hugh was fed up with waiting for The Day.

He wanted a baby too, loved being an uncle, wanted to be a father.

But he hadn't known what that would mean – how it would change his wife. He couldn't cope with the new Jojo, the one who'd sprung up since the triple pain in their lives: her mother dying, their infertility and her father marrying Bess.

In the midst of all of this, he found himself asking one question in his head again and again: why am I not enough for you any more, Jojo?

The facts are horrible, my darling: your beloved mother is dead, and I am so sorry; our much-wanted baby is not on the way; plus your father has married someone else. It's a triad of pain. But you still have me. Is that not enough?

It didn't appear to be.

'Yeah, a pint sounds great, Rob,' he said, grabbing his things.

Waiting in the hallway for the lift were a few people, clearly ready for some fun after a hard day.

Elizabeth, Hugh's old college pal and the family law expert, was there too.

'Just one drink,' she was saying. 'I have a big case tomorrow and need to prep.'

Rob, who was a good-looking guy and not yet married, gravitated in the direction of one of the newer hires, Clio, a young girl who was blonde, clever and apparently destined for great things.

She reminded him slightly of Jojo: she had that same willowy build and fabulous blonde hair, although Jojo seemed very thin these days because she forgot to eat.

Clio was wearing a classic lawyer's grey suit, which was far more formal than the fashiony stuff that Jojo wore.

She gave him a half-smile and Hugh responded with a smile of his own.

She looked young and happy and he tried to remember when he'd felt the same, when Jojo had smiled at him happily.

Somehow, the few pints were dragged out and Hugh found he didn't want the evening to end. The others all had homes to go to, or other more exciting events and then it was, astonishingly, just himself and Elizabeth sitting at opposite sides of the round table in the bar.

'I should go,' said Hugh, not making a move.

'Me too,' said Elizabeth. 'I have to prep for tomorrow.'

But still they sat there.

'Oh what the heck, let's have a quick dinner. Jojo won't mind, will she? And though Wolfie's back from Berlin, he'll undoubtedly be in the studio sculpting and not know whether I'm there or not.'

Elizabeth's second husband was an artist and Hugh was never sure if Elizabeth had chosen him simply because he was the precise opposite of her first husband, a control freak of the highest order.

He phoned Jojo while Elizabeth went off to the loo.

'Hello, darling, myself and a few of the guys are going to dinner, I know it's an impromptu thing.'

It was an impromptu thing, but it wasn't a few of the guys. It was going to be just himself and Elizabeth.

After lying on the phone to his wife, which Hugh still couldn't quite explain, he and Elizabeth walked around the corner to a local restaurant many of their colleagues went to. This was the wisest move, they seemed to agree without any words being exchanged: nobody seeing two colleagues there could ever imagine anything salacious in their having dinner together. Surely if one wanted a torrid affair, one went somewhere one wouldn't be seen, Hugh reasoned. Plus, he and Elizabeth had been friends for years: fifteen years, at least.

There had never been even the slightest spark between them – they were too alike, both unswervingly professional.

Elizabeth was beautifully put together and very corporate, the way an intelligent solicitor like herself needed to be. She dressed in lovely, but very businesslike suits with her shoulder-length dark hair never straying onto her face thanks to plenty of hairspray, and wore what had to be family pearls around her neck. Nobody was going to get the wrong impression about her, although Hugh was sure that with her looks and cool intelligence, she featured in other men's fantasies.

But for him, there was simply something very nice about talking to his old friend, something calming and relaxing. There were no other agendas. No subjects that had to be delicately skirted around like there were with Jojo now.

He felt that hint of guilt thinking about Jojo, but by now

he'd had several beers and felt a little bit anaesthetised from his feelings. All he knew was that this nice intelligent woman was sitting with him, being a friend and he did not have to fix her or make it better. Right now, he could simply be himself.

'I don't normally do this,' Elizabeth said when their bottle of wine had arrived and they put in an order for something to soak up the couple of beers he'd had and the two gin and tonics she'd had.

'Do what?' Hugh said, startled. 'Go out to dinner with a colleague?'

She looked at him levelly. 'Go out the night before a big case, Hugh, you dodo.'

'Of course,' he said and took a large gulp of wine.

Why had he thought she meant anything else? He'd better stop drinking and eat. His mind was addled.

He realised that this all looked bad – more so for Elizabeth than for him.

Reputation was very important for women, far more so than for men. A woman who got a name for herself for going out for drinks with married male colleagues would be branded a certain type of woman – totally unfair and misogynistic it might be, but that was the truth. The rules were different for women.

But he was fed up with things being different for women, fed up with feeling like a second-class citizen.

His heart was broken over what he and Jojo were going through and though he knew that Jojo was the one being pumped full of hormones, he was living with the pain of infertility too. Yet was Jojo being kind to him? Was she worrying over him? Did she tiptoe around him delicately...?

'...I know I shouldn't be moaning to you,' Elizabeth was saying and Hugh tuned back in. 'But it's not working out, with me and Wolfie. He's too different from me. I wanted someone different after Charles and I just fell down the rabbit hole.'

'Oh, Liz,' said Hugh, reverting to the name he used to call

her in college before she got corporated up and went back to Elizabeth. He reached out and grabbed her hand.

'I'm sorry. I had no idea.'

She didn't move her hand and her eyes filled with tears.

'Nobody bloody does. I work and work and come home to no dinner, no shopping done and Wolfie expecting me to leap into bed with him because his day went well, and he thinks what I do is boring. But I'm the one who's earning, I'm the one who's making the actual money, yet he still expects me to do the other stuff.'

She wiped her eyes with her other hand and Hugh handed her his napkin and suddenly, Elizabeth was back and Liz – vulnerable Liz – was gone.

'Sorry,' she said, sounding like a general hyping up the troops before a battle. The troops she was hyping up were her own. 'Don't know what came over me.'

Hugh refused to let go of her hand. 'Liz,' he said, 'I'm your friend, that means something so don't shut me out if you need help.'

She stared him in the eye. 'If we're friends, why don't you tell me what's going on with you and Jojo, and why you look like someone's hit you first thing in the morning before you put your game face on?'

Hugh slumped in his seat.

'It's complicated,' he said.

'Said everyone, everywhere,' retorted Elizabeth.

She moved so that there was more room on the banquette at their corner table, and rearranged the place settings so that he could sit kitty corner to her and rest on the banquette too.

'Slide in here and talk to me,' she said. 'I'll mop your eyes if you cry and you can mop mine.'

And, knowing that this was not a good idea, Hugh moved to her side.

Sixteen

'Life is always either a tightrope or a
feather bed. Give me the tightrope.'
Edith Wharton

Helen looked at the contents of her closet with displeasure. She had many things to wear to the grand seventieth but none of it was new. What if someone, anyone, looked at her outfit and realised this?

'Oh, Helen, so good of you to get a second and third season out of things. Aren't you clever!'

She would die, literally die on the spot if such a thing happened. And imagine if Bess overheard?

She might not mind Edward hearing – after all, he'd been married to Lottie and for all her beauty, Lottie treated clothes as if they didn't matter. Which was all well and good if you were rich or beautiful. Nobody minded what rich or beautiful people wore. They could roll up at great galas in elderly silk dresses or something that looked as if the cat normally slept on it, fling on a few jewels and a slash of lipstick, and people said they were clever and stylish and meant it.

But if someone like Helen – who had no money to speak of and was married to the Brannigan brother who had tried to make a fortune at all manner of things and failed – wore an old dress, people would laugh, no matter that she'd held on to her big diamond earrings despite the crash.

Only the rich or the beautiful could get away with not caring.

Everyone else had to care or face social death.

She phoned her friend and neighbour, Marlene, to discuss it all.

259

Marlene played tennis with Helen and the two couples socialised, but Marlene and Peter had no money to speak of, lived in a quite ordinary house on the same road – at least, Helen thought, White Gables was big, even if it hadn't been redecorated since the year dot – and Marlene thought Helen was the last word in style. Marlene's admiration was comforting in an ever-changing world.

An hour later, Marlene was installed at Helen's lovely dining room table in White Gables – Helen never received guests in the kitchen. Kit was fatally obsessed with his childhood meal of bacon and cabbage and the cabbage scent tended to linger – drinking coffee from the Nespresso and eating biscotti.

'I love these,' said Marlene, dunking hers into the tiny Villeroy and Boch espresso cups.

Helen could never remember if it was acceptable to dunk anything or not – she must check. It was one of those weird things about etiquette: the poshest people did things Helen had been sure were entirely wrong, like that time a grande dame at a hunt ball had got entirely plastered and had gleefully pinched a waiter's bottom. Helen, never at a hunt ball or even on a horse before, had not known where to look.

Therefore, she did not dunk, although the biscotti were hard on her dentures.

Marlene looked to her for advice, after all. 'What do you think you'll wear? That pink dress you got for the races was lovely—' said Marlene, with the faint envy of someone who longed to go to the races but never had the money for it.

'But it's short,' sighed Helen, 'you know the notion of not wearing short to an evening event...'

There had not been much of a rule book in her home in Lisowen, apart from stay out of Daddy's way when he came home out of his mind with drink, and if you had clothes, you wore them because if you didn't someone else would take them. Still, somewhere on the planet, somewhere nice, the place where Helen really wanted to have grown up, there was a rule book, and Helen wished she knew all the intricacies of it.

'You could wear it,' said Marlene eagerly. 'It's the twenty-first century, the silly old rules don't apply any more about evening things and you have great legs—'

'Do you think…? Let's take this upstairs, then.'

They traipsed upstairs and Marlene, who was admitted to the sanctuary of Helen's dressing room only rarely, first admired the orchids on the jardinière on the landing, and then the gleam of the mirrors in the dressing room.

'You must never stop polishing,' sighed Marlene, staring at the wall of mirrors.

'I don't,' said Helen, who did polish but wanted to sound shocked at the thought. 'Mrs P does it. I'm allergic to cleaning products, you know that.'

''Course,' said Marlene, who was equally shocked at having forgotten about Mrs P, a sweet but slightly dim lady, to hear Helen describe her as a bit deaf too.

Imagine having a cleaning lady. Marlene did her own cleaning.

Marlene had never met Mrs P and there was a reason for that: Helen had trouble holding on to help because of her tendency to bitch at them, so Mrs P was the latest in a long line and it was not a marriage made in heaven. Mrs P, actually Paula Porter, came from the estate four blocks away from White Gables, had been raised with a cynical eye and took precisely none of Helen's bitching.

'I'll clean but don't hassle me, love, or I'll be off,' Paula had said on day one, looking her new employer up and down like a bookie evaluating the runners in the four o'clock at Leopardstown. 'Let's face it, you've gone through just about everyone else round here who does cleaning, so you keep out of my way when I'm working and I'll keep out of yours or else I'm outta here.'

Retelling this story would not elevate her in Marlene's mind, so Helen had come up with the ruse of calling Paula Porter Mrs P and making her sound like a sweet lady who was thrilled to be admitted to the glory of White Gables, instead of a woman who swore like a docker and chain-smoked apart from the six hours a week she stood inside the Brannigans' house.

Neither did she reveal the information that Mrs P and Kit got on famously, and when he was there, Paula went into his study to polish and their laughs – Paula's rough and too husky, Helen always thought with disapproval – could be heard all over the house.

'This is the pink dress I wore to the races.' Helen, who knew where all her clothes were because she spent a lot of time in her dressing room inspecting them, pulled out a hanger and held it up like a Dior saleslady holding a 4,000-euro jacket out for admiration.

'Lovely,' breathed Marlene.

They both looked. The pink dress was short, flouncy, just to the knee, and although Helen was proud of her knees and felt she could have modelled, really, if only she'd had the chance, she wondered if it would be rude to wear something short to an evening event.

Even this, even with her legs...

Marlene, giddy with getting her hands on the closet, pulled out a long silver dress, all lace and curlicues, and with a high collar.

'This is beautiful,' she said, almost squeaking with delight.

'A bit out of date,' said Helen, who didn't want to say that it had been cheap as chips and made her look old.

She wasn't old. Sixty-four was young these days. Sixty was the new fifty, really, and nobody said she looked her age. Not like Nora, God help her, who looked older because she hadn't a clue about night creams or using retinol or anything. Who knew what sort of outfit Nora would wear to the party? Some old black thing covered in dog hair probably. That thought, at least, cheered her up.

Not to be foxed by the rejection of her first choice, Marlene put the silver dress back and pulled out a black crêpe. It was like being a stylist, she thought happily.

'Too black.'

The long Schiaparelli pink that Trina said reminded her of a Barbie dress wasn't right, nor was the lilac lamé that Helen couldn't bear to throw out because once she'd had shoulders that could do the halterneck look. Their coffee was cold by the time they'd gone through it all and Helen had sunk into a state of depression.

Not even Marlene's joy at finding treasures like Helen's actual Chanel jacket, which had nearly given Kit palpitations when he discovered how much it had cost, nor the pleated old-gold dress she had bought on a shopping expedition in Browns in London once upon a time, which had been another palpitation event, could cheer her up.

'I suppose they all remind you of wonderful evenings out with Lottie,' said Marlene, putting a comforting hand on Helen's. 'It must be so dreadful to have lost your dear sister-in-law.'

'Yes,' said Helen, wondering if she dare ask Paula Porter to vacuum inside the wardrobes because, honestly, the amount of dust in there. 'Dreadfully sad.'

'I think you deserve something new, something fabulous to make up for the pain,' said Marlene.

Marlene never got anything thrilling to make up for anything and she would never have expected it. Her husband worked in insurance, she ran the house and the PTA, and any money left over went into taking care of their three children. But she had listened to poor dear Helen's sadness over her beloved sister-in-law and knew how difficult it must be to go to a party with Edward Brannigan's new wife.

Helen was loyal to her brother-in-law, of course, but it would be hard.

'You definitely need something new.'

Helen thought of how Bess Brannigan would have made another trip to somewhere exotic to buy her party outfits. New York perhaps. Paris. Milan! Her eyes narrowed at the thought.

It was one thing to get away with beauty and lovely legs when you were young, but when you were older, you needed serious clothes and serious jewellery. Kit couldn't possibly have been honest about them cutting back financially. He was only saying that, she was sure of it.

A little shopping trip was just what Helen needed.

'You know, Marlene, pet, I think you're right. It'll be in memory of dear Lottie. My way of saying: "I haven't forgotten you!"'

John Steele looked at the tour prospectus. It was his worst nightmare. What looked like every American city he had ever heard was in there, with early morning flights, late night flights and more hotel names than he could imagine ever seeing on TripAdvisor. Worse were the lists of interviews, only some of which he was to do when he was actually in the States.

'You'll do an enormous amount over the phone beforehand,' Gavin had said in that self-assured tone of his on the phone the previous day. 'And then there are the Q&A-style interviews and blog tours, that sort of thing.'

'What's a blog tour?' said John, wondering if he'd died and woken up in some alternate universe where the language was different. It was like those dreams of waking up in exam halls naked, without a pen and with absolutely no exam information in his head.

'You don't know what a blog tour is?' said Gavin in astonishment. 'Bloggers are hugely important in the business these days, and you go on their blogs and answer their questions.'

'What sort of questions?' asked John, feeling the sense of unreality grow.

'You know,' said Gavin, 'where you get your ideas from,

advice for other people on how to write books, that sort of thing.'

'But I'm very bad at explaining where I get my ideas from,' John said anxiously, thinking of how his close friends in West Cork teased him about listening in to their conversations and watching too much TV for his books.

'Yeah, I steal it all from *Criminal Minds* and *CSI*,' John would joke back, because how he actually created a book was such a complex thing that it was impossible to explain, and besides, he didn't want to make himself different from his friends in the village. It had been strange enough when he'd got his first book deal and some people had looked at him differently.

'Suppose you'll be the big man now round these parts,' a few grumpy old souls had muttered, and John had said he was still a carpenter and this was a bit of fun, because it was easier than saying writing was his first love but it was a temperamental, tricky love, like an exquisite girlfriend who was neurotic and you couldn't explain to people why you adored her so much.

All this talk of interviews was giving him that acidy sick feeling in the pit of his stomach, the same one he sometimes got when he looked out at the garden, the landscaping of which was nearly finished and the bill for ninety per cent of which was already lying on his office desk, preventing him from doing much work. It stared at him, all the noughts, all the VAT added on. Who'd have thought that a fish pond could be that expensive? And what had they needed a fish pond for in the first place?

When John had been a kid, fish had lived in a goldfish bowl; now they lived in what appeared to be the Four Seasons of swimming pools with all manner of vegetation and other stuff. There was even a hard cover to stop Jake from falling into it. *That* he approved of, but the rest of it...?

Someone had mentioned koi, which were the aristocrats of the fish world and cost thousands. What if next door's tribe of feral cats ate them in a sushi attack?

'You'll get the hang of the blog tour and the touring itself,' said Gavin cheerily, who wasn't the one who'd have to do any of it. 'It's really very easy. And I was thinking you could write maybe a couple of short stories and, most importantly, a Kindle single. Now, as you know, the Kindle single is a very important part of the market: maybe 10,000 words, short, snappy, designed to get people into reading your work. Priced at a couple of dollars max, they are really good for recruiting new readers.'

John had been silent.

'Recruiting new readers' – it made him think of the army recruiting new people to go to war or spy agencies recruiting young brilliant foreign language speakers from universities to spy for their countries. But recruiting new readers, this was a concept he hadn't ever thought about before, which was stupid because, obviously, they needed new people to start reading his books. The way Gavin spoke about the world of publishing and the way Cari had spoken about it were as different as chalk and cheese. With Gavin, it was a military mission: shock, awe, destroy.

Cari had never spoken to him in this way. When they weren't discussing the actual book in detail, they talked about practical parts of the book: the jacket copy, which was the wording on the back of the book and was really important because people only spent about six seconds reading it.

He could remember Cari explaining this to him in her own inimitable way: 'I know,' she'd said, 'you spend years of your life working your fingers to the bone and your brain to breaking point with this precious book and someone has to translate it into a mere hundred highly polished words so that someone en route to a train can get excited and take it to the till… I know the very thought makes you want to vomit, but that's what we have to do. We have to encapsulate the story so that people can grasp it quickly and decide they want to read it. Now of course, honey' – she laughed – 'with your name, they know they want to read it anyway. They love your books – you are brilliant. But we have to give them a clue as to what this one is about.'

Things had seemed different with Cari, more like she cared about the actual writing itself and how he, John, was dealing with it all. She was an editor, plot-analyser, plot-decoder when it was all going wrong, cheerleader, psychologist and main contact in the publishers all in one.

But Gavin was a different beast altogether. It was easy to see how Gavin was climbing up the ladder of publishing and would soon be running something big and wildly important because he had his eye on the main prize and that main prize was a combination of money and power. Making as much money as was humanly possible for the publishers, and himself into the bargain, and earning power along the way.

John felt left out of all of this, like an onlooker.

It was the first time in his career as a writer that he felt he didn't matter.

He'd never felt this with Cari.

He could remember her sitting in his garden on a sunny day, sipping tea and explaining that even though there was a huge amount of teamwork in the business, there was nothing to sell, there was no book to write a blurb about, there was no book to have an amazing cover for *if he did not write the book in the first place.*

'There's a lot of magic in this business,' she used to say, smiling. 'One of my old bosses always said it was all magic, and black magic at that,' and she'd laughed. 'Ivanka Radisky-Clarke was her name. She was fabulous, you'd have loved her, John: Ivanka drank Virgin Marys all morning until noon and then she switched over to Bloody Marys. Marvellous woman, a bit nuts, but I think that helped. And yet when she talked about there being magic in the business, she was right: the magic is in the book, because if the book doesn't work, if the book doesn't touch people and light them up, then there is nothing to sell.

There is nothing for the sales team, there is nothing for the marketing team, there is nothing for any team, there is nothing for me to edit. Always remember, *you* create the magic.'

John Steele looked now at his touring schedule, a schedule that would take him away from his beautiful West Cork haven for nearly five weeks, five weeks of strange hotels, of never being in the same place twice and more flights than he'd care to mention. Afterwards, he'd have enough air miles to go outside the Milky Way if required, but he might go mad into the bargain. And he had to do interviews over the phone and answer questions about his motivation and do blog tours beforehand ... wow.

He couldn't talk to Mags about it. She'd been worried when he'd said he was moving from being edited by Cari.

'But you love her, she grounds you,' Mags had said.

'Freddie said it would be good for my career,' John had pointed out, full of the new vision of himself as a publishing monolith, as proposed by his agent.

He could hardly go to either Freddie or Mags now and say he was full of anxiety, worried about the new book, even more worried about going insane on a five-week-long book tour where he would be wildly out of his comfort zone.

He would have to shut up and deal with it.

Cari couldn't stop thinking about Conal. Four days had passed since their blind date at Jeff's and he had been disturbing her daily – and nightly – ever since. And not a single phone call since that first one she'd ignored, which annoyed the hell out of her because she expected him to call and she'd planned to tell him, no she couldn't possibly go out with him. All of which advance planning was wasted seeing as he didn't call again.

She took to dropping into Jeff's office more frequently than normal, ostensibly to talk to him about work but hoping he might mention that Conal had asked about her or was pining for her but didn't have the courage to phone or *something*.

No joy. Not a word. Either Jeff was losing it – a possibility given his sleep deprivation issues – or Conal really hadn't asked after her. Bummer.

Not only had she screwed up her career, three years out of the game meant she'd lost her ability with men.

She was at her computer, wearily working her way through her endless line of emails – why were there so many? Did they multiply like rabbits in the night? – when Jeff burst in and her first, wildly embarrassing, thought was: Conal has rung and says he must see me now!

Jeff threw his lanky body down onto one of Cari's chairs.

'I love this book, this A.J. Sharkey person. It's brilliant. I love the narrative arc, that simplistic style that lulls you into a false sense of security and then, when you're thinking one thing, another story comes out of nowhere.'

This was the one subject destined to cheer Cari up. She still felt the chill every time she picked the manuscript up. But she needed some sort of go-ahead from Jeff before approaching the author. She'd fought for it, told him how she loved it and so did everyone else in the team, but Jeff needed to be on board too.

'It's got to be a woman but sent in by an agent or unsolicited, remind me?'

Since she'd told him all of this already, Cari sighed quietly. 'I agree, it's got to be a woman but I don't know for sure since they used initials. Also, no agent – off the slush pile. I found it, Declan loves it and so do Alice and Gloria. There aren't many books we all love.'

'Put me down in the "love it" column too, then,' Jeff said, yawning. 'We've got most of it, right? Ninety per cent. Has she/ he written it all? Is there more? Have they sent it to anyone else…?'

That was always the fear – that the fabulous manuscript was on the desk of every editor in town.

'I was waiting for you to get back to me. I'll courier a

response right now. There is no email, which is weird. I mean, who doesn't have email, right?'

'Yeah, get him, her or it in here soon. I just get that feeling when I read it—'

'Me too!' said Cari.

Jeff was clearly finished. He got up to go, then turned back to her.

'Oh yeah, has Conal been talking to you?'

'Er, no,' said Cari, managing what she thought was Academy-Award-level acting in order to sound blasé.

'He wants to take you out to dinner.'

'Oh?' Cari was proud of that 'oh?' Meryl Streep and Helen Mirren would have applauded.

'He said he phoned you but I must have given him the wrong number.' Jeff did some head scratching and Cari wanted to slap him, hard. 'I can give him your home number and your mobile, the right one, OK? You wouldn't mind?'

'Sure, whatever,' said Cari with another award-winning little shrug. 'I'll free up some time in my calendar.'

All afternoon, she had to control herself from slamming her direct dial office phone number on a bit of paper in front of Jeff, who was half asleep, and saying: 'Give it to Conal, NOW.'

Jeff had her phone number, obviously, but he needed a spur. Or a lightning bolt to the head – one or the other.

By evening, she had dispatched a courier to the writer's address with a plea to contact them, a paean of love for the story and the writing, and plenty of enthusiasm for what Cambridge could bring to its publication.

As she always did when she sent such letters or emails, she closed her eyes and said a brief prayer up into the sky and the divinity residing there, asking for help.

'I would love to publish this book,' she murmured, and suppressed the thought that she deserved some good karma after losing her star author, John Steele, so horribly. Karma and destiny were fickle things and one could not bargain one's way into receiving either at a specific time.

Then, she cleared her zillion emails, tidied her desk, and finally made herself face into a second, lengthy explanation to one of the writers on her slush pile to explain that yes, when she said she'd originally emailed to say that she didn't think the book was publishable partly due to the subject matter and certainly at its current length of approximately 4,000 pages, she'd meant it. She added, again, that autobiography was a tricky field.

'As I said before, your life seems very interesting—'

Cari sighed as she wrote this because it really was a red rag to a bull, but then saying, 'Like all of us, your life is a little on the ordinary side and if you want to write that sort of autobiography, then you have to be a fabulous writer and frankly, you're not, my dear, so I don't see this working...' Such a comment would be hideously cruel and she simply couldn't do it.

She was used to people at parties, when they heard what she did, regaling her with tales of their lives and exploits and delightedly telling her it would all make a fabulous book.

'I'd want a lot of money for it, though!' said one man, poking her in the ribs as he said this, as if he were a ball of fire with a story worth telling instead of being a perfectly nice but rather dull man from whom Cari had been stealthily moving away all evening.

'You wouldn't believe my life,' was another variation on the theme, often followed by: 'Do you have someone to do the words?'

'Yes, the words can be hard,' Cari would murmur. 'I know you're going to find this incredible but some people think the words are the hardest bit.'

'Never?'

'I know: amazing, isn't it?'

Cari tried again with the 4,000-page autobiography person.

'Many people write for themselves and not for publication. There is joy to be had in simply writing about your life for your own enjoyment. Think of how lovely it will be for your children to read this,' she wrote, and then thought about the bits about all the lovers, and hoped they'd cut those segments out before handing the epic over to the next generation for posterity.

She signed off and hoped to high heaven that she would not hear from them again. There really was a lot to be said for the returned manuscript and the printed note bearing the legend: 'Thank you for sending us your manuscript. I am afraid it is not suitable for our list. Wishing you the best of luck elsewhere.'

No, but thanks for thinking of us – to the point and polite, which was supposed to stop thwarted would-be writers from storming the place with pitchforks and a grudge.

It was half seven when she left the office and drove home, having decided that Conal had had no intention of phoning her and she must have imagined that white-hot heat of attraction between them. After all, it had been so long since she'd had anything to do with a man, she was bound to be rusty. That was a depressing thought – it was like having had a six-pack of belly muscles and finding out that overnight you were now the proud possessor of a flabby belly.

Well, she was going to stop that, she decided grimly, negotiating a traffic jam with unusual vigour: she was going to start dating again. She'd felt the wild thrill when she'd met Conal. She was still a woman, still a sexual being. Barney hadn't killed off that part of her totally, although she'd certainly felt as if he had.

But no: Cari Brannigan was a woman in her prime.

And if Conal didn't realise it, too bad for him. So there.

She pulled into her parking spot with slightly more speed than normal, slammed on the brakes and was giving herself empowering messages when her mobile phone rang.

It was an unknown number. The one she'd ignored before? This time, she'd clicked 'answer' and found herself breathlessly saying, 'Yes, hello.'

'I figured you were one of those people who didn't answer unknown numbers on their mobile.'

Conal. Excitement rippled through her.

'You could have just rung me at work,' Cari said, and then cursed herself. What sort of cretinous thing was that to say? It implied she had been sitting waiting for him to phone her. 'But this is fine,' she added quickly.

'Good,' he said, clearly doing the man-of-few-words thing.

'So,' said Cari, wanting to regain the upper hand.

'So yourself,' said Conal.

'You rang me for what exactly?' she asked, getting cross. Was this a game? Not phoning for days and then fun and games when he did ring.

'To ask you out.'

Cari's heart literally skipped a beat. She didn't know it could do that without one of Jeff's energy drinks.

'Oh, well, I mean … yes, er … what did you have in mind?' she stammered, hating herself for sounding like a love-struck fourteen-year-old.

'Dinner, where we can get to know each other, because drinks can be code for sitting in a bar and getting through two bottles of wine and I hate that sort of thing,' he said.

'I thought you had just come from France where people like sitting in wine bars and drinking two bottles of wine?'

Good retort, Cari, she told herself.

'Probably why I'm over it,' he said, 'and people don't really drink two bottles of wine in wine bars in France, not couples. Four people perhaps, two – no.'

'OK, dinner,' said Cari.

She liked this man. She really liked him. She didn't want to appear too eager, but she wanted to dispense with all the dating bullshit.

'Where were you thinking?' she said, as she pulled her diary out of her handbag, grateful that she was parked before the phone had rung and therefore she had a chance to check when she was free.

'Tonight,' he said.

'Tonight?' said Cari indignantly. 'Tonight is not suitable. Why would you think I'd be free tonight? Am I the sort of woman who has no friends and—'

He cut her off before she really got into her stride.

'No, I don't think you are the sort of girl who has no friends, but I really want to see you soon, even though I have a work thing early tomorrow – I always have work things early,' he added ruefully, 'but I didn't want to ring you in the office, and I don't want to wait ... and I wasn't sure you wanted to go out with me since you never picked up the first call.'

He sounded unsure and that made Cari all the more keen. For all that he put on a good cool superstud act, this man was nice, really nice.

'You rang?' she said innocently lying. 'There was no message.'

'Yes, I rang. First thing next day. Because I wanted to ask you out quickly, before someone else snapped you up, Cari.'

'Oh,' she subsided, feeling undone and unable to talk properly. 'My hair is a mess and it's sort of late, so we couldn't stay out too long because tomorrow is a work day,' she said. 'But yes, I'd love to go out tonight.'

'I'll pick up you then,' he said.

'There's no need,' Cari replied. 'I mean I can meet you there.'

'I'm not the sort of man who meets women in restaurants,' said Conal in a low growl. 'I pick them up and drive them or get a taxi, now give me your address.'

She had forty minutes to get ready and she raced around the apartment, feeling indeed for all the world like that fourteen-year-old on her first date.

Had she had a first date when she was fourteen? She didn't think so. Mum had been notoriously strict about dating and though there had definitely been some sort of school dance when she *was* fourteen, members of the parents' committee had stood on chairs every ten minutes to peer around and make sure nobody was kissing to the slow songs.

It had been very innocent. Cari hadn't had a proper boyfriend until she was seventeen. Davy. He had been such a darling, not at all the wild boy she had planned to go out with, the sort who had a worn leather jacket and had a motorbike. No, Davy was a jock, but incredibly clever. She'd loved the way he kissed, but he turned out to be not as interested in girls as he was in sports and even then there was a part of Cari that wanted the whole thing, the whole love story... Then Davy had gone off to college in Belfast, which had put the kybosh on the love thing anyway.

She stopped in front of her dressing table mirror and looked at herself.

She fluffled her hair up a bit because she didn't have time to wash it.

After quickly touching up her eye make-up, she pulled on a crimson silk shirt that worked with everything and lifted every outfit including the denim skinnies she was wearing with it. She rolled the jeans up and slipped on high biscuit-coloured slingbacks that didn't hurt and made her feet look long and elegant. Ten minutes and she was done, looking cool and elegant at the same time: no pushover, a clever woman who ran her own life and had a reasonable career.

Not a fabulous career, any more – not since John Steele had been taken away from her, but with a fairly decent career and if this new book turned out the way she'd hoped, maybe a damn good career again.

But still, hidden away behind that façade, was the girl Cari had tried to hide for so very long: the romantic. The romantic Cari Brannigan, forever hiding it behind spike heels and attitude.

The romantic had been flattened as if a steamroller had

driven over her when Barney had walked out on their wedding and Cari hadn't dared let her out since. But there was something about Conal, despite the sharp comments and the teasing, that made her long for romance, that sensed he was the man she was looking for.

'Get a grip on yourself, Brannigan,' she told her reflection, 'this is just a date. You haven't had a date for so long, so don't mess it up and don't go all gooey and romantic, right? And no talking about mummy porn or he'll think you're sex mad. Politics, books, science – all good.'

The restaurant Conal had picked was French, naturally, and when they got there, Conal spoke fluently to the owner, doing all sorts of complicated French cheek kissing and Gallic gesturing.

He'd obviously been there before as there was a certain amount of chatting with the waiters and then the chef had to come out, and for a moment, Cari had felt a bit surplus to requirements until Conal had put his arm around her and said, also in French, something that clearly implied that this beautiful woman was his date.

She knew enough French to pick up some of it, and then they all turned and admired her and made kissing motions to imply that yes, Conal had found the most exquisite creature and suddenly Cari found herself smiling and blushing and wondering where all her plans to hide the romantic had gone.

'I didn't know about this place,' she said as they sat down and several waiters made a great palaver about taking a water order and laying a napkin across her lap.

'I always come here when I'm back,' Conal said.

'You come back a lot then?'

'Yes,' he said, 'to see Jeff and the family. I loved living abroad but you know it can get lonely too.'

He looked wonderful tonight, even better than he had the first night, still the tall, dark Byronic hero, and Cari wondered what he was doing on his own. With that came the unwelcome thought that he probably hadn't been on his own for long and maybe that's why he was now lonely – because there had been a Mrs Conal somewhere in the picture...?

Although Jeff had never mentioned this, better to nail the details of previous women immediately, Cari thought. She wasn't going to be made a fool of twice. Complimentary glasses of wonderful champagne arrived, and as they drank them, Cari decided to start the inquisition.

'Have you been married before?' she asked.

'No. Next question,' he said, the corners of those mobile lips just turning up ever so slightly.

'Long-term relationships?'

'A couple.'

'The most recent?'

He sat back. 'You really want to know this early on in the relationship?'

'Yes,' she said. 'I was let down quite seriously once, which I'm sure Jeff explained to you, so I don't like to mess about.'

'I can tell that,' he said and those glittering eyes seemed to be glittering just for her, taking her in from her flushed face and her emerald eyes down to the lips she'd glossed with a crimson to match her shirt.

'I was let down a few times myself,' he said wryly.

'Really?' Cari asked. 'Tell me.'

'It's boring.'

'Not boring at all,' said Cari.

'No, really.' His fingers toyed with the stem of his wineglass. 'Not boring but painful and let's not talk about anything painful.'

'You are a man of contrasts,' Cari said.

'Late developer,' Conal said. 'I was the guy girls never looked at, stuck with my head in a book or a computer. You know the joke about research scientists? What's the difference between

277

an introverted research scientist and an extroverted one? The extrovert one looks at *your* shoes when he's talking to you.'

Cari laughed gently.

'You've got over that,' she remarked.

'Yes, Paris did help me. Nothing like the City of Lights to open you up to the possibilities of life. I grew up. I like your outfit,' he said, entirely changing the subject. 'You look beautiful. That shocked me the other night – Jeff never told me that.'

'So he told you all the other stuff?' Cari interrupted.

'He told me some of the other stuff,' Conal admitted. 'He told me a little bit in advance of your coming over for dinner, but I've got the rest out of him since then, because I was interested in you. But beforehand, before you turned up at his house, he never said how beautiful you were.'

She felt that little thrill of excitement inside her again and then quashed it.

'Does that line of chat work in France?'

'All the time,' he agreed. 'It's how I get women to fall into bed with me.'

'*Fall* into bed with you?' She laughed. 'That sounds like really sleazy seventies talk to me.'

'Yes,' he said, deadpan. 'I moonlight in sleazy 1970s TV shows. When I'm not doing that, I put bets on, you know: which woman is going to fall into bed with me first...'

She burst out laughing. 'I know you're joking.'

'Busted.' He held his hands up. 'How did you know?'

'All my CIA training,' she said.

'Very good,' he replied.

'You have a tell, like a poker tell,' she went on, not kidding. 'It's that little crinkle up to the left of your eye,' and she reached forward and nearly touched his face and then pulled back. What was wrong with her?

'Keep going on with the interrogation,' he said. 'Then afterwards, I get a go.'

'No, you don't get a go,' Cari said. 'You have Jeff to give you all sorts of background information on me and I have nobody, and you won't tell me your bad stuff.'

'Jeff would give you information,' he said.

'Jeff does not know which way is up since Jasmine arrived,' Cari pointed out. 'He really doesn't know night from day. It's a miracle he's still keeping his job. In fact, I'm keeping it for him,' she added, 'so there is absolutely no point in asking him anything about you, because he'll just tell me something you did that was adorable/desperate when you were both small children and that would be no use at all. So—' She smiled evilly. 'The most recent long-term relationship? Spill your guts.'

As was the norm with wonderful French waiters, they were hovering discreetly, waiting for a break in the conversation before they came forward.

'Let's order and then go back into the analysis of my life,' said Conal and Cari wondered if she was sensing hesitation. Was this the killer relationship he didn't want to touch upon?

They ordered quickly, and Cari decided upon mussels with garlic, not really caring if her breath was going to taste weird and garlicky if he kissed her later, because she was going to be herself and she liked garlic mussels and that was it. He ordered the same thing.

'So we'll both taste of garlic if we have to lean up against a wall and I have to kiss you,' he said.

'Do you also have a bet on with someone about that happening tonight?' Cari asked cheerfully. 'One of the waiters? The owner? Because you are going to be out of pocket.'

He laughed so loudly that the owner stared across at them and grinned, the grin of a Frenchman seeing a fellow man doing well with a woman.

'No,' he said, 'I wouldn't like to put bets like that on for a woman like yourself. You're more of a high-stakes classy casino bet instead of a grubby ten-euro bet.'

Cari raised her glass at him and smiled. 'Nice to know.'

As they ate he told her about a marvellous woman called

Yvette he had been with for two years and how they'd talked about marriage but somehow never quite got there.

'We were *simpatico*,' said Conal, with a distinctly Gallic shrug, 'and yet I don't know, neither of us ever saw a long-term future there. We had a great life – we had friends, people we went to the theatre with, people we went to dinner with, but I just couldn't see it for ever and neither could she.'

Cari didn't like this answer. Was this the woman who'd put the dark look on Conal's face or just someone he was prepared to talk about.

'Do you really mean *neither of you could see a future in it* or that you just told her it was over and then she agreed? Or did she dump you?'

'Ouch,' Conal replied. 'It wasn't like that, it genuinely was mutual. I'll give you her phone number: phone her, ask her. We're still friends. You can't be friends if you hate each other, right? There were a few others but Yvette's the most recent. Now, your go. Tell me about the man who dumped you?'

Cari shuddered. She could hardly blame him because she'd just interrogated him but weirdly and possibly for the first time in ages, it didn't hurt that much.

'I like it better when I ask the questions,' she said.

'I know.'

He patted her hand, a brief touch that felt electrifying and then went back to his food.

'Plus, there's something you're not telling me,' she added. But she would get it out of Jeff.

'Right,' she said, 'the man who dumped me: that would make a good title for a book wouldn't it.'

So she told him about Barney, just the bare facts, making it funny rather than sad and painful – the way it really had been.

Somehow, Conal's hand with its long, piano-player's fingers snaked across the table and entwined itself with one of her hands. 'Do you play the piano?' she asked.

And he laughed. He was laughing a lot, she thought, but

not in a laughing *at* her sort of way – more laughing with her, laughing at the fun of being with her. It was like he got her jokes, he appreciated her.

'I read this thing once,' he said, 'about how differently men and women's minds work, and we are thinking about one thing while women have extrapolated the conversation to such an extent that you are on a completely different topic altogether. So how did we get on to me playing the piano?'

'Your hands.'

They both looked down, and Cari found that both of her hands were on his single hand and she was stroking it as if learning its shape through braille, feeling the strength in his fingers and the sensitivity and wondering – oh, she was wondering! – what it would be like to have those hands touching her.

She wanted to pull away but she stopped herself. This was normal, this is what normal women did. They went out to dinner with men and thought about having relationships with them. Just because she had been so badly hurt and hadn't done this for three years meant that this sort of carry-on startled her a little bit. But no, she was not pulling her hands away, she decided with determination.

'I was thinking that you have long piano-playing fingers.' It sounded a bit daft now in retrospect.

'I did play the piano,' he said and she got the feeling that he liked her hands on his, 'played for years, but once I got to college I stopped and I can't tell you the last time I sat on a piano stool.'

'How wonderful,' said Cari with genuine admiration. 'I've never played an instrument. We were always a bit broke when we were growing up, too broke to buy a piano but Dad said he'd get us something. Then my little sister Maggie began to learn the recorder at school. In case you don't know, it's a bit of a sort of tin whistly type of instrument and could easily be used as a weapon of torture for terrorist cells. Well, it could be, the way Maggie played it. So I said she wasn't allowed to practise and really that put an end to her musical career. I must have been a horrible older sister.'

'I doubt that,' he said, doing that eye-glittering thing at her that made Cari's stomach feel hollowed out as if she were doing a loop the loop on a rollercoaster.

'What sort of music do you like?' he asked. 'Any classical? I have a thing for Chopin.'

'Imagine being able to play Chopin…' said Cari dreamily and she realised that she needed food after a glass of champagne, one of wine and a dose of rollercoaster-ness. She removed her hands because it seemed safer and grabbed her water instead.

More wine was poured when the mussels arrived and they lost themselves in talking about music, and how good the food was. They were both dunking big lumps of crusty bread into the garlicy wine sauce and she was having fun, Cari realised.

Fun and something more.

When the food was taken away, he reached across the table again and took her hands this time. And they kept holding on, it was like they didn't want to let go.

'Is everything all right? You're enjoying yourself?' said his friend, the restaurateur, coming over and giving Cari an admiring look.

There was a time when she'd have given him a tough squinty-eyed glare in return, as if to say, don't look at me like that, sonny boy, but tonight she didn't: tonight she'd beamed under his admiration.

'Oh it was fabulous,' she said, 'those mussels. Delicious.'

'I know,' he said, 'beautiful, fabulous, sensual.'

'Sensual,' agreed Conal, 'that's definitely the word.'

And he looked at Cari, who giggled. Somewhere along the way she'd told him the story about the mummy porn and how Declan, her editor colleague, could never eat another mussel again because of the goings on with shellfish in a recent attempt of *Fifty Shades of Grey*.

'Yes, very sensual, Jacques,' went on Conal.

Cari began to dissolve into giggles and under the table, Conal nudged her foot with his.

'I will leave you two alone then,' said Jacques and drifted off, poetry in motion in an elegant jacket.

'We could always tell him about the mussel story,' said Conal innocently.

'Oh hell, we couldn't,' said Cari. 'I would never be able to look him in the eye again.'

By mutual consent, they waved away the dessert menu and even when Jacques appeared proffering after-dinner drinks on the house, Cari and Conal said no.

Somehow the evening had heated up and Cari was aware of a fire in her belly, a desire she hadn't felt for – well, three years. The careful, cautious woman who hadn't had a man in her bed since Barney had last left it found that she wanted this man in the worst way possible.

She thought of how she'd have cautioned her sister Maggie and her cousin Trina against going to bed with a man on their first date. She thought of how she'd have told any young girl, 'No don't do this, this is a mistake, somebody has to care for you before you let them touch your body, there has to be mutual respect and kindness and...'

'Will we go?' Conal interrupted her thoughts.

'Yes,' she said.

They got a taxi back to her house, Conal's car left in a car park and the financially aware Cari didn't even mention that it was insane to leave it there overnight.

'I know this isn't a good idea,' Conal said, and he wasn't talking about leaving his beloved muscle car in a car park overnight. 'I planned to have no wine and drive you home sedately because this is officially only just our second date and I don't want to rush it.'

'You're right,' said Cari. Blast it, he was right. No rushing it. No flinging herself at this man. She searched deep inside herself for the logic switch and found it, remembering how long it was since she'd dated and how badly that had all turned out.

She stopped at the door and turned to him.

'Let's take this slow. I've been hurt—'

'I understand,' he said and leaned in for a kiss. 'Slow.'

'Slow,' agreed Cari.

She had once thought you didn't truly know a person till you lived with them, but she now knew that was wrong. She'd lived with Barney and she'd known nothing. Her new measuring stick was how they kissed and Conal's kiss was like nothing she'd ever experienced.

He held her gently as if she was something rare and precious, and touched her lips with his, deepening in intensity until one hand was caressing her face as his tongue reached in to tangle with hers, his other hand was around her waist, pulling her close, and she decided that she must have been mad: she wanted him to come in immediately.

'You're beautiful,' he said in a deep voice.

'Don't forget funny,' she murmured into his mouth.

'Funny. Delicious.' The kiss hardened.

'Deliciously weird?' she said.

'Just delicious,' he said and he pulled away, slowly.

'If I don't go now I won't be able to leave,' he said. 'So I will bid you adieu and call you tomorrow.'

'Tomorrow?' said Cari, leaning against her door.

'Tomorrow.'

He waited until she was inside and then kissed his fingers and waved them gently at her.

She grinned and pretended to catch the kiss.

'Where do you want me to put it?' she teased, expecting him to say something sexy.

'In your heart,' he said and he was gone.

In her apartment, Cari danced around for a moment and wished she had someone she could phone to tell them about this glorious date, but the person she'd have liked to have phoned was Jojo, and she couldn't tell her any of this. When you were in the depths of despair, other people's happiness hurt even more.

The next morning, Conal phoned at twenty to eight.

'Just going into a meeting,' he said, 'but I wanted to talk to you first.'

'Remind me never to be a scientist,' Cari said, smiling as she stood at her car, ready to get into it for the commute to work. 'I'm just leaving home.'

'What are you up to this evening?'

'I thought I might wash the kitchen floor or my hair – hard decision to make,' teased Cari.

'How about you leave them both in a state of unwashness and come see a movie with me?'

Cari mentally booked a lunchtime appointment with the hairdressers near the office. The kitchen floor could go hang, not that she'd planned to wash it anyway.

'I'd love it.'

Seventeen

Bess knew that Edward's seventieth was going to be a fabulous party. Catering, flowers, rooms, a band who could cover a repertoire from Glenn Miller to Elvis Presley: everything was organised.

Except for her and Edward. They were in chaos: organised chaos in that they spoke civilly at the breakfast table each day and discussed the events of said days over dinner in the evening. But the spark, the love, had vanished from their marriage. It was as if, Bess thought, Edward had decided that he had to make a choice between her and Jojo. He could only love one of them and he had chosen Jojo.

'What's your day like today?' he'd ask as they sat at the breakfast table, him reading the paper, Bess scanning her diary.

'The usual,' she'd say and she'd long for those early days in their marriage when he'd wonder if she could have lunch with him? If she could skip home early? If they could go to see a film and have dinner?

On those days, he'd have woken her with gentle kisses: Edward always woke before she did.

'Morning sleepyhead,' he'd murmur, feathering kisses along her neck and then kissing her properly, before they'd reluctantly agree that they had to get up for work.

286

Sometimes they showered together, making love before returning to the mundanity of getting dressed.

'You'll kill me, Mrs Brannigan.' Edward would grin at her, towel wrapped around his waist.

'You'll kill me first, Mr Brannigan,' she'd say, swatting his behind and going to get dressed, knowing she had that flush of lovemaking burnished across her face.

None of that ever happened now. No. They were like people married alive, only worse. Because they had so much unspoken between them.

Bess was scared to say anything because she – she who was supposed to be tough as steel – was afraid he'd send her away and then this marvellous love would be over. And she was still hoping.

She went about her days in a haze of pain. Who knew love could hurt this much?

How could she last until the party was over? Because she wouldn't walk out now but when it was over, afterwards, she would quietly disappear from Edward's life.

It would kill her to do it but she had some self-respect left.

She still had her own apartment. She wouldn't take much, although she wanted her crazy painting of the jungle and the tiger. She'd come to love it: it symbolised the new Bess in some way. A woman who'd thought love didn't exist.

It existed all right, she knew that now. But it couldn't last. Hadn't lasted. Jojo would get her father all to herself.

Bess had taken another trip to Lisowen to finalise these last-minute details and now she walked round the ballroom in Lisowen listening to the hotel's banqueting manager reassuring her that everything would be wonderful.

To get here, she'd got up extra early and taken the first flight to Farranfore airport. It was the fourth day trip she'd taken and she felt bone-tired. At the start, she'd had such plans about this party. It was to be a showcase of her love for Edward and now ... Now it felt like a coda to a marriage.

'With the candles glittering off the crystal and the dark red roses, the room will look so beautiful,' the catering manager was saying.

Bess wanted to cry as she admired the beautiful ballroom with its high ceilings and huge mullioned windows, which must have given some poor window cleaner nightmares. Years ago, Edward had looked from the outside in, the poor local kid from a tiny farm staring in, nose metaphorically pressed up against the window as he imagined the great life of the people living within.

Bess knew the Villiers family had been broke for many years before they'd finally sold the property and that scandal had dogged the lives of the last generation of Villiers, one of whom had died on the French Riviera in murky circumstances, something to do with a young girl and an enraged father.

She'd learned all of this from the various people in the castle, many of whom were not originally from the area but who knew of the castle's original owners.

'There was something bad in the last of them,' the reservations lady had told Bess when they'd been discussing the rooms everyone in the family would have. 'If your husband's from round here, he must know about it,' she'd said.

'No,' said Bess. 'They all moved away long ago.'

'Well, it'll be lovely to come back here and see the place as it was once,' the lady said cheerfully.

Bess had nodded. It would be lovely for Edward but not for her. If something didn't change soon, she would be gone from his life.

Lottie would be the one he thought of when he came here again, not her.

Lena was happy they were flying home to Ireland for the birthday party.

'I can't wait,' she kept saying to Paul, dashing round the apartment as she made lists of what she needed to pack and what they'd need for Heidi on the plane. Little Heidi was wonderful on planes: well, she had been on the previous two trips to Ireland, and Lena had been dreading the first one when Heidi was four months old.

Then, hours of internet surfing had left her miserably telling Paul that four-month-old babies and their parents really needed to be secreted in a separate part of the plane to all the other passengers because mothers' message boards were full of dark tales of small babies who wailed non-stop on long flights; of people who'd come up to mothers and screamed at them to keep their child quiet; of those rare parents without babies who sent sympathetic glances in the crying baby's parents' direction.

'My sisters say she's too young for an antihistamine: they make them drowsy,' Lena reported before that first trip home.

'Drug her?' said Paul, shocked.

Lena's two older sisters had big families, four and five children each, and one had practically given birth to her latest child near the soft drinks section of Aldi. They were all wildly laid-back about parenting at this stage, and he realised that mention of something to calm the baby's nerves was probably normal to them.

'Not drug her but there's this stuff and it's for itching and it makes them tired...' said Lena, looking as if she might cry herself. 'I'm just a hopeless mother: I don't know all this stuff...'

Paul put his arm around her and kept a wary ear out for Heidi because it was evening, just around the time when the colic kicked in. Nothing appeared to fix colic and to see Heidi crying killed him. He wasn't sure how he'd cope on a plane if Heidi sobbed all the way. The other passengers could go hang: Paul had enough of his father's strength not to care too much about what other people thought.

'You're a wonderful mother,' Paul said, kissing his wife, and wishing as he so often did that his own mother had been alive to see his baby daughter coming home to Ireland for that first time.

If you're watching, Mum, thank you for everything, he thought silently.

Lottie, with her great emotional intelligence and gentleness, had made him able to understand a little of what Lena was going through.

On that first trip, four-month-old Heidi had not cried non-stop. She had been the model of the perfect child and as they'd disembarked in Dublin, one harassed mother with a toddler who'd treated the back aisles as an Olympic track training field carried him off as he slept, worn out with his efforts, and she shot Paul with a sideways glance.

'Antihistamine medicine?' she said.

Now, for this third trip, Heidi would be a seasoned traveller, although Paul fully expected her to use her new-found moving skills to belt up and down the aisles the whole time.

'I'm so glad you're coming, son,' Edward said to Paul on the phone.

'As if I'd miss it,' said Paul, who was trying to feed an increasingly naughty Heidi her breakfast.

Lena was getting ready for work and they'd already had a fraught shouting match about who was responsible for the main burden of the childcare.

Paul thought he did pretty well but Lena said no, she was doing far more.

Heidi, who had a throwing arm like a quarterback, grabbed her juice beaker and flung it at the wall where the lid banged off and juice splattered all over the recently painted wall.

Paul tuned out of what his father was saying for a moment, something about Jojo and Bess.

It had cost a fortune to get the apartment repainted and Lena had been irritable with him because she felt he should have done it himself. But the office was mental and he'd never been brilliant at home improvements.

'Yeah, Dad, gotta go,' he said. 'See you in a week. Can't wait.'

Edward met his brothers for a round of golf on Saturday morning. Kit loved golf and had once been a single-figure handicapper. Mick was mainly a pitch and putt man, but he loved the chance to whack the ball down the fairway at Edward's exclusive golfclub. He didn't care if he didn't win but when he did, he loved taking the fiver off Edward.

The three men and their wives were then going to dinner that night in the clubhouse. Edward, who'd arranged it weeks ago, was regretting it all.

Not the notion of dinner with Nora – no, he always had all the time in the world for Nora. But the thought of having to be nice to Helen when he was feeling so anxious, and he was sure she'd be watching Bess like a hawk just for the sake of it.

If anyone was going to spot a hiccup in the new marriage, it was Nora. But if anyone was going to loudly comment upon the hiccup, it was Helen.

And right now, his and Bess's marriage was one long hiccup.

He was trying his best to be a good husband, trying to recapture some of the easiness of the early days of their marriage, but it had just vanished. They were like people in a play, pretending to be married.

He knew he had to take responsibility for some of this but it was all so difficult – he wished they'd never planned this damned party in the first place. Perhaps then, eventually, Jojo would have come round to the idea of Bess being his wife and perhaps then, he'd have been able to enjoy simply loving Bess.

But it was too late to back out now. The damage was done.

'Any plans for the day?' Edward had said to Bess before he left that morning. For a long time, she'd been spending her Saturdays in the garden when he played golf.

'I've never gardened before,' she'd said that first day, when he arrived home to find her exhausted, smudged with dirt but delighted with herself because of the flower beds she'd weeded.

'It's very satisfying, isn't it?' she'd said. 'You do a bit and it's done – not like work in the office which seems never-ending.'

'Weeds grow back,' Edward had reminded her fondly, kissing her smudged cheek.

'That's another day's work,' said Bess, satisfied. 'I need a bath. Do you want to share one?' And she'd shot him that sensual, loving glance he simply couldn't resist.

Gardening had been her way of putting down roots, making the home her own, he knew now.

However, she'd stopped the gardening. It was as if she was considering leaving and didn't want to expend any more time on the place. Edward could sense this but he had no idea how to fix it.

'Not sure,' she said brightly, too brightly. Definitely like people in a play. 'I might drop in to the office. I've been neglecting it lately.'

Edward had driven off in a very bad mood.

He'd told her to cut back on work – he'd loved the idea that his wife, who had always worked so hard, needed to work less and delegate work to her partner because she was now married to a rich man. Subtly, she was telling him that she had her own life, her own business. An independent woman could always leave.

He hated the thought of that.

'How's Bess? Up to ninety about the party? Only a couple of weeks to go,' said Mick as he and Edward walked down the third fairway, Kit wandering off to the rough because he'd hooked his drive to the left.

'Not really,' sighed Edward. 'She could organise it in her sleep. She's upset, though because of Jojo and Jojo not wanting to come.'

'Ah,' said Mick, with the wisdom of a man who could see it all. 'Not easy for you, Ed, to sort through it all. It's hard for

292

Jojo, for sure, but you deserve a bit of peace in your life now. Jojo's young, got her life ahead of her.'

'Yes!' Edward wanted to say, 'Yes, but it's making me feel guilty and I can't bear that and yet I love Bess and...'

'Found my ball!' roared Kit.

'What would you do in my shoes?' Edward asked quickly.

Mick gave him a sympathetic look. 'I don't know,' he replied. 'You won't lose Jojo, she'll come round eventually. But you might lose Bess.'

Then Kit took the shot, and came back out onto the fairway, waiting for his brothers to join him, and the chance for more conversation was gone.

Nora met Bess in the ladies' room in the golf club that evening.

'Edward told me you were in here,' said Nora, hugging her sister-in-law. 'Thought I'd say hello before we went to the table. Helen and Kit are here already.'

Bess groaned.

'I nearly pulled out of this, Nora,' she said. 'I can't face Helen. She looks at me as if she's calculating the net worth of everything I own and she will just take one look at me and Edward and know it's not all rosy in the garden. I can't cope with an evening of her looking at me speculatively.'

'We'll cope together,' said Nora, putting her arm through Bess's companionably. 'I'll ask her opinion of what to wear to the party and you can pretend to be listening, fascinated.'

'That seems unfair,' said Bess.

'Look, I'm not interested in clothes but she is, so I let her talk about what interests her,' said Nora simply. 'There's no malice in it. It makes her happy. She loves her clothes and you know I don't care about them. She isn't interested in books or dogs or gardening or a new recipe for bread or any of the things I like, so I make the effort for her and don't let it get to me that it never occurs to her to make the effort for me. It's compromise.'

'I wish everything was as easy to fix with a bit of compromising,' said Bess bitterly. 'It hasn't worked for me. Edward's never going to have a showdown with Jojo. He can't bear to look at me these days because he sees Jojo's face and knows that his being with me is hurting her.'

'And that's destroying your marriage,' said Nora flatly. 'Compromise works for me and Mick. That's how we're happily married. Not that he's an old shoe and I'm an old sock. We work at it. We compromise.'

'You shouldn't have to compromise on everything,' said Bess.

'In business, maybe, but in marriage ...' Nora laughed quietly. 'Compromise and respect rule. When you stop respecting your spouse, when you look or talk to them with contempt, when you deliberately hurt them – those things destroy love and marriage.

'Remember that your husband is not put on earth to make you happy, that's your job. Respect them, understand that marriage isn't easy and compromise is important and then – it can work. OK, lecture over. Let's go and talk gowns ...'

'No, don't go.' Bess held on to Nora. 'I understand what you're saying but it's not that easy. Jojo is literally the third person in our marriage. Edward had no idea how upset she was about me and the birthday party in Lisowen has underlined it for him. He's never said a word but I can tell that it's wrecking everything we have. This isn't about me worrying about Jojo. It's gone way beyond that now.'

Her voice had risen but Bess no longer worried if anyone heard them. 'I honestly don't care if Jojo comes to the party in Lisowen or not. I want my husband back but he's so caught up in this that he thinks that if he loves me, he's betraying his daughter. I don't even think he knows it but that's the truth. He has backed away from me in every sense and he doesn't even realise it.'

'Oh, Bess, I am so sorry. But he loves you, he will come round. You have to show him that it's not worth wrecking your marriage over whether or not Jojo accepts you at this point, Bess. You make Edward happy. Jojo makes him happy. Perhaps you are both never going to be in the same room at the same time without sparks flying, but luckily, she's a grown-up with her own life and not a four-year-old.'

'One problem,' said Bess grimly. 'Edward's not happy any more. Neither am I. Jojo's magic has succeeded. The only way I can tell him what's happening is to tell him his beloved little girl has ruined our marriage and that will go down really well. I can't see us getting over this.'

Nora looked crestfallen. 'Please don't say that,' she said. 'He loves you; he needs you and you love him.'

'It's not that easy, Nora. There's so much stacked against us.'

'Please try, give him a chance. He's such a good man, Bess,' begged Nora. 'He's not good at talking about feelings, Lottie—' She stopped.

'Lottie always said that, did she?' asked Bess bitterly. 'You can say Lottie's name because Lottie is not the one between us. It's Edward's daughter, not Lottie, ironically enough. I thought the dead wife would be the one who'd scupper us but it isn't.'

'Give him a chance,' said Nora, grabbing Bess's hand.

Tears filled Bess's eyes. She couldn't trust herself to speak. All she wanted was to give her husband a chance but he had to respond. Was that too much to ask?

Helen was at the table done up to the nines and looked at Bess as if already assessing the cost of her outfit and jewellery, but Bess gave her a smile.

'Hello, Helen,' she said.

She then sat down beside Edward and reached for his hand under the table.

Surprised, he squeezed it back.

Compromise just a little more, she thought. Understand that Edward wasn't good at explaining his feelings. She wanted this marriage to work, so she'd keep trying. Give him time to see that he could love her and Jojo. And hope it would work.

Eighteen

SECRETS OF A HAPPY MARRIAGE #6

Bleaching your upper lip – that's the biggest secret in your
marriage. Ask yourself, would it break your other half's heart?
If the answer is yes, the secret behaviour needs to stop.

On Sunday morning, Hugh sat on the bathroom floor with
Jojo and felt her sob in his arms.

Not pregnant. For the third time, not pregnant.

The stick lay on the floor and Hugh wondered if he jumped
on it, would it signal his own rage and hopelessness at this
exact moment.

Jojo had woken at six, her eyes feverishly excited.

'It's day sixteen!' she said, as if he didn't know.

Neither of them had slept much the night before but they'd
lain there side by side, each trying to sleep, each pretending
to sleep, he was sure, because they couldn't bear to talk to the
other.

To talk might be to discuss the test and what would happen
if Jojo wasn't pregnant.

He knew Jojo could not bear to imagine this. And neither
could he.

So they'd lain there in silence.

'I can't believe it, I was sure, this time,' sobbed Jojo, her
whole body vibrating with the intensity of her grief. 'Third
time lucky...'

'Me too,' he whispered.

He could say nothing else, offer no hopeful 'next time' conversations because Hugh wasn't sure if he could go through
this again. In fact, he knew he couldn't.

Jojo would kill him if he didn't agree to another cycle, he was pretty sure of that. She was obsessed.

He leaned in to her hair, waiting for the moment when she'd move away from him.

Jojo leaned against Hugh, wishing she was being comforted by her mother instead of him.

Lottie had gone with love and grace and wisdom.

'Live your life, please, my darling,' Lottie had said to her before the drugs had really taken hold and she had become glazed before she died.

Her mother had been ready. It was too soon but she had been ready.

In the same way, the tiny embryos inside Jojo had not been ready to go and yet life hadn't been breathed into them.

She felt hollow with pain. So much that she didn't know if she could bear it any more. Nobody understood. How could they?

'Will you come downstairs with me and I'll make us some tea,' said Hugh helplessly. It was the most useless gesture in the world but he didn't know what to say any longer. Everything had been said.

Every word of pity and sympathy and pain had been ground out.

Jojo shook her head and pushed him away.

'No, you go. Leave me alone.'

Hugh was shocked.

'Jojo?'

'Sorry,' she said, her eyes blurred with tears. 'I'm better on my own.'

In the days following, Hugh felt as if he'd lost Jojo. She looked thinner, if that was possible, and yet he watched her eat and fed her fruit smoothies laced with protein in the morning to keep her strength up. It was like taking care of someone who was convalescing.

Emotionally, she was there – but not quite there.

Over a year ago, pre-fertility treatment, he and Jojo would have sat down and talked out their worries.

They might have taken a cheapie weekend away, hiked a bit up a mountain, which always brought the clarity Hugh liked. Then curled up in a cosy small hotel with nice food, drinks and good books, which cleared Jojo's mind.

How long was it since they'd done such simple things?

That had been the best of their marriage – the simple stuff: the talking, the hugs over breakfast, reading the papers on a Sunday morning, lying in bed at night when they were both too tired to talk and just drifting off to sleep, spooned against each other.

That was what had made their marriage perfect. Now those simple pleasures were gone.

Jojo had changed. Her mother's death, her failure to get pregnant and then her father marrying again: it had all pushed her over the edge.

Hugh had changed too out of worry. He simply wasn't sure they could ever recapture the early days.

He knew marriages went through different stages, from the honeymoon of not wanting to be out of each other's sight for more than a working day to the normality of arguing over who took out the bins, but this... this ennui was different.

They'd heard all that talk about the physical side-effects of infertility treatment but it looked as if Jojo was falling apart emotionally. There were no special injections for that, no emergency treatment for fixing a shattered psyche.

He knew that Jojo would literally kill him if he rang the fertility psychologist to ask if this was normal. That might ruin their chances of another cycle and without the hope of a baby, their marriage would be over. He knew that now.

He just didn't want Jojo lost in this half-world she seemed

to be in. Grief had made her float away from him on a bubble of pain. She showed no sign of caring if she ever floated back again.

He needed to talk to Nora, but he didn't know how to begin. Nora was the closest person to his wife other than Maggie, Cari and her father. Edward was clearly out of the picture now ... and he couldn't talk to Edward because of the Bess situation.

He had to talk to Cari.

He phoned, said he needed her help and heard Cari breathe shakily.

'Oh, Hugh, I haven't known what to do!' she said, sounding absolutely nothing like his normally self-assured cousin-in-law. 'I was in Belfast yesterday at a conference and I phoned her on a whim and she sounded terrible. I said could we meet up but she said no, she couldn't see anyone.'

'She never told me,' he said dully, 'but then she doesn't talk to me either.'

'Hugh, I've been backing off because infertility treatment is such a couples thing, but I've been so worried. This past week, she's barely spoken to me.'

'We were in the final stage, waiting for the pregnancy test,' said Hugh. 'She can't cope with anyone knowing any more. We took the test on Sunday morning – it was negative. She's falling apart and pushing me away.'

'Oh, Hugh,' repeated Cari miserably.

They met at a small café in town in the morning – Hugh had managed to grab a few moments from work and Cari had managed a quick trip out of the office to meet an author.

'We're having one of our girls' nights in at the weekend, you know that?' Cari said. 'I was sort of hoping to get a feel for how she was, because I haven't seen her for ages: she keeps putting me off, saying she can't meet me at weekends. She keeps saying you guys are doing stuff at the weekends.'

'We're not doing anything,' said Hugh glumly. 'She's either

in the shop or she's sitting at home in front of the television as early as she can, not really watching anything, to be honest. Since Sunday, she goes to work without speaking and if she does speak, she snaps at me, like it's my fault.'

'She wouldn't tell me the date of the test,' said Cari. 'She told me the first time.'

Hugh grimaced. 'Incredibly stupidly, we were both too convinced it was going to work the first time – like every lottery ticket purchaser, I guess. I don't know why, but we had this idea because we were young and healthy and we had all these amazing people working with us – we assumed that it was going to happen, we were going to be the one in five or whatever statistic you look at, and we were going to be pregnant.'

He stirred his coffee. He had gone off the taste of coffee, gone off the taste of so much food. Hunger was important, Hugh realised, and when you felt broken-hearted and weary, you had no appetite. 'Then we did the first test and discovered she was not pregnant.'

Cari watched him, waiting. Hugh looked older, tireder. Gone was the jokey friend who could say anything to her and teased her about books she'd published recently, or praised her for one he loved.

'The second time it didn't work, it killed us both. It does something to you, just pulls the rug out from under your feet. Everyone can get pregnant. People who really, really don't want to manage to have babies and you, who do, can't manage it. I don't care what religion you are, or what you believe in, you begin to think it's punishment and that it will never happen, that with each negative result, you're getting another karmic slap on the wrist.'

'You sound like Lottie,' said Cari.

'I wish she was here,' Hugh sighed. 'She could have helped Jojo, could have made sense of it all. I certainly can't. Jojo might say, "It's *us* going through this" but inside her, it's her battle to be a mother. Her biological imperative, her fierce drive to have a baby, perhaps to make up for that fierce love she had for her own mother. I don't know,' he added wearily. 'My feelings sort of fade into the background, and that's hard too. Like I don't matter.' He laughed without humour. 'Just as well I'm not in the divorce law section,' he said. 'I'd really be a hit with my current mood.'

'It's not at that point?' said Cari carefully. Hugh and Jojo had one of the best marriages she knew.

Hugh shrugged. 'Jojo barely talks to me any more. She wouldn't let me tell anyone about this – it had to be a secret and that wasn't fair. I know—' He held his hands up. 'Wildly ironic: a lawyer saying something is unfair, but I needed someone to confide in and Jojo insisted no. I couldn't tell my brothers, anyone.

'The secrecy gets to you. At first, I was so sure it would work out but now, I've begun to see us as part of the other group, the group who try and try and plough all their savings into it and never end up with a baby. And split up.'

Cari put a hand on his.

'Don't,' she said, 'that's not going to happen to you, I have never seen people more in love.'

'Yes,' he said bitterly, 'but this rips through love, this is a scalpel slicing through love, ripping it to bits. Having a baby is supposed to the most natural thing in the world and if it's not the most natural thing in the world, it tears everything up. You know I wanted to stop? I said it to her before we went in for this third cycle. I said we should take a break, because it had affected her so badly, but she insisted. She made me go in. I had to pretend she was fine to the clinic's psychologist when I knew she wasn't, so this is my fault.'

Cari interrupted him. 'It's not your fault, you were just trying to do the right thing.'

Hugh ran a hand through hair that looked too long and messy, another very un-Hugh-like thing. Normally he was so neat, so professional-looking. 'I don't know what the right thing is any more. I need to get her help but I don't know how. This fight between her father, Bess and the whole seventieth birthday disaster in Lisowen isn't helping.'

'Do you think,' Cari said, 'we should wait until after that and then see how Jojo is, because once that's over, it might help her turn a corner.'

They both looked at each other hopefully.

'My mum would be a great person to talk to about this,' Cari added.

'I know,' said Hugh, 'but Jojo was so adamant that nobody else knew.'

Her mum and Uncle Ed could help but if Uncle Ed knew, then Bess would know and Jojo would rather rip off her own leg than let Bess know.

'It's terrible that Jojo hates Bess so much. I know Bess is spiky, and a million miles away from Lottie, but Uncle Ed deserves happiness.'

'I agree,' said Hugh, 'but I dare not ever say that to Jojo or she would totally divorce me.'

'After the seventieth, which is soon. Let's see how she is and make a call then, right?' said Cari.

'OK,' said Hugh, 'till then.'

'I'm going to see her later today – drop into the shop. Pretend we haven't talked?'

'Pretend whatever you like,' said Hugh, 'if you can make her smile, bring her back to me.'

Jojo was folding little T-shirts that just refused to lie flat. The seams were crooked and no matter how she squashed them on the counter and moulded them around the little folding board, they emerged at angles with creases in the wrong places.

'These are useless!' she yelled at Elaine, who had spent the afternoon redoing the window, which was normally Jojo's job.

'But they sell,' said Elaine, who was seeing a new man and

who found that if she thought about him, she could cope with whatever was making Jojo so very... un-Jojo-like.

'Still crap,' said Jojo, hurling the whole lot to the floor.

'OK,' said Elaine, adjusting the angle of a necklace on the mannequin in the window and deciding that it all looked fabulous. 'Spill. Are we bankrupt, the shop has to close and you don't know how to break it to me? Because it has to be something big.'

'I could live without the shop,' said Jojo, sitting on the stool behind the counter.

Elaine was rattled out of her sangfroid for once.

'What is it?' she demanded. 'This is your dream, your baby—'

At that word, Jojo simply crumpled. She leaned over herself as if she had a knife in her stomach and tears flooded down her face.

Elaine was by her side in an instant, proferring some scrunched-up loo roll as a tissue and putting her arms around her friend.

'Jojo, honey, what's wrong? Is it Hugh? Your dad?'

'I'm not pregnant, Elaine, and this is the third time, the third time!'

'The third time you thought you were pregnant?' asked Elaine.

Jojo looked up, eyes red and distraught. 'The third time we've had IVF and it failed,' she croaked.

'Oh hell,' said Elaine, and got to her feet and quickly flipped the shop sign to 'closed' and locked the door.

By the time Cari reached the shop and banged loudly on the door to be let in, Jojo and Elaine were on their second cup of coffee laced with whisky in the back office, sitting on cushions on the foor and Elaine was explaining the benefits of having a puppy.

'Juan has one. A schnauzer,' she said. 'They have to be groomed, which is really the only expense.'

'Apart from the food – and the vets' bills,' said Cari, who had

303

taken care of her mother's dogs on more than one occasion. If there was something weird and sickening in the dead rodent department on their walk, Prancer would eat it and have to have all sorts of injections to sort his intestines out. Not to mention going through a lot of kitchen rolls and making Cari want to gag because whatever went into Prancer inevitably came out.

'Yes,' said Elaine, waggling her cup in agreement. 'I never thought of that. Juan hasn't mentioned it.'

Jojo giggled and Cari hugged her tightly. Thank heavens for Elaine, Juan and whoever had left the bottle of whisky in the office. Jojo was not a spirits kind of girl but seeing her this relaxed, albeit with alcohol inside her, was something to rejoice about. Jojo was wound so tightly, she was like a coiled spring. A little uncoiling had to be a good thing.

'How long have you been seeing Juan?' Cari asked, saying no to the whisky bottle Elaine was proferring. She would have to drive them home afterwards and she was more of a pinot grigio girl herself.

'Two weeks,' explained Jojo, who now knew the whole story. 'She thinks it could be marriage, the whole thing.'

'Marriage, definitely,' sighed Elaine. 'He's perfect.'

'So far,' said Cari, the voice of reason.

And then she thought that she hadn't known Conal for much longer than that, when it came down to it, but she felt wonderfully sure about him all the same. She was not going to rain on Elaine's parade.

'Cari doesn't date,' said Jojo to Elaine, who knew damn well that Cari didn't date and Cari felt a tinge of sorrow that she hadn't been able to tell her closest friend about Conal and how she felt about him.

Later, she decided. Just because Jojo was tipsy now and the spring had uncoiled didn't mean Jojo had gone back to normal. It would take more than a couple of whisky-laced coffees for that. Her news about the delectable Conal could wait.

'How about a sobering-up coffee and I drive you two home?' she said, turning away to text Hugh with the news that for now, at least, Jojo was relaxed. 'You are not going to be able to sell much today.'

'Oooooh!' shrieked Elaine, bounding to her feet. 'My Most Hated Poster. All those women who come into the shop, try everything on and don't buy. I'm putting it up now!'

Jojo collapsed into hysterical laughter. 'Don't let her, Cari,' she begged, before she curled up on all the cushions and closed her eyes.

Kit had begun to hate the sound of the postman. Years ago it use to annoy him because next door's dog, a large creature of indeterminate breed, had gone ballistic every time the postman so much as put a foot into the Brannigans' front garden.

It wasn't that Kit had a problem with dogs – in fact he loved dogs and he'd have adored it if they'd been able to have one. Trina had wanted a pet for years and had begged and begged for some sort of dog, but her mother wasn't an animal person. 'I do not want something dropping hair all over this house,' Helen had said, shuddering.

So the Brannigans had not had a dog, no matter how many times Trina cried at Christmas over Santa not leaving a puppy.

No, what upset Kit about the concept of the postman coming was that the postman rarely brought good news. There were rarely any lovely cheques, although he had invested some money in the Prize Bonds, and occasionally he won 75 euros – which he always kept from Helen, carefully stashed away somewhere. It was his little nest egg and the irony of the man of the house having his own little nest egg in the way that women used to was not lost upon him.

Helen ran through money the way water ran through pipes.

All that spending was filling a hole in her somewhere, he knew.

Once upon a time, Nora had explained it to him, when he

and Helen had been spectacularly broke and he'd got a bit drunk at a family get-together and spilled his heart out to his dear sister-in-law.

That was the lovely thing about Nora: you could say anything to her and she wouldn't repeat it. She wouldn't judge. She'd just try to offer kind and helpful advice.

'Where's the money going?' she'd asked at the time, even though he was pretty sure she knew damn well where the money was going.

The money was going onto Helen's back from the endless expensive shops that she visited all the time, deciding that this dress or that blouse would change everything and finally pull her wardrobe together, make her perfect.

The whole family used to socialise more in those days, the three brothers and their families going on holidays together or having dinners in each of their houses.

It was clear that Nora never minded the fact that she and Mick hadn't an extra penny to their names, and she'd wear the same dress again and again and not be even slightly bothered.

Sometimes she wore one of the crocheted shawls she made and she wore those little bits of crochet with as much joy as if they were things from a posh designer couriered over from one of the world's fashion capitals with the couture house's compliments.

But not Helen.

No, Kit's wife had to have *new* things, the best of everything, something to prove she was somebody.

Nora didn't need things to prove she was somebody.

'I think we were all affected a bit by the past,' Nora had explained to him gently that time. 'It was where we came from, Kit, you know that, and the fact that there wasn't any money around at the time. Lord knows, none of our families had spare money, and for some people, that fear never went away. That fear of never having new clothes or always having to wear hand-me-downs. I think that's what Helen's problem is – the fear of needing something and not being able to get it. It's worse for her because of her father,' Nora added casually, and Kit had shivered at the thought of his wife overhearing this discussion because she had almost convinced herself that her father had been a paragon of virtue instead of a drunk.

'She never had anything because he spent it all on alcohol and she lived with that as well as the pain of being the daughter of one of the biggest boozers around. That has a huge effect on a person: how we start life. Those childhood years are crucial and if you feel scared or anxious during those years, if you feel like you lived in a war zone – which was, let's face it, what Helen lived in – then you're affected for ever. No matter what it looks like to other people, in her head, Helen is always making up for the fact that she was the poor kid with the drunk father.'

'I understand the pathology of it all, but she's making us broke with it,' Kit had said and he'd been sorry as soon as he had said it, because it felt like such a betrayal of his wife.

He knew how hard her young life had been, he'd seen her have nightmares where she woke, wild-eyed and sweating, and told him she'd dreamed of being back in her family home with her father drunkenly shouting and breaking every bit of crockery in the house.

But Nora had managed to move the conversation along gently, as if he hadn't said something disloyal about his darling Helen, as if she understood what he was feeling.

She was an amazing woman, his sister-in-law, and, not for the first time, Kit thought how lucky Mick was to have her. No wonder they had such a strong marriage. They were both such good people, so straight and honest. There would be no things unsaid in their home. Not like in Kit and Helen's where so much was unsaid, so much lost in the miasma of the past where to talk about what had gone before would be to start a war.

'Look, why don't you talk to her Kit, say you're broke, say

you love her having beautiful things and you understand why she wants them, but that for a little while you need to pull the horns in,' Nora advised.

'Yes,' agreed Kit with a firmness he didn't feel. He had never been up to discussing his wife's demons with her. But they had to talk about the money soon. He knew that the hole inside Helen would never be filled, not with designer clothes or jewellery that nobody else had. But they would run out of money soon, and that would break her totally. It would break them all.

'That's it, I'll talk to her about it.'

But of course he hadn't talked to her about any such thing. Woe betide anyone who tried to stop Helen from going to the shop when she wanted to.

It was her due, she felt. She had married into the Brannigan family and even if he was not the rich one of the Brannigan family, Helen felt people didn't know this and would expect her to be dressed in the first stare of fashion, which is why he hated the postman and the bills and the credit card statements.

Sometimes they went through them together and Helen would instantly get defensive.

'Well that was just that little necklace because I was buying a top, and the necklace went so well with it, and I had to have it, I mean really would you deny me that?'

Kit couldn't deny her anything. Next door's dog was long since gone, but Kit knew when the postman came anyway and he collected the post that morning and opened it wearily, knowing what he'd see, knowing that his wife would not have been able to control herself with this big party coming up.

How was he going to tell her the full extent of their financial problems?

Amy was on the phone to Nola when the text came in. Normally, she wouldn't interrupt a phone call to peer at a text but the name on this one had made her sit up: Clive.

'Hold on, Nola,' she said, managing to sound calm. 'It's ... er, a work thing.'

'Are you around? I can drop in for half an hour and I've got wine! And guess what, tomorrow night I can stay the night!'

Amy felt her heart leap. She hadn't heard from Clive for so long, since that horrible day in the lift and in the intervening period, all his interactions with her had been cold and professional. And now this ...

'Nola, I have to reply. I'll buzz you back,' she said hastily.

All her plans for the next day – plans to visit the shops to try to buy a dress for Edward's blasted seventieth party – had gone out the window. Clive could come over and stay the night.

During their whole relationship, he had never managed this, even though he said himself and Suzanne lived separate lives and did their own thing, and honestly it was hardly a marriage at all ...

In the early stages, Amy had asked him a couple of times to stay over in her little apartment – which she'd have cleaned and bedecked with flowers for this very purpose – and she had been heartbroken that he hadn't been able to.

Still, she couldn't push it: people didn't like to be pushed, *men* didn't like to be pushed. She'd read this a lot in magazines. She would let this wonderful life-long love develop naturally, because he might reject her and then ... she couldn't manage that.

At the heart of Amy was an enormous fear of rejection. She tried her very best to keep this fear hidden from her mother, from people she knew, from everyone except perhaps Tiana and Nola.

They understood.

'You fear rejection because of your parents,' Tiana used to say before she went to New Zealand.

309

'I mean, your mother is hardly the touchy-feely type and your dad – he was a sweetie, but he wasn't really around.'

'He did love me, though,' Amy said sadly. 'Does love me.' She thought of the cards he sent but it had been years since he'd visited and he moved around so much, had never had a permanent home abroad where she could go to.

'I'm sure he loves you,' said Nola, the voice of reason, 'but the reality is that when you were a child, he left for the UK and the stripper.'

They all allowed themselves a little laugh at Granny Maura's description of Amy's father's second love. Sometimes laughing was the only way to deal with things.

Sylvia, the so-called stripper, was actually sweet, a little innocent, far too young for Dennis, and was actually one of many young women trying to earn a crust as a perfectly respectable dancer in West End shows.

Whatever she was, it seemed as if being with Sylvia in London was preferable to Dennis than spending time with his daughter in Ireland.

'That's rejection number one,' said Nola, who studied such things for her work on how to make yourself a better, stronger person.

Having Bess as a mother – hard-working with not enough time for emotional closeness with her daughter – created the long-running rejection that was number two.

'At least your mother had something solid behind her,' Tiana used to say when they were comparing the madness of their mothers. 'Mine had her knees worn out on the floor praying the rosary. The more I think about it, the more I think she was quite bonkers. She talked endlessly about hell and Satan and how if we didn't pray, we were doomed. That is not normal.'

'Oh, what's normal, anyway?' sighed Amy, who didn't want to be psychoanalysed by her friends.

Her mother was trying now but Amy had so much going on and she didn't have time for Bess just now.

'Normal's a cycle on the washing machine, honey,' Nola said gently. 'Remind yourself of that every now and then but it's important to work out all your issues too.'

Amy had had her issues worked out perfectly well and she knew them all. But knowing your issues and avoiding the pitfalls they created were two very different things.

That was why she had never told either Tiana or Nola about Clive. They would both hate him and everything he stood for: a married man who said his marriage was over and that all he cared about was Amy and his children. Yet he still was with said wife and children.

He was still never able to spend the night and once, lately, he'd said that he probably wouldn't be able to leave until the children were old enough, which had made Amy cry after he'd gone. How long would she have to wait? And she'd thought financial issues were behind his living with Suzanne?

But a woman who was afraid of being rejected because she had been rejected before never pushed things, which was why when Clive said he couldn't stay the night, Amy would always nod sweetly and say: 'Of course, darling, I understand.'

But now, she thought joyously, now he was going to stay. He must love her.

She had bought new sheets ages ago, just in case: gorgeous ones that felt soft to the touch and she ironed them at high speed, made the bed with love and had to stop herself scattering rose petals on their snowy plumpness. Normally she didn't bother ironing things like sheets. But tonight was going to be special.

The big window of the sitting room of her apartment overlooked Delaney Gardens, which was small and pretty and was always full of children and people walking dogs, the sound of laughter and giggling mixed with the odd little terrier bark or a giggling argument over who was best at playing keepy-uppy with the football.

It was a wonderful place to live, in the pretty community of

Silver Bay, where the houses swept down to the great curving horseshoe that was Dublin Bay. There was a real sense of community and she loved it.

She always felt that Clive didn't entirely appreciate it because he belted into her house at high speed, as if terrified someone was going to see him. Amy would have liked to explain that her neighbours would hardly recognise Clive and what were they going to do even if they did? Put a picture in the paper and say, 'This man spotted going into somebody's house'?

The following evening, she got home from work late because roadworks had delayed the bus, and she was anxious as there was still so much to do. She had to organise the fresh fruit and the slow cooker was bubbling away with a casserole but she hadn't got the hang of the slow cooker yet and sometimes things came out of it wonderfully and sometimes meat came out as if it could be cut into thin slices and used as shoe leather.

If the meal – a slowly cooked Thai curry – hadn't worked out, she was going to race to the supermarket and buy something else. But no, a spoonful comfirmed that the Thai curry tasted lovely.

Fabulous. This was going to be a marvellous night.

She had the quickest shower ever, blow-dried her hair, put on pretty underwear and a lovely dress, floral and the colour of golden apricots to go with her hair, and then left herself with bare feet so she could pad around the apartment, her feet sinking into the lovely rag rugs that were placed on wooden floors she'd stripped and varnished herself.

She lit candles and put on music, singing to herself all the time. It was almost an afterthought to check the letter box and see if there was any post, because she was too excited to think about anything else, too excited to think about what might be there. But finally, it was there.

Not the enormous package she'd half expected: her manuscript back with a 'Thank you, but no thanks', the thing everyone in the online writers' group talked about and dreaded.

Instead, there was a letter from the publishers, a letter that had ludicrously clearly been stuck in the wrong letter box because Mrs Thompson, her neighbour, had scrawled: 'Sorry, Amy, this landed in our box and we were away. It's not your name but your address and I thought you might know what to do with it...'

Amy thought she might be sick. The stuck-on label with A.J. Sharkey and her address on it had 'Cambridge Publishing' and their Irish address inscribed at the top.

It had come weeks ago. Delivered to the wrong apartment in her building, in the first place, then the whole mistake compounded by the fact that she'd deliberately used initials that were not easily identified as either male or female, so that no preconception could be made. Just in case Cari had seen it, she hadn't used the name Reynolds but had gone for Sharkey, her mother's maiden name. Her neighbours hadn't connected it with her and all this subterfuge had resulted in this.

Full of fear, ready for the rejection, she opened it and read, then sat down on her couch and tried to take it all in.

It was a letter from Cari Brannigan, who was – if Amy thought about it – her stepcousin, sort of. A thrill shivered through her.

Cari writing back to *her*! *And what a letter!*

'*Dear A.J.*,' the letter went. '*I wish I knew your proper name because it seems strange writing to A.J. Sharkey and not knowing if you are a man or a woman or two writers. I sense you are a woman, I sense that from something in your writing, but I don't know for sure. All I can say is that I love your manuscript, I love the way you write and so does everyone else in our publishing department. We want to see more, please? You haven't shown us the denouement and I know it must be fabulous.*'

Amy had never fainted before, but as she looked at the letter and felt the thrill of excitement rise from her feet up through her whole body, she thought it was entirely possible that she would collapse onto her floorboards.

There followed Cari's phone numbers, email address and another plea to please get in touch as soon as possible.

Amy had read the letter five times, going over each word, mouthing them silently.

'I love the way you write,' said Cari. *'but I need to know something about you, I need to see the rest of the novel. Is there more, please tell me there's more, lots more? I feel you have got so much in you, I can sense it, please ring me as soon as possible, I want to talk to you, we want to publish your book.'*

It was the letter Amy had dreamed of all her life: for somebody to say she was a writer.

Nobody knew, only Tiana and Nola, and they didn't talk about it because Amy wouldn't let them – she was too nervous of putting the kybosh on her dream. Her grandmother had been a big fan of the superstition of believing it was bad luck to think of further successes because to do so would invite failure and disaster.

Nola was always so encouraging and after a while, Amy had asked her not to keep mentioning various novels she had tried to write over the years because it was embarrassing.

'What's embarrassing about trying to do something amazing?' said Nola in that sparky, can-do attitude of hers.

'It's just that I keep trying things and they don't work out, I have to delete them all and then I just feel like such a moron,' said Amy. 'I'm not telling anyone again.'

'Amy, you're a born creative person,' said Nola, emphasising each word like she was teaching an empowerment course. 'You'll get there in the end. You're honing your craft.'

'I wish,' said Amy, having just junked another 20,000 words of a novel because it simply hadn't worked out. 'Nobody ever said I was creative at school, no one ever read out my English essays, I wasn't one of those kids.'

'Hey,' said Nola cheerfully, 'none of us fitted in. We were the Three Musketeers of Not Fitting In. It's hard to be creative and sparkling in any particular field when you are struggling to get by. Besides, weird teenage years are fabulous fodder for being a writer. Gosh, Tiana should have a go – she has plenty of material!'

Thinking of this made Amy send Nola a text: 'Have amazing news about book, will phone you later.'

She felt guilty not phoning Nola immediately but Clive was coming and she wanted to see him so much, to tell him and to have him share in her excitement.

He knocked on the door quietly and she ran to it, for once not caring that he was knocking in that ludicrously clandestine way.

'Darling,' she said delightedly at the door.

He said nothing but just shoved her in.

'Hush,' he said, 'someone will hear.'

'Who is going to hear?' she said, laughing. 'We're on the second floor. Do you think the police are peeking in to see who I have got coming round to my house?'

She was joyfully happy, her dreams were coming true. And she had someone to share them with.

'You never know who's watching,' hissed Clive.

'OK,' said Amy slowly. 'Clive, I'm excited because I've got some great news.'

Clive shut the door quietly as if the world's secret services, MI5 and Mossad included, were indeed on his tail.

'Just can't be too careful,' he said.

Some little thing inside Amy clicked into place.

'What do you mean you can't be too careful?' she said, staring at him.

She was still holding the letter in one hand: it gave her power. She, Amy Reynolds, aka A.J. Sharkey, was going to be a published author. Publishers and editors liked what she had written. She was not going to be doing a series of dead-end jobs for the rest of her life. She was going to do something she loved.

'And what do you mean, you don't know who is watching?'

'Suzanne is acting really weird,' said Clive, going over to the window and peering out.

'Acting weird?'

'As if she knows something,' said Clive.

And then all the cards that Amy had been building up inside her head, entire villages of little bits of paper laid on top of each other delicately and beautifully, all fluttered to the ground.

Clive was not separated from Suzanne and cohabiting in the same house with her until he had funds to move out. They were not in line for a divorce down the road when the money was sorted/the kids were older/the moon was in Venus. His wife wasn't seeing other people, *he* wasn't free to see other people. He was a married man coming round for sex and adoration and dinner, maybe not even in that order, Amy thought wretchedly.

Had she been absolutely mad? How had she not seen this? And now that she had, she couldn't unsee it.

She didn't know whether it was the power of suddenly having something else in her life or not, but it was all terribly clear to her now. Painfully clear.

'Clive,' she said, as she watched her lover staring out the window in the manner of a man distracted, 'I've something important to tell you.'

This was a little test.

'You know that book I've been working on for a long time?'

'Yeah, your story thing,' he said dismissively.

He tucked the curtains back into place and looked at her and then he smiled and walked towards her, fingers on the buttons of her blouse. Amy always wore blouses or dresses when he came over. They were more feminine, he said.

It was because he liked undoing buttons and stroking the softness of her skin and reaching her bra more easily.

'Yes, my book,' she said, correcting him, 'not my story thing.'

She moved a step back so that his fingers no longer were touching her skin.

'I sent it off to a publisher, they like it and want to publish it.'

'That's wonderful,' he said, moving forward again so his fingers could go back to working on her buttons.

'Yes, it is wonderful,' said Amy, still waiting.

She was waiting for some excitement from him, waiting for Clive to say, 'Darling, I'm so proud of you! This could change your life, you've worked so hard on this.'

But he wasn't interested in her book, he wasn't interested in her life being changed. Instead, he was interested in getting her clothes off and getting her into bed. Without his wife knowing.

That was all she was to him – someone he went to bed with.

Amy had never actually slept with Clive. She had never curled up beside him, happy to have a night's sleep or even a few hours of sleep with her beloved with nothing sexual involved, just the comfort of a human being who loved her, lying peacefully beside her.

She'd never woken up in the morning to hear him pootling around in her kitchen, making her coffee, calling that he could squeeze orange juice and did she want toast before she went to work?

None of those simple pleasures. She'd got caught up in the whole dream of romance and the handsome boss who was thrilled with her beauty and would take her away from all of this. But it turned out that the handsome boss was no prince. He was a frog, or worse. Frogs were probably monogamous.

She had to be her own prince.

'Clive, sit down for a minute,' she said.

'Of course,' he replied, delighted, sitting down on the couch and reaching for her.

Amy deftly moved so she was sitting down on her single armchair.

'Are you still with Suzanne? I need to know before we go any further.'

'Honey, I've told you—' he began.

Amy still held Cari's letter in one hand. Normally she was not a strident person, or a person who was able to stand up for herself. But she thought now of Cari as she'd met her at her mother's wedding: funny, sparky, with a ready wit and a career. Cari would never let a man use her. Never.

With the letter as a talisman, and summoning up all her strength, Amy refused to back down.

'Please tell me the truth, Clive.'

'Amy, lovie, it's... it's complicated,' said Clive, and he adopted that particular face he always wore whenever he spoke about Suzanne, a face that implied great courage in the face of adversity, respect for his poor wife and lots of other things, but none of them saying, 'I love you and I want to be with you.'

'So if I went round to your house now, and asked Suzanne if you two were getting divorced, would she be shocked at the notion or agree that it was just a matter of money and timing?'

Clive went pale and Amy had her answer.

She knew that it was entirely her own fault. She had met this wonderful man and thought he was the answer to all her prayers when in fact he was the answer to someone else's prayers. He was someone else's husband, the father of other children and he would never be the father of her children.

'There is no living-in-the-same-house-but-separated relationship between you and Suzanne, is there? It's not over, the two of you aren't waiting to separate amicably, am I right?'

'Look,' said Clive, raising his hands expansively as if he were addressing a staff meeting, 'you know it's difficult when you're married. You don't understand because you have never been in this position but—'

'What position is that, exactly?' said Amy.

'A senior management position.' Clive's chest puffed up wth his own self-importance. 'People don't necessarily understand what we are going through. The stress ... and you know I love Suzanne and the kids but sometimes marriages get stagnant and I just need something else and ...'

'You needed something else and I was stupid enough to think I was all you needed,' said Amy.

In her head, she heard a mental chorus of her two best friends shrieking at her, saying: 'This man is nothing, nothing! How have you carried on with this?'

Somewhere in the mental chorus was Granny Maura, hissing: 'You should be ashamed of yourself!'

'I am ashamed of myself,' she said out loud.

'You are not going to tell her,' he said, suddenly anxious.

'I'm not going to tell her,' said Amy. 'I'd be too ashamed. But you know what, why don't you go home now and try and keep it in your pants, Clive.'

'I can't believe you are speaking like this,' said Clive, trying to salvage things. 'I'm your boss.'

'Yes,' said Amy, her fingers still clutching the wonderful letter full of Cari's words of praise. She tried to channel Cari Brannigan. 'You're my boss and I'm a junior member of staff, and I feel quite sure that the Met-Ro people would not like to think that you would take advantage of me in this way. What is this – sexual harassment? You being my direct superior and all that?'

Naked fear appeared in his eyes and that fear was a small recompense for all those hours she'd spent waiting for him to call, waiting for him to tap on the door and come round for what she thought was a wonderful romantic interlude and what had really been something quite grubby. And sad. Desperately sad.

'Go, Clive, get out of here. Let's forget this ever happened, just don't do it again to poor Suzanne, she deserves better.'

'Look, you are not serious about complaining, are you?' said Clive, grabbing his jacket. 'I mean that could ruin me, destroy me, I wouldn't have a career, I'd be unemployable and—'

'Just get out,' she shrieked, and he went.

Amy locked the door, wondering what she'd seen in him, because in the flesh he was all those wonderful things that she had read about for years, and yet at heart he'd been weak and he'd used her. She deserved more, she deserved better.

She wanted to tell her mother – inexplicably the desire to explain it all to Bess came over her, but she couldn't. Mum would be so upset, disappointed in her for betraying another woman.

Instead she picked up the phone and rang Nola.

First up, she told Nola about the book. Nola's whoops of joy could be heard for miles.

'Oh, honey, I'm so proud of you, I knew you had it in you. I knew you are a writer, just the way you sit quietly and watch everything, and all the world thinks you're just this quiet shy girl and secretly you're watching everything.'

'Unfortunately, that's not the only thing I have been doing,' said Amy with a grimace, and she proceeded to tell Nola the whole grubby story.

'I feel like crap, actually,' Amy said finishing. 'Dirty and miserable and as if I have been playing in the ash heap. How could I not have known?'

'Because he lied to you. It's that simple. We've all been burned by the wrong man,' said Nola wisely. 'Even me. Yes, I know you think I have it all sorted out but I haven't. I have once spent some time with a man who told me that he was nearly divorced. Just let me tell you, honey, there is no such thing as nearly divorced. It's like being a little bit pregnant. Why don't you book a weekend flight and come to me. We can celebrate your book!'

'I'd love that,' said Amy. 'Let me see what the story is here with the publishers and then ...'

She paused.

'Nola, I'm going to have a book published!'

It was as if the news was finally coming to settle in her head. She, Amy Reynolds, might just possibly, with luck and a four-leaf clover and lots of other stuff, be a success.

Nineteen

'The truth will set you free,
but first it will piss you off.'
Gloria Steinem

Cari and Conal had been out every second night since they'd
met. They'd gone dancing, to dinner, over to Anna and Jeff's
again, and finally, back to the glamorous French restaurant
where Conal had brought her the first night.

Cari had deliberately kept everything slow. She would not
let her lesser instincts rule her brain.

She wanted to know this man before he put a foot into her
bedroom. Just because Elaine was seeing wedding bells after
two weeks of Juan and his dog didn't mean Cari had to be
similarly silly.

And yet the more she knew of Conal, the more she found
she was crazy about him. He was fun, wildly clever, definitely
sexy, and more than slightly obsessed when he talked about his
work, although Cari could uderstand why.

Her boyfriend was officially one of a group of amazing
people in the world trying to cure cancer. Compared to her job,
it was … well, she of so many words could come up with none.

'Inadequate,' she said finally, looking up from her cheesecake
into Conal's sexy grey eyes. 'You make me feel inadequate,' she
said.

'Really?' he looked worried. 'That doesn't sound good.'

Cari shook her head. 'No, it's fine, but your job is so amazing,
what you do so incredible and I wonder do you look at me like
I'm some sort of idiot because I don't understand everything
about your work and you need to be *simpatico* with someone

to have a relationship with them … and, you could get bored with me and run off with some sexy girl scientist—'

'One who wears her hair up and has glasses, but rips them off and suddenly turns into a hot babe?' he interrupted, grinning evilly.

'Yes! Don't tease me.'

'Sorry. I have gone out with fellow scientists,' he said, and she swore she saw a faint darkening of his face, but then it was gone, 'and you tend to talk endlessly about work. Or the people you work with. But with you, I get to talk about art and literature and mummy porn.'

'Stop that.' She threw her napkin at him. 'If you think you're going to make me blush, you've got another think coming, doctor. I have your number now. All talk and no action.'

'Really?'

One of his long arms reached under the table and found her knees, then played a delicate tickling game along the inside seam of her jeans.

'Stop! We'll get thrown out.'

'I think we should go anyway,' he said, and she was pleased to note the hoarse tone in his voice. She was doing this to him, not the hot lady scientists.

'Your apartment, for herbal tea?' he asked politely as they left.

'Herbal tea?'

'OK,' he whispered into her ear, 'something else steamy?'

'Works for me.'

At the door to her apartment, Cari's fingers fumbled with her keys.

His mouth was on her neck and his hands were touching her waist, as he leaned over and laid kisses on her neck from behind.

'I love the way your hair is cut so short that I can kiss the curve of your neck,' he murmured huskily. 'There's something so sexy about it, it's an erogenous zone.'

'Nobody ever said that was an erogenous zone before,' said

Cari, wondering had her key changed because it wasn't fitting into the lock properly.

Somehow she managed to open the door.

The apartment was going through one of its neat and tidy stages, although Cari tried to remember if the bedroom had a certain level of chaos going on from her speedy beautification before going out on the date.

Oh, who cared. She turned around and he was holding her tight, kissing her, his big hands gently cradling her head, his mouth touching hers and it felt so amazing: this man holding her and she could feel that he wanted her and she wanted him so much and it was going to be equal.

She wasn't taking advantage of him, he wasn't taking advantage of her, they knew everything about each other – well, she thought she knew everything about him...

'Stop thinking. You are over-thinking this, I can tell,' he said.

'How do you know I'm thinking?' she said, laughing.

'You said you can tell when I'm fibbing,' he said, 'you know the look in my eye. I can tell by the look in your eye that you're working things out and analysing it. You're an analyst, Ms Brannigan, and you have been hurt but I'm not going to hurt you. I don't jump into bed with everyone I meet.'

'Me neither,' she said, pulling at his shirt.

'No, honestly, it's been a while...'

'I thought men couldn't go without sex,' she said.

'Not this one,' he began, unbuttoning her blouse. 'Not when there's someone special and you're waiting for them, hoping—'

'Oh, stop talking,' she said, kissing him.

Then they were on the couch and their clothes were coming off and Cari found herself saying, 'My bedroom would be nicer.' And Conal, despite the extra pounds that she worried over because of all the chocolate, picked her up as if she were a tiny faery person, carried her into the bedroom, laid her on the bed and made love to her, with what she could only describe as reverence.

She ignored the fact that he had condoms with him. He was being cautious, that was all. It wasn't that he'd been convinced she was a sure thing, right?

The next morning she woke up to feel this large body beside hers and she wasn't scared or anxious or worried: it felt utterly right. A long hairy leg stretched over hers, a face with morning stubble nuzzled into her shoulder and it felt absolutely wonderful. She didn't regret any of it, any of the glorious fabulous passion of it.

'What time is it?' he said in a husky morning voice.

'It's...' Cari looked at her watch '...ten past seven.'

'Oh hell, I have got to be out of here. Early work meetings again. Otherwise I'd stay, honestly, and wake you up properly, Ms Brannigan, because you look so delicious lying there naked but—'

He leaned down and kissed her again, one hand sliding down to circle her nipple. And then he was half lying on her and groaning that he had to get up.

'Go,' said Cari, used to having to think of work. 'Have a shower first or they'll know you spent all night in bed with a strange woman.'

'You're not that strange,' he teased. 'I've spent every spare moment with you for weeks now. I mean, you're strange, sure, but my kind of strange,' and he kissed her deeply before he pushed himself off the bed and headed to the shower.

The running of the water gave her the chance to race to the tiny cloakroom in the hall and brush her hair. She had spare mouthwash somewhere but it was probably in her main bathroom and yet she didn't want to kiss him again with horrible morning breath.

Blast.

Racing back into her room, she sprayed her favourite peony-scented perfume all over herself. He might be asphyxiated, she thought with a giggle.

Then she heard his phone – a piano ringtone from his side of the bed.

It might be this work thing, she thought, although a picture of the person phoning with the name Beatrice flashed up on-screen. Beatrice looking like a skinny thirty-something model in high fashion clinging to Conal.

Still, Cari, fresh with lovemaking and love, grabbed it, going to bring it into the shower to him. But wasn't the sort of smartphone she was used to and somehow, in touching the screen, she answered it.

Noise like someone standing in a factory came loudly through the phone.

'*Chéri*, can you hear me? This line is terrible, we are all wait-ing for the plane on the runway. I miss you. I told you I did and I do. I can come to Ireland if you want.' The voice, honeyed and exotic, pronounced Ireland as if it was a bare one-acre rock in the Atlantic with a shed on it. 'I can meet your family, this new baby, be with you. You there, *chéri*? *Merde*!'

The phone was hung up and Cari started at it in horror.

Yvette was the so-called last lover, but this was Beatrice, Beatrice who was definitely not a work call, who looked as if she worked on French *Elle*, and had been a model in a past life.

Beatrice. The sort of elegant French woman who would have been superglued to Conal. Who *had* been superglued to him and who'd been conveniently left out of the dating narrative. He had lied to her and if there was one thing Cari would not put up with, it was being lied to. Not ever again.

Conal raced out of the bathroom, dragged on his clothes and apologised. He was rushing so much, he didn't notice that as she sat at her dressing table pretending to put on make-up, she was just stalling for time.

'Look, I'm really sorry, I'm really late. I'll call you.' And within three minutes he was gone.

Cari sat there alone and wished she had a cat. An alien baby hairless cat she could hug and cry at. Or even a loan of Juan's schnauzer, even if it did need grooming and feeding and vets' bills paid. Anything so she wouldn't be alone.

Because once again, everything she thought was right had turned out to be wrong after all.

Conal rang at half nine when he was out of the meeting but Cari didn't pick up. So he texted: 'Miss you, sexy girl. You are amazing. I'm crazy about you. Later?'

Later? Cari glowered at the phone, rage and hurt rushing through her. She'd give him later. She'd give him a whack of her mythical baseball bat if she could and if she had one and if…

She sat at her desk and tried to hold back the tears.

Then she blocked his number on her phone and tried to work but it was hard to see emails when your eyes were full of tears. She'd fallen in love with him, like a complete idiot, and he'd lied to her: he had another woman apart from the handy Yvette.

Beatrice. Why had he not told her about Beatrice?

Wiping her eyes, Cari fired up Google. She mightn't be curing cancer but she knew how to research. She'd start with Conal's French lab. Those labs always had fundraisers, and fundraisers involved doctors coming along with dates to talk science to the contributors, and there might be a picture and, therefore, a surname for Beatrice.

It didn't take long at all: Beatrice wasn't from the fashion department of *Elle* France. She was a scientist who worked with Conal.

Beatrice St Antoine.

Petite, beautiful, serious with tortoiseshell glasses in most photos and that blonde mane elegantly tied back. Cari thought of Conal's crack about the sexy scientist with glasses and hair up. Bastard. He hadn't been joking after all.

She really could pick them, couldn't she?

She snapped off Google viciously.

That was it.

She was not even going to speak to him again. Let him see the call from bloody Beatrice. Let him realise it all. Not that he'd give a damn – he could dump handy old Cari if hot, brilliant, genius IQ Beatrice was willing to come to crappy old Ireland for him.

Well, Conal and Beatrice could go hang.

Five minutes later, a call came in on her office line and she picked it up warily. Perhaps she should have asked someone else to take her calls for her?

'Cari?'

It was a woman and she sounded vaguely familiar.

'This is Amy, your aunt-in-law, Bess's daughter,' said the voice.

'Oh hi,' said Cari. She did not need family stuff right now...

'I got your letter. It went into the wrong house and they were away and I only got it last night...' went on Amy, in that soft, sweet voice Cari remembered.

'What letter?'

'About my book. I didn't want you to think I was taking advantage of knowing you, so I used a pseudonym, A.J. Sharkey,' said the voice.

Cari wanted to cry.

'How lovely that it's you,' she said, 'and you haven't sent it to anyone else, have you?'

'No, only you,' said Amy.

'That's wonderful, Amy. We all love it. We want to publish it. Can we meet up?'

Amy wondered why Cari sounded so close to tears.

'Are you all right?' she asked gently.

'Gosh, yes, just... er hay fever,' lied Cari. 'Stargazer lilies in the office,' she added. 'Now, let's set a date to meet.'

*

328

Jeff picked up the call on his mobile from his brother.

'Can you talk to Cari for me?' said Conal.

'Why?' said Jeff, who still sounded like someone who was getting very little sleep.

'Because she won't answer my calls,' said Conal.

There was a pause.

'What happened?' said Jeff.

'That's not really any of your business, bro, but to be honest, nothing bad. We ... er ... I stayed the night with her last night, that's all. And now she's not answering my calls. I just need to talk to her, she's been hurt so much before and—'

'Listen,' Jeff interrupted him. 'I love Cari, she is amazing but if she's not phoning you, she's decided not to phone you. End of.'

Conal laughed. 'You don't see her at all,' he said, in astonishment. 'She would never sleep with someone for one night. She is not that sort of person at all. How can you work with someone like that for so long and not know she's romantic, a believer in true love, a total softie.'

'Cari might have a tender side but she's a cool cucumber,' said Jeff. 'Very good at her job too, very sharp, very clever.'

'I know that, obviously,' sighed Conal, 'apart from the cleverness, she's a total softie hiding under the carapace of cucumberyness.'

'I should hire you with your fabulous ability to make up words,' Jeff retorted. 'If you're that crazy about her and you think she's a believer in true love, why do I have to intervene in getting her to phone you?'

'I ... er ... had to race out of her place this morning?' said Conal.

'You had to race out of her place this morning?' repeated his brother. 'That can't be it. She's a career woman. You wouldn't believe how often we have to get the red-eye to London. No, you did something else.'

'But what?' said Conal. 'I can't come up with anything else—'

'Well, figure it out, bro'. I am incredibly fond of Cari and I don't want to see her hurt—'

'I'm glad you hold my beloved in such high esteem,' said Conal. 'She deserves it. I'm crazy about her, by the way. I guess I'm going to have to try something else. I'm stuck in work all day but I'll camp outside her house tonight if I have to.'

Every month, the four Brannigan cousins had an evening in together. Paul used to complain that even before he went to New York, he wasn't invited, but Cari merely laughed and said they simply talked about men and periods and he'd have hated it.

Tonight, the evening in was due to be at Jojo's but Cari had instantly detected a certain froideur when she arrived and the sensation hadn't diminished when Hugh almost ran out of the house after barely hugging her hello and with a heartbreaking glance in Jojo's direction. So much for the uncoiling session of a few days ago with Elaine, Cari thought miserably.

'I am not in the mood for this,' said Jojo as she and Cari stood in the kitchen and put crisps into bowls, which seemed to be the extent of Jojo's catering abilities. 'I don't want a "let's mani and pedi ourselves for Lisowen Castle", which is what Trina and Maggie want.'

Cari was still devastated over Conal, but at least he'd stopped phoning. He kept leaving flowers on her doorstep every evening with a note and every morning, Cari took them into work and gave them to someone else. The note she put into the bin, unread. She didn't know if Conal had noticed the Beatrice call on his phone yet. If he had and he was still stalking her, it meant Beatrice hadn't come to Ireland yet and she was to be his booty-call until his French girlfriend arrived. Yeah, good luck with that.

If Conal was asking Jeff to be his lookout, he'd know how little she cared for his damn flowers. If he wanted to play pure bastard tradecraft by bedding her while having another woman waiting in the wings, she could play that game too.

Apart from the thrill of finding the new manuscript at work, she was appallingly miserable.

But she would squash her own feelings down to help Jojo.

She resolved to keep the evening light, to cheer her beloved cousin up. She would not mention Conal or the great disaster, even though once Jojo would have been the first person she'd have told.

At least Maggie and Trina were full of chat and, thankfully, full of excitement about the forthcoming party. A herd of depressed elephants could have charged through the room and they wouldn't have noticed.

After Thai take-away food, they sat in Jojo's pretty living room and chatted, Cari desperately trying to invest the evening with some fun for Jojo's sake.

'Would a sitcom of my life work?' she asked idly, sitting sideways on Jojo's armchair, feet dangling as she admired the series of cheap nail varnishes Trina and Maggie had amassed for their pedi/mani session, which was the current fascination between the two flatmates.

'Are there lots of cute men in it?' asked Trina, who had already done a pretty professional job on her hands with a shade of metallic navy blue that had just opened Cari's eyes to the possibility of navy as anything other than a clothing colour.

'No men at all,' lied Cari, fighting the sinking feeling inside her. 'The postman at work tried to nudge his arm into my boobs the other day, though. Does that count?'

'How dare he?' shrieked Jojo.

The two others just looked at Cari's rather large bosom in an assessing manner.

'I would kill to have a chest like yours,' said Trina, who was an A-cup unless she stuck in the chicken fillets.

'Why are none of you worked up about the whole postman thing?' demanded Jojo, getting mildly animated. 'That's sexual harassment. No, you don't work with him, actually, so it's sexual assault.'

'He's looks about ninety,' said Cari, 'and it could have been a mistake but to be on the safe side, I gave him the evil eye so he won't try it again. Plus, I worked in that small publishers in the city centre years ago, the one with the technical guides. I had two bosses take me out for "drinks" and try to get into my pants on my first day. After that, a pervy postman I can handle.'

Jojo shuddered.

'You have been insulated in the nice world of fashion where nobody ever harasses anyone,' Cari said, shrugging. 'The real world is not so nice. I have had men talk to my chest. Lovely men, men I respect, but somewhere in there, they can't help it – it's testosterone telling them to look at the bits of the woman that turn them on.'

She didn't say that she still dreamed of how she and Conal had been skin to skin and how glorious it had felt. His betrayal felt like a huge chasm inside her. Again, why again?

'That's a cop-out, Cari. Like saying we should all wear floor-length dresses so we don't get raped,' said Jojo hotly. 'What about telling men not to rape us rather than telling us how not to dress to get raped. Nobody should stare at your breasts or try to touch them.'

'I think models get harassed,' pointed out Maggie. ''Cos they're so young when they start and people can take advantage of them.'

'I'd like to think that's been nipped in the bud but face facts, girls, sexism exists,' Cari pointed out.

She had done her best to indoctrinate her sister and young cousin into what feminism actually meant and she didn't feel like giving a tutorial at that exact moment.

'Now, back to my sitcom—'

'No men in it, then it's only half a sitcom,' Trina said. 'Unless it's *Orange is the New Black*, which is pretty men-free, right, Maggie?'

'Some men,' agreed Maggie, now engrossed in delicately putting black dots onto her coral and yellow striped manicure.

'The heroine has lots of trouble caused by men and lurches from one disaster to the next,' Cari said.

'And has money,' Trina pointed out, extending one finger at Cari's discarded shoes, which had red soles.

'Has credit card bills due to misery shopping,' Cari contradicted ruefully.

'Ideally, you need another fabulous man, a ride of a man, to come into the plot and make you forget all else: pervy postmen, mean authors, scumbag fiancés,' said Maggie, eyes shining.

Cari knew of a fabulous man but she was never seeing him again. So she made the sort of joke everyone expected her to make: 'But where are they hiding these men? Is there a bunker somewhere with loads of them, hunks of manhood hidden in case aliens invade and we need to repopulate the earth?'

'Ooh,' sighed Trina and Maggie at the same time.

The four of them laughed and Jojo realised she let out some of the tension in her body. When had she turned into this person, this taut woman who couldn't even joke with her cousins. Though she'd had a hell of a hangover because of those two horrible whiskies, that session with Elaine had cheered her up.

As if she could read her mind, Cari caught Jojo's eye.

'So,' Cari said, in that deceptively light tone that meant she had something very unlight to say, 'should I get the whisky out so we can discuss your father's seventieth. Are you going?'

'Ugh, whisky. I must have been mad. I hate that stuff. Two of Elaine's measures and I had the hangover from hell!'

It had been the first time all evening Cari felt as if she was talking to the old Jojo, the one with the sense of humour.

'Please come,' said Maggie. 'I know you don't like Bess, but Uncle Ed's happy and really that's what it's all about, isn't it? Who knows, they may let some of the hidden-in-the-bunker dudes out... You know, the alien invasion repopulation team?'

'It's family only,' said Jojo.

'I think they're asking more people to the grand dinner on Saturday night. You know, business colleagues and that sort of thing. We're the only people in the hotel but they're driving in. There might be some hot young billionaires for me, Cari and Trina.'

'Ones who do not already have a trail of women following them?' laughed Jojo, the tension leaving her finally.

'There must be some out there,' said Maggie, thoughtfully, 'just recently billionaire-y, who haven't got a trail of women yet.'

'Or a lottery winner!' said Trina delightedly. 'Who has never really spent money and needs help.'

'That's more millionaire than billionaire,' said Maggie gravely, as if she'd given it some thought.

Jojo couldn't help herself and she started laughing, the sort of laughter that comes as a release and lets all the hurt out, even if only momentarily.

'I'll do up an advert,' Jojo said, wiping the tears of laughter from her eyes. 'Billionaire/millionaire wanted: must be a bit shy and retiring and need woman who hates tidying her apartment, OK?'

Life was so simple when she was the girls' age – she was falling in love with Hugh, before her mother was sick, before Bess had come along – everything was simple then, except for somewhere along the way it had gone wrong.

Nothing could turn back the clock. Just as it seemed as if nothing could make her pregnant.

Could she cope with going there again? She wiped her eyes again. The tears were half amusement, half plain old tears.

Cari finally cornered her in the kitchen while Trina and Maggie worked on the finer details of their mythical perfect men, who sounded like firemen but drove Maseratis and had black credit cards.

'You've been totally avoiding my calls,' Cari said.

'I'm avoiding life,' said Jojo, trying to sound blithe but Cari could hear the bitterness.

'Elaine's determined to fix me,' Jojo went on. 'All I need is a dog, according to her.'

'Juan still going strong?'

'Amazingly, yes. He came into the shop the other day and he's lovely. Worships the ground she walks on.'

'Hugh worships the ground you walk on,' Cari reminded her.

'He used to. Now he sees this neurotic, baby-obsessed woman and she's harder to worship. Maybe that's who I was all along – that smiley, happy woman was just for the first thirty years and forever after, I am going to be bitter and twisted.'

'You don't have to be.' Cari took a risk. 'Your mother would hate to see you like this.'

'Don't go there,' warned Jojo.

'I have to,' said Cari. 'I'm not the sort of friend who tells you what you want to hear. I tell you what you need to hear. Hugh's hurting too, Jojo. This is not just your pain.'

'He talked to you?'

'He's worried.'

'It's not his place to phone you,' snapped back Jojo.

'What? He needs a document signed in triplicate before he can phone me? We talked because he loves you,' said Cari, an expert in tough love. 'I think he's wondering if he should drag a psychiatrist round here to look at you because he's terrified you're having a breakdown. Are you?' she asked suddenly, in a softer voice.

'Are you supposed to know if you're having a breakdown?' Jojo said. 'Surely you just collapse.'

'It's not like that,' said Cari patiently. 'It can be a slow descent where the person feels helpless and hopeless and—'

'Don't tell me – you edited a book on it once?' said Jojo, stung at the thought of being discussed by Hugh and her cousin, *her best friend*, as if she was falling apart.

'I nearly fell apart after Barney,' said Cari evenly, 'but I didn't. This is worse, Jojo. Worse for both of you.'

'Don't tell me what it's like,' hissed Jojo. 'You don't know. And Hugh doesn't know, either. It's my body that's being bashed with chemicals, not his. Women have the need for children, not men.'

'You edit a book on that once?' bit back Cari.

'I'm living it!' said Jojo.

Cari stilled her breathing. She couldn't mess this up.

'Jojo, you know I love you and Hugh loves you, so don't push everyone away. Jojo, we don't always get what we want in life. I haven't.'

'Neither have I!' said Jojo fiercely.

'Well, deal with it! Because that's what I have to do!' snapped back Cari and collecting her things, entirely surprising Trina and Maggie, who were discussing blond men versus dark-haired men, she left.

Twenty

'New beginnings are often
disguised as painful endings.'
Lao Tze

Cari went towards Jeff's office with the whole of Amy's manuscript. She'd read it three times now and she loved it more each
time. Amy was a genius.

The door was closed but Cari peeked in the glass parti-
tion and it looked as if Jeff was having a nap because he was
slumped back in his seat with his head back and his eyes closed.

Paternity leave should last longer, Cari thought, like maybe
a year or something.

Knocking loudly to give him a chance to wake up, she
opened the door to find Jeff still asleep and Conal lounging
on the small office couch, flicking through a novel.

'Oh.' She stopped dead, manuscript in hand.

'Oh yourself,' said Conal, sitting up. 'I've been calling you
for a week.'

'Why?' said Cari lightly. 'Have you a book you want edited
as well as the indoctrination back in the cooler places in the
country?'

'I don't think I could write a book,' Conal said.

Weirdly, as if she was hypnotised, Cari found herself moving
towards him. She didn't sit on the couch but on the small chair
beside it. She didn't quite trust herself beside Conal. All the
testosterone that came off him in waves made him dangerous.
She was done with him – so why was she even staying in the
room. She could come back and talk to Jeff when Conal had
gone.

'Everyone and their lawyer thinks they can write a book,' she remarked.

'Jeff says that,' Conal replied agreeably. 'Don't know why.'

'Because it's putting words together and people think they can do that.'

'Singing is making sounds come out of your mouth and everyone doesn't think they can do that,' said Conal.

'Bad example,' Cari said. 'Have you see some of the TV shows around? If everyone thinks they can write a book, even more people think they can sing.'

'Listen, Cari, I want to apologise. I should have told you everything. I saw the call from Beatrice—'

Cari held a hand up.

'Enough!' she yelled, frightening herself with her intensity. 'I don't want to hear it.'

Conal stood up and she had to take a step back.

'Why are you running away from me, Cari,' he said, looking genuinely lost for the first time. 'I can explain.'

'There's always a rational explanation, isn't there? Well, I'm not ready for any more life-shattering rational explanations,' she shouted. 'Keep away from me, Conal. It's over. Finished. Done. Call me again and I phone the police. I have had enough explanations to last me a lifetime.' And she left, slamming the door behind her.

Three years earlier

After the debacle in the church, Cari couldn't bear to think about the wedding or the honeymoon.

It wasn't as if she had even known where she was going, was it?

'You've got to find him and talk to him,' Jojo had said a few days after the aborted ceremony, when Cari was still hiding out in Jojo's spare bedroom, refusing to talk to anybody except for her parents, Maggie, Hugh and Jojo, obviously.

Even then, she wasn't really talking much: she was

communicating in the odd sentence and then she'd burst into tears and of course, when you were like Cari, you didn't want anyone to see you cry.

What sort of a fool had she been, how would she not have known there was something else going on?

The details were sketchy, despite CIA-level investigations going on as to what had happened with Barney and Traci and why Barney had broken off the engagement in such hideous style.

Nora had wanted to go round to Barney's house and rip him to shreds, but Mick, who wanted to rip him to shreds even more, had intervened and said that this was not going to be a good plan.

'I have spoken to Owen on the phone,' Mick said, 'and he doesn't know what's going on either. Yvonne's taken to her bed, so no surprise there. Owen says he's sorry, so sorry because he and Yvonne love Cari and they had no idea Barney was doing anything with Traci and as for marrying her... they're as shocked as us.'

Everyone was quiet in the face of such oddness. Why would Barney, who had loved and adored Cari for so long, suddenly run off with her cousin?

Discussions were limited on Traci. Nobody wanted to talk about her, out of respect for Cari, but Cari wanted to talk about her all right. Except the only person she could have any decent conversation with, any decent bitching with, was Jojo.

Cari's plan to let karma be her guide and never bitch too much about anyone had disintegrated along with her unused wedding bouquet.

'She had buck teeth when we were growing up, they stuck out like Bugs bloody Bunny and she was a bag of bones, even then,' Cari recalled with rage. 'Remember when we got those training bras and she couldn't fill one and she was so jealous because I had proper boobs when I was fourteen. She was always jealous of us. I never did understand her, she was never one of our friends. Do you think that was it? Do you think she wanted what I had, that she took Barney because he was mine?'

Jojo had looked at her cousin sadly.

'I don't know.' said Jojo again.

Slowly, information dripped out from the other camp. Barney's mother, Yvonne, and his sister Jacinta were overcome with mortification and upset and had come, waving the white flag, over to Mick and Nora's house.

'We had no idea, you have to believe us,' Yvonne wailed. 'We had absolutely no idea he was going to do that, we love Cari, you know that too.'

'I don't know who I want to kill most,' Jacinta had said, 'him or that stupid cow.'

Nora knew that name calling was going to get nobody anywhere so she stuck with the facts.

'Barney hasn't been in touch with Cari since the wedding, nothing, not a text, not a phone call, nothing. We have tried ringing him but he won't answer any of our phones: not mine, not Mick's; why do you think he did it? It might help Cari move on if we knew what had happened.'

And Yvonne, who couldn't tell a lie to save her life, had looked up at the woman she had expected to be related to only a few days before and said, 'She's pregnant.'

'Ah,' said Nora. 'Seems like he was a busier bee than we'd all thought.'

Yvonne spoke as if reading from a formal statement: 'He just thinks this is the right thing to do, this is what he has to do.'

'He didn't have to wait until our daughter was standing at the altar in front of all her friends and family, did he?' growled Mick.

'No, he didn't have to wait until that moment,' agreed Jacinta. 'I'm with you, Mick, I can't believe he'd do that to Cari, but I could tell he wasn't himself the last few days before the wedding, and it must have been this. I don't trust Traci. If only we could get to the bottom of it, then maybe Traci would go off and everything would be back to normal and—'

'I don't think anything is going to be back the way it was before,' said Nora, trying to be kind. 'A baby's on the way, for a start.

'Cari's had her heart broken and she has been publicly humiliated into the bargain. I don't think there is any way of coming back from any of that. Add to that the fact that Barney hasn't been in touch with her.' She looked upstairs, as if she knew her daughter was sitting on the exact mid-way step of the stairs of the house in Longford Terrace, listening. 'If only he'd come clean and said, "Traci's pregnant and I have responsibilities towards her and towards my baby." If he had said any of that then things would be different, but to do it to her at the altar.'

They were all silent, there was nothing anyone could say.

Finally Cari spoke from her position on the stairs. 'He's a coward, tell him I said that, Jacinta.'

'I wish he'd ring me,' Cari said to Jojo that evening. 'And then I could tell him how much I hate him, because I spend all the time in this room alone telling him that – except he's not here to hear the words. But I practise them over and over in my head: "Why didn't you tell me, why couldn't we have a conversation, why did you leave it until the very last minute?"'

Jojo was at a loss for the answer. Barney had seemed to be in love with Cari, nobody could have faked that and they hadn't all imagined it.

Jojo had never liked Traci, who was skinny, predatory and who, when asked as a child which ice cream she'd wanted, would always answer 'hers'.

In this case, it seemed that Traci had wanted whatever Cari had and she'd got it.

'I think, perhaps, that Barney was scared,' suggested Jojo,

because she was sure Traci had got her claws into Barney and that with the correct effort, the claws could be unhooked.

Cari was not impressed: in fact, she was outraged.

'Nonsense,' she snapped. 'Barney was never afraid in his whole life. I know Traci is a bitch in heels but Barney knew what she was like. He knew what he was getting into bed with—'

And then Cari had to stop in case she had a heart attack at the thought of Barney leaving Traci's bed and coming home to hers. If Cari had fallen in love with someone else, she'd have had the courage to tell Barney about it. She wouldn't have left him at the altar. How could anyone do that?

In the end Hugh brokered the peace deal.

Barney contacted Hugh first.

'What do you want?' Hugh said coldly. After all, he was the one who'd had Cari living in his house on and off for the past three weeks, watching her get thin and white-faced, watching her face get pinched and sadder with every day. He kept waiting for the moment when she'd cheer up and somehow come out of it, reach that Beyoncé moment of female empowerment.

But no, three weeks was clearly not enough time to get over a broken heart.

Tests had proved it took at least six months actually, Jojo had told him, as they lay in bed together holding hands, listening to Cari in the other room crying herself to sleep.

So when Barney contacted Hugh, Hugh was not really keen on having a conversation with a man he considered to be scum of the highest order.

'I just need to explain to somebody, and I need to speak to Cari,' Barney said.

Hugh was at work when he had taken the call: that was partly why he had taken it. He'd looked at his mobile quickly, seen Barney's number, and had clicked 'accept' almost automatically.

'Why haven't you tried to talk to Cari herself?' Hugh asked. 'I'm not the person you left standing at the altar in front of everyone, I'm not the person you let down or pretended to be in love with—'

'I was in love with her, I—'

For a moment Hugh thought that Barney was going to say, 'I still am in love with her,' but he must have been imagining it, because if you were in love with someone, then you married them or you explained things to them no matter what was going on in the rest of your life.

'Why Traci?' demanded Hugh. 'I mean of all the people in all the world you could have cheated on Cari with, why do it with her second cousin?'

'I can't explain it,' Barney said. 'But I never meant it to happen.'

'Says every guy, everywhere,' Hugh snapped back. 'I never meant it to happen, she just ended up on my lap with no clothes on, how did that happen?'

'It wasn't like that,' Barney said. 'I, I loved Cari so much and I can't really explain what happened but I'm trying to do the honourable thing here and—'

Hugh cut him off instantly. 'There is nothing honourable in what has gone on, your behaviour has not been honourable and you're not contacting Cari to explain. Not one single thing you've done has been honourable.'

'I know that,' said Barney, 'I just need to talk to her, not on the phone, either. I'd like to meet her somewhere that doesn't belong to either of us, not your house and I know she's staying there, not our old place – by the way I have moved all my stuff out, she can go back there.'

'And have you moved the wedding presents out?' Hugh asked acidly.

'I got my mum and Jacinta to do that, I wouldn't ask Cari to do that.'

'Great. Nice to hear you have got one decent bone in your body.'

'Give me a break will you?' Barney asked. 'Just ten minutes with Cari, that's all I'm asking, ten minutes.'

Cari sat at a seat outside the café. It was April now, warmer, and people sat outside enjoying glasses of wine, cappuccinos and smoking cigarettes because they couldn't smoke inside. There was a buzz in the air that came from being in the city centre, a buzz from it being early evening on a Thursday when people were going home from work, full of the joys of spring with just one more day of the week to go and then, yahoo, the weekend.

Cari didn't care about weekends any more. She could hardly remember what it had been like when she did. She didn't care that she had got really thin and that her skinniest jeans were hanging off her.

She did mildly care that she looked like a corpse microwaved up when she looked in the mirror and saw that she had big dark purple circles under her eyes, but she didn't really care that much: who was going to be looking at her?

She was damaged goods, the girl dumped at the altar.

She was surprised it wasn't on YouTube already.

She stirred her green tea some more, just for something to do. She'd have liked a coffee but she was sleeping so badly that it was crazy to think of having caffeine at this hour of the day. She had chosen this place because she and Barney had never come here before. It was entirely unsuitable for her work, although it wasn't too far from Barney's, but she wasn't working at the moment, she was still – laugh – supposed to be on her honeymoon, going back on Monday. Now *that* was going to be a complete riot. No matter how much she liked all the people in Cambridge Publishing, it was going to be horrible facing work after the last three weeks. Her colleagues had been there in the church: they'd witnessed it all.

How did a person go back into work after that?

'Hi all, I had three lovely weeks off. Yes, I did lose weight! It's the Dumped At The Altar diet. No, don't try it – it's a bit drastic. So, how are all of you?'

No, that didn't quite cut it.

'Cari.' He was beside her and she hadn't heard him come up, she had been so busy thinking about the hideous past and her empty future.

'Hello,' she said, shocked and then irritated to see that he looked almost unchanged. Barney didn't look as if he had been crying into his pillow every night, he didn't look as if he had lost weight out of anxiety and a complete lack of appetite.

He was still good-looking, still with a hint of the tan from when he'd gone skiing in January with some pals from work. She'd been too busy, hadn't gone. And skiing was so expensive. But maybe he'd been off with Tricky Traci then.

'May I sit down?'

'Of course,' she snapped out.

She moved her chair back away from the table, wanting to be as far from him as physically possible. And if she was too close to him, she might remember that she'd lain in bed with this man, had slept entwined with him for over a year, had promised to marry him and worn his ring on her finger. Had believed it when he said he loved her!

What sort of a moron was she to have believed in him?

No matter what excuse he came up with, it didn't matter. She had made the biggest mistake of her life and she would never trust another man again. Clearly her judgement was appalling.

Jojo thought this was going to be closure but Cari knew it wouldn't be.

Closure was a dumb notion made up by psychologists who justified people going to them for ever, the concept that one day you'd get over something and be able to say, 'OK, that's in the past, I'm better, I've moved on.'

Bullshit.

Cari would never move on, this would never be in her past. It would always be staring up at her, saying, 'You made a phenomenal mistake, your judgement of character is hopeless.'

She glared at the man who'd broken her heart.

'I've only got five minutes,' she snapped, sounding like the woman who did deals and talked to agents in a tough voice.

'Please don't be like that,' Barney said.

It was all Cari could do not to throw her entire cup of boiling green tea at him.

'I will be whatever way I feel like,' she said, 'I have earned that right, I think. You've got exactly five minutes to tell me whatever it is you feel you need to tell me and then I want you out of my life for ever, got it?' She set the alarm on her phone and then folded her arms.

'Fine.' He looked down, discomfited.

Barney was normally confident, full of enthusiasm and energy. Yet beneath the façade of good health, she could actually see none of those things as she stared at him. He was diminished after all. Good.

There had to be a hopeless waster there, didn't there? Because otherwise, she was an idiot.

'I'm sorry I didn't ring you immediately afterwards, I didn't know what to say.'

'Was Traci sitting outside the church in a car, a getaway car?' Cari said. 'Was that it?'

'Almost,' he said.

'Did you come on to her or did she come on to you? I ask just for the sake of it, I'm not really interested,' Cari went on. 'It would be nice to be able to fill in the blanks. I knew there was something wrong for a few weeks before the wedding and you didn't have the courage to tell me. Plus, the night before the wedding you knew the game was up and you didn't have the courage to say it, you couldn't say, "Let's not go through with this." No. You had to humiliate me in front of everyone I care about.'

For the first time, he looked anguished.

'I wanted to say something but I didn't know how. The morning of the wedding, she rang me, said she'd turn up at the ceremony and—'

'She's pregnant, right?' interrupted Cari. 'So this pregnancy didn't just materialise two hours, or twenty-four hours for that matter, before our wedding, did it?'

'No.'

'I thought not,' snapped Cari.

'You see, it's Traci and I honestly thought she was just saying it. I didn't believe she was really pregnant,' Barney said.

Cari took that information in.

He had slept with Traci – obviously, this was apparent to everyone if Traci was pregnant but to hear him discuss her cousin's pregnancy made the vision of him and Traci in bed trample through her brain. Barney had promised to love *her* for ever, not Traci.

How could you ever think you knew a person? Did everyone lie?

Barney was still talking: '…and then she had proof that she was and there was no going back, and I couldn't do that to her, but I couldn't do that to you by lying and getting married.'

'So you couldn't dump her but you thought you might just dump me in the most public manner possible,' Cari said drily. 'Thanks for that.'

'It wasn't like that, I was so confused,' Barney said.

Cari stared at him, the man she had been going to marry. This man who had been so confused by getting another woman pregnant that he hadn't been able to tell his fiancé what had happened. He hadn't been able to end it all with the minimum of pain and agony and humiliation. In a way, the humiliation was almost the smallest part, the fact that she meant so little to him that he'd been able to leave her at the altar, *that* was the hardest part.

'You've done me a favour,' she said, getting to her feet,

smiling a smile that was not one of happiness and owed a lot to teeth-grinding. Her alarm still hadn't sounded but she'd had enough. Time was up.

'You've shown me what guys are like. Thanks for that, Barney, I hope you and Traci will be very happy.'

'Please don't go. There's so much I want to say to you,' Barney said, and he reached out and grabbed her arm.

Cari pulled back as if she'd been burned.

'Don't ever touch me again,' she said furiously. 'Don't ever contact me again, you are out of my life.'

And she walked off.

She was proud that after it all she wasn't crying. She would never cry over a man again.

Twenty-One

SECRETS OF A HAPPY MARRIAGE #7

Never underestimate kindness. Being kind to the person
you love is worth more than a hundred gifts. Kindness
makes us feel loved, supported and appreciated.

It was over: Bess knew it.

Her marriage was over.

Nora's notion of compromise had gone. She and Edward
had managed a certain amount of compromise and trying to
be nice to each other. They'd gone out to dinner instead of
eating at home, and it had been almost like in the old days,
almost.

The party was nearly upon them and Bess was praying that
Jojo would come, and that the presence of Nora and Hugh and
everyone else would act like a balm upon her and it would be
like the wedding: Jojo could be civil to Bess and accepting of
her father's new marriage because she'd done so at the actual
wedding. This was just one event.

Bess was sure things were improving: Nora must have spoken
to Jojo. That had to be it.

And then Jojo had phoned Edward, late one night.

'Hi, Jojo, honey. I thought you had your girls' night in
tonight,' Bess heard him say and she felt the ache of loving
and not being loved in return.

It was the warm, loving way he spoke to Jojo, the way he
once used to speak to Bess, too, as if she was one of the most
important people in his life. But he didn't speak to her like
that now.

The tone he used with her was cool, businesslike.

As if aware of this, Edward took his mobile into his study and shut the door.

Jealousy and then pain shafted Bess and she almost went upstairs and packed a bag then and there.

It was over – she knew that now. She couldn't stay with a man who spoke to her like someone selling him insurance, and spoke to his daughter with love and affection. She hadn't signed on for this. She had signed on for actual love. Togetherness. Respect.

She began to climb the stairs, thinking of what she could take but something stopped her. Fine. Her marriage was over.

She would do this with dignity. She would go to the big seventieth birthday she'd arranged so lovingly for her husband. She would let everyone see the love and care she'd put into it, and then, when she got back to Dublin, she'd take her belongings and move out.

There would be gossip but then, no matter what you did, people gossiped. There was no point in living your life on the principle of whether your actions would cause gossip or not.

'Daddy,' said Jojo and she was crying.

'What is it, my darling?' said Edward, and he wished they weren't on the phone and he was with her.

'I just needed to talk to you. Hugh's out and I had a fight with Cari.'

'A fight with Cari?'

Edward was astounded. Jojo and Cari never fought. They had the odd squabble but they were such wonderful friends.

'Over what?' said Edward, feeling an ache in his chest. He couldn't take much more of this stress. It was truly killing him.

'Over my infertility treatment. Oh, Daddy, we've tried three times and it hasn't worked out.'

Now Edward felt as if he'd been punched in the chest.

'Infertility treatment? Honey, why didn't you tell me? I can't believe you didn't – I love you and I could have been there for you …'

'But you'd have told Bess and I didn't want her to know. Mum couldn't know, you see.'

Edward sat down on his office chair, feeling the grief he'd felt when Lottie was ill. Everything then had been black too, black and collapsing all around him.

This was his fault. He'd failed his daughter all because of his selfishness.

'My darling Jojo, why couldn't you tell me? You can tell me anything. Where are you? I'll come and meet you now.'

'I'm home. Hugh's out and Trina and Maggie have gone. It's just me.'

'I'll be there in twenty minutes,' said her father.

As Edward drove quickly down the drive, he didn't see Bess watching him from a front window.

Nor was he there to see her begin to pack up her clothes. She'd begin to move them back into her apartment. Just some of them. Better to get started now. That way it would be easier when the party was over. She could simply come back here, pack up her last few things and leave the Brannigans for ever.

'You think I'm going? To an awards ceremony that plans to honour an author I no longer edit?'

Cari stood in Jeff's office and glared at him, letting the cold blast of her anger towards Conal, Gavin and John Steele hit poor Jeff like a polar frost.

'You have to,' said Jeff, slumping back in his chair. 'We all have to. Personally, I'd rather chew my own leg off because I hate these bloody award ceremonies but I, as MD, have to go. And you, as editor of *Rock and A Hard Place*, John Steele's latest book, the one that is up for an award, by the way, have to go too.'

'I don't care,' rapped out Cari.

Jeff blinked at her and then sighed.

'Cari, I know this has all been hard for you personally with the John Steele thing and it's been a hit for the office too because now he's not ours, not the Irish team's author any more, but this is a job: if we want to pay the bills, we work and we go to award ceremonies and we grit out teeth. *Capisce?*'

'I don't want to see him again,' yelled Cari, and in her heart, she wasn't even speaking only about John Steele. She didn't care about bloody Gavin either.

She was thinking of Conal, the bastard, who'd gone to bed with her because he had a vacant slot waiting for the whenever-ready Beatrice, who was now only too eager to clamber aboard Conal and his bloody Hard Place.

'Is this about Conal?' asked Jeff.

Cari made a noise that sounded like a growl.

'Did you just growl?' said Jeff, utterly astonished.

'I might have,' said Cari, startled out of her anger. 'Didn't know I could.'

Jeff got up, went to the other side of his desk and hugged her.

'I know I'm not the one you want to hug and if you want to kick him in the nuts, don't do it to me just because I'm here and he's not, but Conal's a good guy, Cari. I'd have never set you up with him if he was a bastard. I care for you. We've worked together for six years now; I'd like to think you trust me.'

'I trust you,' said Cari deliberately, 'and I trust my father, my uncles, my cousin and my cousin-in-law, Hugh. That's about it. Oh yeah,' she added, as she spotted Declan moving past the office window. 'I trust Declan.'

'He's bringing a date to the ceremony,' Jeff remarked, looking at Declan.

'Really? Is he mad?'

Jeff held up both hands. 'He's paying for the ticket – the company only pays for staff and if he wants to show his beloved the people he works with and the industry he works in, then the Stella Book Awards are the place to do it.'

'You mean he wants to show someone us all muttering under our breath when people we dislike win and show them how trollied a bunch of publishers can be when one of their authors wins and free drink is ordered?'

'Beats me,' said Jeff. 'So, you're coming, right?'

'Right,' said Cari, resigned. 'It's the night before my uncle's having this big party in Kerry for his seventieth birthday, so I won't be staying late, OK? I'm driving to Kerry first thing the next morning.'

'If I was a woman, I'd get an amazing dress, just to show to Edwin, John Steele, Gavin and everyone else how fabulous you are,' said Jeff, pleased now.

'What sort of fabulous dress…?' enquired Cari.

'Oh sparkly, and low cut and show off your legs and heels, yes heels! And lots of make-up.'

Cari laughed for what felt like the first time since that morning when she'd got the email about the fact that she hadn't replied to her invitation to the awards ceremony.

'Don't ever become a transvestite, Jeff,' she said. 'You'd have the worst taste ever. It's legs *or* boobs not both at the same time, and if it's sparkly, it has to be classy or you're going into money-for-sex territory.'

'I'm just saying what I'd tell Anna if she had to go to something she hated,' he said, a bit wounded.

'Ah, but if she did,' Cari said sadly, 'she'd have you with her.'

Gavin Watson had never had a panic attack in his life – until today. He'd remembered editing a book about anxiety when he had been just a junior editor, not that he'd bothered too much with the editing because he knew non-fiction wasn't where he wanted to work and it had been terminally boring, but he remembered the details: the feeling that his pulse was going to burst out of his body, the thumping heart, the gasping for breath, the feeling of impending doom.

It had all happened out of the blue: John Steele's agent, Freddie North, had sent an anxiety-inducing email about his most important client.

'John is really worried about this book. And the book tour. Between you and me, Gavin, I'm not sure this new system of editing is working out. John likes brainstorming plot details and talking it over. He's not getting that from you. We need to discuss this urgently. Today. What time are you free?'

Gavin read and reread the email several times, which was where the panic attack had come on.

He was sitting in his office, a very nice corner one in Cambridge House in London, and he'd been thinking that all was pretty good with his world because he had some great books on his list, he had a big trip to New York planned soon, and a wildly attractive new agent at Curtis Brown had smiled at him at a launch the previous night, making him think that he might be in with a chance. Before his fabulous job success, Gavin had never had luck with women but now he felt powerful and on the up: this gave him a sense of confidence and women no longer looked at him as if he was a sleazy guy, which is what he had been called in college. Now, as a publisher and John Steele's editor, they talked to him happily. It was heady this power stuff.

Up until Freddie North's email, life had looked pretty damn amazing and now this.

Quickly, he dialled the agent's private number. Freddie had barely got his name out before Gavin launched into him. Attack is the best form of defence, Gavin found, despite the fact that older, wiser editors had told him a calm head was a great asset in publishing, as indeed in any industry.

'What the hell is going on, Freddie?' he asked.

'Good morning, Gavin,' said Freddie coolly. 'I'll tell you what's going on: John and I are worried that this isn't working out. He's incredibly anxious about this book in a way he hasn't been since his first novel – now that's not good, for any of us.' Freddie paused. 'He hasn't said as much, but I feel it would be better if he had Cari Brannigan back as his editor. She keeps him calm, gets the books out on time and has a brilliant relationship with him. I know you don't want to hear this but I have to think of my client—'

'Well, he can't have her, can he?' screeched Gavin, interrupting. 'I'm his editor, we agreed. It was part of the plan. Like touring – is he pulling out of that as well?'

There was silence on the other end of the line and Gavin had a sinking feeling, knew that touring was no longer on the John Steele agenda.

'We paid him a lot of money and he can't renege on the deal,' he said slowly, trying to put menace in there.

But this wasn't Freddie North's first rodeo and the younger man's attempt at menace meant absolutely nothing to him. Freddie had agented books about the IRA, about Russian dissidents, about arms dealers. Gavin Watson throwing a hissy fit was hardly going to faze him.

'Do you want me to talk to someone else,' Freddie asked, still calm. 'I wanted to go to you first to tell you what's going on but I can talk to Edwin just as easily.'

The managing director, the one man who could pluck John Steele from Gavin's list just as easily as he had plucked Steele from Cari Brannigan's list.

'But John and I get on brilliantly,' Gavin found himself saying, realising it was what Cari had said several months ago.

'I don't see much evidence of actual editing,' said Freddie caustically, 'and he's not happy. John is the talent and it's got to be our aim to keep the talent happy.'

'And sell books,' added Gavin nastily.

'The two are not mutually exclusive,' said Freddie, 'and as

someone who has been an agent for thirty years, I find that happy authors tend to work better. John might write books about a hero who can gut a man with four swipes of a blade, but personally he's an emotional man and he needs to trust you. He also needs to be happy with how you handle his book, happy with the publicity, happy with the marketing, happy with the sales, happy with you, Gavin. Because if you mess that up, when his contract is up, he'll move. It's that simple. And publishers will be queuing up to sign him. You'll be the man who lost John Steele from Cambridge, which will put a dent in your swift climb to the top.'

Gavin felt the panic overwhelm him again. It could all fall apart so easily. He thought of the chummy way he and Freddie had discussed removing John Steele from Cari Brannigan in the first place.

It had been his idea, naturally. John Steele was too valuable to let someone like bloody Brannigan get away with him. He, Gavin Watson, should be the editor of a successful writer like John Steele. One of the company's most successful writers.

Freddie had been amenable to having someone in London looking after John's career, rather than Cari, stuck in the Irish office, away from the cut and thrust of the main company.

Suddenly it looked like it was all falling apart. He had to rescue it, had to sort it out.

'I'll fly down to Cork, see him, talk to him, sort this out,' said Gavin, flattening down all the fear.

'OK,' said Freddie, 'you do that. But we need this fixed within the next few days. I don't want him upset.'

Freddie hung up without another word, and Gavin felt the panic attack recede to be replaced by something more in the line of rage.

He bet that bitch Cari Brannigan had got in touch with John Steele: he knew it! She was the one who was messing this up. It couldn't be him, everyone said he was brilliant. Look at how far he had come in a couple of years. Yes, it was her, meddling, trying to woo his client. Cow.

He pressed a button on his phone and got through to the assistant that he and two other editors shared. 'Miriam,' he snapped, 'I need to get to Cork to see John Steele asap. Check out flights for me, will you? I'll mail him, tell him I'm dropping in.'

Twenty-Two

'May your choices reflect your hopes,
not your fears.'
Nelson Mandela

Faenia Lennox liked to travel light. But due to weather considerations, she'd decided that she'd bring two medium bags to Ireland, nothing too heavy since she was flying from San Francisco to LA, to get the direct flight to Dublin.

There were no sign of her bags on the baggage carousel in Dublin. No sign of quite a lot of bags and an airport person was being harassed by irate passengers as he passed.

'Yours lost too?' said PJ, the young man beside her at the baggage carousel in the airport who'd looked at Faenia's exquisitely cut short white hair, tanned but wrinkled hands, and guessed she had to be about sixty. She was alone and he felt he should help. His mother had drummed into him that it was important to give up your seat on the bus to an older person and this lady – and everything about her shrieked lady – was obviously older and not strong.

'I can travel long distance with just cabin baggage but this time, I put a couple of bags through because of the weather. In this country, it's better to be prepared for anything,' Faenia said with her usual warm cheerfulness.

'So you've been here before?' PJ asked, satisfied with this explanation. She was good-looking for a woman of her age, he thought, but then, in California, it was hard to tell anyone's age.

Women in cut-off shorts and halters could look mid-thirties from behind and then turn around to show off elderly faces with large fake lips and pillowy cheeks.

But this woman wasn't like that. She might be sixty, he reckoned, but she had a youthful, energetic sense about her. She was almost sexy, he thought: then felt shocked at such a notion. He was only twenty-three.

She could be his mother.

His granny.

She was glamorous like a movie star and all that, what with the soft caramel sweater she was wearing and those amazing eyes, bluey green, and they weren't coloured contact lenses, he reckoned. She wore subtle make-up and there again, she was nothing like his granny, who had a perm twice a year and only took lipstick and Revlon powder out for weddings, funerals and Christmas.

'I was born here,' said Faenia, still cheerful, even though it was half six in the morning and to PJ, the flight from LA had felt like a trek across the universe that had taken a month.

The queue for the plane loo had been too big and frantic in the hour before they landed, so he hadn't even got to brush his teeth.

This woman looked like she was ready for anything, with that glossy smile, interested eyes and some sort of tribal necklace yoke on her neck.

'You don't sound it,' PJ said, astonished. 'No trace of an accent. How long are you staying?'

'I don't know. A few weeks or more, maybe. You?'

'Home to stay,' said PJ, who was coming home from LA after three years and had all his stuff in a rucksack and a battered suitcase he'd been given by his friend, Miguel, who said loftily that he would never need it again because he was staying in Tinseltown, come what may.

PJ had wished Miguel luck but didn't hold out that much hope.

Acting was not as easy as everyone said it was, as it turned out. Tips from his waitering jobs were what had made life better in La La Land, as his father had called it. Tips, the golden sunshine and the golden girls, but golden girls wanted to be actresses too and were not interested in Irish actors who'd had bit parts at home and no parts at all in Hollywood.

'Oh, happiness! That's one of mine,' she said, as a nice brown suitcase, nothing fancy though, was flung at high speed from the baggage chute.

PJ hauled it easily onto her trolley.

'Thank you. I can't tell you how grateful I am to you for that. I'd have ruptured some bit of me if I'd done it. I'm Faenia Lennox,' said the woman, holding out her hand.

'PJ Tallon,' said PJ.

They talked idly while the baggage went round.

A Louis Vuitton bag sailed past.

'If I had one of those, I wouldn't put it in the hold,' PJ said with a certain longing in his voice.

He'd gone out with a girl in LA who had a vintage Louis Vuitton handbag and had lovingly cared for it as if it were a small pet.

'People are proud of their nice things,' Faenia said thoughtfully, as an over-made-up woman in murderously high heels and tight leather trousers struggled to get the Vuitton off the carousel. 'And I think if they're feeling a bit insecure, it cheers them up to see proof that they earned this expensive bag.'

'We all feel a bit insecure from time to time,' PJ said ruefully as his battered suitcase made it round to their spot.

'Isn't it lucky that you and I are so well adjusted that we don't need fancy suitcases to cheer us up,' Faenia said. 'I'm being collected once I've got my bags. Do you need a lift?'

Faenia sat in the back of the silver Mercedes as PJ and the driver got the luggage in the trunk. No, she couldn't say trunk any more. She had to remember the European words for things. Boot, that was it. Eighteen years in Ireland, nearly forty out of it and she'd entirely forgotten the lingo. At home – well, in San

Francisco – people still said she sounded Irish and she used to tell them about the lovely village, Lisowen, she came from.

It had been years before she'd done that.

Obviously, darling Chuck had known all about Ireland and her flight to New York, so too had Marvin and Nic. She had never wanted any secrets from the people she loved. But many of her American friends hadn't probed when Faenia gently deflected talk away from why she'd gone to the US at such an early age – and why she never went home.

'Nobody left at home,' she'd lied, and then felt a hollow emptiness at having lied so horribly.

There were people left at home but she was gone so long, had felt the guilt at having run off for so long, that she couldn't go back.

Now, Isobel was using some magic to pull her back to Lisowen and the family.

But home was somehow still Ireland. Weird, that. She must tell Nic—

And then it hit her.

No Nic.

She had left one more message on Nic's answerphone:

'I love you and I want to be with you. It's really up to you now, Nic. I'm going to be away for a while, so if you want to come to the house and get your stuff, work away.'

Faenia thought she might cry when she said that.

Nic would come and pick up the leftover things: clothes, books, whatever.

It was over. Who was she kidding with this last-ditch attempt at getting back together. She'd told Nic it was all or nothing.

Faenia was too old to settle for second best any more.

Once the bags were stashed, PJ and the driver settled into the car and PJ got into the reflective mood that hit people when home was only minutes away after entire years abroad.

'My father will say I've wasted my time in America when I could have been in college studying business,' PJ said wistfully. 'He wants me in the family business, making it more commercially successful. He runs a builders' suppliers. He wants to call it Tallon & Sons.'

'And you don't want to be the & Sons,' said Faenia wisely.

'No. Never did.'

'You haven't wasted your time in the States. No time spent anywhere is ever wasted. You've learned how to stand on your own two feet in one of the toughest towns around. You've worked, you've seen a bit of the world. You can find your own place, be happy to be home, tell them you've missed them and you can tell your dad what you'd like to do. Which is...?'

Please don't say 'more acting', she thought. Having known many actors and lived in California for many years, her opinion of acting was that it was similar to wanting to be a high-wire artist in the circus: better to admire from afar than actually put a toe on the wire one hundred feet above ground without a net.

'It's going to sound stupid,' PJ said. 'My dad would call it totally daft, but I'd like to be a drama teacher—'

Faenia beamed at him and PJ, thrilled to see someone approving, managed a hint of a smile back.

'He likes what is safe and what he knows, but he also knows that you do what you want anyway. Hasn't he had two years to get used to that idea?' she said.

'But when you're home' – PJ gestured out the window to a country that clearly looked familiar to him and like another planet to Faenia after living abroad for so long – 'it's like nothing's changed. He'll think: right, you failed at the acting, now it's time to settle down with the business...'

'You'll find everything has changed,' Faenia interrupted. '*You've* changed. You've learned a lot and now you've come home with this new plan and that's it. You're not looking for handouts. You know how to stand on your own two feet. You might be able to help your dad find the right man for his business. You're a part of it all – just not in the middle of the family business.'

She could see PJ mentally trying out this new theory, telling his family his plans.

She could see those big, strong shoulders relax. He was a kind boy. He loved his family, worried about them.

She thought of her baby boy, born too early to live, the child that had died before he'd been born. That boy would be in his forties now, a lot older than sweet PJ here.

Would her life have been different if her son had lived? She might still be married to Chuck in the lovely ranch in Texas but they might never have had their own children and that would have been hard for Chuck. As it was, she'd nearly died when her baby had come so early and she'd been told other children were out of the question. In the end, that had eaten away at her and Chuck's marriage like woodworm.

She'd grieved over her stillborn son, grieved over her marriage but she'd had her stepchildren – Lola, funny, irreverent and spectacularly kind in her own way, and Marc, grave and professorial, as different from his sister as possible.

They were her second husband Marvin's grown-up children, and even though she and Marvin had been married only a few years before the dementia took him away into a place where none of them could reach him and he'd died three years later, Lola and Marc were a part of Faenia's life and always would be.

But they didn't worry about her the way PJ seemed to worry about his parents – Lola fondly called Faenia an Irish witch who was safe even in the worst areas of San Francisco.

'You don't need to carry concealed,' she'd laugh, coming up tall and strong behind Faenia to hug her. 'You just shoot gangbangers with one of those tough Irish glares and yell that you're going to put a curse on them – those guys are gonna run. Same as you made boyfriends you didn't approve of run.'

'Wasn't I right?' Faenia said, a twinkle in her eyes.

'Oh yeah, you were always right,' Lola agreed. 'Seeing the future: another part of your spooky Celtic repertoire.'

'What about you?' PJ said as the car came off the motorway and began winding round a spaghetti junction of slip roads. 'When's your family expecting you?'

'Oh, they don't know I'm coming,' said Faenia, surprising herself with her cheerfulness. 'It's a surprise.'

'You're coming home and they don't know?'

PJ was astonished. His mother would be up with a cooked breakfast ready to go and she'd texted him twice already to find out when he'd be near the house so she could look out for him. His younger brothers were going to be late into school because they were dying to hug him, and as for his father, well, PJ was going to say the acting thing hadn't worked and he had more secure job training lined up.

But Faenia was coming and nobody knew?

Faenia patted his knee in a kind way. 'Perhaps stay, perhaps not. I kept it to myself because I might throw my family into cardiac arrest if I told them I was coming. It's been quite a while.'

'Since you visited? Well, air fares aren't that cheap ... When were you last home?'

PJ looked out the window at the streams of traffic.

'Nearly forty years,' Faenia said quietly.

Even the driver was lifted out of his professional silence.

'Nearly forty years!' he said. 'You're kidding.'

'You're both young,' Faenia said. 'That amount of time – well – it can fly by, you know.'

PJ caught the driver's eye in the mirror. They were both in their twenties. Forty years sounded like for ever.

'Isn't the rain lovely,' Faenia remarked, as a light March shower dusted the car with sparkling drops and a rainbow shimmered in the sky to their left.

PJ watched her looking out, clearly wanting to change the subject. He suddenly knew who she looked like: Faye Dunaway, that actress who'd been a great beauty in her youth and still had the shimmering hair and the great bones that made people want to look at her face.

PJ had discovered that while he was tall and handsome, with a body honed by time in the gym from training other people, he didn't have the indefinable star quality that made people want to watch him. But this woman did.

The driver was heading to the part of the city where PJ had been born and raised. Traffic notwithstanding, they'd be there in a few minutes.

'Give me your phone number, PJ,' Faenia said, taking out a smartphone and deftly clicking into numbers and emails.

PJ recited his number and email.

Faenia gave him hers as the car pulled up smoothly outside PJ's home. His father's big white van with Tallon's Builders' Suppliers written on it sat on the drive.

'Be firm,' advised Faenia. 'It's your life to live, not anyone else's.'

'Thank you.' PJ leaned forward and hugged her. It seemed like the right thing to do. 'If you're ever at a loose end, you know, give me a buzz and we could have a coffee or something,' he said, a bit awkwardly.

'I will,' she said, with warmth in her voice.

He was halfway out of the car when he stuck his head back in. She'd probably never phone him and he just had to know.

'Just one thing – why are you coming home now?'

'My big brother's seventy,' she said. 'I thought it was time.' She didn't say the rest of it.

'Of course.' PJ nodded, in a way he hoped implied that coming home for a birthday when you'd been away for forty years made perfect sense.

Maybe when you got older, things changed.

365

But he couldn't see himself leaving for forty years, not ever, not under any circumstances.

His front door opened and there they all stood: his family. PJ felt the tug of love for them all.

That could have been it, he thought, waving as Faenia's car began to slide off and he ran to hug his mother and his two little brothers at the same time.

Twenty-Three

'I can only please one person per day.
Today is not your day.
Tomorrow isn't looking good either.'
Anonymous

Jojo was in the shop without Elaine. The place was ghostly: only two customers had been in all morning and neither of them had bought anything.

Elaine would have sold them something, Jojo knew. But how could anybody buy anything off a saleswoman with a face full of tears just waiting to drop.

Perhaps Cari was right – she was on the verge of some sort of collapse. She'd texted Cari to apologise and they'd had a little texting conversation but it had been surface stuff: nothing real. As if they were both too scared to have a proper conversation again.

Now that she'd told Dad what was going on, he kept phoning every day, and dropped round several times during the week, glaring at Hugh when he saw him as if it was all somehow Hugh's fault.

'You told your father?' said Hugh in that neutral voice he was using all the time lately. It was as if he didn't trust himself to speak normally.

'Yes,' said Jojo, as if daring him to query her.

She could do what she wanted. She was the one in pain.

But that wasn't fair, she knew. Hugh was in pain too. Guilt rose in her. She hated how she was hurting Hugh. She'd go and see him at work, hug him, and maybe, maybe it would feel better…

A woman came into the shop idly and Jojo marched to the door.

'Sorry,' she said briskly. 'Closing for lunch.'

'But you don't—'

'We do today.'

Once, Jojo had taken any opportunity to drop into Hugh's office and see him for lunch. That had been in the early, crazy days of their marriage, she remembered.

Now, she never did.

She found a space and a meter, had enough coins in her bag. All good omens. That's what this decision was: a good omen.

Like Elaine reading their horoscopes in the papers in the morning.

She reached the old Georgian building where Hugh's offices were, went in and slipped up the back stairs before the receptionist even spotted her. They could have lunch somewhere simple if Hugh was free. And if he wasn't free, she'd wander round the National Gallery for a while till he had a spare half-hour.

Thinking all of this, she hurried onto his floor, past the desks and up to his office, the door of which was slightly ajar.

No meeting then.

Trying to put a happy smile on her face, a smile that said 'I'm sorry, I need you,' she pushed open the door.

Hugh stood at the window nearest the street, and with her arms around him and her face buried in his neck, was his old friend and colleague Elizabeth.

Hugh's arms were around Elizabeth too, Jojo noted as if from afar.

'Jojo!' Hugh tried to pull away from Elizabeth but she held firm, almost smiling at Jojo.

'It's not – I mean, don't think this is—' tried Hugh.

But Elizabeth had other ideas.

'It is exactly what you think,' she said, her colour heightened.

'You don't deserve him, Jojo. He's a good man and you treat him like shit.'

Jojo stared, dumbstruck.

'Total shit,' went on Elizabeth, on a roll now. 'You don't want Daddy to get married again and you want a baby, and it's your baby and your issues and nobody else is allowed to feel upset.'

'Elizabeth!' Hugh looked stricken and then the formal, decent, everything-by-the-book Hugh Hennessy took over.

He disentangled himself from Elizabeth who stood staring at Jojo almost triumphantly.

'I will move my things out later,' he said in a formal voice. 'I can't do anything else. Except apologise, Jojo. This is not what it seems.'

'Yes it is,' snapped Elizabeth.

Without having uttered a word, Jojo turned and left.

Jojo sat in the car on the way home and felt a clarity she hadn't felt for a very long time. It was like being a computer that had been reset, a slap in the face to a woman screaming hysterically.

For months she'd been caught up in her internal struggles and now she saw that all that struggling and emotional heart-break had brought her nothing. Nothing.

Hugh had loved her and she'd pushed him away. Shoved him away.

Made him feel not just second best but third best, fourth best.

So far down the line that Elizabeth – Elizabeth, it made no sense at all – had been the one he turned to. But then, Jojo had turned to Cari and her father for help, making Hugh know that he came very far down the line: after her, after her desire for a baby, after her grief over her mother. After her hatred of Bess, which was childish and vicious, she knew.

As she drove carefully, fully aware that this was precisely

the moment she should have been going to pieces, she felt an eerie calmness.

And in the calmness came one phrase: it's all your own fault, Jojo.

Cari wanted to pack for the weekend and seeing as she had the book awards the following night, she went home early on Wednesday to get ready.

She was just in the door, when her doorbell rang.

'Delivery,' roared a voice in a thick foreign accent.

Normally deliveries came to the office but plenty of agents had her home address, so Cari, who'd taken off her shoes, padded out to the door and opened it.

Conal stood there.

'Go away!' she howled but he shoved his foot in the door.

'I will call the cops.'

'Please?' he said. 'Just one minute. I've figured out what went wrong – Beatrice called, that was it? You picked it up wrong... She was a woman I went out with for a while but it didn't work with us—'

'She sounded like she was coming right over here pretty damn fast to make it work,' yelled Cari, trying to shove him out the door. 'You never told me. You should have told me! That's the problem. I have trust issues, asshole. You lied to me, bullshitted me about some woman you'd dated for two years and it ended all nicely. "Lovely Yvette, we were like brother and sister... yadda yadda." I told you everything about me, *everything*.'

'I know, just let me explain,' he beseeched.

'I don't want explanations,' said Cari harshly, 'I don't believe them. They're handy ways out of trouble and I don't want to get hurt again.'

'It's not *Madame Butterfly*...' began Conal.

'It fucking is!' screamed Cari, and getting his foot out of the door, slammed it.

She ignored him banging on the door and put the double lock on.

'Go away or I'll call the cops,' she yelled.

In her bedroom, away from the sound of Conal still banging on her front door, she dialled Jojo.

'I need to see you? Can you come over,' said Cari, sobbing into the phone. 'Tell Hugh I'm sorry and I know you're going through so much but if you could just come over for an hour or two I might feel better...'

'I can stay the night,' said Jojo, with a depth of calm that was astonishing even her. 'I think Hugh's left me.'

Cari had stopped crying and ran straight into her cousin's embrace the moment Jojo arrived at the door.

'Jojo, what happened, I can't believe it. No way Hugh's left you—'

Jojo shrugged with terrible sadness. 'He has and it's totally my fault. I wanted our baby, our baby meant more to me than our marriage and I drove him away. We're all supposed to think that marriages are forged in fire like Gandalf's bloody ring, but they're not. They're forged in everyday living: making the other person a cup of coffee, asking them if they're OK and meaning it, being kind, showing them you love them every bloody day in the little things.'

Jojo still didn't cry.

'When one person forgets about the other person and just lives in their own pain, stuck in the grand gesture of themselves, not really caring about anyone else's pain, then there's no hope.'

'Really?' asked Cari, through her own tears. If Hugh and Jojo couldn't make it, who could?

'Yeah, really,' said Jojo. 'Now you've listened to me ad nauseam for two years. Enough about me – you.'

Cari looked glum. 'It's sort of a déjà vu situation...' she began.

For the Stella Awards the next day, Cari wore a dress that made her look like a curvy supermodel on a night out: long and sleek in purple satin, with a halter neck that showed off her sheeny skin, the swell of breasts that needed no bra, and with a hidden slit over one leg that went up to mid-thigh. Her nails were short and painted dark navy, her heels were sky-high.

Jojo had searched through Cari's closet and found it.

'I gave you this: have you ever worn it?'

'Never had the nerve,' said Cari.

'If I have the nerve to go to my father's seventieth—'

'You're going?' interrupted Cari. 'We can go together. Change of heart?'

'I've been a selfish bitch long enough,' said Jojo. 'I've broken up my own marriage – it would be terrible to break up poor Dad's too. So, if I can do that, then you have the nerve to wear this damn dress.'

'Hold on,' said Cari, holding up a hand. 'You cannot get off this lightly. When did you decide to go?'

Jojo looked down miserably.

'When I realised that I have personally destroyed my marriage – although I'd say Elizabeth had a hand in it. Hugh isn't a cheater, he's too decent for that. I think she's always had a thing for him and she just jumped into the vacancy left by me. She might be a wicked old cow, but I left the door open for her to do it,' said Jojo. 'I pushed poor Hugh away, wouldn't let him tell anyone about the infertility and then behaved as if I was the only one suffering.

'When I left town today, I drove out to Mum's grave and I thought of her and all the lessons she'd taught me, and you know what, I've been ignoring them all: to be kind, love others, all that stuff. I've been a bitch, furious with the world for taking her away and then the infertility treatment—'

'Nobody can take that much pain without cracking a bit,' said Cari.

'I know but people do,' said Jojo. 'People have children and lose them. Kids die from cancer. Horrible things happen. If I can't get pregnant naturally, then we could adopt but I wouldn't let Hugh even say the word adoption.'

'Harsh.'

'Stupid,' agreed Jojo. 'What I did to Hugh was terrible but Dad and Bess – I've been trying to make him choose between us. I didn't mean to but I have been, unconsciously. I don't have that right. So that's why I'm going to the party, to make it up to him and her. She probably hates me too.'

'In fairness, you did a pretty good impression of hating her,' Cari pointed out.

'Yeah. So it's going to be a fun weekend. No Hugh and me telling Dad and Bess what a selfish cow I am,' said Jojo.

'Hugh loves you,' said Cari.

Jojo shook her head.'I don't know if he does, Cari. Not any more. He sent me a text that he'd move his clothes out of the house later today.'

'There is no way he'd cheat on you,' insisted Cari. 'I know that I think all men – well, most men – are scum, but not Hugh. He loves you. He's simply doing what he thinks you want him to do. You have to fight to get him back.'

'You think?'

'Oh yeah.'

'Thought you weren't supposed to combine' – Jeff gestured downwards when he spotted Cari at the awards – 'you know, bazooms and leg?' he said.

'I had a change of heart,' said Cari. 'OK, point me in the direction of everyone I need to schmooze.'

'You know who to schmooze better than me,' Jeff said, and loped off.

John Steele watched from his table as Cari Brannigan worked the room like the charmer she was. There was nothing false about the way she talked to people, not like Gavin, who had attached himself to John and Mags early on and was apparently sticking to them in case anyone else tried to get at John. He also, however, displayed his annoying habit of looking around the room for any more important people than the ones he was seated beside.

Gavin was also making great inroads on the wine on their table, even though the dinner hadn't started yet.

'These things are so boring,' said Gavin, gulping up more wine.

'Not if you're up for an award,' said Mags sharply.

She really didn't like Gavin, John knew. Neither did he, he realised.

Jennifer, one of the British team, a woman with a sharp black pageboy haircut and a list of authors like a list of Booker prize winners, sat down beside Mags.

While Gavin looked around the room for important people, Jennifer talked to Mags and John about his new book.

'Is this taking you away from writing?' she said.

'I haven't delivered the first draft yet,' admitted John. 'The plot keeps getting away from me.'

'He needs a bit of brainstorming,' said Mags, as if John's admission was a mistake and she had to cover it up.

'You should meet Gavin tomorrow morning then,' said Jennifer, looking at Gavin with a certain amount of displeasure, as Gavin ignored the conversation entirely.

'I'm going back first thing,' said Gavin, who could look and listen at the same time.

Jennifer's eyes met John's coolly but she said nothing.

John would have loved to have said that Gavin had been to his house but had proved, yet again, to be entirely useless at brainstorming or discussing the plot loopholes. He was basically interested in his own career, not in John's.

John could see Cari leaving one table and looking around for hers. Dinner had been called. He needed to talk to her.

If he could just grab her for a moment and explain the plot problem, then she'd fix it in a moment and he could relax and write the bloody book.

'Excuse me,' he said and shot up from his seat.

Cari decided she'd race to the loo before the dinner proper began. The awards were interspersed between courses so you couldn't nip out to the ladies once it had all started.

She'd just wriggled out of the swing doors into the huge lobby when a voice stopped her.

'Cari!'

It was John Steele.

As this was a business dinner and as she was due up early to drive to Kerry, Cari's drink of choice was orange juice. She was entirely grateful for this right now. With a glass of wine inside her, she might lose her inhibitions and tell John to go forth and multiply in clear Anglo-Saxon. As it was, she smiled professionally.

'Good luck tonight,' she said.

'You look lovely, Cari,' he said. 'Listen, I'm so sorry the way all of this turned out...'

Cari held up one hand, admiring her manicure at the same time. 'It's fine, John,' she said. 'Must rush to the loo. Bye.'

'No, I need to talk to you.'

His hand on her arm stopped her.

'I'm really having trouble with the book – the plot, it's not working out, it's got more holes than one of Mags's bloody bits of knitting and I can't figure out why. I can't get at the magic and...' His eyes glazed over the way they used to when he was discussing plot details and Cari would sit with him, throwing in the odd suggestion until he grinned and he'd say, 'Got it!'

Hauling back her temper because a woman could only cope with so many damned men at one time, Cari gently removed his hand from her arm.

'John, I'm not your editor any more. Gavin is.'

'But just—'

Cari took a step away, making sure he noticed the distance between them.

'You chose Gavin,' she said quietly. 'Not me. You can't run back to me for the tricky little details and let him be your editor. You can't have it both ways. Besides, it's not professional of me to work with you when Gavin's your editor.'

She knew that if Edwin Miller or Jennifer were listening they'd choke, but she didn't care. Let them fire her if they wanted to. Besides, there was nobody listening out here.

'I knew you'd try to get your hands on him,' said a voice, slightly slurred.

Cari and John turned to see Gavin coming towards them.

'Up to your tricks of trying to lure him away with a hot dress, is that it?' said Gavin.

He was definitely drunk.

Suddenly, Cari no longer cared if she was fired or not.

'Gavin,' she said sweetly, leaning in close as if to kiss him.

He stumbled towards her and Cari began her move. It was a very long time since she'd worked on the self-defence book and the writer – a former special forces guy – had come into the office and showed all the girls how to throw a bigger assailant off. But she could remember most of it.

Move in, distract, position your leg so your weight is evenly balanced, lean in, grab your opponent round the waist so you can twist them. Slide your knee to the side, making sure you are hitting your opponent's anterior cruciate ligament and while you shove, twist their body the other way.

It had been a tricky move but not impossible – even in high heels, she found.

'Ouch,' squealed Gavin and he went down, clutching his knee.

'Bad knee?' said Cari solicitously, thinking that Gavin probably wouldn't have damaged anything. Probably.

'Too much wine, I'd say,' she said, shaking her head at John Steele. 'He just tripped over me.'

She yelled over at the bar.

'Man down,' she said cheerfully. 'They're starting early.'

Then, smiling, she said, 'Bye, John,' and walked off.

John Steele had turned away from Cari Brannigan and he was the third man in her life to do so.

It would not happen again.

Getting Gavin on the floor was just… Cari pondered the correct word: fun.

Twenty-Four

'The most effective way
to do it is to do it.'

Amelia Earhart

Gavin Watson had missed a couple of calls on his mobile.

When he finally got around to looking at them, he realised
they were all from Freddie, John Steele's agent. He felt that
weird panicky feeling he had begun to experience lately when
he got any call relating to damned John Steele.

Gavin didn't want to ring the agent on a Friday afternoon.
He had a hangover from the previous evening's awards in
Dublin, a sore knee, plus he had an evening planned, things
to do, parties to go to and Freddie could wait. What could be
that important?

Then a call came through from Edwin, Managing-Director-
of-Cambridge-Edwin, and the sort of person Gavin could not
ignore.

'Hi, Edwin,' he said eagerly, 'how are things? What can I
do for you?'

'You can phone Freddie North,' said Edwin in a deep, low
voice, the sort of voice he used when things were wrong.

It wasn't a voice people heard very often because Edwin
really did have a reputation for kindness and gentleness.

'Phone Freddie, of course,' said Gavin guilelessly, as if he
hadn't ignored several calls from the agent already. 'Do you
know what it's about?'

Gavin had a feeling in the pit of his stomach that he knew
exactly what was up. Things weren't working out between him
and John Steele and there had been several uneasy phone calls

between them. It wasn't just the editing, it was everything, but editing was at the heart of it. Editing wasn't as easy as everyone thought it was – non-professional people thought you just read over something another person had written, said, 'Sure, that's all tickety-boo,' inserted the odd comma and a semicolon for fun, and that was it.

But it was far trickier, you had to develop a relationship with the person and work with them, give them guidance, give them encouragement, have entire conversations about where the whole novel was going, discuss the story arc – stuff that really bored Gavin to tears. He liked the idea of publishing, but editing, not so much.

And last night, John had seemed very out of sorts with him, as had John's annoying little wife.

'John Steele is not happy,' intoned Edwin, still using his deep, dark voice.

'Right,' said Gavin, mentally thinking, well I don't feel very happy right now, either, but tough bananas. John Steele is just going to have to get used to not being happy. Life sucks.

'I can almost hear the thought processes in your head,' said Edwin.

Gavin seriously hoped not. He also wondered why everyone thought Edwin was just an old sweetie. He had to be bloody psychic.

'John is not happy because you are not working with him. You are talking to him about tours and interviews but you are not working with him on his novel, which is your job! He wants an editor. He reached out to Cari Brannigan at the awards last night but she told him she's not his editor and that it wouldn't be professional of her to go behind your back like that.

'This is his fourth book, not the twenty-seventh novel from some bigwig who won't let anyone edit them and considers each word sacrosanct. John Steele wants to be edited, he wants the help. He's one of those writers who needs nurturing. You've heard that word before, Gavin? Nurturing. Now when Freddie and I spoke to you in the first place you said you were up for the nurturing, you said you were up for the phone calls telling him how good he was, phone calls discussing all parts of the plot, you understand?'

'Of course I do,' said Gavin, trying to sound stunned at this implication that he wasn't up for editor of the year at industry awards. 'I've edited many people.'

'Like Evelyn Walker,' said Edwin drily, reminding Gavin of that hideous old woman that Gavin had hated, who'd caused him no end of trouble because his idea of editing and her idea of editing had not gelled.

'Edwin, please don't worry. I'll take care of this. I'll fly to West Cork, we can sort it out.'

'You did that already,' said Edwin. 'The game is up, Gavin, you're no longer editing John Steele. Freddie told me to deliver the message. He was trying to get hold of you himself, but you haven't been returning his calls – which is not a good plan either. At Cambridge Publishing, we return agents' calls. Now why don't you telephone Freddie right now and apologise to him, telephone John Steele and apologise really meaningfully to him and then let me get on with the tricky business of finding an editor for John Steele.'

'Not Cari Brannigan?' said Gavin quickly.

'What have you got against Cari Brannigan precisely?' said Edwin.

'Nothing,' said Gavin, which was true because he didn't have anything particular against her – it was just that she was clever and ambitious and therefore stood in his way. That was all it took with Gavin.

'It will be Cari Brannigan because John wants her back.'

'Whatever makes him happy,' said Gavin piously.

'And I'll see you first thing on Monday morning in my office because we need a talk,' said Edwin. 'John Steele is an important author to us and you could have screwed this up. I only hope we can fix it, I only hope that Cari agrees to edit him again and hasn't already been looking for another job because she hasn't been treated very well in all of this. If she walks, and Steele thinks she's the only editor for him, then he'll walk right after her.'

'Should I phone her too?' said Gavin, then regretted it instantly.

'Hell, no! As I said,' said Edwin, gravelly voiced, 'we'll talk first thing on Monday morning.'

Not much happened in Lisowen village that Mrs Gwen Carlisle didn't know about.

Pregnancy, people who were off the sauce going back on it, affairs, a broken exhaust on the mobile library van – she knew it all. And could be persuaded to tell you all about it under the correct circumstances.

Today, she was up and out of the house earlier than usual because she wanted to be at the church early in order to deliver the latest news. Mass was at ten and half nine was a good time to hit the café for a small tea and to hold court. The church was half a mile away, five minutes in the car, but Gwen had been banned from taking to the roads in her Morris Minor since the incident with the herd of Aberdeen Angus cows.

Mr Ryan was out at his postbox. 'Grand day—' he began, but Gwen was already whisking past.

Mr Ryan was a sweet bachelor who lived on his own in the cottages at the end of Station Road, where Gwen lived in lonely splendour in the old manse, Mr Carlisle having shuffled off this mortal coil many moons ago.

'Grand,' agreed Gwen, as she kept going. Bachelors were rarely any good for gossip. Mr Ryan liked talking about trains (he had model ones) and tomatoes (he had a greenhouse), in that order. No point in wasting good gossip on him.

Lady Lucas drove past in the Land Rover, muck and rust shimmering in the air as she passed. She waved but didn't stop.

Lady Lucas was as bad as Mr Ryan – no time for talking

about local affairs – and she steered as if she was handling a nervous young horse over a tricky jump, so it was safer to say no to her kindly proffered lifts.

Finally, Gwen reached the shops, Clara's Coffee Shop and headquarters central for anyone with a nose for local information.

As if they knew, as if the information had been swirling around in the air along with the bees and the drifts of dandelion heads blown by children aching to be off school, the girls were all there.

They were all, excepting Mrs Tansy Porter, widows and Tansy might as well have been as her poor husband was in his dotage and regularly rolled up at Mass in his combination drawers with the family Bible in one hand, a flat cap on his head, and a worn-out Tansy beside him.

'It's hardly news, is it?' asked Lizzie McGovern, who'd grown up only a hair's breadth away from the small Brannigan farm. 'They're all back for Ed's big party and renting out the whole castle. Sure, we know that.'

'That's not the news,' said Gwen, relishing the fact that, yet again, she knew more than anyone else. 'Fáinne's coming.'

There was a silence, a rarity at these get-togethers where silence only occurred after news of a death or a piece of information so shocking that everyone had to breathe deeply just to take it in.

'Fáinne?' said Tansy, who was old enough to remember them all, older than Edward, even, though they'd all called him Ned back then.

'How do you know?'

'She's staying at The Regal. An American's booked in but called Faenia. Has to be her, has to. Two rooms.'

'Ooh,' said someone.

'Family coming too?'

Faenia had rung PJ up a few days after meeting him and he was completely surprised to get the call.

'Remember me?' said that husky elegant voice he remembered from the airport. 'It's Faenia Lennox, I gave you a lift from the airport—'

'— to my house. Have totally forgotten it,' laughed PJ.

She wasn't sort of the person people forgot.

'How have you been?' he asked.

'Oh, not so bad,' said Faenia. 'I was ringing to ask you a favour, actually.'

'A favour?' said PJ, wondering what he could possibly do to help this woman out.

'I have to go to a family event in Lisowen in Co. Kerry this weekend and I would love it if someone would drive me. I was thinking of you, if you're free. I've got a hire car and everything, but it's a long old way. I'm not much of a driver, to be honest. I'd pay you, of course, that might help.'

'I'd do it for nothing,' said PJ and he meant it.

It didn't matter that he was entirely broke and his father was making irritable noises about when was PJ going to get a proper job, like working for him in the builders' yard, instead of going to interviews about teaching jobs. PJ knew exactly what his father thought about teaching drama and none of it was good.

'Now you're back from chasing the dream, you'd want to settle down,' his father said on a daily basis.

PJ wanted to settle down but in his own way, not in a *settle for* sort of way. Giving up his dream of drama would be settling for and he couldn't do that.

'No, I want to pay you,' insisted Faenia.

'Why me?' said PJ in a rare moment of suspicion. 'It's not as if you couldn't afford to get one of those lovely limos to drive you down, the way you had the limo to pick us up at the airport.'

'I'd like the company for the whole thing,' admitted Faenia. 'You'd be my guest. It's a family party and I don't want to go alone.' She paused and PJ could picture her lost in thought at the memory of the family who'd been unaware of her coming back. A big party with them all might not be much fun, if you thought about it, no matter that she had money. Family could be tricky no matter what age or stage in life you were at.

'In fact,' Faenia went on, 'you'd be doing me the most enormous favour, so I should really pay you double for that.'

On the other end of the phone, PJ laughed. 'There is no need to pay me double for anything,' he said. 'I'd love to come and you don't have to pay me at all.'

'No, I would like to pay,' she insisted. 'And secondly, you're going to need a dress suit.'

'By dress suit do you mean the full monkey suit?' asked PJ, who had worn one precisely twice in his life: once to his big, end of school dance and again to his slightly stuck-up cousin's wedding, but they had both been hired and hadn't fitted him very well to be honest.

'Yes, the proper monkey suit,' said Faenia. 'I'll pay for that too. You see, I don't want to go on my own and if you were there as my guest at the party, it would make me feel better.'

PJ didn't need to think twice. There was nothing romantic in his decision to accompany Faenia Lennox on this trip. She had to be easily in her sixties and his next big birthday was going to be his twenty-sixth. But there was something special about her, something that made PJ feel protective of Faenia Lennox. If she wanted him to go along, then he would.

When Faenia arrived at PJ's house in the rented car, PJ was surprised to see that it was a small car. He'd half expected her to roll up in something glamorous and glossy, some expensive marque of German design with automatic steering and probably the capability to go to Mars. But she suited this neat little Toyota hatchback.

'I didn't know what to wear so I brought a lot of stuff,' she said, indicating the pile of luggage in the back.

384

He laughed as he hung his hired tuxedo in its suit cover on one of the hooks in the roof and threw in a duffel bag.

'You're a bit of a snail, aren't you?' he said, sliding into the front seat and ratcheting it back so it could accommodate his long legs. 'You like to bring all your things with you.'

Faenia grinned. 'You are very wise for one so young,' she said. 'I do like to take my things with me, very perceptive of you.'

'You may call me Yoda for the rest of the trip,' PJ joked, and they set off.

At first Faenia was full of questions. How was he getting on with the job search, was his father still nagging him to go into the family business, and was his mother completely delirious that he had finally come home from America? The job search was going slowly, PJ admitted. His mother *was* entirely delirious he was home from America as was his young brother, and his father – well, Dad was happy he was back, but there had been some very heavy hints being dropped about how drama wasn't a proper career and he must know this by now and surely a job that gave a decent wage like the one that was waiting for him in the builders' yard would be a better bet.

'He just wants to see you settled that's all,' Faenia said. 'Parents are like that. They like to see their kids settled and happy and then they can stop worrying quite so much.'

'Have you kids?' PJ asked.

'No, I was never blessed with any,' said Faenia lightly. 'It wasn't meant to be. My second husband had children himself but they were nearly grown-up when I met them. I'm very close to them, though.'

'Second husband,' said PJ, pretending to be surprised but not really being surprised at all. Faenia had an air of glamour and excitement about her and it was quite normal for people like that to have been married several times, certainly people from the West Coast and he had met enough of them in his time in LA. 'How many times were you married?' he asked.

Faenia laughed her deep throaty giggle. 'That's what I love

about the Irish,' she said. 'They ask you these things. People in California ask too, you know. I think we are very similar really, that's why I settled down so well there. People in Ireland and California will ask you absolutely anything. And New Yorkers are the same, utterly upfront – there's nothing they won't ask you: what you earn, whether you are thinking of leaving your husband, and if you *are* leaving your husband, can they have his phone number.'

It was PJ's turn to laugh. 'Ah now,' he said. 'I met a few mad people all right, but I never met anyone who asked that.'

Faenia hadn't been able to get a room in Lisowen Castle, obviously.

'The place is jam-packed and the family have booked it all out,' Isobel told her.

'That's fine, that's what I expected,' Faenia said.

'I've booked you into The Regal,' Isobel said. 'The two rooms like you asked.'

Isobel hadn't blinked an eye when Faenia had turned up with PJ, who was probably young enough to be her grandson, never mind her son.

'This is my friend, PJ,' Faenia said proudly, when they finally rolled up at Isobel's house early in the afternoon on the day of the big party. 'We haven't known each other long, but he has taken on the big job of driving me around and taking care of me, because I can't get the hang of these Irish roads and driving on the other side. At least half the drivers don't use their indicators, they just launch themselves wherever they want to go.'

'Some people do see the indicator switch as more of an ornament than an actual aid to driving,' Isobel agreed.

'Delighted to meet you,' PJ said formally to Isobel. He had taken in the information that Isobel was the police sergeant's wife and was behaving with great formality.

'Ah, you can stop that,' said Isobel kindly. 'There's no need.

Plenty of people around here suck up to me and, honestly, I have no power over the law.'

'I suppose not,' said PJ thoughtfully. 'It's just that you always imagine that in a small town that—'

'— that the sergeant's wife is going to know every bit of dirt and tell him who to arrest?' laughed Isobel. 'Not a bit of it, I'm afraid, although there have been times when I have felt the need to arrest a few people myself. But still, my husband is the one who is a guard, not me. Now, a cup of tea? I won't offer you a drink since you are driving,' she said to PJ and twinkled her eyes a little.

They made it to The Regal by four and it was a lovely hotel, nothing like the castle, mind you, which Faenia had already Googled to see it in its new incarnation. With its glamorous décor and spa, it was nothing like the place she'd remembered from her youth.

The rooms in The Regal were nice and clean, plus there was a swimming pool and PJ decided he'd go down and do a few lengths before the evening.

'Are we eating at this thing or what?' he said to Faenia, which was a perfectly normal question and yet threw her.

For a brief moment Faenia had wondered if she was completely mad to have driven all the way down to Kerry when nobody knew she was coming, to a party where she actually had no answer to the question of them staying for dinner.

She and PJ were not on the guest list, but she didn't want to tell him this.

They might be eating and they might not be eating. She wasn't sure which.

'We could have a little pre-party snack before we go,' she said thoughtfully. That would cover all the bases.

While PJ swam, she sat in her room, unpacked and checked her email for any message from Nic. There was none, had been none since that first text where Nic had said: 'Where are you, I came to see you and you were just gone. I can't believe you did that. Where have you gone?'

There has been a few little x's, but that hadn't been enough for Faenia.

Nic knew how the phone worked and, incredibly, it worked in both directions. You didn't send random text messages wondering where they were.

No.

You rang them, with worry in your voice and wondered where the heck they were because you were sick with anxiety, and they were about to call 911, thinking you had been kidnapped. Or else you said that if it was your fault, you were sorry and, please, could you start again. They had made mistakes but it was over now.

That was what you did with someone you loved when you had messed up as seriously as Nic.

But then, Nic had some serious decisions to make and it seemed they hadn't been made yet. Perhaps never, and Faenia would have to live with that, live with a broken heart.

She dressed carefully. The gown she had chosen to wear was one she had owned for years and it was quite timeless: a silvery sheath that had been cut so well it hid a multitude of sins. Faenia had once been very slender but she had the inevitable thickening around the middle that women of her age developed. She still had great legs though. Nic had noticed them first thing.

'I bet you were a dancer when you were younger,' Nic had said early on, in those delicious courtship months.

Faenia looked at herself in the mirror and wondered at what she was doing here, about to meet people she hadn't seen for forty years, away from the one person she loved in the whole world, a person who couldn't love her back properly.

PJ must think she was mad, coming on this wild goose chase

across the country when she couldn't answer the question as to whether they would actually eat at the party or not.

He didn't know they didn't have proper invitations, that they were going to crash Edward Brannigan's seventieth birthday party. But then Faenia had always been brave.

Bess looked around the beautiful presidential suite in Lisowen Castle, knowing it had been completely redecorated since Lottie and Edward had been there before. It was amazing that she could say Lottie's name now – Nora had done that for her. Nora had allowed her to break through that strange barrier and say Edward's first wife's name, Lottie.

Lottie who loved art and painting silly statues with yoghurt and using railway sleepers all over the garden even when they were lethal because people slipped on them. Lottie who'd had a tiny greenhouse in the back of Tanglewood, where she had grown tiny hopeless little seedlings. When she'd been sick, she obviously hadn't been able to do anything with her greenhouse and when Bess had moved in, she had found it overrun with weeds and broken panes of glass and she hadn't felt sorry at all.

She'd just ordered people in to take it all away. But now, she realised, she should have seen this was another woman's life, a life that had been snuffed out too early.

Lottie was everywhere. Too late, Bess realised that there was room for her *and* Lottie in Edward's life and that the threat to her marriage was not Edward's dead wife but his very much living daughter.

Jojo had hated her on sight and did not want Bess joining the family. That had wrecked Bess and Edward's marriage.

This was nothing, Bess reflected, like getting married first time round and doing everything fresh. She didn't know why she hadn't realised this before, but she had run into her second marriage, thinking only of herself and Edward and not seeing the bigger picture, because there was a much, much bigger picture.

She wouldn't have minded if the beautiful suite in the hotel hadn't been touched beause she didn't fear the memory of Lottie.

When you lay in a bed with your arms around another human being and you knew they had made love to a different woman for many years, you could not banish those thoughts. It would be impossible.

But you needed space to make your own memories. That's what she and Edward had needed: the space to make their own memories but it was too hard to do that with the antipathy Jojo showed her.

Nora had said there was something going on in Jojo's life and Bess didn't know what it was, might never know what it was. But she knew she would not remain in this marriage if Jojo always hated her.

And she could not stay when Edward's loyalty to his daughter made him treat Bess differently.

Life was too short for that. She loved Edward but she deserved more.

And besides, she needed to make changes in her own life, changes with her relationship with Amy. Nora had made her see that. They'd had lunch together since their meeting in Nora's house and it had been fun.

One one level, Nora was nothing like many of the women Bess had known over the years. Nora was straightforward, funny, said what she thought and genuinely had no agenda. She cared deeply about her niece, Jojo, and wanted her to be happy.

And then she'd done her best to explain Jojo to Bess.

'Edward should be doing this, but I don't know if he can, I don't know if he's aware of it. Lottie was the person with emotional intelligence in that family and Edward was fighting the battle at the office, being the best he could be, being the alpha male bringing home the bacon. Have I mixed my metaphors there?' she asked, and Bess laughed.

'Probably,' she said, 'but keep going, it sounds great.'

'Tell me about your daughter.' Nora had said with her unerring sense of getting to the heart of the matter.

Bess, who never cried, felt herself welling up. What was it about Nora Brannigan that did this to her?

'I don't have a very good relationship with my daughter and I don't know why.'

'Tell me about her. I saw her at the wedding, but we didn't talk a lot,' said Nora. 'Is she shy?'

'Shy?' Bess wasn't sure if her daughter was shy or simply had learned a long time ago to keep her mouth shut and to keep out of the way, because when you did that you didn't get into trouble.

'I pushed her very hard when she was young,' Bess said slowly, poking her salad around on her plate. 'My mother didn't live with us, but took care of her sometimes. My mother pushed her hard too. She – my mother – was one of those women who had been let down by men, well, she felt she had been let down by men. My father was not the great earner she had been led to believe and when he died she went back to work and it made her bitter. I think a lot of that got into Amy's psyche or maybe it didn't. Maybe she just needed to get away from me and my mother telling her she had to work hard, make something of herself, stop messing around.'

Nora didn't say anything. She had a knack, Bess noticed, of not saying anything at important moments.

'You'd have made a great therapist,' Bess said, grimly staring at her new friend.

'I know,' said Nora with a certain cheerfulness. 'People have said it before.'

This weekend, Bess planned to talk to Amy to see if she could do something about their relationship. After all, what did she know about Amy's life other than to criticise the work she did? She didn't know Amy's friends, she didn't know if Amy dated. Amy could be gay, transgender, interested in heading off to another planet on a mission never to return and Bess would be the last to know. And of course whose fault was that? Bess's fault.

The man appeared with the luggage and Bess told him where to put it.

There was no sign of Edward, he was wandering around reception greeting members of his family delightedly, hugging them, and Bess hadn't been quite ready for that. She'd meet them all later, but first she needed to go to a quiet place and prepare herself to face all the Brannigans together. For seeing Jojo and not being Lottie. For being herself.

She loved her husband very much but this was going to be difficult. This weekend was more than Edward's seventieth birthday celebration – this weekend was going to be her last weekend with the Brannigans.

Cari and Jojo arrived late, shattered after the drive.

'Oh gosh, it's Aunt Carmel,' said Jojo as they checked in. 'I'd better go over and say hello to her. She'll think it's very rude if I don't. Mum would have killed me if I ignored Carmel,' and Cari watched, slightly open-mouthed, as her cousin sailed across the foyer.

'Cari,' said a voice, and Cari turned around to see her Uncle Edward bearing down upon her.

'Where's Jojo and Hugh? Any sign of them?'

Cari was not going to be the bearer of the bad news.

'She's gone over to see Auntie Carmel,' she said.

'Oh, Carmel,' said Edward, peering. 'Lovely woman, daft as a brush but Lottie was very fond of her.'

He looked around anxiously, as if afraid Bess might be there and had heard him using his dead wife's name.

Cari felt a pang of pity for Edward – forever locked in trying to please both Bess, who had never met Lottie and was undoubtedly sick to the teeth of her, and Jojo, who wished for Lottie with all her heart. It was just as well she'd given up on the whole notion of men and relationships: it clearly wasn't worth it.

Jojo thought she'd have been poleaxed with grief as soon as she stepped into Lisowen Castle, thinking about the last time they had been there when Mum had been alive and it had been such a happy occasion.

But she hadn't. She had gone beyond that.

Her darling mother was dead. Life had to move on.

Her mother had tried to tell her that when she was dying.

'I know, Mum: I need to live my life, carry on,' Jojo had parrotted, sick with grief and instead of doing just that, she'd messed it all up.

She'd pushed Hugh into having the third treatment when he hadn't been ready, when she hadn't been ready, and this was the result. Personal annihilation. She'd pushed him away from her, too. Not for one moment did she think he was having an affair with Elizabeth. Hugh was no Barney. He loved her but she'd pushed him too far. And now he was gone, all his stuff out of their shared house and nothing but a formal letter, as befitting a lawyer, left on the table saying he'd be in touch about the house.

But she was coming back from the dark side – she could never have told anyone else this or they'd have locked her up for sure, but she was convinced that her mother was giving her strength. She could feel her mother's spirit all around her, telling her the truth: that her pain was to do with grief – a person had to grieve properly and she hadn't.

She'd gone straight from her mother's death to trying to get pregnant, as if having a baby would somehow make up for the loss of her beloved mother.

Then when that failed, she'd raced into starting fertility tests, then a laparoscopy, and then finding out that she had a problem. All the time, she'd pushed Hugh to do what she'd wanted and because he'd loved her he'd gone along with it.

She missed him, Jojo realised. She missed Hugh so very much.

Amy looked at herself in the changing room mirror of the hotel pool and smiled.

'Ah, it's always a good sign to smile at yourself in the mirror,' said the woman. 'Do you know, they say that when a woman looks in the mirror, she sees all the things that she thinks are wrong with herself and that when a man looks in a mirror, he sees all the things he thinks are right.'

Amy beamed at her new friend.

'You are absolutely spot-on with that analysis,' she said. 'I've spent my whole life looking in the mirror and seeing the things that are wrong and, really, what's wrong with me? Two arms, two legs, etc, all working!'

'That's the girl! You're beautiful in that swimsuit,' said the woman. 'It looks like an expensive piece.'

'My first expensive swimsuit ever,' Amy revealed. 'Normally I'd spend about a tenner on them and when you spend a tenner, you get a tenner's worth of a swimsuit,' she added ruefully.

'We have to treat ourselves sometimes,' said the woman, tidying up the towels and giving a quick polish to the top of the sink. 'Now, you should try out that jacuzzi. It's fabulous. Not that I'd have a go myself but everyone seems to love it.'

'I will, I promise,' said Amy.

She went into the swimming pool area and decided that she would sit in the jacuzzi first of all. The new her – full of confidence and never buying the cheap option or telling herself what was wrong with herself ever again – did things like wander confidently into jacuzzis, no matter who was there first.

She sat at first with her back to the pool and looked out of a beautiful picture window from which she could see acres of parkland falling away. It was a very clever conceit to have the swimming pool in the basement and yet with these big windows carved out of the earth so swimmers and jacuzzi-goers could look out.

The beautiful hot water caressed her and she thought how wonderful it was and perhaps when she got money for her book…

Just then, Cari appeared.

'Hello!' said Amy, delighted.

'Hello, favourite author,' said Cari and smiled because it felt utterly truthful. She loved Amy's work and she was so over John Steele. Even if he wanted her back now she wouldn't go to him.

Cari sank into the jacuzzi with Amy and let the heat warm her bones.

'This is glorious. That drive is murder.'

'I got the train,' said Amy.

'You should have come with us,' said Cari. 'Unless you love the train. Do you want a lift on the way home?'

'Yes.' Amy beamed.

They talked books until they were both semi-pruned, then they did a few half-hearted lengths, and finally Cari said they'd better go and get dressed.

Cari hadn't bought anything new for the party – instead she was wearing an outfit she adored, which was not at all feminine but which suited her. She'd bought it in the post-Barney years: it was cut to look like a man's tuxedo suit only she wore it without a white shirt but with a delicate black lace camisole underneath. The combination was both sexy and feminine despite the masculinity of the cut, and she wore the highest heels she had.

She went up to her room, hotel slippers flopping all the way, then showered the chlorine out of her hair and made herself up.

She would not think about damn Conal, she thought.

Perhaps she needed therapy as well as Jojo – anti-man therapy, to deal with the anti-man pheromones she was clearly giving out.

A text pinged on her phone and she had a quick look. It was from Edwin.

'Cari, need to talk to you regarding John Steele. It's about Gavin and perhaps you could give me a call. Don't worry about the time, phone any time.'

Cari stared at the text, the corners of her mouth beginning to turn up. Jeff had been right after all. Gavin had messed up editing John Steele as she and Jeff had known he would.

John was a lovely man, but anxious and needing assistance, reassuring talks and brainstorming. Gavin couldn't brainstorm to save his life and he didn't do reassuring and helpful talks. Well, unless he did them to his own reflection each morning after he shaved.

A moment of wildness hit her and she sent a text back to Edwin: 'Edwin, I'm at a big family party – could I call you tomorrow?'

It was a tiny bit childish but she couldn't help herself, and yet a text pinged back almost instantly. 'Fine, any time after 10.'

Ha!

Her thoughts were confirmed. If Edwin was that keen to talk to her that he'd chat on a Saturday, clearly Gavin had screwed up and John Steele was possibly her author again. If she wanted him.

She thought about it. John Steele wanted an editor in London, and no, she didn't want to move to London.

She allowed herself one quick call.

Jeff sounded sprightly. He must have managed half an hour of a snooze.

'I have news for you,' she said. 'I think they want me back on the John Steele case, I think Gavin has messed up.'

'Told you he would,' said Jeff, sounding remarkably pleased

with himself. 'Yes, that's one big surprise today,' he said and then added mysteriously, 'but there may be more.'

'What more, what do you know?' demanded Cari.

'Just wait and see,' said Jeff enigmatically. 'Bye, Ms Fabulous Editor,' he said and hung up.

Cari dressed, feeling light-hearted. She hadn't got the chance to tell Jeff that she was thinking of turning down John Steele. Because she didn't want to live in London any more. She was happier here, where she had back-up.

To think she'd been dreading this weekend because she was worried about Jojo, and anxious about seeing Traci and Barney. She was ready for them: she was all fired up because Jojo was on the mend – even if the Hugh situation wasn't ideal – and she herself was on the up.

But Jojo and Hugh would get back together: Cari knew it. They were one of life's great couples, one of the few. Like her parents, she thought, biting her lip. It was just a pity that Cari couldn't manage that herself. Still, she'd have a great career, right?

And this weekend, even if the dreaded Traci raced over to Cari first thing – which was perfectly possible – and said, 'Oh, sweetie, it's so lovely to be here with you!' Cari would just smile.

What Cari hated most was insincerity and Traci could represent Ireland in the Olympics in the insincerity stakes, but Cari didn't care any more. Clearly that's what Barney liked and he was stuck with it now. Barney knew all about Traci's insincerity himself. No baby had been born to Barney and Traci. An early miscarriage, someone had helpfully told Cari.

But it didn't matter, not any more.

Barney said he was going for a walk. It was the only way he could get away from Traci and try and meet up with Cari.

Traci was already angry with him because he'd refused to stay in Lisowen Castle.

'I don't know why we can't stay there,' she'd raged. 'There's a spa, a pool. There's nothing here,' she'd added with distaste, looking around what she considered a second-tier hotel in the village.

The Lisowen Arms was pretty, but poolless, spaless and didn't have five stars above the door. Traci liked the finer things in life and would do anything to get them.

'I just think it's fairer if we don't stay in the castle,' Barney said. He found that repeating things with the broken record technique recommended for dealing with either annoying people or children worked very well with Traci.

He drove out of the car park and was at the castle in moments. As he walked in, he was aware it was early and he probably wouldn't bump into anyone there for the family party. They were probably all getting ready in their rooms, or coming up from relaxing swims.

At reception, he asked them to ring Cari Brannigan's room.

'Who shall I say is calling?' said the lovely receptionist.

'Er, could you just connect me briefly?' said Barney, squirming. He'd anticipated this and had an excuse ready.

'I'm here as a surprise,' he added to the receptionist. 'I don't want her to know who it is, you know.'

'OK,' said the receptionist, who was actually used to people coming in with weird requests and as long as this good-looking man didn't want to race down to Ms Brannigan's bedroom – which was strictly against hotel regulations – then she'd put him through.

Although, thought the receptionist, she wouldn't mind if this man raced down to her bedroom, she sighed, she wasn't there to think such thoughts. She was there to make a living and look after herself and the kids. Plus, he had a weak chin.

'Someone on the line for you, Ms Brannigan,' she said when she got through to Cari's room.

The receptionist clicked a couple of buttons and then

gestured to a courtesy phone on the other end of the desk: 'You may use that phone, sir,' she said to Barney.

He picked it up and said hello.

'Hello,' said Cari and he felt that pang, the pang from listening to her voice for the first time in three years.

That last horrific meeting after the wedding had made him feel about two feet tall and he'd hated hurting her, hated that he had been taken in by Traci, hated that he wasn't now with the beautiful Cari Brannigan, because he loved her.

He knew that now. He'd discussed it with Yvonne, his sister, and Yvonne had called him all sorts of names and said, 'You are a complete muppet, Barney. And Traci is a muppet too or maybe she's the one with her hand up your rear end working your arms.'

'Thanks, sis.'

Yvonne had adored Cari and she'd been right. He adored Cari too. He just wasn't sure why it had taken him so long to tell her but now this was kismet, fate: this weekend and their being asked was the perfect time to tell her.

'Barney? Where are you?'

'I'm in reception. Can you come down and see me?' said Barney.

'You're in the hotel?'

'We were invited to the party,' said Barney.

'I know,' replied Cari. 'I just don't know why you came.'

'Because Traci wanted to,' Barney replied.

'And whatever Traci wants she gets, including other people's fiancés,' said Cari acidly.

'Could you come down and see me?'

'I've just come back up from the swimming pool,' said Cari, 'so no. I have to get ready for tonight, and no, I don't want to see you. Why don't you just go away.'

'Please,' he said, 'please.'

'Five minutes,' Cari said, thinking she must be mad. 'Five

minutes in—' Her mind cast around for somewhere she could possibly see him where nobody else would notice.

Her plan for meeting Traci and Barney this evening had included ignoring them totally and sailing around in her lovely evening outfit, letting everyone see she was ignoring them.

'There is a small billiards room off the bar,' she said. 'See you there in five minutes *for* five minutes.'

She hung up and adjusted her lovely evening suit and elegant camisole. At least, she thought, she looked good. She'd got her hair newly cut, her fingernails and toenails were painted, and she'd had her eyebrows shaped.

'Take that, Traci,' she said, looking at herself in the mirror.

The one-time love of her life was sitting in a chair in the billiards room when she walked in and he got up as if to hug her. Cari held up her hand.

'Stop right there,' she said. 'I don't know what you are here for, Barney, but get it over with quick.'

'I'm here to tell you I love you and I'm sorry and – and it was all a mistake me and Traci and...'

Cari sat down heavily on a chair near the door, which slammed shut behind her and she was glad of that because she didn't really want anyone else to witness this.

'So after two and a half years of no contact and you being married to someone else, you now love me and want to be with me and I'm supposed to go along with that?' she said with a fake smile. 'Did you get dropped on your head recently?'

'I needed to tell you, tell you everything,' Barney said, sitting down, not beside her but on the other side of the door, and letting his head hang.

He still looked as good as ever, Cari realised, but there was something not so masculine about him, certainly compared to Conal. *That louse.* At least Conal hadn't promised to marry her and love her for the rest of his life, she thought. He'd taken her to bed, made her see stars, and then left. But, still there had been no promises of forever love. And he was ten times hotter than Barney.

'Are you listening to me?' said Barney. Cari looked up. Clearly Barney had been speaking all the time and she'd been thinking about Conal and, well, she was never seeing Conal again, so that was completely ridiculous but still—

'I'm trying to explain what happened with Traci.'

'Yes, Traci,' said Cari. 'Go on, what about her? She's wildly manipulative and she wanted what I had, do I have that right?'

'You have that right one hundred per cent,' said Barney.

'Why are you still married to her if she's such a peach? We have divorce in this country, just leave her.'

'It's not that easy,' Barney said.

'Never is,' agreed Cari, doing her bored voice. 'What exactly do you want to tell me?'

She looked hard at him and realised with a sense of pure joy that she was so over this man. It felt good. It wasn't that she'd been crying in her sleep for him for the last two and a half years but his memory, his essence, had hung over her life and the way he'd left her at the altar had certainly left a dent in her psyche.

Seeing him here, looking much less gorgeous than Conal – *bastard* – made her realise that she could move on even if it wasn't with Conal. Maybe that was the trick: keep finding new men to annoy the hell out of her and eventually she'd be immune to them all. She'd have enough men antibodies in her system to deal with them.

'She wasn't pregnant at all, it took me ages to figure that one out, but she just decided she wanted to marry me and she did,' said Barney. 'She said she'd had a miscarriage but she didn't.'

'Barney, I used to think you were an intelligent guy,' said Cari.

'I don't know,' he mumbled, 'she trapped me and...'

'Trapped you in bed,' added Cari brightly. 'You see that's the problem, Barney. I could understand if Traci wanted you and went after you but in order for the whole plan to work, she had to get you into bed. You were engaged to me, about to be married to me and you should have said "no thanks, keep your clothes on, Traci", but you didn't. You said yes. So that's where it all falls down, this loving me schtick. I'm sorry that you found out that she's manipulative and I'm really sorry that you don't like being married to her, but if you want out, I would advise you to lawyer up and in the meantime, leave me alone.'

She got to her feet and stretched. She felt good. The swim had loosened up her muscles. She smiled at Barney, who looked a bit shell-shocked that this conversation wasn't going as planned. She wondered who else she could sort out today. She might possibly ring up Gavin in London and tell him he was a useless moron and was a hopeless editor to boot. Yes, she might do that, or was there anyone else annoying she could say smart things to.

'But you don't understand,' begged Barney, 'I love you.'

Cari gave him a pitying look.

'Sorry, Barney, that's too little too late. Three years too late. I don't love you any more.' She was about to say, 'I think I love someone else,' but given that that someone else was no longer in her life, what was the point?

'See you around and enjoy the party,' she added with a little smile before slipping out of the room.

Bess had found Amy.

'I need to tell you that I'm going to be leaving Edward after the weekend,' she said, 'I just have to go, I can't stay with him any more.'

'Why?' said Amy.

'It's over, this marriage is over, I must have been mad to think about it from the start. Your grandmother was right, love doesn't happen, love is some mad concept that people have.'

'No, Mum,' groaned Amy. 'Don't say that just because of

Jojo, she'll come round. Mum, I'm not letting you walk out on this marriage.'

Stunned, Bess sat down on the bed meekly and stared at her daughter in astonishment. 'Great that you want to get involved, Amy, but it's too late.'

'Edward is a good man and he's good for you,' insisted Amy. 'He's bringing out your softer side.'

'What if I don't want my softer side brought out?' demanded Bess.

'You need it,' said Amy. 'I'm sorry your softer side wasn't more in evidence when I was growing up, but I can understand why that might not have been the case.'

'I failed you,' said Bess and burst into tears.

Amy was not used to the sight of her mother crying. But she knew their relationship had to change and now finally she had the strength, the courage and the self-belief to change it. She sat on the bed beside her mother and hugged her.

'Now listen,' Amy said, 'I love you, we have never been very good at saying stuff like that but I do, so let's start again, you and me, and with Jojo try and understand where she's coming from and poor Edward too.'

'So it's poor Edward now, is it?' said Bess. 'I didn't even think you liked him.'

'I always liked him,' said Amy, 'it was just easier to stay out of your way and get on with my own life, but that's not really a good plan is it? You need me and I'm here.'

Bess sobbed into her daughter's shoulder. 'Thank you, Amy,' she said. 'But I still have to go. Will you be there for me...? I know I haven't been the best mother but I can try?'

'Let's both try,' said Amy, hugging back.

Somehow, Bess repaired her make-up and when Edward arrived, Amy hugged her mother one more time and left.

Bess felt so on edge that she instantly turned the television on to hide the sound of silence.

'You look nice,' she said to her husband when he was finally ready. The words sounded like a death knell in her head. This was their last weekend together. It still hurt, would hurt for a very long time.

'So do you,' said Edward, feeling the pain in his chest. How could he tell her? How?

He knew what he'd promised Lottie when she'd been dying but Jojo was his beloved daughter and he couldn't turn his back on her. He needed to be there for her and if that meant giving up Bess, he would have to do that. But oh, he wanted to cry when he thought about it.

Bess had brought so much love into his life. He adored her, loved her. How could life be this cruel, how could he lose two women he loved?

There was a knock on Cari's room door, and dressed but still not wearing her high heels, Cari went over to answer it. If it was Barney and he'd tracked her down to profess his love again, she would stab him. She wrenched open the door and began: 'For the last time, Barney, get out of my life—'

But it wasn't Barney.

If she had been the fainting sort of girl, she'd have fainted on the spot because standing there, wearing the most divine dinner jacket and looking as if he should be in an ad on the TV selling cognac or chocolates, was Conal.

'What are you doing here?' she asked, stunned.

Were all her exes turning up tonight? Had a pact been made with the devil? Was Davy, the guy she'd gone out with seventeen years ago, going to roll up too and say he really loved her, even though they'd split up when he'd gone to college in Belfast, when they'd both had spots?

'Can I come in?'

'Can you come in?' she said, exasperated and outraged in equal measure. 'Is there a new sign on my door saying "Disturb me, please!"'

She looked up at the door: 'No, I thought not. So why don't

you and your Milk Tray man/James Bond suit get the hell out of here. Because there is no booty call to be had here tonight.'

'Nice outfit,' said Conal, looking her up and down with those assessing eyes and totally ignoring her.

'Did you not hear what I said?' shrieked Cari, and she began to lose it. She wanted to cry, scream and hit him with her fists.

'I heard all right but I was just ignoring it because I thought I'd let you get it out of your system.'

She went for him then, fists flying and she whacked at his chest with rage. She'd never understood women who'd hit men before but now – *now* she got it totally. How dare Conal turn up and wreck her head after how he'd treated her before? How dare he be here and—

He grabbed her wrists and held them easily but gently.

'Easy, tiger,' he said, 'I deserve that and it's totally my fault, I'm sorry, sorry, sorry.'

Cari blinked at him, 'Sorry? You're saying sorry?'

'I'm saying sorry, yes,' said Conal. 'Do other men not say sorry when they screw up?'

'Not in my experience,' snarled Cari. 'Or if they do, they do it three years too late.'

Somehow he'd managed to get her inside the room and he shut the door with his foot. 'I screwed up and I'm really sorry. I missed out on the total disclosure part of our relationship.'

'You got that right,' she said.

'I'm sorry. That's all I can say, Cari: sorry I didn't tell you all about Beatrice and the whole thing and how I don't love her and how I love you.'

Cari blinked.

'You love me?'

'That's what I said. I love you, Cari Brannigan. Beatrice was a fling and yes she's fabulous-looking, and hot, and women are totally threatened by her—'

'I was not threatened by her!' shrieked Cari. 'I answered your phone and she began talking as if you'd merely left Paris with

405

arrangements to meet her here as soon as possible for some horizontal jogging. That's not being threatened – that's having it made clear to you that your boyfriend is two-timing you. And I've done that, got the T-shirt, thank you very much!'

'Apologies,' said Conal. 'Beatrice always talks like that. It is over between us, was over when she phoned. She is a one-dimensional woman, Beatrice-dimensional. Everything is about her – her career, her family, what she wants. It took me about a week to see we made good friends and bad lovers, but she didn't like taking no for an answer. We broke up months ago. Ask Jeff, he knows and he would never lie to you. When I came here she kept phoning. I never asked her to come to Ireland with me, never, cross my heart. And by the way Jeff told me you whacked a guy in his cruciate ligament and got him on the floor at some awards ceremony – I need to hear about that.'

He got down on his knees.

'Do you need a knee replacement?' she asked. 'Or are you just hoping to escape a cruciate attack?'

Conal laughed.

'I'm not producing a box,' he said, 'just in case you thought I was. There is no ring hidden in these pockets, no standard Tiffany solitaire secreted about my person, so you don't misconstrue my meaning. Not that I don't like the idea of a Tiffany solitaire, but I don't want to freak you out just yet. Next month a ring, though? I don't want you getting away from me again.'

Cari blinked again.

'For real?'

'For real. I just wanted to tell you I love you, and that I apologise for not telling you about Beatrice,' Conal went on, 'and I just thought maybe if I did it on my knees that would be better and then you could poke me in the chest with your spiky heels and you'd feel better too, because you love those damn heels, although I don't know why. I'll even let you bash me around the head with them.'

Cari couldn't help it – she started to laugh.

'I'm not wearing them,' she said and she pulled up the hem of one of her trouser legs to show him her bare foot. Then, a wicked idea hit her, so she quickly lifted her foot, put it against his chest and shoved, but it wasn't a hard enough push and he was too strong. Instead of her knocking him over, he grabbed her ankle and suddenly she was thrown back onto the bed.

'Whoof,' she said.

He landed heavily beside her.

'At the risk of getting walked on with the heels of death for sounding chauvinistic, that's more like it,' he said. 'I think you and I do our best conversing lying down.'

'Spoken like someone who leaves money on the mantelpiece,' said Cari. 'What am I talking about? You *didn't* leave money on the mantelpiece.'

'I couldn't afford you,' he murmured. 'You're worth millions. No, I'm speaking as someone who is crazy about you,' said Conal, 'someone who screwed it up seriously in the beginning and doesn't know how to make it up to you but keeps trying. I can't sleep or think straight and why wouldn't you return my calls?'

'Because I have been out with enough assholes,' said Cari.

She didn't know how much longer she could keep this tough act up. It was hell being beside him, hell having him try and apologise to her in her lair, so to speak, and she really wanted to put her arms around him, lean her head against his chest and tell him she'd missed him. She wanted to explain that he'd hurt her by not telling her about the beautiful, batty Beatrice, and didn't he realise how she – she who had been dumped at the altar – would view that?

'I have trust issues,' she said quietly. 'I need to trust you.'

'You can,' he whispered, and then he kissed her slowly. 'Sorry,' he said, moving away briefly and he kissed her some more until Cari put her arms around him.

'Sorry,' he said, 'sorry, sorry, sorry. Please ask Jeff, ask my mother, ask Anna, ask Jasmine – even she knows about crazy Beatrice. And she's only a few months old.'

'She can't talk yet, bozo,' said Cari.

'She would say: gurgle, gurgle, Beatrice crazy, gurgle, Conal loves you.'

Cari couldn't help it: she laughed and then he was kissing her neck, moving the jacket aside to touch the softness of her collarbone and slide the silky straps of her camisole so his tongue could lick a hot trail along her throat.

'It's OK,' she said, her hands tangled in his air, her mouth close to his. 'You can stop saying sorry.'

'Really?' he said. 'Oh good.'

'Afterwards, you have to resume it again, for like, two years. Sorry, on the hour every hour.'

'I can do that,' murmured Conal. 'But two years – just not long enough. I'll need more time.'

'OK, cowboy, I'll look in my diary and see how long I can give you,' Cari murmured back and wondered if anyone would mind if she was late for the party.

Twenty-Five

There's magic in marriage. It can happen in a heartbeat
and it runs like a river of life through your veins.
It's infinitely precious, and it needs nurturing.

Faenia walked slowly into the Lisowen Castle restaurant and
looked around for the big table.

'Cool place,' said PJ.

'Yes,' said Faenia faintly. She could barely believe she was
here.

Forty years later. Maybe it had been a mistake...

And then she saw Edward, him first, as ever, because he was
the tallest. And as if he could feel her eyes on him, he turned
and looked at her and his hand went to his mouth.

'Fáinne? Is it you?'

She nodded and walked over but Edward ran over and lifted
her off her feet.

'I can't believe you're here,' said Edward, holding on to Faenia
as if letting go of her hands might mean she would run away
again for another forty years.

'You just vanished and I tried looking for you.'

'I knew you would,' she said, 'I just had to get away.'

'But why?' said Mick. Faenia turned to look at the brother
nearest in age to herself. She could still see the young scamp
and his lovely face and those kind eyes.

Thank goodness he'd married Nora, gorgeous Nora, who
still didn't give a damn about what sort of old dress she had
thrown on because Nora's white hair was sticking up like a
brush, she was wearing a necklace with pretty shiny stones in it

that someone else must have given her and earrings that didn't match at all, and she was beaming at Faenia.

Faenia beamed back. She'd missed them all so much. Why had it taken her so long to come back?

'And this is Bess,' said Edward pulling forward a dark-haired woman in a sheath of emerald-green silk that Faenia recognised as being a very expensive dress.

'She's my wife.'

'Bess,' said Faenia, reaching forward to hug the woman who stood stiffly.

Oh, all is not well here, she thought, and it was nothing to do with her coming back. Nobody said Lottie was dead but Faenia knew it anyway. Isobel had filled her in on all the details. There was always someone in Lisowen who knew what was going on, always a person who would keep in touch with the Dublin papers and who'd died, who'd married, and someone who kept an eye out for the gossip columns of news of the rich and famous. And certainly Edward Brannigan appeared to have been famous and yet he was still her big brother. The crowd of people around them diminished as if someone had gone along whisking people away saying, go on, shoo this is family.

'I'm Helen,' said a voice, a slightly self-important voice and a small, slim woman wearing far too much make-up pushed herself forward and stood in front of dear Kit.

Faenia loved Kit but he'd always been the weakest of her three brothers, the one who'd fibbed to get himself out of trouble at school, the one that Edward and Mick had to protect for all that Mick was younger.

'I'm Kit's wife.' The made-up woman held out a beautifully manicured tanned hand, fake-tanned to a faintly orange colour, Faenia noticed. Faenia noticed those sort of things.

This Helen didn't have the warm vibrancy of dear Nora or even poor Lottie, whom Faenia could barely remember because she had been younger than the rest of them when Faenia had left. But in the reports over the years, Faenia had never heard anything but good about Lottie.

'And the children,' she said, 'now tell me who is who.'

'I'm Cari,' said a tall, dark-haired girl with the same sparkling emerald eyes as Faenia herself, and a wide smile. She was attractive, Faenia thought, and clever and funny and was this the one who had been jilted at the altar? Isobel had had some news about that. It was dreadful, Isobel had said in an email – 'Some young pup left her at the altar and went on to marry a cousin, I think.' Faenia wondered if the cousin and the scurrilous young pup were here tonight and thought possibly not because that would be a little hard for any woman to take.

But this Cari didn't look too much put out – the tall, sexy man standing proudly beside her was probably why.

'I'm Conal,' he said, preferring a strong hand. 'Cari's intended.'

'Intended for what?' Cari demanded of him.

'See what I have to put up with?' said Conal with a wicked smile.

'Intended my backside,' she muttered to him and Faenia smiled. Young, sparkling love.

She reached out to shake hands with this Cari, but Cari pulled her into a hug. 'It's amazing to meet you,' she said, 'I never knew you existed.'

Faenia laughed. 'You're Nora's daughter, for sure,' she said, and Nora laughed, the same loud, vibrant laugh.

'You've nailed it perfectly there, Faenia,' she said. 'We slightly wrote you out of the history because we didn't know how to handle it.'

'That's understandable,' Faenia said, 'I wrote myself out of the history.' She thought for a minute about what all this meant and realised that all those years of therapy had worked. She'd run away at high speed because of what had happened and yet here, now, her family were welcoming her back with delight, except perhaps for Helen, who didn't look too delighted at anything.

Faenia was introduced to Paul, Edward's son, and his wife Lena and a darling little baby named Heidi whom she had to pick up immediately.

'She should be in bed,' said Lena, 'we have a babysitter and everything but she refused to sleep – probably knows there's a party on.'

Faenia agreed, thinking of how blithely she talked about babies as if she knew what she was talking about when, sadly, she had never had one.

'And Jojo,' said Edward suddenly looking around. 'Where's Jojo?'

'Here,' and there was a beautiful blonde woman who looked anxious but had a big smile on her face.

'So you're Fáinne, the one they tried not to tell us about.'

'Because she left,' said Nora, crying, 'and we didn't know what to say.'

Faenia hugged Nora.

'I was pregnant,' she whispered. 'I didn't want to cause trouble, you know what it was like then, and I went and once you go—'

'It's easier to stay away,' said Nora.

And Faenia nodded.

'Well,' interrupted Helen of the orange skin and the calculating eyes, 'here is my daughter, Trina.'

Trina, a minxy gorgeous creature with long dark hair appeared with another girl who could have been her twin.

'And Maggie, my other daughter,' said Nora.

Both the younger women looked as if they were having a ball, delighted with the party, with themselves and possibly having already had a couple of cocktails that made them giggly and smiley and bright-eyed. Maggie smiled at PJ as if she'd been at sea, manless for a month.

The girls had the Brannigan dark hair and the eyes and they looked so full of happiness.

'I'm sorry I stayed away so long,' said Faenia.

'But why?' said Mick, sitting down. For a second, he looked older than his age, older than a man in his sixties and Faenia was acutely aware that she had missed much of his life. 'It's a long story and maybe now isn't the time to discuss it,' she said gently. 'Plus, this is a celebration, isn't it?'

Bess got to her feet. There was something about this rush of emotion that was killing her: she'd thought she could take the weekend here by Edward's side but she couldn't, she'd go now.

Hoping nobody would notice her, she slipped away, but Edward was too fast for her.

'Where are you going?' he said quietly, away from the hubbub.

Her eyes met his.

'You know where I'm going,' she said quietly. 'It's over, I can't compete with all of this. I can't make Jojo even like me and you're too guilty to let our marriage continue. I deserve better, Edward. So I'm going.'

'Please, Bess—'

And then Edward Brannigan felt the strange pain in his chest again, the tightness, then a terrible pain, and he clutched his chest and fell to the ground.

'Edward!' Bess stood looking at him and then fell to the floor beside him, holding his hand, weeping.

Lena was on the floor in a flash checking for breath sounds while Paul roared for someone to ring for an ambulance.

'I think his heart has stopped!' shrieked Lena. 'Massive heart attack.'

'Oh, Jesus,' said Paul.

Mick was so pale he looked as if he might possibly have a heart attack too.

Jojo raced over, and threw herself as close to her father as she could.

413

'Dad,' she said, 'Dad, please don't die!'

At this, Bess bit heavily on her lip and moved aside. It was time for her to go. He wouldn't want her here no matter that she was feeling as if her heart was breaking with pain.

'No,' said Jojo, pulling Bess back. 'You have to stay.'

'Why?' cried Bess.

Jojo took both of Bess's hands in hers. 'Because you're his wife and he loves you.'

A member of staff appeared holding onto a box. 'I'm Fiona, I'm trained in CPR, first aid and use of the defibrillator.' She held up a phone, 'I'm onto the emergency services now. They'll talk us through this.'

'Are you sure?' said Lena, moving reluctantly out of the way.

'Absolutely sure,' said the woman. 'Somebody has to hold the phone up to my ear, though.'

Lena held the phone up to the woman's ear.

'Edward, is it? Edward, I'm Fiona, we're going to help you. The ambulance is on its way.'

There was no response from Edward.

The first aid responder leapt into action, listening for breath sounds and checking Edward's heartbeat.

'Right, we'll start CPR,' Fiona said.

They sat together, Jojo and Bess, on opposite sides of the bed in ICU and waited for someone to throw them out. Both women were pale but Bess looked as if she might faint any minute. Jojo kept watching her in between watching her father. Paul had been in, along with Mick and Kit.

'It's going to be OK,' Jojo said. 'Dad's strong, isn't he, Paul?'

'Yes,' said Paul, who was crying on and off and kept having to go outside.

'It's my fault,' sobbed Bess, 'I told him I was leaving...' and Jojo moved from her side of the bed to sit beside Bess and hug her. How could she have hated this poor woman? She felt the guilt weigh heavily upon her – it was her fault that her father was here, her fault entirely.

'It's my fault,' said Jojo. 'I put him under so much stress. I am so sorry, Bess. So sorry. I know you love him—'

Bess couldn't respond. It didn't matter any more. What was the point in screaming at Jojo?

Edward would die and it wouldn't matter that finally Jojo had forgiven her or got over her strop or whatever. He would be gone.

Gone for ever. Her life would have no meaning. She might as well be dead herself.

Silently, Bess began to cry.

'No, he can't see you cry!' said Jojo fiercely. 'He will recover, won't you, Dad? We need you. Listen to me, you two,' said Jojo fiercely, to both Paul and Bess. 'He is not going anywhere, are you, Dad?'

She grabbed her father's hands and held them gently so as not to dislodge the lines feeding drugs and fliud into him.

'When Mum was dying, she told me that she wanted you to have more life, another person in your life and you found her, Dad. You found Bess and I'm sorry I didn't understand that, really sorry. It's my fault we're all here but you've so much to live for. You have Paul and Lena and baby Heidi, and if my treatment ever works' – both Bess and Paul stared at her in astonishment – 'Hugh and I might be able to give you a grandchild too. So wake up right now!'

One of the machines began to beep, Edward Brannigan began to move and the nurses shoved them out of the way.

'Outside, for a moment, please,' one of the nurses said.

Outside the ICU, Paul wanted to talk to her but Jojo said she needed to make a phone call first.

'Hold onto Bess, will you?' she said. 'I'm worried about her.'

'You're worried about Bess?' he whispered.

'Yes,' she whispered back. 'Leopards can change their spots, especially stupid, childish leopards. Now grab her and put her in a chair before she falls.'

Jojo rounded the corner to get some privacy and dialled her husband's number.

'Hugh,' she said when he answered. 'I know it's a big ask, but do you think you could come to Kerry? Dad's in hospital: he's had a heart attack and I need you.'

'I never cheated on you with Elizabeth—' began Hugh fiercely.

'I know you didn't,' said Jojo, and the emotion of it all got to her. She hadn't cried as she'd sat in the hospital beside her father's bed. She didn't want him to wake up and see her crying, but the tears came now. 'I know you better than that, Hugh, darling. But let's not double date with Elizabeth and Wolfie ever again, right?'

Bess was allowed back in first and she held Edward's hand.

He was improving slightly, the doctor said. But he must be kept quiet. No more yelling.

'I love you,' she whispered to him.

He tried to speak but she couldn't hear him at first.

'What is it, darling?'

The grasp on her hand got tighter.

'Don't leave me,' he said so quietly she could barely hear him.

'I won't,' she said and she kissed his forehead gently. She was going nowhere.

As her husband slept, Bess listened to the steady beep of the machines that told them Edward was stable and she thought about Lottie: a person whose presence could have hung over Bess's newly married life like a shroud, except that it hadn't.

There had been no pronouncements from Lottie from the grave about the house, the family, traditions. No diaries of pain and family anniversaries to be held in such a particular way.

Lottie had left with grace and courage, had told her

heart-broken husband that he needed to find someone else. She had had the courage to do that, even as she lay dying.

And she'd been able to say it to Jojo.

Outside, Jojo sat beside Paul on the hard hospital seats and thought about her mother, near the end.

They'd been in the hospice. Lottie hadn't wanted to die at home.

'I don't want you to see my death filling every corner,' she told them all.

Alone, she turned to Jojo. 'Your father will need someone else, another wife, darling.'

'No!' Jojo hated how loud she'd said it but she couldn't help the basic revulsion at the thought of another woman taking her mother's place.

'Men are not so strong as us, darling. I don't want him to be lonely. You have Hugh and Paul has Lena. You'll have families, lives and he will have only memories.'

Jojo had thought Bess had married her father for his money but she knew now that she'd been totally wrong. Bess adored her father, which was what her mother would have wanted. Her own grief had got in the way and she was ashamed of that but she would make it better – for her father, for Bess and for Hugh, who loved her so much.

Edward opened his eyes slowly. He wasn't sure where he was but he felt so tired, as if he couldn't have moved to save his life.

Two faces came into focus. First, Bess, her lovely dark eyes wet with tears as she saw him waking up. And then, beside Bess, Jojo.

'Welcome back, darling,' said Bess.

'Dad, we love you,' said Jojo. 'I'll get Paul. He's asleep on a chair outside.'

'You're here together?' whispered Edward, because all he could do was whisper.

Jojo held up one hand and he saw that she was holding Bess's hand with it.

'Together,' she said and smiled.

'Is Fáinne OK?'

'Yes,' said Bess, 'Nora was taking care of her but now she's in here taking care of Aunt Helen, because Uncle Kit is having an angina attack over his double mortgage.'

'It's the gambling,' said Edward, still whispery. 'Between him and the horses and Helen and the shops, I don't know how they have any money.'

'Nora's calming them both down,' said Jojo.

'What would we do without Nora?' said Edward in his whispery voice.

'What would we do without you?' said Bess, leaning in to kiss him.

Jojo came round the other side of the bed and kissed his other cheek.

'I'll leave you two together and wake Paul. Then I'll phone the hotel and tell them you're awake and doing well.'

'Doing miraculously,' said Edward and his eyes were shining wet as he looked at the two women he loved.

Faenia lay back in her hotel bed and listened to her mobile phone with relief. Edward was awake and doing well.

'And Bess and Jojo are sitting by his bed, happily, taking turns to go out and get tea,' said Nora delightedly. 'Bet you didn't think your return was going to be so jam-packed, Fáinne,' Nora went on.

'I like a bit of excitement as well as the next woman,' said Faenia, 'but brothers having heart attacks – that's too much excitement. I feel so guilty—'

'Edward was under huge stress,' Nora said. 'You coming

home was perhaps a final blast but things have been very hard for a long time. Second marriages are not easy on kids.'

Nor were third relationships, particularly when those relationships were a little more complicated, Faenia thought sadly.

When she'd hung up, she wondered was it worth checking her answering machine back home again.

She dialled in, expecting nothing but cold calls from insurance salesmen and aluminium siding people but there was Nic's voice, the same soft ladylike voice that had made Faenia turn that first time she'd heard it.

Nic or Nicolette as her family knew her, was a Southern lady born and bred. A daughter of the American Revolution and a lady who knew how to offer Southern hospitality. She wore elegant clothes, had blonde curls, her *grandmère*'s pearls always around her neck, drove a reconditioned classic Mercedes coupé, wore St John knit suits and kissed Faenia in a way that made Faenia's heart contract with pure love.

But Nic had grown-up children and grandchildren.

'They won't understand,' she said. 'I've never told them about the way my life has changed, the way my feelings have changed. I was married to their father for thirty-five years and they can't see any other life for me than a widow lady with her own art gallery and friends to go to the theatre with. I can't do this to them, Faenia, I just can't. They think you're my friend, nothing more.'

The months since had nearly killed Faenia but there was nothing she could do. It was Nic's decision and she couldn't fight her.

Faenia could understand it. She'd never so much as looked at another woman all her life. She'd been married, had two husbands and then, when she thought sex was long gone from her life, she met Nic and realised, with a huge shock, that she was attracted to this woman.

She'd gone back to a therapist she'd seen for years to discuss it.

'I can't be a lesbian,' she'd said. 'This makes no sense. I'm not saying this because I'm homophobic but – but how?'

'It's more common than you'd think,' the therapist said, with that Zen-like calm that had helped Faenia so much. 'There is no choice element in it and it's a growing phenomenon. Late-blooming lesbians – there's a new label for you.'

'I work in a business surrounded by labels and I'm not threatened by them,' Faenia had said, smiling. 'I just don't understand it.'

'You are attracted to this woman?'

'Yes.'

'Sexually?'

'Yes.'

'And you think she might be attracted to you?'

Faenia nodded. 'Absolutely.'

'We can't choose who we are attracted to. This transition is out of your control.'

Faenia had asked Nic for a coffee: she had to know if she was imagining it. And sitting in that coffee shop with Nic, she had suddenly known for sure that she was wildly attracted to this other woman. Their hands had brushed when they both touched the bill at the same time and when Nic's fingers reached hers briefly, it was like an electric shock shooting through her.

'I don't know what to say,' said Nic. 'I'm sorry…'

'Why are you sorry?' said Faenia, feeling a surge of love and joy. This was wonderful, exciting and Nic was the most incredible woman in the world. Who cared what the label said: Faenia never worried about labels. What counted was how you felt about something new, not what someone else had written on it.

*

'Honey,' said Nic now, in a message that had been left the previous day, 'I can't do this any more. I went by the house and you're gone. I understand if you don't want to see me or talk to me, but please call. I couldn't live with myself any more. I felt like Judas, so I told them. I told them all. And guess what, Melanie had guessed. "Mom, what took you so long to say it?" she said. I felt like a college kid coming out to her parents. She says we're part of a big demographic. We're a demographic, honey. So call me, please. If you still want to.'

The hotel curtains weren't totally shut and morning sun was beginning to stream in through the crack in the fabric. It was nearly eleven at night in San Francisco. But what the hell, she'd wake Nic. Some things couldn't wait.

Epilogue

In the bridal suite in Lisowen Castle, Jojo zipped up Cari's cream dress.

'Easier than all the little buttons last time,' she said gently.

'Closure, right?' said Cari, half-turning to grin at her. 'Making sure I am clear of all the pain of the past before I move on? I edited—'

'— a book on it. Yeah, I know. Is there anything you didn't edit a book on,' Jojo teased, as she fastened the tiny popper fasteners on the wide skirt's tight, cream satin belt.

'I have stayed out of children's fiction and my knowledge of epic ship battles in the eighteenth and nineteenth centuries is pretty bad,' Cari said thoughtfully. 'The ship thing is huge. All hideous life below deck, cannon-ball wounds and people getting scurvy.'

'Lovely. Trust you're taking a couple of those novels on honeymoon?'

Cari grinned. 'I am only taking seven books. Conal's astonished. I told him I usually took ten for a two-week holiday, so I said he had to amuse me the rest of the time.'

'Betcha he'll take you up on that.'

'Yes,' sighed Cari. 'I know marriage is not just about making love but hey, it's fun, right?'

'Yes,' agreed Jojo, thinking of Hugh.

For so long, sex in their marriage had been part of a desperate attempt to make a baby. And then, sex had been off-limits as Jojo either waited to get pregnant via IVF or mourned not getting pregnant.

Actual making love had fallen so far off the scale that everything else had gone with it: affection, touching, hand-holding, a gentle kiss on the cheek. And affection made up a huge part of marriage.

Now that they'd turned off the whole baby-making part of the deal, their marriage had recovered and lovemaking was just that: two people making love to each other.

'Now, twirl and show me.'

Cari twirled.

Jojo hated crying because her make-up had been so beautifully done, yet she welled up at the sight of her darling cousin in her second, for real, wedding dress.

This time, Cari wore a cream silk dress with a fitted bodice, a sweetheart neckline and tiny cap sleeves. The bodice swept down to a tiny waist and then flared out into a fairytale princess full skirt made with gossamer-light silk and decorated with hand-sewn roses.

'You look beautiful,' Jojo said huskily.

'No crying at my second wedding,' joked Cari. 'At my third, maybe, when I've gone overboard with the plastic surgery and all.' She went to the mirror and looked at herself. 'Faenia has the most incredible taste.'

'Yes,' agreed Jojo. 'I look at her work and I realise I know nothing. The people she's dressed—'

'—and the clothes she's dressed them in,' sighed Cari. 'Incredible. Do you think she'd write a book...?'

The week they'd spent in San Francisco with Faenia and Nic had been so much fun for many reasons. Ostensibly, they were there to find the perfect wedding dress for Cari, but they'd managed to fit in visiting so many wonderful places, spent ages in Schiffer's, the department store where Faenia worked, and Cari had adored being in the city where Armistead Maupin, one of her favourite writers, had set his glorious series of books.

'I loved those books, too,' said Nic, and across her head, Faenia and Cari had exchanged a grin.

'Stop smirking at each other,' said Nic, who may have looked like a delicate Southern rose with those fluffy blonde curls and wide-eyed blue stare, but was as sharp as they came and didn't miss a thing. 'Yes, how ironic, I liked a book with many gay characters and I was afraid to say I was a lesbian in case my children would hate me. So sue me, girls!'

'Families can take news about their parents strangely,' said Jojo with a grimace. 'Thinking they have a life beyond you is not always easy to take.'

'But you're over that now, honey, aren't you?' said Nic, patting Jojo's cheek in a motherly way.

'Yes,' said Jojo, leaning against the other woman and enjoying the motherliness.

'Every girl misses her mama when she's gone,' Nic went on, 'but Faenia and I can be stand-in mamas. Your US mamas.'

'Thank you,' said Jojo happily.

She had a wonderful relationship with Bess now. So much better once she'd realised that whatever else Bess was doing in her father's life, it wasn't trying to replace her mother. And Bess did love Jojo's dad, adored him: it was obvious. He was happy with her and Jojo was happy for them both.

'Can we come in?'

Jojo went to the door and Bess, Nora, Faenia and Nic stood there eagerly.

'Oh look,' said Nora, and she didn't mind crying because of any amount of make-up. She'd already wiped half of it off and she hated mascara, anyway. It all rolled down your face, she felt.

'That dress suits you as if it were made for you, Cari,' said Faenia, beaming.

'Perfect princess dress,' said Nic in appreciation, 'but no tiara. Honey, I thought we'd agreed on—'

Faenia kissed the woman she loved on the cheek. 'You and your tiaras,' she said. 'We are going for simple and classy.'

'And beautiful,' said Bess, beaming.

'What's not classy about a tiara?' demanded Nic, pretending to pout.

Everyone laughed.

'Where are the bridesmaids?' asked Cari, tweaking her hair a bit.

Nora laughed. 'Well, your sister is still having an intense discussion with PJ even though I keep reminding her that she has bridesmaid duties. Trina doesn't like the way Amy's hair was done and she's redoing it, and that's it. The hairdresser is not happy, I can tell you.'

Bess shot a look of gratitude at Cari, and Cari smiled back. She understood.

Thank you for making Amy a bridesmaid, for making her part of all of this, Bess was saying.

The first time she'd said it, Cari had said: 'Amy has brought me so much joy in work with her book, which is going to be a hit, I just know it, and I wanted to make it plain that the whole Brannigan clan are together, always.'

Bess, whom Cari had mistakenly thought was a bit of a tough nut, had welled up at that and hadn't been able to speak. Tough nut indeed: more of a meringue, Cari decided.

'Thank you,' Bess had finally managed to say.

There was another, tentative knock at the door.

Bess peered out.

It was Helen, wearing not a new dress but one of her old ones.

She still looked lovely, but that faintly supercilious look Bess had hated was gone. Helen had hit the real world with a bang.

Her and Kit's home would have been sold if Edward hadn't stepped in and paid the mortgage off.

'Ooh you look gorgeous, Cari,' she said, inserting herself into the room as if she might not be welcome.

'Come on in,' said Nora, who was now sitting on the bed.

'We wondered where you'd got to,' said Bess, and was rewarded by seeing Helen relax.

Nora was teaching her: not by actual lessons but by just watching. Compromise, she reminded herself.

Outside in the bar, the men were waiting.

Hugh and Paul were playing with little Heidi, who was now moving at speed and needed a sprinter to keep up with her.

'She loves you,' Paul remarked to his brother-in-law.

'I love kids,' said Hugh. 'We're on the adoption register now. It's not an easy road in this country because we can only adopt from a few countries and the waiting time is long, but whatever it takes and however long it takes, I don't care—'

He grabbed Heidi and cuddled her, while she squealed with her high-pitched laughter.

Edward, Mick and Kit wandered in after a little walk around the grounds.

'I don't know how you can wear these outfits, Ned,' said Mick, pulling at his bow tie.

'Blame your daughter for putting you into it,' teased Edward. He wondered when Bess would be out of the room. He had a gift for her – a necklace for her wedding outfit. A tiny diamond heart on a platinum chain. Nothing that anyone else would notice but he knew she'd love it.

Conal came back from pacing outside.

'Is she ever going to be ready?' he said anxiously. He wanted a ring on Cari's finger and he wanted it official as soon as possible.

His brother Jeff patted him on the back. 'Welcome to being married, little bro,' he said.